D0034328

Also available in Headline Feature:

TOM CLANCY'S NET FORCE
Tom Clancy and Steve Pieczenik

TOM CLANCY'S NET FORCE: HIDDEN AGENDAS
Tom Clancy and Steve Pieczenik

and

TOM CLANCY'S NET FORCE EXPLORERS
Tom Clancy and Steve Pieczenik:

The Deadliest Game
Virtual Vandals
One is the Loneliest Number
The Ultimate Escape
End Game
Cyberspy
Shadow of Honor
The Great Race

Tom Clancy's Net Force: Night Moves

Created by Tom Clancy and Steve Pieczenik

First published in 1999
by HEADLINE BOOK PUBLISHING

A HEADLINE FEATURE paperback

10 9 8 7 6 5 4 3 2 1

All characters in this publication are fictitious and any resemblance to real persons, living or dead, is purely coincidental.

ISBN 0 7472 6116 4

Typeset by Avon Dataset Ltd, Bidford-on-Avon, Warks

Printed and bound in Great Britain by
Mackays of Chatham, Chatham, Kent

HEADLINE BOOK PUBLISHING
A division of the Hodder Headline Group
338 Euston Road
London NW1 3BH

www.headline.co.uk
www.hodderheadline.com

Acknowledgements

We'd like to thank Steve Perry for his creative ideas and his invaluable contributions to the preparations of the manuscript. We would also like to acknowledge the assistance of Martin H. Greenberg, Larry Segriff, Denise Little, John Helfers, Robert Youdelman, Esq., Richard Heller, Esq., and Tom Mallon, Esq.; Mitchell Rubenstein and Laurie Silvers at BIG Entertainment; the wonderful people at The Putnam Berkley Group, including Phyllis Grann, David Shanks, and Tom Colgan. As always, we would like to thank Robert Gottlieb of the William Morris Agency, our agent and friend, without whom this book would never have been conceived, as well as Jerry Katzman, Vice Chairman of the William Morris Agency, and his television colleagues. But most important, it is for you, our readers, to determine how successful our collective endeavor has been.

'The history of the sword is the history of humanity.'

Richard Burton

'Putting on the spectacles of science in expectation of finding the answer to everything looked at signifies inner blindness.'

J. Frank Dobie

PROLOGUE

Friday, April 1st, 2011 – 2:15 a.m.
Outside Sahiwal, Pakistan

The middle of the night, and still the temperature hovered near ninety. The humidity was so high that sweat did not evaporate and, having nowhere else to go, sour perspiration soaked the men's black uniforms. Only April, and already a new record high for this date in the Punjab, almost a hundred and fifteen, with more of the same predicted for tomorrow. Pah.

Three men in sodden black camouflage clothes lay in the darker shadow of a row of stunted bushes a few dozen yards from the railroad tracks, waiting.

In the distance, the sound of the train's whistle announced that it was on its way.

'It won't be long now,' Bhattacharya said. Fat as he was, the others sometimes called him Ganesha, after the elephant god, though they did not say this to his face. However corpulent he might be, Bhattacharya was quick to anger, equally quick to move, and once moving, a formidable opponent.

Until two years ago, Bhattacharya had been an officer, a colonel. Then, at a garden party in Panipat, he had stabbed another colonel who had insulted him. It was only the lucky presence of a doctor that had saved the fat man from a murder charge. As it was, what he'd done was enough to have him stripped of his rank and arrested – and offered jail or a transfer to the Special Unit.

Like similar covert organizations around the world, the Special Unit did not officially exist. None of the men carried regular army-issue weapons or gear. Their assault rifles were surplus Chinese AKs, their pistols German, their sheath knives were from Japan. Their communications equipment came from New Zealand, their boots from Indonesia, their clothes from Australia. No man had upon his person any item that would officially identify him at all, much less identify him as an Indian soldier.

During an operation, no man was to allow himself to be captured. If such an event became likely, a quick suicide by gun or knife was expected. This was not as heroic as it might seem. Anyone who refused to do his duty would soon be dead anyway: before embarking upon this mission, each man had taken a slow-acting poison. If he returned from the mission, he would be given the antidote, and would suffer only a few days of flu-like misery. If he did not return for any reason, he would die a lingering and painful death, the effects of which made suicide seem a picnic in the park. Better to choose the quick exit, if it came to that.

When there were dark military things to be done in India, the SU was called upon to do them. Most countries had such units, though most would quickly deny such an accusation.

This mission was as dark as any. Sneaking into Pakistan for a covert operation was a risky proposition at best. Packy was a touchy one, and given the current political situation, it was easy to understand why.

Next to Ganesha lay Rahman, around forty, a man of no particular caste from New Delhi. Rahman was long and lean, the opposite of Bhattacharya. Rahman was familiar with this area of Pakistan, having once been a member of India's Border Security Force, the BSF foot-stampers who faced the Pakistan Rangers across the wire at the Wagah Post. There, each evening, both sides danced the mutual show of stylized aggression that marked the daily lowering of the flags and ceremonial blatting of the bugles. Crowds came from miles to see the mock-battle, cheering each side on as if it were a soccer match.

The third man was Harbhajan Singh and, naturally, he was called The Sikh. Although Singh was certainly not an unusual name for a Sikh, he had in fact been named specifically for the particular soldier who had achieved *moksha* – enlightenment – while patrolling the border with China in the 1960s near Nathu-La. All they had ever found of that Singh were his snow goggles, his helmet, and his rifle. To this day, Singh's ghost still patrolled the area. The Chinese often saw him standing on top of a mountain, or walking across the surface of a stream. The Army had not believed the story for a long time, until a visiting general offered disrespect to the ghost, and for his attitude was promptly killed in a helicopter crash on his way home. From then on, the new commanders of the region were most careful to send their personal cars to the area once a year, to offer Singh a ride to the train station for his annual leave. And a seat would be booked for the ghost on the train, too. It must have made for an interesting trip to have been the driver of the car, though no one had ever claimed to see Singh riding in the car or on the train.

All of which was fascinating, but did little to alleviate the discomfort this Singh felt under his beard and turban from the night's tropical heat. Even though his great-great-grandfather had lived near Lahore, only a few miles north of here, Singh had spent much of his life in Madras, on the Bay of Bengal, and while that city was certainly warm year-round, at least there were sea breezes to offer relief. Too, he had lived several years in Calcutta, and that had been hotter than Madras, but even Calcutta was not baked as was the Punjab. The hottest place on earth, so it was said. He could believe it.

'There it is,' Bhattacharya said. 'See the light, there?'

Singh and Rahman nodded and murmured their agreement. Along the track, the other 'mercenaries' would be gathering themselves for the attack. There were sixty of them, and while some would probably die during the assault, they would be missed only by their comrades. You did not join the SU unless you were alone in the world, no wife, no family, no ties to anything. You were expendable.

The train's whistle bleated again, drawing nearer.

Singh gripped his AK-47 clone and took a deeper breath of the fetid and hot night air. He was not a very good Sikh, had not been for many years, but he was moved to repeat God's name a few times anyway. No harm in that.

The train came into view. What the engineer could not see ahead was a set of angled derailing plates that had been artfully welded to the rails, right where the tracks curved and banked a hair to the left.

The special train from Multan to Lahore was about to make an unscheduled and most abrupt stop.

Singh held his breath as the chugging engine hit the plates. There came a loud *clang* and a scream of protesting metal. The engine jumped the tracks, plowed into the ground, and ripped up great chunks of earth. More crashing noises filled the air as the engine slammed onto its side and kept skidding.

The following five or six cars also leaped from the rails and tumbled about like a child's toy. More noise and great clouds of smoke and dust billowed into the night.

Singh was already on his feet, running toward the still-moving train. Some of the cars stayed on the track, and one of these, a boxcar with doors closed, loomed right in front of him. The door opened, and five Pakistani Rangers leapt out.

Singh fired, waving his weapon back and forth, hosing the soldiers. Next to him, Rahman's weapon also spoke, as did Ganesha's, and the Pakistanis went down, cut dead by a sleet of jacketed metal.

Sorry, Packy, better luck next time around.

More guns went off, the darkness was lit by muzzle flashes and exploding grenades. White phosphor blossomed, and red flares spewed.

There were as many soldiers defending as there were attacking, but the SU troops had surprise – and a train wreck – on their side. Within moments it was all over. A few wounded yelled in pain but were quickly silenced by gunshots. Singh, Bhattacharya and Rahman went to their assigned boxcar. It was empty, but that did not matter. They set their explosives, activated the preset timers.

'Go!' Rahman said. 'Quick!'

The three of them joined the other fleeing SU troops. They had only seconds to get clear. There was no time to find and disarm the charges even if there had been anybody still alive here with such a mind.

A gun went off to the left. Singh twisted and raked the spot where he'd seen the muzzle flash, spraying quick three-round bursts from the AK, and heard a scream. One of the Pakistanis, playing dead. Dead for real, now.

But the Pakistani's last shot had found a mark.

Bhattacharya went down.

Singh skidded to a stop, though Rahman kept running.

The fat man was hit in the chest, high and slightly off-center, and the camo was already soaked with blood, a dark and wet splotch in the night. The fat man looked up at Singh. 'I'm done,' he said. 'Help me out here, Sikh.'

Singh nodded. 'Yes.' He pointed the assault rifle at Bhattacharya's forehead, squeezed the trigger fast, got off one round. The man's body spasmed and went limp.

No time to stand around and offer prayers. Singh ran.

A few seconds later, light and noise shattered what was left of the hot and clammy night. The exploding train could be seen for miles by any who happened to look.

It was felt, in a different way, around the entire world.

1

Friday, April 1st
Hampton Court, England

The palace, whose first royal occupant had been Henry VIII, back in the 1500s, was huge. The stone buildings themselves covered more than six acres, with ten times that much walled-in lawn and gardens around the structures. The chambers were mostly big, with high ceilings, tall windows; a couple had stone fireplaces large enough to walk into without bumping your head. Many of the rooms were empty save for giant wall hangings and baroque chandeliers. A few had monstrous canopied beds or chairs and desks in them. There were art galleries hung with age-muddied paintings. Much of the section they were in at the moment, called the King's Apartments, had burned in a sudden fire in the mid-1980s, and had since been restored to what it supposedly looked like in the 1700s.

Alex Michaels glanced around in awe. It was hard to imagine that anybody had ever actually *lived* in such a place.

It had cost them fifteen Euros each to be admitted

to the palace, not counting the ride on the tube from London. They'd strolled across the Thames on the Hampton Court Bridge to the main entrance. Michaels had traveled over the years, more so since he had become Commander of the FBI stand-alone unit Net Force, but he had somehow never made it to England until now. He and Toni had decided to add some vacation time to the week they had been allotted for the International Computer Crime Conference. They needed some time off; things had gotten a little rocky on a personal level the last few weeks.

So here they were, in the huge house of kings and queens, and, vast as it was, Hampton Court Palace was not big enough to contain Toni Fiorella's simmering anger. Michaels expected it to burst out any second, to blast him and whatever room they were in to a blackened crisp. They weren't married but it seemed the honeymoon period was nevertheless coming to an end, much as he did not want that to happen.

Fifteen Euros, that was a lot to be allowed to walk around inside a musty castle for a couple of hours. If it hadn't been for the calculator built into the electronic virgil on his belt, Michaels would never have been able to figure out what that was in real money. Multiplying fractions was not his favorite pastime.

He pointed out the security beam generator to Toni, set into the support that held the drooping velvet ropes supposed to keep the tourists from sitting in the antique chairs. 'Step over that and I bet we'll hear an alarm scream.'

Toni said nothing.

Oh, Lord, what have I done now? 'You okay?'

'I'm fine.'

Michaels drew in a long, slow breath and let it escape silently as they walked. A costumed man who looked as if he might be from Henry's court stood under a painting of an ugly couple and two much better-looking dogs, explaining to a tour group the significance of the painting. The man had what Michaels had been told was a posh accent, nary a dropped aitch, very upper class.

Before he and Toni had become lovers Michaels had been married and divorced. There was a way that a woman said, 'I'm fine,' the tone clipped and brusque, that meant she was *anything* but fine. He had learned not to go any farther down that road unless he was *really* ready to hear what was wrong, sometimes at a decibel level equal to standing in front of the speakers at a This is Your Brain on Drugs rock concert. Would Toni yell at him in the Great Hall? Or would she wait until they were in the smaller Tudor rooms where Cardinal Wolsey once pursued his studies? Right at the moment, if Michaels dared to touch her, he was almost sure his fingers would get burned. She was pissed, and he was pretty sure it was at him.

Why wasn't life simple? Two people love each

other, they get together, and live happily ever after?

Probably what Anne Boleyn thought when she hooked up with the fat man, said his inner voice.

He told his inner voice to shut up.

She waited until they were outside, strolling across a damp and chilly lawn toward the North Gardens and the carefully tended hedge maze before she said anything. He was watching her out of the corner of his eye, admiring her athletic walk, her beautiful face and figure. She had been his assistant ever since he'd been at Net Force and she was very good at her job. She was also almost a dozen years younger than he was, a bright, tough, nice Italian girl from the Bronx who was an adept at an Indonesian martial art called *pentjak silat*. She had been teaching it to him, and although he was getting better at it, if push came to shove and she was *really* angry she could wipe the floor with him and never break a sweat. That was an odd sensation, knowing the woman you loved could kick your ass if she felt like it.

When she spoke, her voice was quiet, even, no anger apparent in it. 'Why did you send Marshall to the OCIC meeting in Kabul?'

Michaels took another deep breath. Why hadn't he sent her? Because Afghanistan was not a place he wanted Toni to be. It was backward, women were fourth-class citizens, after men, boys, and horses, and there were frequent terrorist attacks on foreigners, particularly Americans. He did not want to put her at risk. But he couldn't say that straight out. Instead, he said, 'Marshall wanted to go. I didn't think you did.'

'I didn't, particularly,' she said.

'Well, so there it is. You didn't have to. No problem, right?'

He should be so lucky. She said, 'I was up. I should have gone.'

'But you just said you didn't *want* to go.'

She stopped walking and stared at him. God, she was beautiful, even when she was mad at him. Maybe even more so when she was mad at him.

'That's not the point. I was up, you should have sent me, whether I wanted to or not. Why didn't you?'

He had a pretty good memory, a necessary requisite for prevarication, but even so, when it got right down to it, Michaels was not a very good liar. Oh, sure, he could tell somebody their hair looked nice when it didn't, or smile and nod at a superior's bad taste in clothes without blurting out his sentiments, but beyond simple and harmless white lies designed to spare feelings he had no real talent in games of deceit. She had caught him, he had tried to slip past and couldn't, so he wasn't going to try to lie his way out of it. He shook his head and went for the truth: 'Because I didn't want to send you into a place where you might be at risk.'

'That's what I thought.' She started walking again.

He went after her. 'Look, Toni, I love you. Is it so wrong to want to keep you out of harm's way?'

'For a lover, no. I'd be unhappy if you didn't want that. But for a colleague in the intelligence community, yes, it's wrong. You know I can take care of myself.'

'Yes,' he said. He knew; he'd seen that demonstrated a few times. She was better able to take care of herself when things got physical than he was, but even so, she wasn't Superwoman.

'I want you to treat me like one of the boys.'

He smiled. 'That would be a trick. I can't think of you that way, and if I did, well, I wouldn't be interested. I like girls. You in particular.'

She gave him a tiny grin in return, a quick flash. So she wasn't totally pissed off at him. 'I meant at the office. I very much like being treated as a woman when we're on our own time.'

'I understand.'

'Do you? You really need to, you know. I want you to hold my hand when we walk in the moonlight, but not when we're at work. You need to separate your personal life from your work life, Alex.'

'Okay. I will. Next time you're up, you go, no matter where it is.'

She flashed a bigger smile. 'Good. Now, you suppose we might find some chocolate somewhere?'

They both laughed and he felt a great sense of relief. Neither of them had been to England before, and one of the things they noticed early on was that there were chocolate candy machines everywhere, in stores, train stations, even pubs. It had become a running joke between them, finding chocolate. They both expected to gain thirty pounds and have their faces break out before they returned to the States.

His virgil played the first few bars of Aaron Copland's 'Fanfare for the Common Man'. He had an incoming telecom. He pulled the device from his belt and saw that the caller was from the office of the FBI's Director.

'That's cute,' Toni said, meaning the music. She waved her finger as if directing an orchestra.

'Jay must have sneaked into my office and reprogrammed the ringer again. Better than last time, when it was George Thorogood's 'Bad to the Bone'.

'Ta dah dah dah dah *dump*!' Toni sang.

'Everybody I work with has a warped sense of humor,' he said. 'This is Alex Michaels.'

'Please hold for the Director,' a secretary said.

Toni looked at him, and he held his hand over the virgil's microphone. 'Boss.'

'I sure wish Walt Carver hadn't had that heart attack,' Toni said.

'I think he's glad he did. It gave him an excuse to retire and go fishing. It's only been a month, we should give her a chance—'

'Commander, this Melissa Allison. I'm sorry to interrupt your vacation but we have a situation . . .'

Her face appeared on the virgil's liquid crystal

display screen, so he tapped his send-visual mode and held the unit so he could see the virgil's cam thumbnail of his own face in the screen's corner.

Allison, forty-six, was a thin redhead with a cool-bordering-on-cold voice and demeanor. She was a political appointee, a lawyer with no experience in the field but an encyclopedic knowledge of where dozens of political bodies were buried. The rumor was that certain high-ranking members of Congress had prevailed on the President to offer her the FBI directorship vacated by Walt Carver, so she'd keep quiet about things better left that way. Outside of a couple of meetings and a few memos, Michaels hadn't had to deal with her yet.

'Go ahead.'

'Some hours ago an unidentified military force attacked a Pakistani train near the Indian border, killed a dozen guards, and then blew the train to pieces. The cargo was a top-secret shipment of electronic components on their way for use in the Pakistani nuclear bomb program.'

'I thought there was a non-proliferation treaty between Pakistan and India.'

'There is, but neither country pays any attention to it. The government of Pakistan is convinced the attacking terrorist force was a special unit of the Indian Army.'

'Do they have proof of this?'

'Not enough to start a war. Not yet – but they are looking hard.'

Michaels looked at the tiny image of the Director's face. 'With all due respect, ma'am, what's this got to do with us? Shouldn't the spooks be on the hot seat?'

'They are, but if they and the Pakistanis can be believed, there was no way anyone could know about the train and what it carried. The terrorists had plenty of time to get into position for the ambush and the Pakistanis say this wasn't possible.'

'Obviously it was,' Michaels said.

'The liaison with the CIA tells him there were only four people who knew about the shipment and the route. The crates were unmarked, and the workmen and train personnel who loaded and were delivering the materials didn't know what they were carrying.'

'Coincidence, maybe? They attacked a train at random?'

'Nineteen trains passed that point in the twenty-four hours prior to the one that was destroyed. Only one carried anything of strategic importance.'

'Then somebody told.'

'The Pakistanis say not. Nobody had a chance to tell, once the operation began. Three of the four who knew were together, and the other one, who happens to be the head of their secret police, didn't get around to decoding the computer message telling him about the shipment until an hour before the attack. Some kind of computer failure on his end had his system down. Even if he had wanted to tell, there wasn't enough time.'

'Somebody intercepted the message and broke the code, then,' Michaels said.

'Which is why it concerns us,' she said. 'The security encryption was supposedly bulletproof, a factored number hundreds of digits long. According to the CIA, it would take a SuperCray running full time, day and night, about a million years to break the code.'

Great, Michaels thought. He said, 'I'll have my people look into it.'

'Good. Keep me informed.'

Her picture disappeared as she broke the connection.

Toni, who had been listening, shook her head. 'Not possible,' she said.

'Right. The difficult we do immediately. The impossible takes a little longer. Come on, let's go see the maze.'

'You going to call Jay?'

'It can wait a few more minutes.'

2

Friday
London, England

The waiter arrived with a Bombay gin and tonic and set it on the table next to the overstuffed leather chair where Lord Geoffrey Goswell sat reading *The Times*. The Japanese markets were going to hell in a handbasket, the American stock market was holding steady, and gold futures were up.

The weather forecast for London called for rain on the morrow.

Nothing about which to be concerned.

Goswell glanced up. He watched the servant tarry a moment to see if there was anything else required, and gave the waiter a military nod. 'Thank you, Paddington.'

'Milord.'

The waiter glided noiselessly away. There was a good man, old Paddington. He'd had been delivering the paper and drinks here at the club for what . . . thirty, thirty-five years? He was polite, efficient, knew his place, and never intruded. Would that all servants were half as well-mannered. A man to be remembered with a nice tip at Christmas, was Paddington.

Across the short stretch of dark and worn oval Oriental rug, reading a trash paper like *The Sun* or *The New York Times* or somesuch, Sir Harold Bellworth harrumphed and blew out a fragrant cloud of Cuban cigar smoke. He lowered his paper and looked at Goswell. 'Can't believe what the American President said today. I don't understand why they put up with that kind of bloody nonsense over there. If the PM did that, he would be tossed out on his ear, and rightly so.'

Bellworth, eighty-two, was class of '47, eight years older than Goswell.

Goswell smiled politely at the older man. 'Well, they're Americans now, aren't they?'

'Mmm, yes, of course.' Here was a standard answer that neatly answered so many questions. There was the British way, and then there were all the . . . *other* ways. Well, they are Americans, aren't they? Or French, or German, or for God's sake, Spanish. What else could one *expect* from foreigners, save the wrong way of doing things?

'Mmph.' Harry lifted the paper and went back to his reading.

Goswell glanced at the big round clock over the bookcase. Half past five already. He should have Paddington call Stephens, he supposed. It would be a slow drive to The Yews, especially on a Friday evening with all the rabble streaming out of the city for their weekly two-day holiday, but there was no help for it. Normally he would just stay at Portman House in the city until Saturday, then enjoy the leisurely drive to his estate in Sussex, but that scientist fellow of his, Peter Bascomb-Coombs, was arriving for dinner at half nine, so there was no help for it. Given the traffic, Goswell would be lucky to make it in time as it was. He folded the financial section and put it next to his gin and tonic, picked up the drink, and took a large sip. Ah. He put the glass down.

A moment later, unbidden, Paddington appeared. 'Milord?'

'Yes, have Stephens bring the car round, will you?'

'Of course, milord. Some tea and sandwiches for the trip?'

'No, I have a dinner when we get to the country.' He waved one hand in airy dismissal.

Paddington left to find the chauffeur. Goswell stood, pulled his watch from his vest pocket, and checked its time against the club's clock.

Harry looked up from his paper again. 'Off, are we?'

'Yes, a meeting with my scientists at the country house.'

'Scientists.' Harry delivered the word in the same way he would have said 'thieves' or 'whores'. He shook his head. 'Well. Cheerio, then. By the way, have you cut down that bloody yew behind the greenhouse yet?'

'Certainly not. I expect to nourish its roots with you any time now.'

Harry gave a wheezy smoker's laugh. 'I'll dance on your grave, you young upstart. And warm my hands from that bloody yew as it burns merrily in my fireplace, too.'

The two men smiled. It was an old joke. Yews were often planted in graveyards and, because they seemed to always grow largest in such locations, it was thought that the minerals from the decomposing bodies were good for the plants' roots. The big yew behind the greenhouse on Goswell's estate was eighty-five feet tall, if it was an inch, and probably four hundred years old. He had been threatening to feed Harry to it for years.

He glanced at his watch again. A minute or so fast, but close enough. The watch was a gold Waltham, of no great value, but it had belonged to his Uncle Patrick, who had died during the Blitz, and it had come to him as a lad. He had better timepieces that ran dead-on, Rolexes and Cartiers and a couple of the handmade Swiss things that cost as much as a new car. The Waltham was a simple machine. It did not offer the date, nor the market news, nor could it be held to one's ear and used as a telephone. It was no more than a watch, and he rather liked that.

He slipped the Waltham back into his vest pocket

and started for the exit. By the time he reached the street, Stephens would have the '54 Bentley waiting. He preferred the Bentley to the Rolls, as well. It was basically the same automobile, without that ostentatious grille, and being ostentatious was not something a gentleman *did*, now was it?

He would listen to the BBC News on the way out of the city. See if the wogs in India and Pakistan had started shooting at each other over that little . . . entertainment he had arranged. That would be lovely, if they would just bomb each other back to the time of the Raj, and the Empire had to come back and help them along to civilization again.

There would be justice, wouldn't it?

Friday
Somewhere in the British Raj – India

Jay Gridley rode the Net, master of all he surveyed.

Right at the moment, he was in a VR – virtual reality – scenario he had designed especially for this new assignment Alex Michaels had called him about. In RW – the real world – he sat at his computer console inside Net Force HQ in Quantico, Virginia, his eyes and ears covered with input sensors, hands and chest wired so that his smallest movements could be turned into control pulses. But in VR, Jay wore a pith helmet, khaki shorts, and starched khaki shirt, along with knee socks, stout walking shoes, and a Webley Mark III .38 revolver strapped around his waist. He sat upon the back of an Indian elephant, inside a *howdah*, next to the local Rajah. Overhead, the afternoon sun broiled everything it saw, smiting men and beasts and vegetation alike with withering heat. Ahead of them, brown-skinned natives in loincloths beat upon metal plates with sticks, rattled rocks inside cans, and chanted loudly, to spook and drive from the chest-high grasses the tiger who might be hidden there.

Jay smiled at the image, knowing it was not politically correct, but unworried. He wasn't likely to run into anybody he knew while playing this scenario, and besides, he was half Thai, wasn't he? Once upon a time, one of *his* great-great-grandfathers or uncles would probably have been barefoot down there in the grass, in what had been Siam, making noise, praying to assorted gods that the tiger would go the other way. All things considered, it was better to be in the shaded little hut up on the back of a ten-foot-tall elephant, with a Nitro Express double rifle racked right next to you, than it was to be on the ground beating a plate with a stick. And there was that extra, a small boy perched on the elephant's rump waving a fan on the end of a big pole to provide a warm but welcome breeze for you and the Rajah.

First class all the way. The only way to travel.

What Jay was actually hunting was information, but keyboarding or voxaxing queries for coded binary hex packets wasn't nearly as much fun as stalking a man-eating Bengal tiger.

Of course, they hadn't *seen* the big tiger yet, and the beaters had been thumping and rattling for a long time, relativistically-speaking. The Rajah was apologetic. 'So sorry, Sahib,' he alliterated, but it wasn't his fault. You couldn't flush it out if it wasn't there.

Oh, yeah, there were lesser beasts running from the hunters. Jay had seen deer, pigs, all manner of slithering snakes, including a couple of eight-foot cobras, and even a young tiger – but not the big cat he'd hoped to find. The tiger had come and gone – maybe burning bright, but certainly leaving no easy trail – had gutted its prey and disappeared. The VR prey in this case was a goat inside a stainless-steel and titanium cage with bars as big as a body-builder's legs. A tyrannosaur couldn't chop through those barriers even if his big ole teeth were made from diamonds, no way, no how. The goat – actually an encrypted file giving the time, location, and other particulars of a train shipment in Pakistan early today – should have been monster-proof. But *something* had ripped the bars open as if they were overcooked noodles, gotten inside, and Mr Goat was history.

Jay hadn't believed it at first, sure somebody had managed to get a copy of the one-time key, which was how these encryptions worked, but after he'd gotten a look at the cage – the mathematical encryption – he could see it had been forced open, no key involved. This was not some kid's DES, used to hide a porno file from his parents, but a decent military-grade encryption. While not unbreakable in the long run, whoever had cracked it had done so in less than a day.

And that, of course, was just not possible. No computer on Earth could do that. A dozen SuperCrays working in parallel might manage it in, oh, say, ten thousand years, but in the few hours since the message was sent and it was broken, it couldn't be done. Period. End of story. Here, let me tell you another one . . .

Jay took off his pith helmet and wiped the sweat off his forehead with one arm. Hot out here in the Punjab and, shade notwithstanding, the little elephant house didn't have AC. He could have designed that in, of course, but what was the point? Anybody could cobble together a bastard scenario full of anachronisms; artists had to maintain a certain kind of purity. Well, at least every now and then they did, just to show they still could.

How could this break-in have been done? It couldn't – at least, not using any physics *he* knew.

It reminded him of the old story during the early days of aeronautics. Some engineers had done studies on bumblebees. Based on the surface area of the bees' wings, the weight and shape of the insect, and the amount of muscle and force it had available, they had determined, after much slide rule and pencil-on-paper activity, that it was flatly impossible for such a creature to fly.

Bzzzzt! Oops, there went another one . . .

It must have been terribly frustrating to look at a paper filled with precise mathematical calculations about flow and lift and drag, to *know* that bees couldn't fly, and then have to watch them flitting from flower to flower, oblivious to man's certainty they simply couldn't *do* that.

The obvious deduction was that the researchers had missed something. They went back to their bamboo slide rules and pencil stubs, did more observations, filled dozens of legal pads, and eventually they figured out how the synergism of bee flight worked.

If you already have the answer, you damn sure ought to be able to at least figure out the question. Bees had been flying about their business for millions of years despite what anybody thought otherwise, and that had to be factored in . . .

So here was a file that couldn't be forced and yet it had been broken open like an eggshell in the hands of a giant. What was it Sherlock Holmes had said? 'When you have eliminated the impossible, whatever remains, however improbable, must be the truth.'

This break-in couldn't be done by any method Jay Gridley knew about and, modesty aside, he was as good as anybody when it came to computer rascalry. But since it *had* been done, then there must be a new tiger out there in the tall grass. All he had to do was figure out what it looked like, find it, and capture it. Without getting eaten.

He grinned again. That brought up another bit of hunting wisdom. The recipe for rabbit stew?

First, you catch a rabbit . . .

Friday
Stonewall Flat, Nevada

Mikhayl Ruzhyó squinted into the desert sun. Although he was relatively fair-skinned he had tanned since he'd moved here, and now he was the color of good holster leather, lines etched into his face, veins prominent on his bare arms. The days were not as hot here in Nevada as they would be in a couple of months, and the nights were still chilly, but it was warm enough. He stood in front of the small Airstream trailer he had towed to the five-acre plot of sand and scrub weed he had also bought, feeling the hot wind play over him. He was more or less alone. Only one of the other five-acre 'estates' within a mile had a structure on it, and that was a green plastic dome lined with what appeared to be aluminum foil, full of packets of freeze-dried food, the kind campers and hikers used. Ruzhyó had picked the simple padlock keeping the place shut and checked it out within a few hours of locating this property. Every couple of months, an old man who drove a large GMC pickup truck would arrive at the dome, unload more of the freeze-dried packets from the vehicle and store them in the building, then lock up and drive away. Ruzhyó wondered why the old man brought the stuff out. Was he storing it against some future catastrophe? Worried about a war? Or plague? Or was it part of some commercial venture?

It was hard to determine the motivations of Americans at times. Back home in Chetsnya, even in Russia, he had never seen old men hoarding this kind of food. Of course, maybe that was because nobody thought such things were worth hoarding. Or they couldn't get it if they did.

Ruzhyó shrugged mentally. No matter. The dome was the only building close by, and the next structure past that was a cabin near the small river that was a dry bed most of the year, almost three miles away. The cabin belonged to a Methodist church, and it had been used by hardy campers only three times since Ruzhyó had lived here, never for more than two nights at a time. None of the campers had hiked close enough to speak to him.

He was grateful for the solitude. Since retiring from wet work, he'd had few occasions to even talk to people, much less kill them. He had money banked he could retrieve as needed, using a computer card. Once a week or so he drove almost two hours into town and bought his supplies in one of several large supermarkets where he was totally anonymous; he did not chat with the clerks when he checked out. He filled the car's tank with gasoline and drove home. He passed Death Valley on the west, and turned off the highway onto a dirt road that led to his trailer. The nearest town, if it could be called such, was Scotty's Junction. A military gunnery range dominated the land to the east.

Ruzhyó had paid cash for his car, a Dodge SUV, used but not too old, and had done the same for the trailer, both of which he had purchased through classified ads in a Las Vegas newspaper. The land he had acquired using one of the safe names he held and, to avoid arousing undue interest, had given a substantial downpayment to the seller and paid monthly notes from the same account since, automatically deducted on the first of each month. His profile could hardly be much lower.

The trailer had a generator and batteries, even air conditioning, but he used the cooler rarely. He relished the heat.

He could not say he was happy – had not been since the cancer had claimed Anna, and did not ever expect to be so again – but he could say he was content. His life was simple, his needs few. The biggest project on his agenda was building a natural stone wall along the perimeter of his property. It might take ten years but that hardly mattered.

Or he had been content, until today. As he scanned the rock terrain, the dust and heat-hazed hills in the distance, he knew something was wrong.

There were no signs he could see to tell him what the problem was. No helicopters had flown over, no dust clouds betrayed vehicles trying a stealthy approach. He lifted the powerful binoculars and did a slow scan of the surrounding countryside. His five acres was on a rise, slightly higher than most of the surrounding country, and he had a good view. He could see the old man's dome from the front of the trailer. He looked at it now. Nothing.

He walked a few yards up the gentle incline behind the trailer, until he could see the roof of the Methodist's cabin and the dry riverbed. No activity there.

He lowered the binoculars. Nothing to be seen, no cause for concern, but in his gut he felt that something was wrong. He headed for the trailer. He had weapons in a flat box hidden under the floor in the bedroom. Perhaps it was time to take them out and keep them handy?

No. Not yet, he decided. There was nothing at which to shoot. Perhaps the feeling was wrong; perhaps his gut was merely troubled by a badly digested meal, or a parasite.

He gave himself a tight smile. He had not survived as long as he had by entertaining such rationalizations. At his best, he had been like a roach seeing a sudden light in the night. Run first, worry later. It had kept him alive when many others in his profession had died. He had learned to trust it over the years. No, something was wrong. Whatever it was would manifest itself sooner or later. Then he would deal with it.

He went into the trailer.

3

Saturday, April 2nd
Las Vegas, Nevada

Colonel John Howard, the Commanding Officer of Net Force's military wing, had two surprises waiting for him at the airport when he exited one of the old refitted business Lears they used for short hops in-country. The first surprise was that US Army Tactical Satellite Operations – shortened to USAT, or sometimes informally called Big Squint – had definitely ID'd their target as the man Net Force sought.

This was not a major eyebrow-raiser, since Net Force had already suspected his whereabouts, or they wouldn't have asked USAT to route a bird to footprint the guy. It was, however, good to have it confirmed.

However, the second surprise *was* something of a shock: Howard was about to be promoted.

Military rank was a strange beast in Net Force. Officially, all of the officers and men under his command were 'detached' National Guard, no matter what their prior branch of service. This was a name-only organization, a place for the paper-pushers and mouse-wavers to slot them, and unconnected to the Guard or US Army in any real sense. It had to do with using military troops in civilian situations as much as anything, generally not allowed in domestic situations, but it also had to do with some strange tax law that came out in the new code's recent revisions. He didn't understand it, his boss didn't seem to understand it, and his accountant didn't understand it, but there it was.

Because of this, Net Force officer rank was more or less frozen. As CO, he could promote grunts – but only up to NCO. Howard knew he could have stayed in the regular army, and even in peacetime eventually retired a grade or two up from where he was now. Being an African-American helped, there still being enough white-liberal guilt floating around to slant things his way now and again. He never expected to get any higher than bird colonel when he retired and joined Net Force however, even though the money – and, more importantly, the opportunities for action – were much better. His direct boss was a civilian, so when it came to brass, he was pretty much it.

Julio Fernandez, his top kick for as long as he'd been with Net Force and for a long time before that, delivered the news with obvious glee.

'Say again, Sergeant?' Howard said.

Fernandez stood in the hard shade of the gamp leading to the private hangar. He grinned. 'Which part didn't the Colonel understand, sir?'

'Let me rephrase that, and be succinct, it's already getting warm out here: What the hell are you talking about?'

The two of them walked toward the hangar.

Fernandez laughed. 'Well, sir, the word is that the Colonel will be, within thirty days from 1 April, offered the rank of Brigadier – that's a grade superior to Colonel and inferior to Major General, sir – in this bastard National Guard outfit he dragged me into.'

'Held a gun to your head, did I?'

'If memory serves, sir.'

Howard smiled. 'Come on, Julio, what are you talking about? I haven't heard squat about any promotion, not a whisper.' He tried to keep the excitement from his voice. Fernandez could be funny, but he wouldn't joke about something like this. Howard had always wanted to be a general, of course, but he'd given that hope up when he bailed from the RA.

'That's 'cause you ain't engaged to the most beautiful and bright woman in the western hemisphere, and probably the eastern hemisphere, too, John. A woman who can make a computer sing, dance, and do back flips without straining her pinkie. I saw the order myself, and it's as official as can be.'

Despite his sudden rush of adrenaline, Howard said, 'Lieutenant Winthrop isn't supposed to be snooping in certain areas now, is she?'

Fernandez opened his hands, spread his fingers, and held them in an I-give-up gesture. 'What can I do? I'm just a sergeant, she's my superior. What I know about computers you can put in your ear, with room left over for your finger. Besides, what's the point in being part of the world's best geek team if you can't poke around in the stuff wherever you want? It's real. Congratulations, John.'

'Thanks, though I'll believe it when I see it.' He felt his spirit soar. *General* Howard. Now there was a term.

Fernandez chuckled, reading his mind.

Howard recovered, damped down his excitement and ego. 'How *is* Joanna?'

'Pregnant as a crowded maternity ward. Not due until September, and I have to tell you, I don't think I'm gonna survive it. One minute I'm her angel and I can do no wrong, the next minute she takes my head off 'cause I'm *breathing* too loud. She eats catsup on mashed potatoes, and sprinkles salt on her ice cream. She pees forty-nine times a day.'

Howard laughed. 'Serves you right. When are you going to make an honest woman out of her?'

'June the first, so I have been told. She'd rather wait a year; it supposedly takes that long to set up a wedding, though that doesn't make any sense. Failing that, she wants to get married before the baby is born, and she doesn't want to look like a brood sow, so it's got to be by then. It's not up to me, I'm just the groom.'

'Weddings and pregnancies are like that, Julio.'

'I do get to pick the best man, though. You interested in the job?'

Howard nodded. 'Are you kidding? I wouldn't miss watching the infamous Sergeant Julio Fernandez tie the knot for all the tea in India. Got a sex on the baby yet?'

'A boy.' He grinned.

'Picked out a name yet?'

'Five of them: Julio Garcia Edmund Howard Fernandez.'

Howard stopped walking and looked at his friend. 'I'm honored.'

'Not my idea, blame it on Joanna. Got a couple of grandfathers in there, too. Me, I'd have named him "Bud" and let it go at that. You get to be a godfather, too – another of her crazy ideas.'

Howard smiled. He was going to be best man at his best friend's wedding, godfather to a boy wearing one of his names, and promoted to a general in the Net Force version of the army. You didn't get many days like this one.

'I hate to spoil the moment, but how about our fugitive?'

'No spoilers there, sir. He lives in a trailer out in the middle of nowhere, all by himself, doesn't even have a dog. Most ambitious thing he seems to be doing is building a rock wall along one edge of his property. He keeps a zero profile, doesn't socialize, doesn't talk to anybody, far as we can tell. Just piles up local rocks. Hard to believe this is an ex-Spetsnaz wet work specialist with forty-four confirmed deletions to his credit.'

'Well, if Vladimir Plekhanov can be believed – and the interrogation shrinks assure me that he can – the man who calls himself Mikhayl Ruzhyó is somebody whose skills are *not* limited to stacking rocks in the desert. We want to do this by the numbers, nice and clean, and gather him up gently enough so he's alive to answer some questions.'

'No problem, piece of cake. Though I thought the Russians were our friends these days.'

'I believe that is a facetious comment, Sergeant. You know as well as I that the more we know about our friends, the better off we are.'

'Amen.'

'All right. Let's see what Big Squint has for us.'

'Command post is in the coolest corner I could find, General.'

'Let's wait on that promotion until I see it in writing, Sergeant.' He grinned.

'Something funny, sir?'

'I was just picturing you as a Lieutenant.'

'You wouldn't!'

'If I was a general, they'd have to listen . . .'

The worried look on Fernandez's face was priceless.

Saturday
The Yews, Sussex, England

Major Terrance Arthur Peel – 'Tap' to his mates – stood next to Lord Goswell's greenhouse, behind the main house, watching as the beat-up black Volvo arrived. The groundskeeper's trio of dogs – a pair of border collies and an Alsatian – set to barking.

Peel liked dogs. He'd rather have one of those in a tent with him in the bush than the most sophisticated alarm available. A dog would let you know when you had company, and a well-trained dog could tell the difference between your friends and your enemies. *And* he would rip the enemy's throat out if you set him to it, too. Unlike people, good dogs were loyal.

The Volvo pulled to a halt, and the door squeaked open on the right side, disgorging a tall and spindly man of fifty, hair gone gray, with more ethnicity than perhaps his name would imply: Peter Bascomb-Coombs had a bit of the hooknose in him. Peel had done the background check himself.

Bascomb-Coombs wore an expensive, if ill-fitting, ice cream suit, a yellow silk shirt and blue tie, and handmade, pale gray Italian leather shoes. Certainly none of his ensemble was cheap. The shoes alone had to set him back three, four hundred quid. His Lordship did not stint on what he paid his favored employees, and Bascomb-Coombs was favored, Jewish roots or not.

Not that the scientist's ethnic background mattered. It didn't affect the man's brain a whit, and whatever else he was, Bascomb-Coombs was as bright and shiny a penny as they came. Brilliant, a certified genius, so far ahead of the rest of his field that he was like an Einstein or a Hawking – in a class by himself – except that he couldn't keep track of a sodding social calendar. He was supposed to have been here for dinner *last* night, and he had simply gotten it wrong. And even if this *had* been the proper day, he was still half an hour late.

The stereotype of the absent-minded professor certainly had a basis in fact, if Bascomb-Coombs was the indicator. Goswell himself had shrugged off the slight. One had to suffer such things – what could one expect from the working class, geniuses or not? Goswell wasn't entirely foolish, save for his mania about the Empire, and he certainly had sense enough to know that Bascomb-Coombs was too valuable to toss away because he got a dinner date wrong.

Peel smiled and adjusted the black SIG 9mm in the Galco paddle holster on his right hip. He was a big enough man so the pistol was easily concealed under the white linen Savile Row sport coat he wore. Six-two, fourteen stone and a bit, and still in fighting shape. Naturally, his Lordship wasn't the kind of man to have some thug in camouflage clothes standing about with a submachine gun, menacing guests. Peel, though retired from His Majesty's service under a cloud, was presentable. Good regiment, decent schools, still fit at forty-five, able to choose the right fork at formal dining if need be. An educated, civilized man, he could chat with the rich and famous and not seem out of place. He'd be a colonel by now had it not been for that . . . unpleasant business in Northern Ireland on his final tour. Bloody country, bloody savages living in it.

The small com unit in his jacket pocket cheeped. That would be Hawkins, at the gate, confirming the arrival of the Volvo at the house, checking to be sure no terrorists had boiled from of the car's boot to blast Peel.

'G-1 here. Package arrive?'

'Roger that, G-1. We are green at the house.'

'Copy green. All clear here, as well.'

Peel looked at his watch, a black-faced Special Forces analog with glow-in-the-dark tritium inserts, a gift from his men when he retired. None of them had been happy to see him go. The rest of the security team should be reporting in about . . . now . . .

'R-1. No activity here.'

'R-2. Got a couple of the fat man's cows chewing cud over here, otherwise clear.'

'Rover-3. Fence is clear from Grid 4 to Grid 7.'

'Gate-2. Slow as bloody Christmas out here.'

Peel acknowledged each of the gate guards and

rovers as they called in their reports. He had ten men, all ex-Army, spread out over the perimeter. This was not nearly enough for realistic coverage in a shooting situation, but most of His Lordship's enemies weren't the kind of men who would try to storm The Yews. More likely they'd skewer him with sharp bonds or pointed hostile stock deals.

He grinned. Of course, His Lordship had enemies who didn't know they were on *his* list, and now and again, they had to be . . . *attended* to, in a circumspect manner, of course. Which is how Tap Peel came to be in His Lordship's service. It was because Peel's father and Lord Goswell had been classmates at Oxford, of course, and that the senior Peel had managed a knighthood of his own before he died. One kept these things in the family, or, failing that, among the chums.

Looked like rain to the north. Supposed to do that in London today. A little shower wouldn't hurt the vegetation hereabouts, either, though the troops would bitch about it. Well, there was a soldier's lot, wasn't it? If you signed on, you signed on rain or shine, cold or hot, and that was that. God knew he had stood in enough downpours, water running into his collar, cursing the officers who had posted him wherever he happened to be.

He smiled. It was a great life, being a soldier. Too bad this was as close as he could come these days. Well, unless he wanted to traipse off to some third-world republic to be a hired mercenary. Hardly. In his grandfather's day, a soldier-of-fortune had been a more-or-less honorable profession; but now, a fool without any military service could answer an ad in an American magazine and wind up protecting your rear in some African jungle. Thank you, no. British fighting men were an odd lot, to be sure, but far and away a better class of soldier than one would find by advertising in a bloody *magazine*.

He supposed he should move inside now. Dinner would begin shortly, and there would be a round of drinks beforehand. Bascomb-Coombs was a white-wine sort of fellow, and His Lordship did not feel comfortable with men who did not drink, so Peel would go and have a sociable whiskey.

His Lordship hated to drink alone.

So, a short one, two fingers, no more, to make sure his head stayed clear.

He grinned again. He had certainly had worse duty.

4

Saturday
Washington, D.C.

The National Boomerang Qualifying Championships were being held at the new Clinton High School track and field ground, and Tyrone Howard was thrilled just to be there, not to mention how ecstatic he was to actually be a *contestant*. Sure, it was Junior Novice Division, and he was only in one event, Maximum Time Aloft, but still, it was pretty amazing. He'd only been seriously throwing for six months.

Next to Tyrone, his best friend, Jimmy-Joe, blinked through thick glasses at all the contestants doing warm-ups. 'Yo, slip, isn't this, like, dangerous? Happens if you get cracked on the stack with one of these things? This ain't VR, it's the real O'Neal.'

Jimmy-Joe was VR all the way, same as Tyrone had been just a few months ago, but Tyrone thought maybe he was coming along okay on this . . . outside stuff. It had taken him a week to convince his friend to leave the computer and go to an actual competition. He said, 'So you get knocked over and wake up with a bump on your skull. Hey, you could short out a REM driver and get brain-fry, too, hillbilly.'

'Oh, yeah, right I could. Past a triple-fail safe and with like a half milliamp of vamp? Couldn't fry a piss ant's egg with that. Not the same as getting whopped on the head with a big ole stick, slip.' Jimmy-Joe shook his head. He gleamed in the sunshine. He had to wear skinblock to walk to the bus in the mornings, and it took him two weeks in the sun just to darken from bright to white. Something of a contrast for Tyrone, who was a nice chocolate color even if he stayed inside all the time. Which he hadn't been doing much of late. He'd been a hardwired compuzoid, sure enough, and good at it, too, until that whole business with Bella blew him out of VR and into RW. Being jettisoned by her had done a doody on him, sure enough. His thirteenth year had been hard, that was a facto, Jacko.

'All right, you got me here,' Jimmy-Joe said when Tyrone didn't reply. 'Frame the game, slip. What's all this twirly stick-dick about?'

Tyrone grinned. 'Okay, there are two basic kinds of boomerangs. One is a stick that comes back when you throw it. It might do a lot of fancy stuff on the way out and back, or not, depending on the type. They can range from the basic model that looks like a cross-section of a banana up to helicopter-like things with six or eight blades.

'The second kind is based on the abo war sticks,

and it doesn't come back, it just keeps on going until it drops – or hits somebody in the head. A war boomerang can go farther than anything else as heavy that you can throw. They fly due to gyroscopic precession caused by asymmetric lift. The lift comes from rotation combined with linear motion.'

'Code interrupt that last transmission, slip! Put it in *my* native tongue.'

'It flies because it turns into a wing as it spins; it comes back because the wing angle is different in different places.'

A tan and black Alsatian ran past, chasing a hard-silicone Frisbee Jackarang.

Tyrone shrugged out of his backpack, pulled out his basic Wedderburn. 'See how the edge is slanted on this blade, on the inner aspect? But on this side, the trailing edge has the slant? When it spins into the wind, the push is different every time the thing rotates, so it starts to curve. You throw it right-handed, like this–' Tyrone showed him the grip, with the concave side forward and the end up – 'and it flattens out and curves to the left.'

Jimmy-Joe looked at the boomerang. Hefted it. 'Hmm. I could code a pro, put in the factors – weight, RPM, speed, aerodynamics, all like that – and make it work exactly the same in VR.'

'Welcome to the past, slip. Serious throwers all have their own scenarios, since B.C. days. I've got exacts for each of my birds. But the program is just the map, *these* are the territory.' He opened his backpack to show his friend his other boomerangs. He had three classics, and three MTAs, ultra-thin and light, rosin-impregnated linen L-shaped blades designed for maximum flight time. His favorite of these was the Möller 'Indian Ocean' model, a standard Paxolin model he had gotten pretty good with.

He indicated the Möller. 'I'll use this one for my event.'

'Hmmp. Doesn't sound as hard as DinoWarz.'

'Analog real-time is different than digital, hill-billy. Talkin' muscle memory, judging wind speed, temperature, all like that.'

Jimmy-Joe wasn't impressed. 'I could program all that in. One session.'

'Yeah, but you couldn't walk over there and throw this and make it work.'

The dog ran back with the Frisbee in its mouth and dropped it at the feet of its owner, a tall dude with green hair. 'Good girl, Cady!' Green-Hair said. 'Go again?'

The dog barked and bounced around.

'And the event you are doing is which one?'

'Maximum Time Aloft. You throw, it twirls up and around, a judge puts a stopwatch on it. Everybody gets a throw, the bird that stays up the longest wins. You have to catch it when it comes back or it doesn't count, and it has to land inside the fifty-meter circle. You want something light and with a lot of lift. The current record is just over four minutes.'

'Feek that! Four minutes twirling around? No motor? Come on.'

'That's just the official record. There are guys who have put one in the air for almost eighteen minutes, unofficially.'

'No feek? That doesn't seem possible.'

'I scat you not.'

Tyrone held up the Möller. 'My best with this is just over two minutes. If I could throw that today, I could probably make the Junior National Team.'

'That'd be DFF.'

Tyrone smiled. Yep, data flowin' fine. Too bad his dad wasn't here to watch. Dad had been real helpful when Tyrone had gotten started, even had an old boomerang at Grandma's house he'd found. Of course, Dad couldn't keep up with him now but that was okay. He was not bad – as dads went.

The PA system blared to life. Tyrone's event was up.

Tyrone swallowed, his mouth suddenly dry. Practice was one thing, competition was another. This was his first, and he suddenly felt a need to go pee, real bad, even though he had gone just ten minutes ago.

Despite his indoor pallor, Jimmy-Joe seemed to be getting into the spirit of things. 'So, when do you do your thing?'

'I'm eighteenth. There are thirty-odd throwers in my class. Some of them have come all the way across the country for this, and some of them are real good.'

'You gonna watch the others?'

'Oh, yeah. Might see something useful. Plus I want to know what time I have to beat.'

'You know some rude dude has, like, three minutes, that helps you?'

'Just like knowing what the high score in DinoWarz does.'

'Copy that.'

There were several other events underway at the same time – distance, accuracy, Australian – and Tyrone and Jimmy-Joe found a shady spot under a dealer's canopy and watched the juniors.

First guy up was a tall, lean kid with a shaved head. He threw a bright red tri-blade – not the best choice for this event – and Tyrone clicked his stopwatch. Forty-two seconds. Nothing.

The next guy was a short, stout kid with a Day-Glo-green L-shape, looked like a Bailey MTA Classic, or maybe a Girvin Hang 'Em High. Or it could be one of the clones, you couldn't really tell from this far away.

Tyrone clocked the flight at a minute-twelve. No winner here, he was pretty sure. Winds were light, from the northeast, so he wouldn't need to tape coins or flaps to his blades to keep them from getting batted down.

Third thrower up was a girl, as dark as Tyrone was, probably about his age, and she had a Möller, same model as his. She took a couple of steps, leaned into it, and threw.

The bird sailed out and up, high, hung there for what seemed like forever, spinning, drifting, circling back. It was a beautiful throw and an exemplary flight. Tyrone glanced away from the bird at the girl. She was looking back and forth from her stopwatch to the bird, and she was grinning.

As well she should. When the bird finished its lazy trip and came down, the black girl had a two-minute and forty-eight second flight to her credit. That wasn't going to be an easy time to beat.

They watched eight more throwers, none of whom came within thirty seconds of the third girl, then Tyrone had to go and warm up for his own throw. His mouth was a desert, his bowels churned, and he was breathing too fast. This ought not to be scary, it was something he did every day the weather was good, threw his boomerang, dozens of times. But there weren't several hundred people watching him practice, and today he only got one throw that counted . . .

Just let me break two minutes, he thought, as he approached the throwing circle. *Two minutes won't win, but I won't be last and I won't feel like a fool. Two minutes, okay?*

He pulled a little commercial pixie dust from his pocket and rubbed it between his left thumb and first two fingers, letting it fall to check the wind direction. The glittery dust sparkled as it fell and showed him that the wind had shifted a hair toward the north, but still was mostly northeast. He dropped the rest of the dust, pulled his stopwatch and held it in his left hand, and took a good grip on the Möller with his right. He took three deep breaths, exhaling slowly, then nodded at the judge next to the ring. If he stepped out, he'd be disqualified. The judge nodded back, raised his own stopwatch.

Go, Tyrone.

He took another deep breath, one step, leaned, snapped his wrist, and put as much shoulder into it as he thought the bird could stand. He was careful to make sure it didn't lay over to the right, and he put it as close to forty-five degrees as he could.

He clicked the stopwatch.

Two minutes and forty-one seconds later, his bird gave it up. He caught it safe, double-handed clap, and that was that.

Tyrone grinned. There were still a dozen more throwers to go, but he had beaten his own personal record by more than thirty seconds, and he was in second place. No matter what happened, he was happy with that throw.

As Tyrone started back toward where Jimmy-Joe waited, the black girl who was in first came over. She was athletic-looking, muscular in a T-shirt and bike shorts and soccer shoes, a little plain-looking. Not in the drop-dead-beautiful-class that Bella had been in. And still *was* in.

'Nice throw,' she said. 'You'da leaned a little more to your left, you'da gotten another ten, twelve seconds out of the flight and beat me.'

'You think?'

'Sure. The Möller'll do six minutes, so they say. I've thrown a 3' 51" in practice. Hi, I'm Nadine Harris.'

'Tyrone Howard.'

'Where you from, Ty?'

'Here. Washington.'

'Hey, really? Me, too. Just moved here from Boston. I go to Eisenhower Middle. Or I will go next week.'

Tyrone stared at her. 'No feek?'

'Nope. You heard of it?'

'I *go* there.'

'Wow! What are the chances of that? Hey, maybe we can throw together sometime! Last school I was at, nobody else was a player.'

'I hear that. Exemplary. Let me give you my E-mail address.'

When Tyrone got back to where Jimmy-Joe stood, his friend was looking around on the ground. 'Lose something, white boy?'

'Oh, I was just looking for a big stick.'

'A big stick?'

'Yeah, slip, for you. To help keep the women away.' He waved in the direction of the departing black girl, pretending to be hitting at her with an imaginary stick.

'Ah, shut it down, dip, she's just a player is all!'

'I can see that.'

'You spend too much time in the pervo rooms, JJ. Get a life.'

'Why should I? Yours is so much more fun.'

Tyrone swatted at him, but his friend danced away. He moved pretty fast for such a little creep.

Later, when the juniors were done, Tyrone watched the portable computer sign they'd set up to flash the results. Unofficially, he already knew he was third. Some guy from Puerto Rico had slipped in between him and Nadine with a time three lousy seconds longer than Tyrone's. Even so, third out of thirty-four at a national competition, and with a new PR, that wasn't bad. He'd made the US team.

The sign started to blink, then it went blank. A second later, an image of some kind of flag appeared, waving in a VR breeze.

Tyrone glanced at his friend. 'Hacker got 'em. Why don't you go and offer to fix it?'

Jimmy-Joe's eyes lit up. 'You think?'

Tyrone laughed.

Saturday
Las Vegas, Nevada

'Got a problem, Colonel,' Fernandez said.

They were at the staging area, getting the trucks loaded for the drive into the desert. A dozen troops, men and women, hauled gear and made ready to begin the run.

'We haven't even made first contact with the enemy yet, Sergeant. Not the local police, is it?'

Sometimes they called the locals in, sometimes not, depending on the situation. This time, there weren't any cops close enough to the target's location to worry about, and the Clark County Sheriff's Department didn't need to know because it was out of their jurisdiction by a long way.

Fernandez shrugged. 'It's the computer. Take a look.'

Howard drifted over to the tac-comp, where a tech named Jeter sat and cursed under his breath.

'It appears to be the Union Jack,' Howard observed.

'Yes, sir,' Jeter said. 'It is. It's *supposed* to be the sitrep feed from Big Squint, with a three-dee layout of the target's location.' Jeter thumped the monitor with one hand. 'This is what happens when you buy your electronics wholesale from the damned New Zealanders, begging your pardon, sir.'

Howard grinned. 'I trust you to clear it up before we depart.'

'Yes, sir.'

Howard looked away, took a deep breath and let it out. He looked at his watch. He wondered how Tyrone had done at the boomerang competition. He was tempted to call but he knew better. Shielded com or not, it was unwise to give away your position in a tactical situation, and not a good habit to get into. He'd call his son when they got this target acquired and neutralized. He was a good kid, Tyrone, but he was also a teenager. Life was getting complicated for the boy and it wasn't going to get any easier. How could a father protect his son from that? He couldn't, and that was painful. The days when Daddy was all-knowing and all-wise were gone. He'd never given it much thought, but now it was staring him in the face: his son was growing up, changing, and if he wanted to maintain contact with him, he was going to have to change, too. That was a strange feeling.

'Got it,' Jeter said. 'We're back on track.'

Worry about child-rearing later, John. Keep your mind on the business at hand.

'Good. Carry on.'

5

Saturday
London, England

Toni Fiorella climbed the narrow, creaky stairs toward the second floor of the four-story walk up. The place she wanted was on that floor, over a small appliance shop in an area called Clapham, between a brick-red Indian Tandoori restaurant and a Charity Shop with boarded-up plywood windows. The buildings and the area in general were run-down. Not as bad as the worst of the Bronx, maybe, but not a place you'd want to take your old granny for a stroll after dark. Unless your granny was maybe a dope-dealer – and armed.

As she neared the top, Toni caught the odor of sweat, stale and fresh.

The heavy wooden door was unlocked.

Inside were fifteen or sixteen men and five women, all dressed in dark sweat pants, athletic shoes, and white T-shirts. The T-shirts had a black and white logo on the back, with a smaller matching version over the left breast: a Javanese wavy-bladed dagger – a *kris* – set at about a thirty-degree horizontal angle, bounded on the top and bottom by the words *'Pentjak Silat.'*

The twenty-odd people were doing *djurus*.

Toni grinned. The forms weren't the same as hers, since this version of the Indonesian martial art was not *Serak* but a variation of *Tjikalong*, which was a western Javanese style, but it looked similar enough that there was no mistaking the *djurus* – the forms – for karate *kata*.

The school itself was hardly impressive, nothing as nice as the FBI gyms at home. The ceiling was high, maybe fifteen feet. The floor was dark wood, old and worn, but clean. Folded in one corner of the large room were fraying blue hardfoam mats that also showed much wear, plus a couple of heavy punching bags wrapped in layers of duct tape. A brown wooden door had a sign on it that indicated it led to a bathroom – a loo, it was called over here. Exposed pipes, for water or heat or whatever, ran across the back wall about ten feet up, and the metal had been painted alternating colors, red, white and blue. A large roof support in the middle of the floor had what looked like an old mattress wrapped around it and held tight with half a dozen red and blue bungie cords. A double row of fluorescent lights graced the ceiling. An exhaust fan whirred in one of the windows, blowing the odor of sweat into the evening.

It was your basic large workout room, no frills.

A tall man dressed the same as the students

walked around, observing their form, correcting stances, offering praise when it was merited. He was not quite muscular enough to be a bodybuilder but he was broad-shouldered and narrow-hipped. He had short gray hair with some brown left in it. He wore aviator-style glasses. A first look might say mid-thirties, but Toni guessed he was in his early fifties, based on his hands and the smile wrinkles at the corners of his eyes.

'Hello,' he said in a clipped British tone. 'May I help you?'

'Hello. I'm Toni Fiorella. I called earlier?'

'Ah, yes, the American visitor. Welcome! I'm Carl Stewart, and these are my students.' He waved at the assembly. 'We're just about to finish with *djurus*.'

'Don't let me get in the way. I'll just stand and watch if that's all right?'

'Yes, of course.'

'Thank you, Guru.' Toni moved to stand next to the stack of mats.

'All right, then,' Stewart said to the class. 'Any questions about the *djurus*?'

A few hands went up. Stewart answered the queries about various moves from the forms. He was patient, not condescending, demonstrating the correct move to show how it was done.

He was smooth, balanced, tight. In *silat*, the ability to perform a *djuru* precisely wasn't always an indication of fighting ability, but you could tell a lot about a person by watching them move.

Carl Stewart moved as well as anybody Toni had ever seen. And she had seen more than a few fighters over the years.

Interesting.

For the next half hour or so, Stewart worked on self-defense applications from the forms, showing how they would apply against an attacker, then putting the students into pairs to practice. There weren't any belts to denote rank, same as in most *silat* styles, but it was obvious after a few minutes who were the advanced and who were the beginners.

This was her weakness, Toni knew. She'd had plenty of advanced training from her guru – as the Indonesians called their teachers – but she hadn't spent much time in group situations, either as a student or an instructor. Guru had always told her she needed to teach to get the full benefit of *silat*. She had only just begun that.

After about thirty minutes, Stewart put the advanced students into a series of controlled semi-freestyle match ups. One student would be the attacker, the other the defender. He allowed the attackers to throw full power punches and kicks, but only to the chest or thigh, where a missed block would merely be painful instead of seriously damaging.

She watched as the current pair of students faced each other. The defender was a thin man with long black hair, the attacker a short and squat red-haired fellow. The thin man turned so his right side was toward the attacker, his feet wide in a deep open stance; his left hand was high, by his face, the other hand low, to cover his groin.

Red tapped his right fist, to show that would be his attacking weapon. They stood about six feet apart, and they circled each other slowly.

Red lunged, shot a fist at the center of Thin's chest. Thin pivoted slightly, did a scoop block and a backfist with his right hand, then followed up with a grab and *sapu*, a sweep, that upended Red and put him on the floor.

Not bad.

Red came up, gave Thin a fist-in-the-palm salute, and they reversed roles.

Thin punched. Red ducked under the punch, put his right shoulder into Thin's belly, stepped through and *biset*, a heel-drag, and took Thin to the floor.

Not bad at all. These would be the two senior students, Toni guessed.

Stewart waved the students off. Then he looked at Toni. 'We have an American *silat* practitioner with us today, class. Perhaps she'd like to demonstrate how her style works?'

Toni smiled. She'd half expected this. Since she was in jeans and running shoes and a short-sleeved cotton pullover, she was dressed to move. 'Sure,' she said.

'Joseph, if you would?' Stewart nodded at Red.

'Joseph is my senior student.'

Toni nodded and gave Stewart, then Red, the fist-in-palm bow. Relaxed, hands low.

Red circled to her left. She did a back cross-step, turned to follow him.

Red lunged, bracing his right punch with his left hand, set up for the wipe if she blocked.

Toni dropped to the floor, caught Red in the belly with a short left thrust kick, hooked her right foot behind his right knee and thrust with her left again.

Red went over backwards as Toni rolled up and did a heel scoop – a hackey-sack kick over his head, slapping it with her left hand to show the connection.

Red waited to see if she was done and, when she stepped back to show she was, came up with a big grin. 'Nice move!'

Stewart also wore a smile. Her move had been flashy but it had worked against his senior student, so he ought to be impressed.

'Very good, Ms Fiorella.'

'Toni, please, Guru.'

'Mightn't I ask if you would feel up to performing *kembangan*?'

Toni nodded. Of course. *Kembangan* was the 'flower dance' and, unlike forms of *kata* in most martial arts, was a spontaneous expression of a *silat* player's art, nothing prearranged. An expert never did the same form twice. Unlike *buah*, the full speed and full power dance, *kembangan* softened the moves, using the open hands more than fists, and turned the motions into a dance suitable for demonstration weddings and social gatherings.

If you really wanted to see how good a *silat* player was, you watched them do *kembangan*. In the old days, when a fight was imminent but the contestants didn't want to maim or kill each other, they would sometimes offer each other *kembangan* instead of actual combat. Experts could recognize who would have won the fight by the skill they displayed during the dance, and there would be no need to come to blows. If you were defeated in *kembangan*, you apologized or made right whatever the problem was, and that was that. It would be dishonorable to continue against an opponent of much lesser skill, and foolish to challenge one who was obviously much better. Of course, the best dancers would sometimes deliberately put small errors into their routines, to lull an opponent into thinking they were less skilful than they actually were. In *kembangan* competitions, only if the players considered each other to be of like abilities did the game progress to sweeps or strikes.

Toni took a deep breath, allowed it to escape softly. She made a full, formal bow to the guru, did another cleansing breath, then a third, and began.

There were days when you were off and days when you were on. Today, her flow was good, she felt the energy coursing through her, and she knew she could do a clean dance without major mistakes.

Halfway through, she deliberately misstepped a hair, allowed her balance to drift slightly off before she recovered.

One did not wish to embarrass the guru in charge of a school one visited by being perfect. It might make him look bad in front of his students, and that was impolite.

A minute was enough. She finished the dance, bowed again. It was a great one, she knew, one of her best. Her guru would be proud.

The class broke into spontaneous applause.

Toni flushed, embarrassed.

Stewart smiled at her. 'Beautiful. An outstanding *kembangan*. Thank you . . . Guru.'

Toni gave him a short nod. He acknowledged her skill by calling her 'teacher.' Now *she* was curious. It was a bit forward but she said, 'I would be pleased to enjoy your *kembangan*, Guru.'

The students went quiet. It wasn't a direct challenge, but there was a broad hint: I showed you mine, now show me yours.

He smiled wider. 'Of course.'

He offered her a formal bow, different from hers but similar in intent, cleared his wind and mind, and began. Stewart's best days would be behind him. At fifty, she knew he would be past his physical peak, on the downhill slide. That was the nature of human physiology. His knowledge might be greater but his body would be half a step behind, and steadily, if slowly, losing ground. Her own guru had been amazing, but she'd been an old woman when Toni started, and there were places she could no longer go. Stewart was still in good shape to look at, and certainly better shape than most men his age, but he would have lost a couple of steps by now. She should have made a couple more mistakes in her dance, she thought.

With Stewart's first series of moves, Toni realized she was wrong.

If you play decent guitar and you see a tape of Segovia practicing, it makes you want to cry. Because you know you'll never be that good.

Stewart was the martial artist equivalent of Segovia.

Toni watched, mesmerized. The man moved as if he had no bones, as if he was a drop of hot oil rolling down a clean glass window, smooth, effortless – and utterly amazing. She had never seen anybody perform *kembangan* as well.

At about the same point in his dance as Toni had done, Stewart offered a bobble. His foot came down a hair crooked, he had to shift his weight hurriedly to recover.

Toni didn't buy it for a second. This man, who was old enough to be her father, would not make that kind of mistake. He'd given it to her, a gift, so *she* would not lose face.

She was thrilled. If push came to shove, Stewart was superior to her. He was the perfect opponent, the one her guru had always trained her to face:

bigger, stronger, probably faster, and with technique that exceeded her own. In *silat*, you didn't practice to beat attackers who had no skill, you strived to learn how to defeat those who were as good as, or better than you. If you could prevail in those circumstances, you had the essence of the Indonesian system.

If she and Stewart fought, *he* would win. There was no question in her mind.

As soon as she realized this, Toni wanted to do it, wanted to test him, to be bested – and to learn from it.

Stewart finished the dance and bowed. The students wanted to go wild with cheering and clapping, but he held up a hand to silence them. He gave Toni a military bow, a slow nod.

Toni said, 'I'm going to be here for a week or so longer. I would be honored if you would allow me to attend your classes, Guru.'

'The honor,' he said, 'would be mine.'

Oh, boy!

Saturday
Somewhere in the British Raj – India

Jay Gridley used a big silver machete to hack his way through leafy vines that draped low across the jungle trail. It was hard work, chopping at the bush, and the heat and humidity enveloped him in a miasmatic fog that kept him drenched in sweat. The wooden handle raised blisters on his hand, and the stink of cut branches and vines was so cloyingly . . . *verdant* it was alive with greenness.

It wasn't comfortable, this hack through the jungle, but there was no good way to make this tracking scenario a cake walk. No matter what he created, it wasn't going to make the job easier. If he made a haystack, the needle he'd be looking for would be microscopic; if he created a beach, he'd be trying to find a sand-colored *smudge* on a particular grain of sand. It was hard, period, end of mission statement, we don't need to see his ID, move along.

But he was getting closer, nonetheless.

A fat albino python sunned itself on a big branch to his left, well off the trail, no danger. Gridley grinned. It was the dog that didn't bark in the night that had pointed him in the right direction. The player who had broken the encrypted code in Pakistan was better than anybody Gridley had ever gone up against, no question. Better than the redneck from Georgia, better than the mad Russian, and – as much as he hated to admit it to himself – better than he was. This guy was a master – he'd *have* to be to do what he did – and he had not left a trail.

Well, not exactly. The tiger had left an Also – a Trail Of Omission, 'TOO', thus brought to 'also' – a concept that was impossible to convey to anybody who didn't know the VR field in and out, and exceedingly difficult to understand if you did know. It was lot like trying to make sense of subatomic physics, it was counter-intuitive. The tiger who had eaten the goat went this way because there was no trail and . . . because nobody *could* have gone this way.

Gridley hacked at a branch with heart-shaped dark leaves as big as dinner plates. The branch fell. The weight of the double rifle slung over his shoulder was oppressive, the belt with the holstered Webley revolver dug into his side. There was no trail here, but he was *sure* the tiger had gone this way. He cut another branch, tossed it aside—

He was right. It *had* gone this way.

He got only a glimpse of it as it leaped. A flash of orange and black, huge teeth, a paw as big as a dragon's.

Then the tiger slapped Jay Gridley's head with that monstrous paw and the world went red – and away.

6

Sunday
London, England

Alex Michaels came out of a troubled dream to the sound of his virgil playing the Aaron Copland fanfare. He sat up and glared at the device where it sat next to his bed in the recharger. What was cute in the afternoon wasn't so funny at two in the morning, even when it woke you from a nightmare about your ex-wife.

Next to him, Toni stirred.

Michaels got up, grabbed the virgil and killed the call tone, then headed for the bathroom. Once there he turned on the light, shut the door, and activated the phone circuit. After glancing at himself in the mirror, he left the visual mode off. Naked, with a sleep-wrinkled face and pillow-hair, wasn't his best look.

The call was from Allison's office.

'This is Alex Michaels.'

'Hold for the Director, please.'

Yeah, right. Wake him up in the middle of the night, but couldn't be bothered to make the call herself?

She came on almost immediately.

'Michaels, we have a situation here. One of your men, a . . . Jason Gridley? has had some kind of stroke. He is in the hospital.'

'What?'

'He was found when the shift changed at the controls of his computer.'

'A stroke? But – how? He's a kid! There's no history of stroke in his family.'

'You'll have to ask the doctors about that.' There was a pause. 'I understand that Gridley is your point man on virtual-reality scenarios.'

'Yes.' Jesus, a stroke? Jay? He couldn't get his mind around that. Jay was in his twenties.

'Could this have had anything to do with the investigation we are conducting into the situation in Pakistan?'

What was she talking about? 'No, no way. You can't get hurt by a computer in VR mode, even with the power jacket at maximum, there's not enough juice. Why would you even ask?'

'Because a British Intelligence computer operative and one in Japan have also had cerebellar events similar to Gridley's, both of them in the last few hours.'

'Not possible. I mean, it's not possible that they were caused by their computers.'

'Nonetheless, Commander, it seems a striking coincidence. I am given to understand, unofficially, that these two computer operatives were also investigating the Pakistani situation.'

'Jesus.'

'Perhaps you might want to cut your vacation short.'

'I–yes, you're right. I'll book a flight out as soon as I can get one.'

'Good. Keep me informed.'

Michaels stared at his reflection in the mirror. Never a dull moment.

'Alex?'

He opened the door. Toni, fogged with sleep and beautifully nude, stood outside the bathroom. 'Who are you talking to?'

'The boss.'

Then he gave her the bad news about Jay.

Saturday
Las Vegas, Nevada

'Son-of-a-*bitch*!'

'Should I take that personally, Sergeant?'

Howard smiled at Fernandez, but the expression was tight and forced. He could well understand his friend's frustration. He was pissed off, too.

The tactical computer was down. It had flickered back to normal operation from the British flag a couple of times, but then had lost the satellite signal and had been unable to regain it. The techs had fiddled with things, and it turned out not to be their system, but USAT's. Howard had talked to the OOD there, but it wasn't going to help. Major Phillips was polite, but terse: His system was acting up, and begging the Colonel's pardon, but he had his hands full trying to unsnarl the bastard and could he have somebody call him back asap?

That had been hours ago, and still the feed wasn't accessible.

Howard looked at his watch, then at Fernandez. 'Okay, that's it. We're scrubbed. Tell them to stand down.'

As he expected, his top kick wasn't happy with that. 'Colonel, we don't need the feed from Big Squint. This guy is in the middle of the desert. We can eyeball it.'

'Negative, Sergeant, that's not the protocol.'

'Sir, troops have been taking territory without satellite coverage for thousands of years. It's one guy alone in a *trailer*, we got two squads and enough gear to fill up a boxcar! How hard can it be?'

'Come on, Julio, you know the rules. There's no leeway for emergency bypass here. Like you said, it's one guy. He's been there for months, he doesn't know we're here, and we've got the roads in and out covered. He's not going anywhere, and even if he wanted to, he couldn't. This is as by-the-numbers as it gets.'

Fernandez mumbled something.

'Say again, Sergeant?'

'Sir, this is bullshit. If twenty troops can't take down one man without help from big bird, we ought to turn in our uniforms and retire. Go sit on the bank of a catfish pond, drown worms, and wait to die. Sir.'

Howard's grin this time was real. 'I hear you, Julio, but it's our protocol for this op-sit. The RA guys will fix their system sooner or later. Tell the troops to take the night off. Go see the casinos, watch a show, enjoy the lights of Vegas. Be back here at 0600 and we'll reset.'

Fernandez shrugged. Unexpected liberty was always good, and this was, after all, Las Vegas. A man with a little money in his pocket could get into all kinds of trouble without having to work too hard. 'Well, sir, since you put it like that, I suppose we'll just have to suffer through the wait.'

'And remember, you are practically a married man now, Sergeant.'

'Yes, sir, of course. But I'm not a *dead*, practically married man. I can still look.'

The two grinned at each other.

Howard headed toward the nearby motel where Net Force had booked enough rooms for his troops. It still felt weird, to be bivouacked not in a tent under the stars but at an air-conditioned motel. It made more sense, of course. A military group camping anywhere around here would draw more attention than it would with its vehicles garaged and its troops tucked away out of sight.

He planned to call home and talk to his wife and son, grab a shower to wash some of the heat and dust off, and maybe find a nice restaurant for some dinner. They had good food in Las Vegas, especially at some of the casinos, and it was cheap, too. They figured they were going to get your money at the slots or the tables, so they might as well make it attractive to stay there and eat, to give them more chances at it. And you could play keno right at your table while you chowed down. Most places served breakfast, lunch or dinner twenty-four hours a day. Once you stepped into the wonders of Gambling Land, time stood still. They didn't leave a lot of clocks around to remind you that you needed to be getting along home, either.

It had been a few years since he'd been here, but Howard didn't think it would have changed all that much. You could stick the kiddies in free daycare, or turn them loose in Warner Bros. World or the Hard Rock, and go lose their college education money. Fun for the whole family and a long way from the old days when the mob ran everything.

The motel was low-key and also cheap, Net Force being like most other government agencies that way. GS employees didn't need to be staying at the best hotels on the taxpayer's credit card. It didn't look good, especially at election time.

There was an old-fashioned mechanical slot machine next to the Coke machine, and Howard shook his head at that. He wasn't a gambler. Oh, he'd buy a lottery ticket now and then, or put a fiver on a soccer or baseball pool. He would root for the Orioles, maybe even cover a friendly bet on them, but he wasn't infested with gambling fever. The odds always favored the house, and the only way to look at games of chance as far as he was concerned was to consider it as entertainment. You wanted to play in the casinos, you took a few dollars and spent it, just as if you were paying for dinner and a show. Once it was gone, that was it, you quit, end of story. You didn't dig into your pocket to win back what you'd lost, and if you happened to come out ahead by the time you were supposed to leave, you went home and put the money in the bank.

His father had taught him that. If you play somebody else's game, most of the time they are going to win. Better to spend your money where it will do you some good.

Howard's room was small, clean, and the water pressure in the shower was not as bad as he'd expected. After he cleaned up, he unpacked his duffel, slipped into a pair of no-iron khaki slacks and a short-sleeve shirt, and found some clean socks and his old loafers. Always paid to take civilian clothes if you were working anywhere near a town. One minute you were a soldier, the next you were a civilian. With the variation in hairstyles these days, nobody could tell by looking.

So, call home, visit with the family, then grab a bite to eat. And after that? Maybe come back to the room and read. After all, he had to get up early, and even though the malady he'd had a while back that made him feel old and tired had been cleared up, the days when he could party all night long and then go straight to work without missing a beat were long past. If he was going to be up and ready to roll at 0600, he was going to have to get to bed at a decent hour.

He grinned at himself in the mirror. Maybe Fernandez was right; maybe he should retire and go drown worms in a catfish pond.

Nah. Not yet.

Sunday
Quantico, Virginia

When Jay Gridley awoke, he had a moment of panic: Where was he?

There was an IV going into his left hand, a tube running from his penis into a bag attached to the side of the bed, and wireless pickups stuck to his chest and his head. There was a cuff around his left upper arm. He wore one of those shortie open-backed gowns.

A hospital, okay, he got that. And something must have happened to him for him to be here. An accident?

He couldn't remember. He started to look at his

arms and legs more carefully, to see if anything was missing or damaged. No, they were there, and he wasn't feeling any pain—

A tall, short-haired brunette in green scrubs appeared next to the bed. She took Jay's right wrist in her hand and looked at her watch. She was about thirty, very attractive. She smiled at him. 'Hey,' she said.

He couldn't feel her fingers on his wrist. In fact, he couldn't feel his right arm at all. Couldn't even relate to it. As if that arm she was holding belonged to somebody else. What—?

She said, 'You're in the Neuro Ward at the base hospital. You had a CVA, a cerebrovascular accident. A stroke. My name is Rowena, I'm the floor nurse this shift. Do you understand?'

A stroke? How could that be? He said, 'I understand.'

But what came out of his mouth instead was a horrible, slurred, slack-lipped sound: 'Awo unnersan.'

His incipient panic expanded into full-blown terror.

The nurse put her hand on his chest, on the left side. He felt that. 'Easy. Your doctor is on the way, she'll explain it all to you, but listen, don't worry. You've got some transient paralysis on the right side. It's going to go away. What happened to you was not major. The drugs you are on are going to fix the damage, it'll take a few days, maybe a couple of weeks, okay? But you are going to be all right.'

Gridley felt his panic abate a little. He was going to be all right. He clutched at that, trying to get a tighter grip on it. He was going to be all right.

Unless she is just telling you that so you don't lose it, his inner voice said.

Another woman entered the room, a short, heavy-set bleached-blonde. She also wore green scrubs, and she carried a flatscreen. Without preamble, she said, 'I'm Dr West. Sometime yesterday afternoon you had a small CVA – a stroke. There were no clots or major bleeders apparent on the CAT- and MEG brain scans, and the cause is idiopathic. That means we don't know what caused it. Your vital signs are normal, your blood pressure, respiration, and pulse are all fine, and your blood chemistry is within normal limits. Aside from the CVA, everything is great. You have what we think is a transient hemiplegia or hemiparesis, and we expect full resolution of that. You following me?'

Gridley nodded, not wanting to hear his own voice.

'Good. You'll be here for a day or two, then we'll let you go home. Physical therapy starts this afternoon; somebody will come in and show you some exercises.'

The doctor glanced at her watch. 'Got to run. I'll check in on you later, with a bunch of medical students. People will come and go, draw blood, give you meds. Try to get some rest.'

Dr West handed the flatscreen to Rowena and left.

Get some rest?

Yeah, right. Part of his brain had exploded and he was supposed to *rest*? No way. Not gonna happen. He didn't want to just lie there and worry about it, either, but what choice did he have? He was tubed and wired and he wasn't going anywhere.

Lord. How could this have happened?

7

Sunday
The Yews, Sussex, England

Applewhite brought Goswell's tray and set it on the table. Vapor rose from the teapot's spout – it was a bit cool out here in the garden, but crisp and bracing. Goswell nodded. 'Thank you, Applewhite.'

The butler poured a cup of tea, adding one lump of sugar and a squeeze of lemon. 'More scones, sir?'

'I think not. A telephone, if you would.'

'Certainly, milord.'

Applewhite produced a mobile from his jacket pocket before Goswell could even take a sip of the tea. He shook his head. Technology. A mixed blessing, to be sure, but fortunately, one which had served him well, financially and otherwise.

'And what was our scientist fellow's name again?'

'Peter Bascomb-Coombs, milord.'

'Ah, yes, of course.' Goswell repeated the man's name into the phone, then held it to his ear. It rang thrice.

'Yes, what it is?' He sounded irritated. Well, of course, these kinds of fellows always did.

'Geoffrey Goswell here.'

'Oh. Lord Goswell.' That changed his tone quick enough, eh what? 'What may I do for you?'

'Not much, my boy. I was ringing you up to see about that, ah . . . small matter we discussed recently over supper.'

'Ah, yes, well, it is proceeding apace. There have been a couple of minor setbacks, but I have taken care of them, and we should be back on schedule right enough.'

He was properly cautious, the scientist. Even though Peel had assured him that his mobile phone and the scientist's were both secure against eavesdroppers, Goswell hated to have things of this nature spoken aloud outside the confines of his own home.

He nodded, then realized the man couldn't see him because this mobile didn't have cameras and what-not connected to it. 'Right, then. And those, ah, curious fellows you spoke of?'

'They are no longer curious. They have other things to occupy their minds at the moment.'

'Very good, then. I'll ring off now.'

Applewhite appeared and took the mobile, put it away. 'Will there be anything else, milord?'

'Yes, see if you can hunt up Peel, would you? I'd like to have a word with him if he's available.'

'At once, milord.'

Applewhite departed to fetch the major. That, at least, would give Goswell time enough to sip his tea before it got cold.

From the corner of his eye, Goswell caught a motion. He looked directly that way and saw a rabbit over in the flower bed, nibbling on some greenery. Cheeky bastard! He wasn't fifty feet away! Of course, the dratted rabbits never came out when he had his shotgun at hand; they were smart enough to know that wasn't wise. His vision was not as keen as once it was, but he could, by God, still pot a thieving rabbit at fifty feet with either barrel of his Purdey fowling piece, thank you very much. He considered calling Applewhite and telling him to collect his shotgun so that he could blast the offending rabbit, but decided against it. It was too lovely a morning to ruin with shotgun noise, satisfying as it might be to teach the bunny some proper manners. Better to have the caretaker loose his dogs on the things. They seldom caught one, the dogs, but they had such fun chasing them, and the rabbits tended to clear off for a time thereafter.

He sipped his tea. When Peel approached, the rabbit decided to remove himself. Perhaps it somehow knew that Peel was an excellent shot with his ever-present pistol and that to stay might be unwise.

'My lord?'

'Morning, Major. Do sit down and have some tea.'

'Thank you, my lord.' Peel seated himself. A decent chap, the image of his father, old Ricky. He poured himself a cup of tea, black, no sugar.

'I've been thinking about this scientist fellow of ours.'

'Bascomb-Coombs,' Peel said.

'The very one. I've been thinking perhaps we should keep a close eye on him, if you know what I mean. He is valuable enough, but with the things he has tucked away in his head, we wouldn't want to have a falling out, now would we?'

'I shouldn't think a falling out is likely, my lord.'

'Well, no, hardly. But one must be diligent and prepared, what?'

'I understand completely. As it happens, I have anticipated that you might feel this way, so I've set a watch upon our Mr Bascomb-Coombs.'

'Have you? Excellent. You're a good lad, Peel.'

'Thank you, my lord. I appreciate your confidence in me.'

Goswell smiled and sipped at his tea. It was good to have men like Peel around, men who knew how to do things without having to be led by the hand. Men of decent breeding who wouldn't embarrass one with social blunders or rash actions. More like him and the Empire would never have sunk so low.

'Should Mr Bascomb-Coombs ever think to become a problem, my lord, we are of course prepared to deal with him in an . . . *expedient* manner.'

'Ah, well, very good, then. Have a scone.'

Peel smiled and gave him a short nod. Such a good fellow to have around. Pity about all that Irish business. Still, the regiment's loss was Goswell's gain. Would that he had another dozen like Peel. Good help was so hard to come by these days.

'Excellent scones, my lord.'

'I'll have Applewhite tell Cook you said so.'

This is how a gentleman was supposed to breakfast. On a sunny spring day at one's country estate, on tea and good scones, in the company of decent fellows. Indeed.

Sunday
London, England

Toni and Alex sat in a small restaurant near their hotel, having coffee and breakfast. She said, 'We have a flight leaving from Heathrow at noon. I couldn't get us on the Concorde, or on a direct, so we'll have to change planes at Kennedy for a cropduster to Dulles.'

Alex sipped his coffee, then said, 'You could stay here. There's no need for you to kill your vacation.'

'Stay here by myself? What fun would that be?'

'Well, this *silat* class you found sounds interesting.'

'Two hours in the evening. If you go, I'm going. You'll need me at work.'

He stirred his eggs around with his fork, not really interested in eating them. 'Over easy,' he said. 'If these things had been fried any harder, you could play hockey with them.'

'I'm sorry about Jay,' she said.

'The doctor said he would be fine. Probably no lasting effects.'

'Even so.'

'I can't believe that he was injured due to something that happened in VR.' Alex stared at his eggs, silent.

'You saw the reports from the Brits and the Japanese. Same thing happened to their people, and they were both poking around in the same area Jay was.'

'It still doesn't seem possible.'

'Neither does breaking the code for the Pakistani train. Whoever did that is leaps and bounds ahead of us. They know things we don't.'

'There's a cheery thought.'

She looked at him. He seemed terribly glum. 'Something else on your mind, Alex?'

He prodded the eggs a final time, then put his fork down. 'Well, yeah. I didn't want to bother you with it.'

'Go ahead, bother me. What?'

'I got a notice from my ex-wife's lawyers on an E-fax this morning.'

'And . . . ?'

'Megan is suing for total custody of Susan.'

'Oh, no.'

'Oh, yeah. Maybe I shouldn't have decked her new boyfriend.'

'You said she was planning to do it before that.'

'Yes. But that probably didn't help. Or that I said

if he slept over again with Susie in the house, I'd throw an adultery charge at her.'

'You were angry.'

'Uh huh. And stupid. She's not a bad woman, it's just that she knows how to get under my skin.'

'Don't make excuses for her. She's a bitch.'

He smiled. 'Unfortunately, she's a bitch who is the mother of my only child, and she wants to take my daughter away. To have that bearded teacher become daddy instead.'

'What did your lawyer say?'

'What lawyers always say. Don't worry, he'll handle it, Megan won't win.'

She reached across the table and took his hand. 'It'll work out. You're too good a person, any judge will see that.'

He smiled again, turned his hand up and squeezed hers. 'Thanks. I love you.'

'That's why I'm here.'

She had loved Alex for a long time, and even though he could sometimes be exasperating with the way he bottled up his emotions and tried to shield her from things, in the grand cosmic scheme of things, these were minor problems. They'd get them worked out, eventually. She was sure of it.

Sunday
Las Vegas, Nevada

Despite his resolve to get to bed early, the wee hours found John Howard, after a long hike, standing in a parking lot outside the Luxor Hotel and Casino, staring into the sky. A crisp, dry wind whirled among the cars, stirring dust. The parking lot was surrounded by palm trees and other vegetation not native to this area. The Nevada summers were hot enough to convince the trees they could thrive – as long as they were watered – but the palms looked somehow uncomfortable as they stood around the edges of the concrete, swaying in the breeze, as if they knew they didn't belong here.

From the apex of the giant black pyramid that was the Luxor, a tight ring of spotlights, focused into one large ray, beamed straight up into the night. The heat from the laserlike column that shot up was intense enough that it sucked air and dust into itself, shoving it heavenward in a fountain of photons. Night had to watch Las Vegas from a distance – the city didn't allow the dark to come in.

Howard observed the boiling light beam. A moth that ventured too close to that white column would find itself roasted and blown halfway to the moon real quick.

There was something incredibly decadent about the whole city of Las Vegas, and the Luxor was a good example of it. More than four thousand rooms, at least half a dozen theme restaurants, a casino that never shut down, an Olympic-sized swimming pool, plus a boat voyage to the Land of the Dead, right in the atrium. It was ancient Egypt by way of Walt Disney, and for a dollar you could tug on the arm of an Egyptian deity and take a chance on the big pay-off. Place your bets, ladies and gentlemen, place your bets . . .

He had gone in and looked around and been amazed, but also overwhelmed, by it all. Here outside the massive structure, whose entrance was marked by a giant obelisk that shamed Cleopatra's Needle, and guarded by a sphinx in much better repair than the big one in Egypt, Howard got a sense of how truly rich the United States was. A nation that could produce such places as this, designed for leisure, for entertainment, for the millions who could afford to come and play here, well, that said a lot about such a country. He could hardly blame the owners whose goal was to separate suckers from their money. They had done a great job, but as attractive and over the top as it was, there was something . . . repellent about it at the same time.

Las Vegas called to the party-loving hearts in people, the *carpe diem*, grasshopper, be-here-now-and-devil-take-tomorrow psyches. But it also called to the dark side, the desperate, the greedy, the addicted. It was plastic and neon and all that was cheap and shoddy about America. But it was also fun.

Howard laughed and began the hike back toward his own motel room. Getting to be a philosopher in your old age, eh, John? Next thing you know, you'll be sitting in a dark room contemplating your navel.

He laughed again. Well. Maybe not just yet.

Sunday
Stonewall Flat, Nevada

Ruzhyó awoke from a troubled sleep, coming alert all at once as he had learned to do years ago in *Spetsnaz*. He listened, but heard nothing out of the ordinary. After a few minutes, he got up, went to the bathroom, then walked to the door of the trailer and opened it. Naked, he looked into the desert.

The night was clear, and stars beyond counting hung in the sky, hard, glittery pinpoints. A breeze blew and stirred the scrub and sand, but there was nothing else moving. No signs of life.

He rubbed at his chin. He had not shaved in several days, and perhaps it was time to do so.

A moment later, he closed the door. Something was wrong. Danger lurked outside his door and even though he could not see or hear it, he knew it was there.

He sighed. Now it was time to take the guns out and make ready. There were other things to check, too, preparations he had made when first he arrived. If Death had come to claim him at last, he would not feel sorrow, but if he lost the battle, he would do so trying his best to win. Though rusty and not used of late, all he had left was his craft. He would display it as best he could.

Ruzhyó went back to the bathroom. He would wash his face and shave, then he would get dressed and make his preparations for war.

8

Sunday
London, England

Michaels and Toni were checking out of the hotel to catch a taxi to the airport when the desk clerk said, 'It might be a good idea if you rang your air carrier, sir.'

'Oh?'

'Yes, sir. We've just had word that there's been something of a problem with flight schedules out of Heathrow. And out of Gatwick, as well, I'm afraid.'

The clerk, as it turned out, was a master of understatement. Michaels' attempts to connect with British Airways were unsuccessful. All incoming lines, he was told by a recording, were temporarily busy, and would he please try again later?

While he was doing just that, Toni caught him by the arm and pulled him over to a television set in the hotel pub. The BBC had broken into regular programming for a special bulletin. Apparently nearly all the computer systems at the world's largest airports had gone bonkers. These included not only the ticketing and reservation computers but the flight-control systems and auto-nav landing beacons as well. A quick check showed problems in Los Angeles, New York, Dallas-Fort Worth, Denver, Sydney, Auckland, Jakarta, New Delhi, Hong Kong, Moscow, Paris, and London. Passenger air travel at major terminals around the world had been brought to a virtual halt in a matter of minutes. Airline personnel were trying to manage but without computers the process was next to impossible. In many places, you couldn't buy a ticket or get a seat assignment. If you could, there wasn't likely to be plane waiting – assuming you could find the proper gate – and if you *did* find a plane, it wasn't going to be going anywhere any time soon.

Today, at least, man was apparently not meant to fly.

'Jesus,' Michaels said.

'It's a mess, all right. And you know what?'

Michaels nodded sourly. 'Yeah. Somehow, it's going to become our mess.'

He knew he shouldn't have said that, knew that the bored god who stood watch for fools was ever alert for just such comments. The response wasn't long in coming.

'Commander Michaels?'

Michaels found himself staring at a tall, green-eyed woman of maybe thirty. She had short, dishwater-blond hair, and was dressed in a dark, conservative suit, with a skirt almost to her knees, and sensible flats. When she took a step toward him, he figured she was a gymnast. Or a dancer, maybe. Very nice . . .

'Yes?'

'My name is Angela Cooper, I'm with MI-6.' She pulled out a wallet with a holographic ID and showed it to him. 'Would you and Ms Fiorella be good enough to accompany me? Minister Wood and Director-General Hamilton would like very much to have a word with you.'

'We're supposed to catch a plane,' he said.

Cooper nodded at the television, then gave him a small smile. 'I'm afraid that's unlikely in the near future, sir. And if we are going to repair that problem, we could use your help. We've cleared it with your Director.'

Michaels looked at Toni. She raised her eyebrows in a what-the-hell expression.

Well, why not? It would probably beat sitting in a crowded waiting room at the airport. Besides, he had heard a lot about the MI-6 building; it would be interesting to see it, if nothing else.

Something about Angela Cooper grated on Toni. As Cooper drove the three of them through the London streets in the big right-hand-drive Dodge toward Vauxhall Crossing, Toni tried to pin it down. The woman was attractive, polite, and well spoken. She was probably about the same age as Toni, give or take a year, and if she was an agent with MI-6, they probably had a lot in common. On the face of it there didn't seem to be any reason to dislike Ms Cooper. Maybe it was chemistry. Or maybe it was the expression on Alex's face when the woman had accosted them. That quickly veiled look of male interest. Alex said he was in love with her, and Toni believed him, but men were hard to fathom at times. If she hadn't been standing there, what would Alex's response to the tall dirty-blonde have been? Would he have flirted? Done more?

She didn't like herself for feeling jealous. There was no reason to believe Alex was unfaithful, even in his thoughts, but it was how she felt. Nobody ever said love was logical. Or if they did, they lied.

'This is Vauxhall Bridge Road,' Cooper said. 'It's a straight shot across the Thames from here. You'll see our building coming up on the left, just there. It's right off the tube station.' She pointed, and Toni leaned forward from where she sat in the rear to look.

The MI-6 building was an imposing and – for London – quite unusual-looking structure. The stone appeared to be cream-colored and there was lots of green glass – windows, Toni assumed.

Seated in front next to Cooper, Alex said, 'I thought internal security was MI-5's responsibility. That MI-6 handled matters in foreign countries.'

'Rather like the FBI and CIA?' Cooper said. 'Well, to a degree, yes. But there is some overlap. Over the last few years, MI-5 has shifted many of its resources to focus on Northern Ireland and against organized crime and benefit fraud. The consensus at HQ is that this computer threat is probably foreign, which gives us some small leeway to look into it. We're all on the same team, after all.'

Alex smiled. 'That doesn't sound a lot like the FBI and CIA.'

Cooper smiled back at him, flashing her perfect teeth. 'Yes, of course, we have our interdepartmental rivalries as well. And MI-5 – we call it Security Service, SS – does get a bit sticky if we tread too hard on their territory. But our ministers are rather put out by all this business, and so SIS – that's us at MI-6, the Secret Intelligence Service – are helping out a bit. The truth is, our computer system is better than SS's, so we're rather on point. Although I suspect we are somewhat behind you in the States in that regard. We've heard very good things about your organization over here. You're an offshoot of CITAC, aren't you? InfraGard?'

She was referring to the old Computer Investigations and Infrastructure Threat Assessment Center the FBI had created in the mid-nineties to deal with computer crime.

'Not exactly,' Alex said. 'But there's a connection, yes. You've obviously done your homework.'

Cooper smiled again, another high-wattage, even-toothed white flash.

Toni definitely did not like her, no question, and if Alex didn't stop grinning like a fool at everything

Ms Cooper said, he was going to be in trouble.

Obviously done her homework. Yeah. Right.

Sunday
Stonewall Flat, Nevada

Ruzhyó's preference for a handgun was a small caliber, like those he had grown accustomed to in *Spetsnaz*. In fact, such weapons were as efficient as the bigger bores the Americans preferred – if one could place the shot properly. A .22 in the eye was easily worth a .357 round in the chest, and it was much easier to shoot the smallbore pistol well – there was almost no recoil, little noise and muzzle flash, and a longer barrel made the weapon more accurate.

Americans were generally taught to shoot for the center of mass, and a bigger bullet was an advantage, given the relative weakness of all handguns, but they could have taken a page from the Israelis or *Spetsnaz* in that regard. With enough practice, head shots came naturally.

When he had come to stay here in the desert, Ruzhyó had bought two guns, both used. The first was a target pistol, a Browning IMSA Silhouette model, based on the company's Buck Mark design. It was a straight blow-back semi-auto, held ten rounds in its magazine, and had a nine-inch barrel topped with a Tasco ProPoint sight. The sight was electronic. It created in the field of vision a tiny, red, parallax-free dot. Operation was simple: You chambered a round, turned the sight on, and put the dot on a target, and if you squeezed the trigger with care, that dot was where the bullet went. At ten meters, he could center-punch a dime with the Browning. At a hundred meters, with the gun propped on a secure rest, Ruzhyó could hit a hand-sized target all day long. He had, in practice, hit a human-sized target at almost three hundred meters – once he zeroed in and knew how much the bullet would fall and drift. Even such a small pellet like the Browning spat would be disconcerting if it hit you solidly at that distance. Not the best choice for long-range gunnery, but in theory the ammunition he used, CCI Minimags, could fly a mile and a half. A rifle was a better weapon, of course, but the pistol could be hidden under a coat if need be, and still be used to strike a man in the head at distances well beyond that at which most shooters could operate most service handguns.

The other weapon in his small arsenal was a Savage Model 69 Series E 12-gauge pump shotgun. Also bought on the gray market, in a different town than the pistol, the shotgun was not as good a piece as the more expensive makes that used double-rail slide actions. Having only a single connector from the pump, which was less efficient in case of a jam, the weapon held five rounds – his preference was for #4 buckshot – but it had the short-barreled configuration the Americans called a riot gun, and was close enough to what he wanted when he went looking.

He could have bought a good hunting rifle and scope to increase his range. If, however, somebody wanted to assassinate him from five hundred meters out with their own high-powered rifle, he had better ways of dealing with that than a long-distance sniper duel. He had circled the trailer at ranges where a good shooter could see and hit him, and there were only a few places with a proper line of sight on his home. He had marked these, and installed at these places certain defenses. Of course, they could take him while he was away from the trailer, but one could only cover so many contingencies.

Last night he had cleaned and oiled both guns, then loaded them with fresh ammunition. He had also loaded four spare magazines for the .22, and he had ten extra shells for the 12-gauge in loops on a belt he could strap around his waist. If he had to use the shotgun to defend himself, the situation would be close-quarters, bad, and he probably wouldn't get a chance to reload; still, one could not be certain. At that point, it would likely be a matter of selling himself as dearly as possible. He might lose, but if he could help it, the winner would not leave unscathed.

He had done what he could. He could have tried

to run, but it was probably too late for that. Whatever was going to happen was going to happen, and he was as ready as he was going to get. Now it was a matter of waiting.

He was good at that, waiting. Right now, he would get some sleep. He might not get the chance again for a time. Or ever.

He moved to his bed, set the shotgun and pistol on the floor nearby, and, next to them, a small radio transmitter. He stretched out. He took several deep breaths, relaxed as much as he was able, and, in a few minutes, fell asleep.

He dreamed of Anna.

9

Sunday
Las Vegas, Nevada

'How far?' Howard said.

'About twenty minutes,' Fernandez said.

'Turn the air conditioner down a couple of notches, it's not that hot.'

Fernandez said, 'But you don't want to let the heat get ahead of you out here, John. Probably be ninety by noon, and you know how these trucks suck up the sun.'

'If this goes as planned we'll be on a plane for D.C. by noon.'

'Never hurts to be prepared,' the sergeant offered.

Howard shook his head. He and Fernandez were alone in the command car, a sand-colored Humvee Special. 'Automatic transmission, power steering, air conditioning, and you're worried about staying ahead of the heat? You're getting soft in your old age, Julio.'

'Perhaps the General would prefer to ride in his horse-drawn carriage next time? I'm sure old Nelly would be more to the General's liking.'

'Well, at least she wouldn't complain about the heat.'

'And you could limber up your buggy whip if she did. One of many in your front closet, I am sure.'

Howard smiled. 'Okay, let's hear it again.'

Fernandez shot a quick glance heavenward. 'Sir. We've got three two-man teams – that is to say, two-*person* teams – hunkered down watching out there in Cow Skull Gulch. If Ivan sticks his head out the door and we so desire, we can pot him like Davy Crockett barking a squirrel. We've got the Big Squint footprint for eight a.m. start-op, and we've got a National Guard chopper on standby if we need it – which we won't – over at Nellis. We've got two squads of bored, combat-ready troops in the transports fore and aft, and we got one broken-down *Spetsnaz* guy in an Airstream trailer in the middle of nowhere who can't run and can't hide.'

Howard nodded. 'All right.'

Fernandez caught the edge of his worry. 'What, John? You and I could go in and grab this sucker by ourselves – and you could stay in the car. It's just one guy, no matter how good he might be.'

'Probably what the Germans thought about Sergeant York,' Howard said.

'Jesus. You worry way too much.' Fernandez clicked the AC control down a couple of notches. 'Maybe your brain is froze. So how did Tyrone do in the boomerang thing?'

It was not the most artful change of subject he'd

ever heard, but Julio was probably right; he ought not to be worrying about this one guy in the desert. Go in with the protocols, hit their marks, and it would be a big anticlimax, they'd drag the guy in and let the headshrinkers go to work on him. 'Came in third.'

'Really? That's pretty good for his first time, isn't it?'

'Yes, it is. Beat his personal best, and he was prouder of that than he was the placing.'

'He should be. You're not so bad a father – for an old guy. I might have a few questions for you once I change my own status in that arena.'

Howard smiled. He could imagine the first time Julio and Joanna's baby ran an unexpected fever, or spit up something green, or got colic. He'd made a few of those panicky late-night calls to his mother back when Tyrone had been a newborn.

'Something funny, John?'

'Oh, yeah. You at two in the morning with a crying baby. I'm going to have Joanna video it.'

He took a deep breath and let it out slowly. This was normal operation jitters; he always got them before the guns went to lock-and-load. Maybe if he'd been in a real war zone with some battlefield experience under his belt it would be different. He was sure it must be.

Sunday
Quantico, Virginia

Jay Gridley sat in a motorized wheelchair, staring at two men playing ping pong. His idea of lying around for weeks in a hospital if something happened to you was apparently behind the times. They had guys who'd had heart surgery *last night* up and walking today, pushing IV poles up and down the halls. Apparently, moving was better than lying still when it came to after-effects of big problems. Some of them, anyhow.

His parents were on their way to see him, they'd be here this afternoon, and he wasn't really looking forward to that. They'd be upset, and wanting to take care of him, and he . . . he . . . uh . . .

What had he just been thinking?

Another surge of fear washed over him, coating him with one more layer of sticky sweat. The physical thing, that was bad, yeah, but they said that would respond to treatment, and in a few weeks he'd be his old self, could walk, talk, do the funky chicken, but his mind didn't seem to be working right. He kept running his thoughts together into a big hodgepodge, a slipsum, and then losing them altogether.

That scared the hell out of him. He could interface with VR with a bad arm and leg, hell, with no arms or legs at all – out if his brain didn't . . . if his brain didn't . . .

Didn't what?

He was afraid, and for a moment, he didn't even know why he was afraid – but then it came back. His mind. His brain. His thoughts weren't tracking. It was like trying to do calculus as you were falling asleep, you couldn't concentrate, couldn't keep the train on the track, couldn't . . . couldn't hold on to it!

He had to get to a VR set and get online. He had to see if he could still do the most important thing in all the world. It wasn't just his job, it was his life. He couldn't imagine himself unable to access computers.

He flagged one of the nurses passing through the rec room. He didn't try to talk, that still scared him, too, but he made the two-handed sign for a VR set – forefingers over his eyes, thumbs over his ears.

She nodded. 'Sure. Just down that way and to the left. Come on, I'll take you.'

He waved her off, then used his good hand to operate the wheelchair's joystick. He would find the computer himself. Plug in, and see what he could do.

If he could do anything at all.

Sunday
The Yews, Sussex, England

Major Peel leaned back in the chair in front of his desk, in an office provided by His Lordship in what had once been the groundskeeper's cottage. Three hundred years or so ago, during the Reformation, the cottage-cum-office had been built – as a Catholic church. In those days, with the Church of England cranking up to full steam, it was worth your neck to be caught practicing Catholicism in some parts of the country, so the faithful rich built small sanctuaries behind their manors and secretly gathered with a select few to worship. As long as they were circumspect about it, and as long as the lord of the manor was sufficiently wealthy and well thought of, local officials turned a blind eye to the practice.

The fact that the King wanted a divorce was no reason to give up generations of cherished belief and ritual, snap, just like that.

The window over Peel's desk wasn't stained glass, but it had that triple-hump Father-Son-Holy Ghost shape inset into the mortared stone, and the desk itself sat upon the spot where once had been an altar.

Peel looked at the computer screen, watching the video, and listened to the report from Lieutenant Wilson, one of his best men. Wilson led the team they had covering Bascomb-Coombs.

'You're certain he doesn't know he's being observed?'

'Certain, sir. He might be smarter than an auditorium full of dons at Oxford but he doesn't track very well in the real world. We've stayed away from fiddling with his computer hardware and programs – he does have those rigged with safeguards we don't want to try – but we've got spycams planted all over his house and office. There are units in the ceiling over his work stations in his lab and at his home that zero on his keyboard and monitor. He can have the best security in the world in the system, but all we have to do is watch him type or listen to him vox his codes in. And we've also got recordings of everything he sees onscreen.'

'And this business with the airports is untraceable?'

'Yes, sir. Everything this chap does online is untraceable. He's rigged some way to overload a virtual-reality headset – we don't have a clue how he did that – and he's put several snoopers into the hospital with some kind of stroke.'

'Really?'

'Yes, sir. There is one small worry we've come across. It seems that MI-6 has contacted the head of the FBI's computer crime unit, Net Force. He's here in London, working with them.'

'Already? That was fast.'

'Apparently he was in town, attending a conference or some such.'

'Hmm. That bears watching. Keep me posted.'

'Sir.'

'Anything else?'

'Nothing concerned with the project. But there's a small item you might find interesting. You remember Plekhanov?'

'The Russian who was going to take over Asia? Of course.' They'd earned a nice piece of change doing a little training for one of Plekhanov's groups.

'After his capture, there were a few loose ends,' Wilson continued. 'The most notable of which was the *Spetsnaz* wet work agent, Ruzhyó.'

'Ah, yes. Nasty piece of work, that one. Got away, did he?'

'Apparently only temporarily, according to what Bascomb-Coombs has learned. It seems they are about to collect Mr Ruzhyó, somewhere out in the American west.'

'Too bad for him.'

'Just thought you'd find it interesting, sir.'

'Yes, well, keep me up to speed on new findings.'

After he clicked off, Peel looked up at the old window. Interesting developments in all this business. While it was not the regiment, it did have its moments. Indeed it did.

Sunday
Stonewall Flat, Nevada

'All set?'

'Yes, sir,' Fernandez said. 'Sniper teams in place, ground troops to their positions. The place is surrounded, and the Strike Team is making dust for the trailer now. Off-road, in case he's got it mined.' Fernandez grinned, to show he wasn't serious about that part.

The two men stood in their modified SIPEsuits next to the Hummer, parked half a mile back on the main road – the only road – leading to Ruzhyó's Airstream. Howard had his visor up, and used his silicone-armored field-grade ten-power Leupold binoculars, sweeping back and forth slowly, looking at the target. 'No sign of him. He must not be an early riser.'

'His problem,' Fernandez said. 'Our boys'll be there in a minute, a few flash-bangs, some emetic gas, and Mr Assassin wakes up half-blind, puking last night's dinner, and in deep feces. You should have let me lead the team, no point in both of us missing all the fun.'

'You're about to be a married man with a child, Julio, and if you think I'm going to explain something happening to you to Joanna, forget it. Better get used to sitting at a desk.'

'That'll be the day.'

'Sooner than you think, Sergeant.'

He looked at the trailer. So far, so good.

Ruzhyó was already awake when he heard the sound of the approaching vehicle. He came up, strapped on the belt with the extra shotgun shells, then picked up the shotgun and slung it over his shoulder by the nylon strap. He collected the pistol and the radio control unit, then walked to the window over the sink. He set the Browning down, hooked the control to his belt, and looked out.

A squat, squarish, dun-colored truck rolled toward the trailer at a good speed, coming up the slight rise ten meters to the left of the driveway, paralleling it. A cloud of pale dust billowed behind the truck.

A military assault? With the driver staying off the road to avoid mines? Smart. If they were military they'd probably be wearing light armor, so his guns weren't going to do him much good unless he was very precise with his shooting. Something to keep in mind.

He took a couple of deep breaths and let them out, found a glass and ran a little water into it, rinsed his mouth, then spat into the sink. He put the glass down, stuck the pistol into his belt, and walked to the door.

Guests had come to call, and it was time to put out the welcome mat.

He pulled the radio control unit from his belt.

There were four buttons on the device, each of which controlled a signal made stronger by a booster hidden in the satellite dish installed on top of the trailer.

He sighed, and pushed the first button.

'What the hell is that?' Howard said.

A circular wall of gray appeared from the ground around the trailer, roiling up into the still-cool morning air. The dark gray cloud obscured the trailer in a matter of seconds.

'He's got smoke,' Fernandez said unnecessarily into the LOSIR headset built into his helmet. 'Slow it down.'

The leader of the Strike Team said, 'No shit.'

Howard was aware of the exchange in his own headset but he was dropping his visor and switching his helmet's viewer to IR.

Not much help: whatever was making the smoke was also making some heat, and he couldn't see through it.

He called up the feed from Big Squint's footprint, but the computer-augmented satellite image didn't show anything inside the ring of smoke, save the trailer.

'He's still inside,' Howard said. 'So far. Proceed with caution.'

'Copy that,' the Strike Team leader said.

Ruzhyó looked through the window over the door.

The smoke bombs had obscured the trailer from view. In another few seconds, they would finish smoking and explode into white hot flares, which ought to confuse any sensor devices pointed at him.

He looked at the second button. Nodded to himself. He hadn't killed anybody in a while, but this attack was obviously military in origin, and those men and women hiding at the sniper points would be soldiers and prepared to shoot him dead if so ordered. They knew the risks of combat. And if they did not, they were about to find out.

Hidden at nine places where a sniper might conceal himself for a field of fire centered upon the trailer were twenty-seven antipersonnel units buried in large paper cups turned upside down and covered with a thin layer of sand and soil. These were variants on the old Bouncing Betty; a small compressed gas charge would pop the cigarette-pack-sized APU's up five or six feet, where a second, stronger charge would explode and blast a handful of steel bb's all around itself in a devastating pattern. An unarmored man standing within a few yards of the APU would be cut down, dead or seriously wounded. Even with armor, some of the pellets could find a seam or unprotected spot and cause dangerous or even fatal wounds.

He pushed the button.

Howard's LOSIR com came alive with startled yells and screams, overlaid with the sounds of small explosions, both online, and then a second or two later, echoing across the terrain.

'Report!'

'We got a mine here, Colonel, Spalding is hit and bleeding!'

'We got blasted at S2, sir, dusted us pretty good, no injuries!'

'Reader is down, her face is a bloody mess!'

'John – look.'

Howard looked at the smoke, saw bright lights flaring through the haze. What the hell was going on here?

When the first of the smoke bombs burned down to their magnesium pots and flared, Ruzhyó opened the trailer door and stepped out. He had only fifteen yards to travel, but he needed to be in position before his heat sig would be the only one in the area. In case they had sat or high overfly surveillance.

He hurried.

The hidey-hole was disguised by a sheet of plywood, lined all around with heat-reflectives and absorbent deadstrip material. He'd glued dirt and brush on top of the board, and once in place it was virtually invisible, and solid enough to walk on. The chamber was only a meter wide by two meters long, but he wasn't planning on staying there that long.

In the hole, he squeezed a cold chemlume and got enough light so he could see to power up the battery-operated TV monitor. A camera on top of the trailer – also hidden inside the satellite dish – and a second camera in the garbage dump behind the place gave smoke-shrouded and grainy, but serviceable, views of the trailer and the area around it, including his 4 Runner.

The car was loaded with things necessary to make the rest of his plan work.

Give it a few more seconds for the smoke to clear.

'Smoke is clearing,' came the report over Howard's LOSIR.

'Proceed with extreme caution,' Howard replied.

'You still want him alive?'

Howard gritted his teeth. He had four wounded – so far – and according to the medic, two of them hit hard enough they needed to be gotten to a hospital PDQ. The Guard 'copter was already on the way.

'Yes. Alive, if possible. But protect yourselves as necessary. I don't want anybody else going down, understand? If you have to shoot, you shoot.'

'Yes, sir.'

Now, Ruzhyó thought. He pressed the third of the four buttons on his control unit.

'Heads up!' Fernandez said.

Howard looked. A vehicle zoomed out of the smoke, coming up the road. Ruzhyó's SUV.

'He's running for it!'

The chatter of subgun fire echoed. Howard

brought his binoculars around to frame the fleeing vehicle. He saw pockmarks appear on the metal where the bullets hit. What an idiot! Did he think he could just hop in his car and drive away?

Ruzhyó pushed the final button.

Before Howard could adjust the focus on his binoculars and get a look at the driver, the car blew up. The ground shook where they stood and the blast wave rolled over them with a noise like the end of the world. A fireball rose inside a mushroom cloud like a miniature atomic bomb. This wasn't the gas tank going up, the car had been rigged with big explosives.

'Holy shit!' Fernandez said. 'What the hell did he have in there?'

When the smoke cleared a bit, there was nothing left of the car except part of the frame and two flaming, smoking tires. More burning debris was scattered for hundreds of meters all around.

Howard stared. Jesus Christ! What a fuck up!

'Looks like you were right to be worried, Colonel. I stand corrected.'

Howard just shook his head.

10

Sunday
Lhasha, Tibet

Jay Gridley sat crosslegged on the floor, wrapped in an orange robe, the smell of patchouli incense heavy in the cool air. The thin reed mat under him did little to stop the cold radiating from the flagstones into his backside, and his shaved head was chilly. Through an open window, he saw snow piled ten feet thick, a blanket that shrouded everything in crisp, glistening white. A wordless vocal chant echoed in the background, a low and pulsing drone; light inside the massive chamber was provided by hundreds of candles.

At the front of the room, seated in full lotus on a short wooden platform that put him only a few inches higher than the monks, was the head monk, Sojan Rinpoche. The man was also bald, probably seventy, and had smile wrinkles that didn't quit. Gridley could see why after a few minutes of listening to the guru speak. He smiled a lot.

At the moment, the old man was talking about some kind of Buddhist deity:

'—in Sanskrit, he is called *Yamantaka*. In China, they call him *Yen-an-te-chia*. In Tibet, we speak of him as *Gshin-rji-gshed*. Everywhere, we know him as He Who Conquers Death, one of the Eight Terrible Ones, the *drag-shed*, Guardian of the Faith, and patron of the *Dge-lugs-pa*.

'He is terrible to behold, this manifestation of *Mañjusri bodhisattva*. Long ago, during a mighty battle in Tibet, *Gshin-rji-gshed* took his form to engage and defeat Yama, God of Death. He has nine heads, thirty-four arms, and sixteen feet. He is the Horror to Behold, the Mighty Terror, the Trampler of Demons.

'He is,' the old man said, smiling, 'not somebody you want to fuck with.'

Gridley did a mental doubletake at the last sentence. That seemed weird, coming from a Tibetan holy man.

He sighed. This was the old man's scenario – if indeed he was an old man and not somebody faking it – and he didn't much care for it. Too austere. And now that he was here, he didn't really understand why he had come. What was it that he had hoped to find?

The nurse. The nurse had told him to look this guy up. After he had ripped the VR set off and thrown it on the floor because he hadn't been able to concentrate without losing it. Oh, he could still use VR, but only in a passive, customer sort of way. He couldn't create it. He couldn't manipulate it. He would begin okay, but after a minute or two he would drift, and the imagery failed.

A computer operative who couldn't run a computer. A VR worker who couldn't work VR. He was screwed. His life was over.

But the nurse – she was some kind of Buddhist or something – had given him this guy's web address, told him to check it out. He'd helped others, she'd said.

Gridley had nothing to lose so he went. But he didn't see how *Gshin-rji*-whateverthehellhisname-was was going to help squat.

As if reading his mind, the old man clapped his hands once, and the monks, save for Gridley, all vanished. The room around him swirled and shifted, and he found himself sitting in a comfortable armchair facing the guru, who also sat in an chair. In place of the orange robes, Jay wore slacks, a pullover sweater, and motorcycle boots, and the old man wore jeans and a workshirt. The Tibetan's legs were crossed at the ankles, he sported Nikes, and he had that big smile again. He looked like somebody's kindly old grandfather come for a visit.

'Better?' he said.

Gridley blinked. 'Uh, yeah, I guess so.'

'A lot of folks want the monastery imagery. It makes them feel as if they've found the real thing. That Tibet, unfortunately, only exists in the movies these days.'

He regarded Jay with a straight, direct gaze. 'You have a problem.'

'Yeah.'

'Your aura is fractured.'

Jesus, *auras*? Time to bail—

'That is to say, you appear to have some difficulty concentrating. Drugs? Or a medical problem? Tumor? Stroke?'

How the hell could he tell that? Nothing like that showed in VR!

'Uh . . .'

'Take your time. You want to check out, come back later, that's cool.'

Jay shook his head. 'You don't seem like any guru I ever heard of.'

'You want the monastery back?'

'No, I – it's just that—'

'Expectation,' the old man said. 'That one is a killer. You had a idea, an expectation of what I was supposed to be, so whenever I pop off and do something that doesn't fit, it's confusing. And you're already confused enough, right?'

'Uh, yeah, right.'

'Well, we'll get to that. First things first. What shall I call you?'

'Webnom or realnom?'

'Doesn't matter, just something you'll answer to.'

'Jay.'

'Okay. Call me Saji. You came for some clarity, right?'

'I – uh, I'm not sure.'

Saji laughed. 'What you mean is, you didn't come for all this Buddhist bullshit, demons and Dharma and all. But you do want clarity.'

'Yeah.'

'Well, being a Buddhist doesn't get in the way of that; in fact, it helps. But we'll get back to that later, too. First things first. The nature of your injury?'

'They say I had some kind of stroke.'

'Fine, we can deal with that.'

'I'm glad you can.'

'Not me, *we*, Jay.' He tapped his right temple with one finger. 'Our brains have a lot of built-in redundancies. You get a short in one spot, it's entirely possible to reroute the signal to a place where the wiring is better. You might not even need that but we'll see. I'm going to ask you a series of questions; you respond however you like.'

'Okay.'

'What is eighty-seven minus thirteen?'

Christ – arithmetic?

'Yes, arithmetic. To start out.' He grinned.

Jay sighed. When you're at the bottom, the only way you can go is up.

'Seventy-four,' he said.

'And who is the President of the United States . . . ?'

Sunday
Stonewall Flat, Nevada

'What have we got, Julio?'

'Sir, not much. We've come up with some bloody pieces of scorched bone, something that looks like burnt hair, and a couple of teeth. Whatever he had in that car did a job on him. I doubt they'll ever find all of him.'

Howard sighed. Yes, indeed. He wasn't looking forward to writing this report.

'All right. Finish the trailer, leave two men to watch the site, and we'll get the lab boys out here. Pack it up and let's go home.'

'Yes, sir.'

Howard looked at the crater where the target's car had gone up in the blast. This wasn't the plan, but at least they had taken him down. The man had been a professional killer. Aside from whatever else he had done, Reader was in bad shape, and three others were wounded enough to need hospital time. The target deserved to be questioned and imprisoned for a thousand years but this would have to do. Quick and rough justice. Howard could live with it.

He turned away, and headed for the Humvee. Julio had been right to keep the air conditioner turned up. It was hot out here and getting hotter.

Damn, he hated this.

* * *

In his burrow, Ruzhyó tried to sleep. It was hot and he was exhausted but he couldn't relax enough to drop off. He had considered wiring the trailer so that it would go up with the car, but had decided against it. Perhaps somebody could get some use from it. It had been, for what it was, a good home for him. And more importantly, anybody who remained behind to watch would surely use the place for shade from the hot sun, or even go inside to run the air conditioner.

From inside, there was no window that looked directly upon Ruzhyó's hiding place; he had made certain of that.

By now, they would have found the remains of what he had left inside a sterilized and vacuum-sealed plastic carton for them to find: Leavings from a barber shop's trash; several uncut bones, raw meat, and blood mixed with anticoagulant made from rat poison, all from a pig. And the final touch, a human skull from a high-school biology skeleton, stolen and wrapped tightly inside the pig's scalp, packed with the pig's brain. Such things would not fool a pathologist for an instant, but someone who had just seen a car blasted to smoking bits might think the fragments of bone and blood and brain were human. And they might think so long enough to allow him to escape.

Nothing was certain but it was a chance.

The cameras showed men getting into vehicles

and leaving. They would post a guard, probably no more than two or three soldiers. It would be hot, and the guards would remove their helmets or some of their armor, or go inside the trailer. When they did, he would be ready. They would have checked the trailer for explosives and, finding none, would feel safe.

Pistol held loosely in his hand, Ruzhyó tried again to sleep. Even a few minutes would be good. He was so tired.

Sunday
London, England

MI-6 HQ looked just like any other modern office building inside. Michaels wasn't sure what he'd expected, especially given that Net Force HQ also looked like some typical corporate structure; still, he half expected to see James Bond or Q or somebody skulking through the halls on the way to do the King's business.

They sat on a comfortable couch in the office of the Director-General, Matthew Hamilton. Along with Hamilton were Angela Cooper, Minister of Parliament Clifton Wood, and himself. Toni had stepped out of the room to call the FBI Director.

'—would be in our mutual interests to resolve this matter as soon as possible,' the Minister said.

'I agree,' Michaels said, 'though I don't understand how we can be of much help here. You have your own people.'

Wood and Hamilton exchanged quick glances. Hamilton cleared his throat and took the lead. 'Well, yes, but you see, that's something of the problem. Both MI-5 and MI-6 want to jump right on this, and there tends to be some . . . professional rivalry.'

Cooper gave Michaels a brief flash of a smile. So much for her downplaying of such things.

'It is our thought that a joint task force with the head of Net Force in charge might move things along faster. Neither Security nor Secret Intelligence want to give up their autonomy to each other, but with a third-party ally . . .' He let it drift to a stop, raised his eyebrows and spread his hands.

Michaels nodded. Politics. Of course. And there was more than met the ear here, too, if they were willing to bring in a foreign service to mitigate the situation. He couldn't imagine the FBI and the CIA allowing British Intelligence to come in and take over a joint operation. No, there was a *lot* more going on here than they were telling.

The door opened and Toni stepped back into the room, clipping her virgil to her belt as she entered. She gave Michaels a short nod.

So. The Director had put them on the hook.

He nodded back at Toni, then looked at Hamilton. 'We will of course be happy to help in any way we can.'

That brought smiles from all three Brits.

Michaels wished he felt like smiling. What he wanted to do was go home. He had Jay in the hospital, the legal problems with his ex-wife, and whatever else might have gone on while he was away.

His virgil cheeped. Michaels frowned. It was set to refuse all but Priority One calls. He pulled the unit from his belt and looked at it. Incoming call from Colonel Howard. 'Gentlemen, if you will excuse me for a moment?'

The MP and MI-6 Commander both smiled and nodded again.

Michaels stepped into the hall. Maybe it was good news.

11

Monday, April 4th
Washington, D.C.

Tyrone Howard headed for his locker, keeping an eye out for Essay, the terror of the hall. Since Bella had dumped him, Tyrone's semi-connection to Bonebreaker LeMott, Bella's jock high-school boyfriend, had become uncertain. Essay knew that his chances against Bonebreaker were zippo, and so for a while just being Bella's friend had conferred a certain kind of immunity against the brain-dead thug. Essay – from the initials S.A., which stood for 'sore ass,' which came from Brontosaurus – would just as soon thump you as look at you, and Tyrone's chances against him in a fight were also zippo, so it paid to be on the alert.

He made it to the locker without seeing Essay. Maybe he'd been kicked out of dear old Eisenhower Middle for smoking again. That would be nice.

He was dumping his carry bag into the locker and not paying attention when somebody said, 'Hey, Tyrone!'

He turned. It was Nadine Harris, the boomerang girl.

'Hey, Nadine.'

She drifted over through the traffic flow, moving gracefully, like a swimmer treading water. 'You got morning schedule, too. Exemplary.'

'Yeah. Who's your anchor?'

'Peterson,' she said.

'He's okay, I had him for Media One. What kind of register you got?'

'Eng Two, Math Three, BioScience One, Media Two, Physical Three, History Two.'

'That's pretty heavy redge for the quarter,' he said.

She shrugged. 'Not so bad. I tested high 'cause my last school was a couple steps ahead. How about you?'

'Eng Two, Math Three, Media Three, Comp Four, and, uh, MH One.'

'Talk about my redge being heavy, whee-doggy, Ty! Comp Four? I didn't think you could take that unless you were in high school. And MH? Isn't that Military History?'

His turn to shrug. 'My dad is military. I thought I'd check it out – he's told me some interesting stuff. He used to throw, and there's a section about throw sticks in the class.'

'No feek? Wow. A *dad* who throws? He any good?'

'Well . . . not really. He, like, did it as a kid, had a couple of wooden 'rangs, entry-level plywoods. But he knows all kinds of things about battles and stuff like that, and how the abos used to use their sticks in fights.'

'Exemplary,' she said.

While they were talking, Tyrone felt a strange sensation, as if he was being . . . watched. He glanced around, being careful not to be too obvious. Maybe Essay was around and had targeted him . . .

Belladonna Wright cruised down the hall with two of her girlfriends, and she was looking right at Tyrone.

His shoulders went tight, his face hot, his bowels loose. He wanted to run and hide under a rock.

She was as beautiful as ever, Bella was, maybe more so, and his memory of sitting on her bed kissing her, putting his hands on her body . . .

Don't go down that path, Tyrone. It will show. That would be embarrassing cubed.

But it was already too late. He slacked his grip on the carry bag, allowed it to hang lower, in front of his crotch.

'You okay, Tyrone?' Nadine said. 'You look like you just swallowed a bug or something.'

'Ah, no – I mean, yes, I'm okay. I – uh, just remembered something I forgot to do. A chore. At home.'

Lame, Tyrone, blankwit slipbrain lame!

Bella steamed by like a battleship with two escort destroyers, awesome to behold in her beauty. She didn't look at him any more when she passed.

Nadine must have caught something in his face because she turned to look. 'Whoa. Who is *that*?'

'Belladonna Wright,' Tyrone said. He fought to keep his voice from squeaking. He almost made it.

'Out of my league,' Nadine said. 'Killer wallpaper.'

'Wallpaper?'

'Yeah, you know, it doesn't have to do anything except hang there and be pretty. Bet she gets invited everywhere, just to be looked at. You know her?'

'Not really,' Tyrone said. He had *thought* he knew her, but he'd sure been wrong. She'd tossed him like a dirty sock.

'The beautiful get it free. When you're like me, you have to work for it.'

'What, "like you"? You aren't ugly or anything.'

She gave him another little shrug, looked away. 'Put me next to that one–' she nodded in Bella's direction – 'I'd disappear.'

Tyrone didn't say anything but it was true enough.

'I hope she doesn't have a brain, too. That would be the dregs – gorgeous *and* smart.'

She didn't have to worry about that, Tyrone knew. Bella wasn't completely dull but she wasn't the sharpest knife in the drawer, either. He didn't want to say that, though. Even after what she'd done, that seemed . . . disloyal, somehow. Besides, if word got back to Bonebreaker that Tyrone was doing oral graffiti on Bella, that would be bad. She might have half a dozen guys in orbit, but

Bonebreaker was definitely one of them. Tyrone kept track. And they didn't call him 'Bonebreaker' for nothing.

'Hey, I gotta go,' Nadine said. 'Keep a line open, okay? We'll get together and throw sometime.'

'Yeah,' he said. 'We need to do that.'

He watched her go. She had a muscular step, athletic and graceful, but she wasn't in Bella's class for looks, for sure.

Well, fine. Bella was history as far as he was concerned, gone, past, done, and he wasn't looking for a replacement. Maybe he and Nadine would get together and throw 'rangs; that was okay. She was good at that, he could learn from her, maybe. It wouldn't be so bad to have somebody who was into the birds to work out with, even if she was on the plain side. She had an arm and she could make a 'rang fly, that was the thing. He didn't have to kiss her.

Monday
Quantico, Virginia

'Colonel?' It was Julio.

Howard looked up from the holoproj image over his desk, the report upon which he was laboring. There wasn't any way to make it sound good, what had happened out there in Nevada. The only consolation was that he hadn't lost any of his troops. Reader was going to need some extensive plastic surgery on her face, but she'd pull through. When she'd heard the launch pop, she'd been prone, facing away from the APW, but she'd turned to look. Her face shield was down, but because of the angle a couple of the pellets had zipped under the bottom of shield, a freak of bad timing. If her head had been inclined a centimeter or two more, the Lexan would have stopped the shrapnel. As it was, she was lucky the pellets hadn't gone deeper into her skull than they had. No brain damage—

'I hate to have to tell you this, John, but we've got a real problem.'

'Worse than yesterday?'

'Yes, sir, afraid so.'

'Wonderful. Spill it.'

'Lindholm and Hobbs are dead, both shot in the head at close range, small caliber rounds.'

'What?'

'Their transport is gone. We've got teams in the air, deputies and state police on the ground looking, but no sign of it so far.'

Howard stared at him. How could this be?

'Forensics says the teeth and skull bits we brought back are human, but they came from somebody who's been dead a long time. The blood and other bones, that piece of brain, they all belong to a member of the domestic *Suidae* family – a pig.'

The implications hit Howard, fast and hard.

'He's alive. He wasn't in the car.'

'Yes, sir, that's the only thing that makes any sense. He must have hidden somewhere – I've got a search unit combing the area – waited until our men were offguard, then deleted them and stole their ride.'

'Shit,' Howard said.

'My sentiments exactly. We underestimated this guy, bad, John. He foxed us.'

'Not 'we,' Julio. Me. The buck stops here.'

Fernandez stared at the floor. He knew.

Howard stared into space. This was terrible. In the years he'd been running the Net Force military arm, he'd had several troops wounded in brush firefights, but he'd never had one killed. And now, because he had screwed up, he had two soldiers down. Oh, man!

And worse, the guy who had done it had gotten away.

Now what was he going to do?

Monday
London, England

'You sure you don't want to go?' Toni said.

'I'd like to, I really would,' Alex said, 'but I need to go over all this crap.' He waved at the laptop on the bed table.

'I could stay and help you.'

'I appreciate it, but you can't read it for me, you might as well take a break while you can. Go, work out, burn off some tension. You'll feel better, and you can spell me later. This class is important to you. I saw your face when you got back from it. Go. Have fun.'

She nodded. She could see his point. She really did want to go to *silat* class, and Alex was right, her mind did work better after she exercised. 'Okay,' she said. 'I'll be back in about three hours.'

He leaned over and kissed her lightly on the lips, then smiled at her. 'Take your time. I'm not going anywhere.'

The cab ride though London to the school in Clapham was an adventure in itself, and by the time Toni got there, it was growing dark. Still, she was fifteen minutes early, time enough to change and stretch before the class started.

Inside, eight or ten students were warming up, doing *djurus* and practicing two-person drills. Toni went to the bathroom, changed into sweat pants, wrestling shoes, a sports bra, and a T-shirt. She joined the other students and began doing leg-stretches. She could still do the splits, front and side, but it took longer to warm into them than it had when she'd been fifteen. Leg flexibility helped, not so much in the *Bukti*, but it was a definite advantage in *Serak*. The basic turnaround required a drop from a high stance to a low one as you twisted, and the lower the better. Tight hamstrings made that hard to do.

Guru Stewart arrived, already dressed to work out. He came over to Toni. 'Glad to see you made it, Guru. I'm sure we have much to teach each other.'

Toni smiled. 'I don't know how much I can teach you, Guru, but I sure have a lot I can learn.'

He returned her smile, and she felt a small sense of triumph at being able to make him grin.

Stewart walked to the front of the room and turned around. 'All right, then. Shall we get started?'

Toni felt a rush of energy as she lined up to bow in. Until now, all of her teaching had been private. She'd never actually gone through a formal class from beginning to end. She was thrilled at the chance to do it.

Michaels pored over the small flatscreen's holoproj logs, scanning files related to the British investigation of the hacker's assault. It was tedious work, made worse because they spelled things wrong. 'Labour,' 'colour,' like that. He kept mentally correcting the odd words when he came to them, and it slowed his scan speed.

His virgil announced an incoming call.

'Telecom from Angela Cooper,' the virgil's voxchip said. He had switched the device from Jay's musical joke to vox, unable to listen to the fanfare after hearing that Jay was in the hospital.

'Connect,' Michaels said.

'Commander Michaels? Angela Cooper here. I have some Eyes Only material to add to your reading list. Might I bring it round?'

'Sure. I'll be here for the rest of the evening.'

'Shouldn't take that long. I'm in the lobby.'

He grinned. 'Come on up.'

There was a tap at the hotel room's door two minutes later. Michaels opened it to see that Cooper could dress down as well as up. She wore a pair of snug-fitting blue jeans, ox-blood Doc Martin boots, and a black scoop-necked blouse. She carried another flatscreen, but if she was armed he couldn't see where she might be hiding a taser or a pistol in those clothes. Very attractive.

'Commander.'

'Come in.'

She did, and offered him the flatscreen. 'Not much new here, but there are a couple of things we've received from the Pakistanis you might want to look at.'

He took the flatscreen. 'How goes the airline snafu?'

'Better. Most of the affected computers have been restored. You still wouldn't want to be flying into Rio tonight unless your pilot was very good indeed, but the situation is improved. They lost a freight jet at Auckland International, three men killed, but so far no other crashes involving loss of life.'

He nodded.

The MI-6 agent looked around. 'Nice room. Ms Fiorella about?'

'No, she's at a martial arts class.'

'Ah. Remind me not to get on her bad side. Well, I should be going, I don't want to interrupt you in your work. We're very happy to have you aboard, sir.'

'Call me Alex, please. All this 'Commander' and 'Sir' stuff is for the office.'

'Right. Then you must call me Angela.'

She glanced at her watch.

'Got a hot date?'

She blinked. 'What? Oh, oh, no. I was just wondering if I had time to grab a bite to eat before I'm off to my sister's. I'm supposed to babysit with my niece this evening. She's eight.'

Michaels smiled again. 'About my daughter's age.'

'I didn't realize you were married.'

'Divorced, actually.'

'Sorry.'

'Don't be. It was a relief. Except for Susan – that's my daughter – everybody is better off.'

'I understand. I was married briefly myself. Awful experience, especially toward the end. No children, fortunately, though I do enjoy them. Lucky for me, my sister's done all the work. Being 'Auntie Angie' who gets to bring presents and spoil the child is ever so much more fun. How's the food here in the hotel, is it passable?'

'They make good roast beef and Rueben sandwiches in the pub,' he said. He looked at the two flatscreens with the secret information. 'I could use a break myself. Mind if I join you?'

'Not at all, please do.'

She smiled, and for a second, Michaels felt a stab of discomfort. Toni was gone and here he was about to dine with the beautiful Ms Cooper.

Well, it wasn't as if he was about to dine *on* her. They were just having a sandwich, that was all. A man had to eat, didn't he?

Right. Sure.

He collected the second flatscreen. He wouldn't feel good about leaving them in the room, even though both were password protected. Given some of the villains Net Force had gone up against that didn't seem very much protection.

Angela walked to the door, opened it, and smiled at him again. It seemed a warm smile to him.

Just a sandwich, that was all. He had Toni, a woman he loved, and that was all he needed, thank you very much.

12

Tuesday, April 5th
London, England

Peel stopped into a sandwich shop on Oxford Street, a place open at odd hours so that you could eat lunch at midnight if such was your pleasure. After Army field rations, anything on relatively fresh bread stood well by comparison, and he was fond of the egg salad they made here.

He took his sandwich, a packet of crisps, and a can of cola to one of the small circular tables by the window. As he ate, he watched the passersby, mostly civilians scurrying about on their business. The birds were nice, and high platform shoes were apparently in vogue again. Some of the teenage girls who clopped past the sandwich shop wore shoes with soles a good six inches thick. Amazing what people would do to themselves in the name of fashion.

Peel liked sex well enough, though he didn't feel much like spending time with the women afterward. Or before, actually. There were always girls of the evening about where soldiers spent off-duty time, and if one took the proper precautions against disease, one could enjoy as much female contact as one could afford. With his current job he could afford as much as he could stand, which translated into sessions of an hour or so once or twice a week. Different bird each time, from assorted outcall services, so as not to establish a pattern that an enemy might track. A man who thought too much with his small head might well lose the larger one.

As he started on the second half of his sandwich, entertaining some vaguely erotic thoughts, he got an ugly surprise:

Peter Bascomb-Coombs appeared next to him. The man smiled, and said, 'You don't mind if I have a seat, do you, Major?'

Without waiting for an answer the scientist slid onto one of the high-backed chrome and plastic stools. He waved at the sandwich. 'Any good?'

Well, here was a nasty coincidence: How had Bascomb-Coombs come to be here? He'd not been to this place as long as he had been under surveillance, some weeks now. Well, all right, Peel could brush it off as happenstance . . .

As if reading his mind, the man said, 'No, I didn't just happen by, old chap. I came to see you.'

'Really? About what?' Peel managed. He put the remainder of his sandwich down, his appetite suddenly gone. He wiped at his lips with a napkin. His sense of danger was piqued. How could the man have known he was here?

'About mutual benefit,' Bascomb-Coombs said.

'I'm afraid I don't follow you.'

'Come, come, Peel. Were you really taken in by my absent-minded scientist act? I suspect not. Just as I have been aware of your surveillance of my person since the beginning.'

'Professor, I'm afraid I don't know what you are—'

'Let's dispense with the fencing, shall we? How much?'

'Excuse me?' Peel stalled, trying to make sense of this suddenly too-knowing apparition. This was definitely a bad show.

'To have you on my *team*, Major. You and I both know that Goswell is off his trolley with his mad scheme to bring back the glory days of the Empire. He really imagines that setting the third-world wogs at each other's throats and stirring up the Americans and Chinese and Russians will somehow cause Britain to rule the waves again. Surely *you* cannot believe this?'

Peel was not stupid. The foundations of his job had just shifted, an unforeseen and formidable earthquake had rattled them, and things were, of a moment, changed. He was a pragmatist; best to see where this was leading. He said, 'No, of course not.'

Bascomb-Coombs smiled widely. 'I thought you were smarter than that. You see, His Lordship has me in this neat little pigeonhole, the idiot savant, the boy genius who forgets to do up his fly when he leaves the loo, and he needs to go on believing that.

Right now, he controls my project though I will remedy that soon enough. Sooner or later your watch team might get in my way, so I decided that it would be best to deal directly with you. Your men are loyal, are they not?'

'They are,' Peel said.

'Good, good. So the only question is, what will it take for you to continue to tell Goswell what a halfwit I am when I am away from my computer? I shan't require the deception much longer but timing is critical just now.'

Peel was a military officer, he had seen action. There were times when you had the luxury to sit and meditate, to plan your attacks and defenses, and there were times when you quickly aimed and fired your weapon and thought about it afterward. He made his decision on the spot: 'A piece of your action,' he said.

The scientist flashed another of his high-voltage smiles. 'Ah, you *are* smarter than I imagined. You don't even know what "my action" is.'

In for a penny, in for a pound. He said, 'That hardly matters, does it? Goswell pays me a good salary but my kind of work has a limited timespan. I can't say I look forward to a small retirement cottage in Farnham or Dorking in twenty years, to spend the rest of my days puttering in the garden and pruning the roses. That's what Goswell will provide for me. I expect you can do better if I work for you?'

'Oh, yes, Major Peel. I can do much, much better than that. I can give you enough money to build a *city* of cottages, a different one for every day of your life. And an army of servants to prune the roses for you.'

'You have my interest,' Peel said. 'Please, go on.'

Tuesday
Jackson, Mississippi

Ruzhyó sat on a bed in a Holiday Inn, watching the news on the television. There was nothing on it about him, nor about the deaths of the two soldiers in the Nevada desert. This was as he expected. The organization responsible for the attack on his trailer would take pains to keep the failure covered up, at least from the public. In this way, the Americans were much like the Russians. What the public did not know could not cause a problem. There would be a search, of course, and they would want him alive, so that he could suffer for his deeds. They had come for him because they had known who he was. Perhaps it would have been better had he shot the Net Force Commander when he'd had the chance?

No, that would have been unprofessional by the time it came up. Plekhanov was caught, and eliminating the man who caught him would have served no purpose. The dead man would have been replaced quickly in any event, and his organization would have had more reason to hunt for a killer of one of their own than for one of the Russian's henchmen – who might not even have stayed in the United States.

So, once again, he was on the move, one step ahead of his enemies, who were surely on his trail. He felt tired.

But he also felt a grim kind of satisfaction. The old skills had not atrophied completely. When called upon, he still had some of his abilities. He was not as good as he had been five, or even two years ago, but at his best, there were few who could stay with him. Even diminished, he was better than most. This was not egotistical, just plain fact.

He sighed. He had several identities left to him, and money hidden in various places, both real and electronic. What was he to do now?

Maybe he should go home. To Chetsnya. To see the old villa once more before he died.

He had thought about doing that often but never acted upon it; the American desert seemed to suit him. But the end was growing near, he could feel that. While one place was as good as another when Death came, maybe there was something appropriate about meeting it where Anna had been claimed. And if it didn't matter, then the farm was as good a place as any, yes?

Home. He would go home. And if they found him there, then that would be the end of it.

Tuesday
The Surface of Luna

'The moon?' Jay said. 'You brought me to the *moon*?'

Saji laughed, something of a feat given that there wasn't any atmosphere to breathe or to carry the sound here. Or there wouldn't be in RW. He said, 'It doesn't get much quieter than here. I need you to be undistracted by sensory input. Would you rather a dark cave? Or an isolation tank?'

Jay shook his head. 'No. I guess it doesn't matter.'

'Precisely. Find a comfortable spot and sit, and we'll begin.'

Jay shook his head. A comfortable spot on the surface of the moon. Sure.

But he walked through the gray dust, bounding into the air – well, no, he couldn't say air, could he? – with each step, until he came to a rocky outcrop that seemed remarkably chair-shaped. He sat.

Saji had vanished but he left behind a Cheshire-cat smile that faded as he said, 'Just remember what I told you.'

Jay found himself alone, on the moon, and it was very, very quiet. The idea was for him to sit and let his thoughts run, then use the meditation technique Saji had taught him to control them. The technique sounded easy enough; all he had to do was to count his breaths. Easier than that, he had only to count the out-breaths. One you got to ten, you started over again. How hard could it be?

Jay closed his eyes. One . . . two . . . three . . .

This felt really stupid. Couldn't Saji have come up with a better scenario than the fucking moon? It was so . . . oops. He was drifting. Saji had warned him about that. When a thought intruded he was supposed to take a deep cleansing breath, gently push it aside, then go back to the count. Okay. Okay. He could do that. Move, pal.

One . . . two . . . three . . . four . . . five . . .

How could this do anything? Just sitting and counting? What was the point? It didn't do anything that – aw, hell, there he went again.

One . . . two . . . three . . .

He saw the tiger, just a flash, and Jay stopped counting because the next out-breath didn't happen. Jesus, the tiger—!

He opened his eyes. Nothing to see but the dead dry moonscape, nothing to hear except his own heartbeat. Which, he noticed, was speeding up. Damn. This was a lot harder than it sounded—

Ping! A single, crisp note played.

He had an incoming call, and it wouldn't have been put through unless it was one of three people: his mother, his father, or his boss.

The moonscape vanished. Jay sat on the couch in the hospital room. He reached for the com.

Tuesday
London, England

'How are you, Jay?' Michaels said.

'I've felt better, boss,' came the reply. But it was slurred and almost unintelligible. The effects of the stroke.

Michaels had his visual mode on, and the hotel room's com gave him a decent-sized picture of Jay. He didn't look much different, maybe a little slackness on one side of his face was all.

'I'm sorry I didn't call sooner. Toni and I have been drafted by MI-6 to help out with this thing. You know about the other ops who were injured like you were?'

'I heard.'

'You remember anything about your line of inquiry that might help?'

'Sorry, boss, no. I don't remember anything but a tiger.' He shook his head. 'Don't even remember for sure if it's connected to this.'

'Okay, don't worry about it.'

'I want to work on this, boss, but . . .'

'When you get better, if we haven't caught this guy yet. We've got everybody in the civilized world chasing him. We'll get him.'

'I don't think so, boss. I've never ... seen ... anything ... like it.'

Just the strain of this short conversation was wearing him out, Michaels could see that. 'Get some rest, Jay. We'll keep you posted.'

He clicked off. Jesus, what a mess.

His virgil announced an incoming call. He looked at the ID. Cooper.

'Yes, hello?'

'Commander. Ah, Alex. A quick call to bring you up to speed. Our technical people have come up with a scenario that might explain how a VR headset could cause brain damage.'

'Really?'

'Yes. Apparently it *is* theoretically possible. I don't have the electronics or the mathematics to understand it but the simple explanation is that certain of the solid-state components in the hardware might be programmed to act as capacitors. They could store the micro-electric current like a camera's flash attachment does, then release it all at once. If, somehow, this discharge was focused and directed, it could indeed short out neural pathways. Theoretically, they say, because they can't do it.'

'Is somebody that far ahead of the rest of the computer world?'

'Apparently so.'

'I don't much like the sound of that.'

'Nor do we. And so far we haven't a clue how to

trace whoever it is. We're hoping your expertise will help.'

Michaels sighed. Yeah, right. His best expert had his brain fried by whoever it was they were hunting. That sure as hell didn't make things easier.

'Discom, then,' Cooper said. 'I'll see you at HQ later?'

'Yeah, I'll stop in.'

After she had broken the connection, the virgil rang again. Lord, it was a parade. This time it was Melissa Allison. Just what he needed.

'Commander.'

'Director.'

'Anything to report?'

Well, yes, we don't know our ass from a hole in the ground, as far as all this goes. But he said, 'No, ma'am, nothing substantial yet. MI-5 and -6 have made their systems available and we are getting up to speed.'

'Keep me informed of your progress.'

'Of course.'

He put the virgil back into its charger as the bathroom door opened and Toni, wrapped in a towel, came out in a cloud of vapor from her shower. 'Did I hear the phone ring?'

'Oh, yeah,' he said. He looked at her, smiled. 'But let's talk about that after.'

She smiled back at him. Undid the towel and dropped it. 'After what?'

'Come here.'

'What is the magic word?'

'Come here, quick!'

She laughed.

Once she was close enough to grab, he did, and whatever thoughts he might have had for the next few minutes were short-circuited well shy of his brain.

13

Tuesday
Quantico, Virginia

The obstacle course wasn't busy, and after a hundred crunches, fifty pushups and a dozen chins at the beginning, John Howard wasn't even close to burning off his frustration. He didn't really feel like running the course. He was too tight, too pissed off, too . . . something. He wanted to hit somebody, hit them hard enough to knock their teeth out, spray blood in all directions, and watch them fall, preferably onto something sharp. It didn't help that who he was maddest at was himself. He had screwed up, big time, and that promotion he had allowed himself to dream about was likely to be rescinded before he ever officially saw it.

Too bad, but when it got right down to it, that didn't matter as much as the two dead soldiers. Losing men in battle, in a firefight, that was one thing. Losing them in a supposedly secure area to a single man who made you look stupid, that galled. Losing them at all . . .

So he stood there, watching the odd FBI trainee

or Marine pass him for the obstacle course, feeling impotent.

So far there hadn't been squat on Ruzhyó since he'd disappeared. Oh, yeah, they found the truck, in front of a supermarket in Vegas, windows rolled down, keys in the ignition. He could be anywhere in the country by now, hell, anywhere on the planet. Net Force had the best computers crunching all flight information, train and bus schedules, rental cars, automobile and motorcycle sales, even car thefts in and around Las Vegas, but so far they hadn't come up with anything to match the fugitive's profile.

He wanted this guy, wanted him as bad as anything he had wanted in a long time. If he found out where he was, Howard was going to hop on a plane, officially or unofficially, whatever it took, and go get the sucker.

'Colonel?'

He shook himself from the red fog he'd allowed to envelop him and turned. Julio.

'Got something you might find interesting.'

He was grinning.

Damn. Good news, at last.

Tuesday
The Yews, Sussex, England

The news on the telly was, as it always seemed to be these days, disgusting. The American President was going on about 'moral fiber,' a subject about which he certainly knew little, if anything. Presidents in the U.S. were notorious for their lack of self-control, from Warren G. Harding, to Kennedy, to Clinton. The idea that the leader of a country with such slipshod spiritual and moral values could hold forth on how *any*body should behave was patently ridiculous. Especially when the leader himself was known to have the sexual ethics of a mink. The current U.S. president was as bad as any – he just hadn't been found out yet.

Goswell nodded at the telly. Well, yes, he would have to do something about that now, wouldn't he? He would put in a call to his man, see if there wasn't some way to use the new toy to find out what the President had been up to. If records existed in a computer anywhere – and surely they must – the scientist could get them. Give the Americans another scandal to drool over, and get the bastard so busy defending his so-called honor that he wouldn't have time to meddle elsewhere.

Meanwhile, he had another call to make. 'Applewhite?'

The butler appeared next to him. 'Milord?'

'A telephone, please. And one with a dial, if you would.'

'Yes, milord.'

The butler went to fetch the telephone. Goswell hated to do such business but it was the nature of reality that a man was sometimes forced to do things he would rather not. If he was to stay afloat in stormy seas.

Applewhite returned with the phone. It looked like one of the old Bakelite rotary dial models he had used as a boy, but it was just a replica. Inside, it was full of electronics as modern as any, and there was no thick black cord connecting it to anything. It was a wireless model.

As he took the phone, he said, 'Any sign of that rabbit?'

'Cook said she saw him when she went to the garden this morning, milord.'

'Ah, well. Fetch me my shotgun, then. We'll just go and see if we can't give the little bugger something to think about.'

'Yes, milord.'

As the man trundled off to the lockbox where the guns were kept, Goswell dialed the number for the man he wished to reach. It rang once on the other end, and the voice that answered was gruff:

The words came out as an uneducated-sounding: 'Whot's it, then?'

'Goswell here. You have some information for me?'

'Roight, Guv, I 'ave.'

'The usual place, then. Say . . . seven?'

'Gawt it.'

Goswell cradled the phone's receiver, sighed, and shook his head. A pity to have to deal with such men, but this wasn't something that could be delegated.

Applewhite returned, the open shotgun cradled in one arm, with a pair of the custom-made brass and waxed green cardboard shells in hand. Two shots was all Goswell allowed himself per adventure. If he missed, then the rabbit would live to raid the garden another day. It was only fair.

The gun was a handmade Rigby Bros. fowling piece, but certainly suitable for bunnies, a 16-gauge side-by-side double with Damascus-twist barrels. The water-patterned steel was beautiful but not up to modern ammunition, so he had his gunsmith make loads that the weapon could digest without blowing apart. They produced quite the smelly smoke, the shells did, when touched off. The smith, George Walker, said he could substitute Pyrodex for the black powder he used and the smoke would be lessened, but Goswell didn't care all that much. A couple of blasts of #8 birdshot would take Mr Rabbit right out of the game – if he could but draw a bead on him. That was the trick, for the rabbit seemed to know when Goswell was armed and when he was not.

Applewhite held out a pair of earmuffs. Goswell glared at the butler.

'The doctor insists, milord.'

Goswell nodded. 'All right, give me the blasted things.' Secretly, he approved of the earmuffs. These were electronic hearing protectors, produced by one of Goswell's own companies in France – Devil take the Frogs – and he had to admit they were useful devices. A circuit in the headset sensed incoming noise, and immediately shut it out, reducing the loud blast to a small *pop*! However, when they were not picking up explosions, the muffs actually amplified regular sounds, so that one could hear better than normal. Truth be known, Goswell's hearing was not what it had been, and he was seriously considering the implants that would bring back his ability to pick up normal conversation, which had faded appreciably. The implants were apparently good for five or six years, using microbatteries that were somehow recharged by the vibrations of sound upon them. He knew a few chaps and one old lady who had undergone the surgical procedure and all of them had been most satisfied with the results. Perhaps he would have it done. He had already had the laser surgery on his eyes, didn't even need his reading glasses unless he was very tired. It was a mixed blessing, technology, but now and again it did offer something worthwhile.

'After I pot this rabbit, have Stephens bring the car round. I'll be going to the club.'

'Yes, milord. Good hunting.'

Goswell smiled. 'Thank, you, Applewhite. I will get the rascal, indeed I will!'

Tuesday
London, England

Peel drove toward the meeting place where Bascomb-Coombs had directed him, still somewhat unsettled by this new twist in his fortunes. And fortune was certainly smiling upon him. Bascomb-Coombs had caused this morning a new account to be opened at an Indonesian bank, a numbered account upon which Peel could draw. And therein was the sum in Indonesian rupias equivalent to one million Euros.

Just like that, Peel had become a millionaire, and the promise was for much more, if he performed his new duties adequately.

The small office suite was off Old Kent Road, not far from the old South Eastern Gas Works. Not a place Peel would have picked but perhaps that was just as well, for none of Peel's investigations had spotted the building.

He turned into the car park, shut the engine off, and walked to the two-story squarish gray block. The windows were barred, and a guard sat behind a desk just inside the lobby. The guard checked a computer screen, matched the name and face to

Peel's, and buzzed him through a locked door to a stair.

Peel climbed quickly, reached the second floor, and turned down the hall toward the office at the end. As he passed other offices, some with windows in their doors, he observed that they all appeared to be quite empty.

The last door on the right was unlocked; he opened it and stepped inside.

'Ah, Major, right on time. I appreciate that. Come in, come in, let me show you around.'

There didn't appear to be much to see. In one corner was a computer desk, a holoprojector and work station upon it and a leather rolling chair in front of it. A small fridge and stove sat to one side, and there was a fold-out couch next to that. A sign on a door beyond the couch identified it as a loo.

Peel raised one eyebrow, as if to say, Show me *what*, sir?

Bascomb-Coombs smiled. 'Doesn't look like much, does it? But the real works are elsewhere, of course, at Lord Goswell's computer facility in Chelmsford. We are hooked into it telephonically, and to answer your question, yes, quite undetectably. I can do from here what I can do at Chelmsford, and nobody will be the wiser.'

'If you'll excuse my ignorance, Mr Bascomb-Coombs, just what is it exactly that you do? I mean, I know about the device, what Goswell has told me of it, and I have seen the results, which are certainly quite impressive, but I'm not up to speed on how it works exactly.'

The scientist laughed. 'And I doubt seriously I could explain it to you. Turner's Dictum is that 'A thing can be told simply if the teller understands it properly,' but I'm not sure I entirely understand it myself. And please do not take offense, but I doubt that you have the mathematics and physics to comprehend it if I did have it all. At this stage, my computer is rather like a kitchen match. I can use it to light a fire but I'm not totally conversant with the chemical processes that make it work.'

He smiled, and Peel smiled back. Had the man just called him stupid?

'I'll give you a basic lesson, if you want. You are somewhat familiar with ordinary computers?'

'Somewhat.'

'Then you know that most computers are Turing engines that use Boolean logic based on binary operations. You have O's and 1's – quantum bits of information called Qubits – and these are the only choices. It is either one or zero, period. In a quantum computer, however, one can get superposition of both at the same time. It doesn't seem reasonable on the face of it, but in quantum parallelism one can use all the possible values of all input registers simultaneously.'

Peel nodded, as if he had a fucking clue what the man was talking about.

Bascomb-Coombs went on: 'Using Shor's quantum

factorization algorithm, one can see that factoring a large number can be done by a QC – quantum computer – in a very small fraction of the time the same number would take using ordinary hardware. A problem that a SuperCray might labor over for a few million years can be done in seconds by my QC. So for a practical matter like code breaking, the QC is vastly superior.'

Peel nodded. 'If so, why isn't everybody using these QCs?'

Bascomb-Coombs laughed again. 'Oh, they would very much like to! But it isn't something one whips up in an old mayonnaise jar out in the woodshed. The problem is that the coherent state of a QC is usually destroyed as soon as it is affected by the surrounding environment. What this means is, as soon as you turn it on and try to access it, you destroy it. A bit of a trick to get around that. They've tried all kinds of things over the years: lasers, photon excitation, ion traps, optical traps, NMR, polarization, and even Bulk Spin-Resonance – quantum tea-leaves, this last.

'Wineland and Monroe worked out the single quantum gate by trapping beryllium ions. Kimble and Turch polarized photons and did the same thing. NTC had some early success with nuclear magnetic resonance, and Chuang and Gershenfeld applied Grover's algorithm for a 2Q model, using the carbon and hydrogen atoms in a chloroform molecule. But the problem has always been multiplicity and stability. Until my unit.'

'How did you manage that, if it is so hard?'

'Because I am smarter than they are,' he said. It didn't sound like bragging and, given the results, apparently it wasn't.

'I lost you back when I said "Qubits," didn't I?'

'Before that, I'm afraid,' Peel admitted.

Bascomb-Coombs smiled. 'Don't feel bad, Major. There aren't a handful of physicists in the world who would understand how I've done what I've done, even with the working model in front of them. Your talents lie elsewhere. I shouldn't want to try and knock you about in a dark alley, nor go against you on a battlefield.'

Peel acknowledged the compliment with a nod. 'Quite.'

'Anyway, what it all means is that I've got a computer that can do wondrous things, and picking locks is at the top of its list. Short of pulling the plug and removing it from any incoming communications, there isn't a computer on Earth I can't break into. Money means nothing when you can enter any vault at will. Military secrets are at our beck. Nobody can hide anything from us.'

'Really? Then why aren't you king of the world?'

The man laughed yet again. 'I like you, Peel, you are so refreshing after years of mealy-mouthed scientific types. The simple answer is, the computer isn't perfect yet. It has a few glitches, and now and again it goes down. About half the time I use it, actually. So I am loath to waste my up-time on frivolous things like money and power – at least until I get it more stable. That's where I'm spending my energies, on the system. Because Goswell owns the physical unit and has it quite well guarded I can't turn down his requests just yet. But the time is coming. And I'll need men with your skills with me.'

Peel thought about the million Euros in the Indonesian bank. He was already richer than he'd ever expected. His father, title notwithstanding, had been a land-poor duffer who'd lost even that before he died. A million Euros was nothing to sniff at but if he stuck with this strange character, the chance of more was distinctly possible.

'I am at your service, Mr Bascomb-Coombs.'

'Oh, do call me Peter, Terrance. I'm sure we're going to get along just fine.'

14

Wednesday
Seattle, Washington

Ruzhyó rode the underground train through the SeaTac airport toward his gate. He was booked on a British Airways 747 to London. He had taken a bus from Mississippi to New Orleans, a Stretch-727 from there to Portland, and a Dash 8 from there to here. Had anybody been able to follow him to Mississippi, they would have seen a similar travel pattern from Las Vegas to Jackson: He had rented a car and driven to Oklahoma City, then caught the first of three short commercial flights south- and eastward from there. A pursuer might have expected him to continue east or south, to Miami, say, and instead he had reversed his direction. Once in London he would fly to Spain or Italy, from there to India or Russia, and from there, home.

If you were being chased, it was not wise to run in a straight line – especially if the hounds were faster than you.

The train was full, and when it stopped again to load more passengers, Ruzhyó got up from his seat and offered it to a young and very pregnant woman carrying two bags. He and Anna had wanted children, but that was not to be.

The woman thanked him and sat. He held onto a railing and watched the wall pass in front of the windows.

The train stopped, the passengers alighted, and Ruzhyó headed for his gate. He was hours early, but he had nowhere else he wanted to go. He would find a sandwich shop; a bathroom to attend to his needs; a place to sit and perhaps to sleep. In the military, one learned to sleep whenever the opportunity arose, and sleeping in a comfortable chair was easy.

The flight to Heathrow was a direct one, only nine or ten hours, and he was booked in the center cabin, as a man would be travelling on business. He wore a medium-price suit, a pale blue shirt and tie, and carried a briefcase full of magazines and blank paper to augment the image. He was just another corporate wheel in the machine, nobody to look twice at.

British Airways wasn't as bad as some, certainly much better than any of the Russian or Chinese internal airlines. His last flight on the English carrier had been dull enough, save for the touchdown. The big jet hit the runway hard enough to deploy the oxygen masks and to shower passengers with luggage from the overhead bins. No one had been hurt, but it had been something of a surprise.

Perhaps they had been letting the stewardess practice her landings. Or maybe the pilot had fallen asleep . . .

He mentally shrugged. He had hit harder. Once, during a monsoon, the JAL flight he was on had landed in Tokyo hard enough to collapse the nose gear, sending a shower of sparks past the passengers' windows despite the wet pavement. Once, on a flight to Moscow, the vintage turbo-prop Russian plane upon which he had been travelling had landed safely, but hit a refueling truck as it taxied to the gate, killing the driver and throwing to the floor half a dozen passengers who had unbuckled and left their seats in too much of a hurry. Bones had been broken on that one. And once, after he had alighted from a small Cessna at a remote field in Chetsnya, the little craft had taxied away toward the runway to depart, rolled over a landmine sixty meters away and been blown to pieces.

He had ceased worrying about such things long ago. If your number was up, then it was up. Until then, the old saw was true: Any landing you could walk away from was a good landing.

A little pub in the terminal had Rueben sandwiches on the menu, and he ordered one and a beer. The television set was on, a sports channel. Hideously ugly women, puffed up like human toads and stained dark brown, paraded back and forth on a stage, flexing their muscles. They looked like men in bikinis. Backstage, one of the women was interviewed, and when she spoke her voice was deeper than an operatic bass singer's.

Amazing what people would do to themselves. Ruzhyó had once trained briefly with Russian Olympic track athletes, and he knew something of the chemicals they used to enhance their performances. The male steroids these women bodybuilders took left them with permanent changes – deep voices, acne, hairy faces and bodies, and enlarged sexual organs. It was fine to pump up when one was twenty-five, but what would these poor women look like at fifty or sixty? He shook his head. No eye for the future.

'Jesus, would you turn that shit off?' one of the other bar patrons said to the man behind the counter. Several of the other men raised their glasses in support. The counterman shrugged and changed the channel.

Ruzhyó ate his sandwich and drank his beer.

Wednesday
London, England

MI-6 had given Alex and Toni a fair-sized office with full access to their computer systems. Well, at least insofar as this particular problem went. Toni had come across plenty of off-limit files.

Alex was down the hall, conferring with

Hamilton. Toni was alone in the office, cross-referencing airline computer data, when Angela Cooper tapped at the open door.

'Come in,' Toni said.

'Sorry to bother you, Ms Fiorella, but Alex wonders if you might join him and the Director-General for a word?'

Alex? She was calling him 'Alex'?

'Sure,' Toni said. She logged out of the work station. Cooper stood there waiting, smiling, but looking somehow impatient.

'This way, please.'

Toni felt short and dumpy next to the blonde, who wore a dark green suit with the skirt hemmed a couple of inches too high above her knees, and sensible pumps with two-inch heels. She had good legs though, and maybe if Toni were tall and leggy she'd showcase them, too, instead of wearing a plain blue silk blouse, jeans, and walking shoes. Well, she hadn't packed for work, had she? After the conference, at which she'd worn both suits she'd brought and then sent them to the cleaners, pretty much all she had in the way of clothes were casual things. It was supposed to be a vacation, wasn't it? But she'd call the cleaners and get her work clothes back. She wasn't going to let Ms Cooper here make her look any worse than she had to.

'Sorry about interrupting your vacation this way.'

Toni pulled her thoughts away from clothes and back to the moment. 'What? Oh, well, it's not your fault. We got to see a little of your country anyhow.'

'Different from the States, isn't it?'

'You've been to the US?'

'Oh, yes, of course. A few work trips. And I spent a summer at UCLA back when I was a student. Lovely climate, I got my first real tan there.'

I bet you did. Toni imagined Cooper in a bikini. She would be striking. The line of men hitting on her would form quickly in the SoCal sunshine. She'd have to carry a stick to keep them off – unless she wanted the attention, and probably she did. She was the type.

'Alex said you are from the Bronx?'

Oh, did he? What was Alex doing telling her that? 'Yes. I'm afraid New York isn't anything like California.'

'I spent a week in Manhattan once, late in August. The heat and humidity were fairly awful.'

'It's worse in September.'

Ten paces went by without any more conversation. The silence was just getting awkward when Cooper said, 'I understand that Alex is divorced and has a daughter. Have you met her – the daughter?'

Jesus, what was Alex doing, telling her stuff like this? And when had he had a chance to tell it? Next thing you knew, he'd be giving this woman pictures of him and Toni in bed together! She said, 'No, I haven't met her. Talked to her on the com a few times. Seen pictures of her. She lives with her mother in Idaho.'

'That's out west, isn't it?'

'Yes. Out west.'

'Ah, well, here we are, then.' She indicated the door with one hand.

'You aren't coming in?'

'Afraid not, other duties. I'll see you later.'

Cooper turned and left, a hint of a sway in her hips as she walked.

The bitch.

Inside, Alex stood next to a table with Hamilton, both of them examining hardcopy photographs under a bright light. Alex looked up at her. He didn't smile. 'Toni. Come check this out.'

She moved to stand next to him. The pictures were spysat overflies of some kind of military installation, computer-augmented for color and dimension. There was what appeared to be a pair of ICBMs on railcar launchers at one end of the complex. 'What am I looking at?'

Hamilton said, 'This is the experimental rocket station in Xinghua, near the coast of the East China Sea. The Chinese have been developing a new long-range nuclear missile here.'

He tapped the ICBM in the photograph. 'Last evening, a computer put two of the working prototypes on alert and began a ninety-minute countdown to launch. The missiles were aimed at Tokyo.'

'Lord!' Toni said.

'Precisely. The computer was locked out, they

were unable to shut it down. Fortunately, both warheads were dummies, and also fortunately, technicians were able to abort the launches manually. The Chinese, while not normally forthcoming about such things, are terrified. Someone bypassed their computer safeguards and codes and lit the fuses from outside. U.S. spysats that keep the station under observation saw the prelaunch movements and the U.S. military scrambled stealth fighter bombers from their base on the South Korean island of Cheju-do. If the Chinese missiles had lifted, the stealth jets would have tried to shoot them down, and they would very likely have bombed the station to prevent any further launches.'

Toni stared at Alex. He looked grim.

'Even without the nuclear payload, a pair of rocks that big dropping into the middle of downtown Tokyo would have caused considerable damage,' Alex said.

'And it's our airline hacker?' Toni said.

'Or somebody just like him. I can't believe there are two of them.'

Toni shook her head.

'We've got to run this guy down, fast. And our best tracker, Jay, is out of commission.'

'Never rains but it pours, eh?' Hamilton said.

Toni looked at the man, then back at Alex. Bad, this was definitely bad.

Wednesday
Washington, D.C.

Tyrone had figured out that if he got to the soccer field immediately after his school shift ended, the field would be empty for forty minutes before the next shift arrived. Forty minutes was plenty of time to get ten or fifteen good throws in.

He stood near the middle of the field, testing the wind with a wet fingertip. There was a pretty good breeze coming in from the north, and he decided to tape a couple of pennies to his MTA boomerang, to keep it from getting wind-whipped. That took only a minute, then he was ready.

He angled himself against the wind, took a couple of deep breaths, and shook out his shoulder to loosen the muscle. He'd been considering lifting weights – the top throwers were all in good shape, and he could use a little more power in his arms. The balance was tricky. If you threw too soft, you didn't get any time aloft, and if you threw too hard, you could get a fast nosedive. But there were times when you needed a little more strength, like now, when the wind was gusting, and at his size Tyrone didn't have any extra muscle. He didn't need to be Hercules or anything, but a little more mass wouldn't hurt.

He made his first throw, to check the angle of the blades and see how the taped coins balanced. The

Indian Ocean glowed in a red blur as it spun, but wobbled off-center and augured in too fast. He retrieved the 'rang and adjusted the angle on the blades by carefully bending them up. He moved the coin on the long arm in toward the angle a few millimeters, retaped it, then tried another throw.

Better, but still off a hair. Well, he could spend all day adjusting the thing, especially in gusty conditions, and it was close enough for practice.

He was on his seventh toss, having finally gotten above a minute for flights, which was about as good as he expected in the wind, when he heard Nadine yell at him.

'Yo, Ty!'

She came across the field, shrugged out of her backpack, and removed from it her own MTA, a long L-shaped blue-and-white striped model. It was a Quark Synlin. He'd never seen one up close, but he'd seen holos, and he saw a couple at the tourney, from a distance, so he recognized it right off.

'Man, how'd you come by that? I thought Quark quit the business.'

'He did, but there are a few still for sale. My mother told me if I could show her I could handle the top-of-the-line 'rang, she'd loan me the money for it. When I won the contest, she figured I was ready. It came air express this morning.' She held it out. Tyrone took it from her as if it was a live baby, holding it carefully.

'How does it throw?'

'Dunno, I haven't had a chance yet. Why don't you give it a try?'

He blinked at her. 'You need to be first, it's yours.'

'No, go ahead. You're already warmed up.'

'Yeah?'

'Sure.'

He wet his finger, checked the wind.

She said, 'Medium-hard, angle up fifty, don't lay over. Better to over-vertical. Five to ten into the wind.'

He nodded. Set his stance. Took a good breath, reared back, and made the toss.

The big Quark zipped out about fifty meters before it started to make its turn, gained height – a lot of height, thirty, thirty-five meters – then started to shift from perp to flat. It bounced a couple of times on an updraft.

'Man, *look* at that!'

It was a beautiful flight, wind and all. It just seemed to hang there forever, and it finally came down within twenty meters of where he'd made the throw, slightly down field. He did an easy slap catch.

Tyrone didn't have his stopwatch, but Nadine had hers. 'Two-minutes-fifty-one,' she said. 'Not bad.'

'Yeah not bad! That beats my PR!' With that time, he would have beaten her at the tourney, too. Damn!

He looked at the boomerang, then smiled at Nadine. 'Thanks.' He handed it back to her. 'Your turn. We've got like twenty minutes before the soccer geeks run us off.'

'Time enough for two throws, you think?'

'You *wish*.' They both laughed.

Nadine was all right. Especially for a girl.

15

Wednesday
Alamo Heuco Mountains, New Mexico

Jay Gridley stood on a patch of high desert listening to the silence among the rocks and scrub growth. The sun was a blinding mallet, hammering everything beneath it into the dead ground. It looked like the middle of nowhere, and if you headed directly east, west or south, you'd leave the U.S. and hit Mexico; from here, the nearest border was only a mile or three away.

Next to him, Saji stood, looking much more like a Native American than a Tibetan. He wore faded blue jeans, cowboy boots, a long-sleeved workshirt, and a ten-gallon white hat with a rattlesnake skin band around it.

'Smell the water?' Saji said.

Jay, dressed much like Saji, but with a shadier, wide-brimmed Mexican sombrero, shook his head. 'All I smell is desert. Dust, sand, and baked rocks, that's it.'

Indeed, every step they took kicked up more reddish-brown dust, fine as talcum powder. It coated his boots and clothes, stung his eyes and nose, and made breathing hard. There was no wind, so at least the dust settled quickly. A very realistic scenario, and it was Saji's – something like this was still beyond Jay's capabilities.

'Okay, let's see if we can cut some sign.'

Jay shook his head. 'How did you learn all this tracking stuff?'

Saji smiled his idiot's grin. 'Jerry Pierce, a Navajo buddy of mine, is a Son of the Shadow Wolves. Tracker for the Border Patrol. He taught me about this, I taught him about the Middle Way.'

'A Navajo Buddhist?'

'Why not? Buddhism doesn't get in the way of most other religious beliefs – at least not the ones that aren't militantly monotheistic. Come on.'

The two of them walked carefully over the sandy ground. After a few yards Saji said, 'Stop. You see it?'

They were maybe ten feet from the edge of a steep drop, a cliff that went down sixty, seventy feet. 'See what? The end of the world?'

'Nothing quite so dramatic. Right there in front of you.'

Jay strained his eyes, staring at the ground. Here were three things: Hard pan dirt, a single broken blade of pale green grass, and a weathered, dusty, reddish rock. The ground here wouldn't hold a track. 'I don't see anything.'

'Not anything?'

'Okay, fine, I see *some*thing. There's a patch of hard dirt, a rock, a piece of dead grass. That's it.'

'Look around. Any other vegetation?'

Jay raised from his crouch, glanced at the area around him. 'There's something looks like a creosote bush about ten yards that way.' He moved toward the cliff edge, peered over it. Nothing growing down that way. 'Nothing close. There's a big cactus way the hell over there. It's desolation row here.'

'Okay, think about that for a minute.'

'No offense, Saji, but if I could think for more than thirty seconds without going blank-stupid, I wouldn't need you!'

'Close your eyes, count your breath.'

Jay sighed. He did as he was told. One . . . two . . . three . . . what . . . did . . . I . . . see . . . ?

He opened his eyes. 'The grass.'

Saji nodded. 'What about it?'

'It doesn't belong here. How did it get here? There's nothing else around like it.'

'Good. Could it have blown here?'

Jay shook his head. 'No wind. And if it had been here very long, it would have been dry as a bleached bone, but it's still green.'

'Which means?'

'Something put it there. Maybe it fell out of a shoe or was stuck to somebody's pants leg.'

'Very good. Now what?'

Jay considered it. Saji had told him, but he couldn't remember it. Okay, think logically, Jay. It was hard, but it wasn't like he had to do any major programming, just take the next small step. Which would be . . . ?

'Spiral out, look for tracks in any dirt that will take them?'

'Good. Let's see it. Careful – you don't want to obliterate any sign.'

Jay spiraled out from the grass, moving slow, looking for tracks. He couldn't spot any for fifty feet in a circle around it. He shook his head. 'No tracks.'

'You sure?'

'Hell, yes, I'm sure!'

Saji waited for a few seconds.

'Sorry. I'm on edge.'

'No problem. Look over here.' Saji led Jay to a patch of dust, pointed at it. 'There.'

'Come on. That dirt is perfectly smooth, not a mark on it, you can't tell me you see a track there!'

'Carpet People,' Saji said.

'Come again?'

'They wear pieces of cut carpet on their feet, booties over their shoes, that don't leave tracks. You see a perfectly smooth spot in the desert, it's wrong. Look there, next to it. See the wind riffles? The rain pox? The way the dust is uneven, here and here? Now look back at that spot, there.'

Jay looked. Yes. The dust was perfectly smooth.

'Get down to ground level, get the sun to the side.'

Jay did. Yes, he could see a slight edge around the smooth spot, a rough oval shape. 'I see it!'

'Sometimes, what you have to look for is the absence of something that *should* be there. Sometimes it will be very subtle, like this no-print footprint. Our quarry passed this way, heading north, staying close to the cliff edge. A man tracking him on horseback wouldn't get too close to the drop, even if the horse would let him. That big cactus you mentioned, way the hell over there?'

'Yeah.'

'I bet he stopped there to rest in the shade.'

'How could you possibly know that?'

'It's to the north. There's no shade behind us for miles. After walking out here in the hot sun for a couple of hours, your half-cooked feet wrapped in carpet booties over shoes, moving slow so as not to disturb the dust, wouldn't *you* stop in the shade to take a drink?'

Saji started walking briskly toward the barrel cactus.

'Uh, Saji? Don't we need to be careful of stepping on sign?'

'Nope. If he went to the cactus, we don't need to know how he got there. He didn't go over the edge or we'd see the buzzards circling his body. He didn't come back our way. He went to the cactus. We'll pick up his trail there.'

'Right,' Jay said. 'You're the boss.'

'No, Jay, *you* are the boss. I'm just a guide.'

He moved off. Jay followed him.

Wednesday
Jackson, Mississippi

John Howard stood staring in the Holiday Inn room where Mikhayl Ruzhyó had spent the night before. The maid hadn't cleaned the room yet; Ruzhyó had paid for two nights and put a Do Not Disturb sign on the door before he left. Even so, the room hardly seemed to have been occupied. The bed was made, the single used towel had been refolded and put on top of the unused ones. A paper-wrapped glass in the bathroom had been rinsed clean, dried, and put back where it came from. And if he had used the crapper, the man had even folded a new point on the remainder of the toilet paper roll when he was done.

'No impact camper,' Fernandez said. 'Wish my bride was so tidy.'

Howard chewed at his lip. 'I suppose it was too much to hope he'd leave a map with a destination circled, along with his airline reservation number and flight times.'

'We'll get him, Colonel. We traced him this far, we'll pick up his trail from here, too. Looks as if he is heading east.'

'Maybe.'

'Maybe he is heading east, or maybe we'll get him?'

'Both.'

Wednesday
The Yews, Sussex, England

Peel stood outside the old church that was now his office, staring at Lord Goswell who was still traipsing around carrying that ancient shotgun, trying to find one of the rabbits that had been raiding his garden.

The old boy considered himself quite the hunter. Peel had heard all his hunting stories a dozen times. Back in the early sixties, when such things were still routinely done, Goswell had gone on safari to Africa. There, he had taken an elephant, a lion, and a leopard, along with assorted wildebeest and springbok and other smaller game animals. Of course, His Lordship's eyes and ears had been a lot sharper and younger fifty years ago, and he'd had an army of bearers to carry his gear, not to mention a local white hunter to find his targets. With that kind of stalk, one just showed up and pulled the trigger when told, and if one missed the shot, the white hunter would save one's arse. Hardly the same as tracking a wounded Cape buffalo into a bamboo thicket alone, was it?

Just at the moment, the old boy, who was half-deaf and blind, was probably as much threat to his own feet as he was to any lurking rabbits. He had been hunting bunnies on and off for months, and while he had fouled the air numerous times with that black powder cannon of his, he had yet to hit anything other than the ground – or once, the side of the tool shed.

Goswell wasn't an awful man, merely a prime example of his class. Born rich, educated at the best schools, with all the right connections, the man had never had to want for anything. He'd married well, had the usual half-witted inbred children, who'd also married well. One or the other of them would come to call now and then, more often apparently since their mother had died a few years back. Even a couple of the grandchildren came round to see the old boy, and he doted on them, of course. It was true what they said; the rich were different, especially the old-money rich. They expected certain things as their due, never considered otherwise.

The old man whipped the shotgun up, aimed – but held his fire. Lowered the weapon and muttered to himself.

Peel grinned. Well, he could find out how it felt to be rich. He had a million in the bank, he could quit right now, invest the money conservatively, and live very comfortably off the interest for the rest of his life, without ever touching the principal. There was security, especially for a man who had always expected to die with his boots on. But he could do even better by simply continuing to work for Goswell. Everything the same – except that his reports about Bascomb-Coombs would change somewhat. His men would continue to follow the computer expert, save at certain specified times. One watcher would be taken off, thinking another would replace him, only that wouldn't happen. There would be a gap, as long as Bascomb-Coombs needed, and Peel would fill it in when he wrote up the reports. Not bad work for a million, altering a few schedules.

The old man wandered around the corner out of sight and, as he did, Peel reflected that the big sound-suppressor headphones made Goswell look rather like some kind of geriatric alien.

Peel glanced at his watch. About time for his men to check in.

Of course, the deal with the Jew scientist would eventually involve more than just keeping His Lordship in the dark; he knew that. The other shoe would drop, and it would certainly involve work somewhat more strenuous than altering a computer log. And while Bascomb-Coombs seemed convinced of his invincibility when it came to his Qubits and all this quantum nonsense, if somebody kicked in the door and started shooting, it would take a man who knew how to shoot back to save his brilliant arse.

Well, Peel had done that for a long time, first for the Queen, then her duffer son the King, and for a lot less money than he was getting now—

A bomb went off. Half a second later, another blast followed.

Peel dropped into a gunfighter's crouch, looking

for danger, his hand automatically darting to his pistol. He relaxed when he saw the greasy white cloud of smoke swirl past, and heard the old man cursing. 'Bastard! You filthy thieving bastard!'

Peel grinned. Missed another one. He straightened, shot his cuffs, and went to make sure the old man was all right. Just because he was betraying Goswell's trust didn't mean he shouldn't be civilized.

16

Thursday, April 7th
London, England

Michaels decided to accept Toni's invitation and go along to the *silat* class. He ought to work out, he'd been neglecting his practice the last few days, and God only knew when they'd get home and back into a normal routine. So far they had zip on this new threat. He'd probably feel a lot better if he exercised, developed a good sweat.

'You've got the long stare,' Toni said.

She sat in the seat across from him in the cab, and he smiled reflexively at her. 'Sorry. I spent most of the afternoon counting figurative paperclips. I'm not any closer to this guy than I was before. I feel stupid.'

'Why do you feel as if you personally are responsible for catching the mad hacker? Dozens of governmental agencies around the world are chasing him, and none of them are any further along than we are.'

'Yeah, but I sit at the top of the pyramid in the can-do U.S. of A. Nobody is eyeballing the Portuguese or the Tasmanians and expecting *them* to track this guy down. We're the only superpower left.'

'Hi ho, *Silver*!'

He blinked at her. 'Huh?'

'How the Lone Ranger got his name. Tonto nursed him back to health after the Butch Cavendish gang ambushed the ranger troop. He came to, asked about the others. Tonto said, 'Him dead, all dead. You . . . only ranger left. You . . . lone ranger.'

'Really?'

'Truth. You know what it says on the barrel of the Cisco Kid's gun?'

He blinked at her. 'What?'

' "Don't make me hurt you." '

He smiled at her. 'How do you know stuff like that?'

'A misspent youth. Older brothers who collected everything from cars to old '78 rpm vinyl records. I can tell you about Hopalong Cassidy, Roy Rogers, and Gene Autrey, if you want. Want to know about Red Ryder's sidekick?'

'Maybe not,' he said.

'You don't want to hear about Li'l Beaver?' She batted her eyes at him and smiled.

'Well . . . yeah. But . . . not in front of the cabbie.'

They both laughed.

The *silat* school was a dump, in a ratty neighborhood that made Michaels wish he had brought his taser. It was clean enough inside, though, and the students were polite when Toni introduced him.

The instructor, Carl Stewart, arrived, and Michaels met him, too. Seemed like a nice guy, a few years older than Michaels, in pretty good shape. A little taller, a little grayer, a little wider across the shoulders and thicker through the arms. He wore bifocal aviator glasses, and Michaels wondered why he wasn't wearing contacts or droptacs instead.

'Toni tells me you've begun studying *silat*,' Stewart said. 'Are you going to join the class this evening?'

'If that would be all right, yes.'

'Certainly.' He smiled at Toni, she smiled right back, and Michaels felt a little pang of . . . something.

Jealously? No, of course not. He trusted Toni.

The class began, and Michaels dutifully went up and down the floor practicing the two *djurus* he had learned. He stole quick glances at Toni, saw her footworking first the *tiga*, then the *sliwa* – the triangle and square – for her *djurus*. She looked very sharp.

Stewart paused in front of Michaels. 'You seem a bit distracted, Mr Michaels. It would be better if you concentrated on your own form.'

Michaels flushed, nodded, said, 'Sorry, Guru.'

Steward nodded, smiled, and moved along to watch other students.

Good thing this wasn't sitting Zen exercise, or

he'd have gotten whacked with a stick, Michaels thought. He refocused on his moves but he felt awkward. He'd only been doing this a few months and much of it still seemed anti-intuitive and unnatural.

After about fifteen minutes of *djurus*, Stewart called a halt and took questions. Even though his students were doing different forms forms those Michaels had been doing, he heard a couple of things about stepping in balance, and keeping his hips corked that Toni had stressed.

'All right, then. Let's work on combinations,' Stewart said. 'Toni? Let me use you.'

Toni offered Stewart a quick bow. The hand position was slightly different than the bow Stewart returned. Toni's right fist was held in front of her chest suppinated, the left hand cupping it from the side; the knuckles on Stewart's fist faced into his cupping hand.

'A right punch, please, here.' He touched the tip of his nose.

Toni stepped in and shot a fast right punch. If it had connected it would have surely broken his nose. He slapped her arm with both hands, fired an elbow at her ribs, twisted, stepped, punched at her ribs again, then swept her front foot out and upended her. He caught her around the chest with one arm before she fell. 'Okay?'

'Yes.'

'Again please, slowly.'

Toni repeated her attack, and Stewart did the block-elbow-punch, sweep combination again, and kept her from falling with an arm around her chest.

Right across her breasts, Michaels noted with a small feeling of irritation. Was that really necessary? Toni could fall without hurting herself; he'd seen her hit a hard floor and come up like a rubber ball. This floor had mats all over it.

Toni grinned at Stewart, and the expression was one of pure joy. Michaels had seen that look a few times, usually right after a sexual climax – his or hers.

He did not like seeing the look now.

He mentally chided himself: Get a *brain*, boy! This is a martial arts class! He's not copping a feel, he's demonstrating a way to beat the crap out of somebody stupid enough to attack him!

Yeah, well, okay.

'Any questions?'

Michaels decided he had one. 'Why didn't you hit her in the face instead of the ribs?'

Stewart smiled – as did most of the class. Michaels caught it but didn't say anything. Stewart caught his look though.

'Sorry, Mr Michaels, but I've been telling the class that you can do all the damage you need to an attacker most of the time with body shots. The Indonesians seldom go for the face; the biggest headhunters are . . . westerners.'

Michaels nodded. But that pause before

'westerners' told him that Stewart had started to say something else, and Michaels would bet dollars to pennies that the something else was 'Americans.'

'All right, pair up and let's try it. Toni, give me a hand watching?'

Toni said, 'Yes, Guru.'

Michaels found himself standing across from a skinny kid with a short crewcut and a pair of nose rings who looked to be about seventeen. The kid said, 'Giles Patrick.'

'Alex Michaels.'

'Want to defend first?'

'Sure,' Michaels said.

The kid stepped toward him in slow motion, his punch floating toward Michaels at about an eighth-speed.

Michaels blocked, got the elbow in, then stalled. What came next?

'Left punch to the ribs, here,' the kid said.

'Right, right. Let me try it again.'

The kid launched his molasses attack again, and Michaels got the block, elbow, and punch in, but when he tried the sweep, he was off-balance and the kid's foot stayed on the floor.

'Got to square your hips,' the kid said, 'Twist in, shoulders and hips facing the same way.'

'Right.'

'One more?'

'Sure.'

This time, Michaels got all four of the moves, and

the kid went down with the sweep. All right! He felt pretty good about that.

Toni moved to stand next to him. 'Looked pretty good, Alex, but when you block the punch, do it more upward, like so. Giles?'

The kid grinned and came at Toni; this time he put some speed into the move.

Toni moved easily, deflected the punch upward, giving herself plenty of room for the elbow into the armpit.

'Thanks, Toni.'

He caught a hint of a frown from her but she nodded and moved to watch the next pair of students.

Frowning? For what? Calling her 'Toni?'

'Okay if I give it a try?' Giles said.

'Uh, sure.'

Michaels set himself and attacked. The kid did a one-two-three-four! and Michaels hit the mat, hard. He came up fast.

'You all right, Mr Michaels?'

'Yeah, fine. And call me Alex.' Bad enough he was getting his butt kicked; he didn't need to feel like somebody's grandfather.

He set himself for another attack. It was good to burn some tension off and all, but so far he couldn't say this class was the most fun he'd ever had. Not at all.

Lord Goswell stood in front of the big seascape that

had decorated the east wall of the Smaller Room of his club for as long as he'd been coming here. It was a large oil, eight feet tall by twelve feet wide, done in actinic, watery blues and grays, a wave-tossed sailing ship in the eye of an electrical storm, lightening illuminating the frantic sailors trying to keep the wooden vessel afloat. Very dramatic, what, with almost photographic realism. He swirled the ice around in his nearly empty gin and tonic glass and was rewarded by the appearance of Paddington and his tray. 'Another, milord?'

'Why not? Tell me, do we know who painted this?'

'Yes, milord. It was painted by Jeffery Hawkesworth, in, I believe, 1872.'

'It's quite good. A painter I should know?'

'No, milord. He was one of the few civilians killed by the Zulu in South Africa at Rourke's Drift, in 1879. He painted but a handful of canvases. The Club came by this some years after he died, a legacy from his brother, Sir William Hawkesworth, who was knighted by Her Majesty Queen Victoria for services in India.'

Goswell nodded. 'Interesting.'

'Shall I fetch your drink now, milord?'

'I don't suppose you'd consider quitting the Club and going into service with me?'

'You do me a great honor, milord, but I should have to decline. It wouldn't be proper.'

'No, of course not. Carry on.'

He watched the servant leave. Drat. You couldn't

buy that kind of loyalty. A pity. Bought loyalty was generally worth less than you paid for it.

Paddington returned, bearing another perfectly frosted glass upon his tray.

'There's a telephone call for you, milord.' There was a mobile telephone on the tray next to the glass.

Goswell took his glass and telephone. He nodded. 'Thank you, Paddington.'

Speaking of bought loyalty . . . Once Paddington was out of earshot Goswell activated the receiver. 'You have the balance of what I need?'

'Roight, I 'ave gawt it.'

'The usual place then. Half an hour.' He shut the phone off.

Goswell stared at the painting, sipping at his fresh drink. A pity this artist had been brought down by some bloody savages. He might have gone onto really great work. Of course, the Royal Army had taught the blackmoors a thing or two during that set-to at Rourke's Drift, hadn't they? A handful of soldiers against thousands of natives, and the troops had, by God, stood their ground and given an account of themselves, hadn't they? Taught the bloody niggers a thing or two about British resolve, by God!

He raised his glass in salute to the painting. 'Cheers, old boy.'

17

Thursday
London, England

Physically, Toni felt pretty good after the workout, though she was a little peeved at Alex for trying to get overly familiar with her in class. He was feeling insecure, she could tell, so he'd kept calling her 'Toni,' instead of 'Guru,' and he'd reached out to pat her on the shoulder or smile at her a couple of times, and she was sure that he did it just to let everybody know they were more than student and teacher. That was fine when they were alone in the gym at home but here it was inappropriate. It had a 'She can kick your ass and she is mine!' flavor to it, and Toni didn't much care for that. She loved him, but sometimes Alex could be such a . . . little boy about things.

Of course, most of the men she knew were that way, and he was less so than most. And he did love her, so she could maybe cut him a little slack.

There was something else on his mind, though. He was pensive about something, and she couldn't tell what. It could have been the whole situation at work but it didn't feel that way.

She needed to talk about both things. How to bring them up without starting a fight was the trick.

Having a lover who was your boss and your student got complicated at times. She'd never thought about that before they had gotten together. probably because, in her heart of hearts, she'd never really expected they would get together. She'd wanted it, more than anything she'd ever wanted, but it had not seemed destined to happen. And then it had, and it had been wonderful, but not picture-perfect.

It was easier to have something in your imagination than it was in reality. All couples had problems. Her parents had been married since just after The Flood, and they loved each other, but even they fought. It wouldn't have been healthy not to. Still, Toni hadn't had any real long-term relationships before, and every time she and Alex got on each other's nerves, she sweated it. She was afraid she was going to lose him. She was afraid that they'd grow apart. She was afraid that she'd had too high an expectation about how things would be, that the reality wouldn't measure up.

The class had been good, though. Guru Stewart was as good a teacher as he was a practitioner. He would take a moment from time to time, while the students were working with each other, to show Toni a move. Their arts were similar enough that she could see the use of what he was giving her, and she much appreciated it.

As the class had been winding down, Stewart had said, 'We should work out together, either before or after a regular class, before you leave town,' he said. 'We could teach each other a lot more if we could concentrate on it.'

She was thrilled. 'I'd like that,' she said.

Now, as she and Alex rode in the cab from the school back to the new hotel that MI-6 had sprung for, Toni realized just how much she had been enjoying the *silat* practice. It was simple, straight forward, no hidden agendas. You worked your body along with your mind, and it kept them both focused on simple things: strike *here*, step *there*, get a good base, use your angle and leverage.

Much less complex than dealing with people's emotions, even your own. Perhaps especially your own.

Back at their hotel, as they were getting out of the cab, Michaels said, 'We're being followed, did you notice?'

She didn't look around, but at him. 'What?'

'There's a man in a gray Toyota parked across the street and back a hundred feet. He was behind us on the way to the *silat* class. I'm pretty sure he was with me on foot when I went out to grab a sandwich at lunch today, too. It would be an awfully big coincidence if this guy just happened to be there every time I went out.'

'British Intelligence?'

He nodded at the uniformed doorman as the man opened the portal for them. He felt sweaty and smelly after his workout but he smiled at the doorman as if he and Toni were dressed for a royal wedding.

'Could be, I suppose. If we had one of them digging around in *our* secrets at Quantico, I'd have the FBI on their tail, to make sure nobody grabbed them up and squeezed something out of them.'

'You don't sound convinced,' she said.

'Well, if we were having one of theirs followed, I'd make sure the field op doing the work was somebody they wouldn't spot – assuming we didn't want them to spot him. The Brits ought to have guys who are as good as ours at *sub rosa* surveillance. This is their town, they know it. By all rights, I shouldn't have seen him.'

They crossed the lobby and reached the elevator. Toni beat him to the button.

'Maybe they wanted you to see him. Let you know you were being protected.'

'Be better just to tell me I was being covered, wouldn't it?'

'Would we tell them?'

'Maybe. Especially if we thought they'd figure it out anyway.'

The elevator arrived and *chinged*, the cast bronze doors opening with ponderous grace. The operator smiled at them. Good thing the new hotel he and

Toni had transferred to was being subsidized by the British, otherwise the Director would have a stroke when she got the bill.

'A friendly test? You used to be a field op yourself.'

'Yeah,' he said, 'but I've lost a few moves since then. Oh, I look in the rearview mirror a couple times when I'm driving, and glance around every now and then. I'm not completely asleep since all that business with the Selkie came down, but I don't put a lot of effort into it. Not as much as I should. No, this guy just isn't very good. I can't believe MI-5 or -6 would send him out and think I wouldn't notice him.'

'Maybe they just don't want to waste a good man on you. Sent in the second team because they figure you're an ugly American who walks around with his head in a thick and blinding ego fog.' She smiled.

'They might be right. but I think I'll give Angela Cooper a call and see what's what.'

They got into the elevator. The operator said, 'Floor?'

'Four, please,' Toni said. In place of her normal faint resonance of the Bronx, she had a passable imitation of a posh British accent. 'Four' came out 'Foah.' Michaels blinked at her.

In their suite, Michaels used his virgil to call Cooper. Toni started the hot water running in the shower, and he watched her strip off her sweats as Cooper came online. He caught her at home, and she had her camera on. She wore something red and silky, what he could see of it. His view stopped just below her shoulders. He flipped his own cam on.

'Alex! What can I do for you?'

'Answer a question honestly.'

'Of course.'

'Are you or MI-5 having me followed?'

'We certainly aren't. I doubt that SS is, but I can check. Hold on a moment.' Her cam froze, and the word 'holding' appeared on his thumbnail screen.

Toni peeled her panties off, pulled her sports bra off over her head. She turned and gave him a glorious frontal view, then waved bye-bye as she stepped into the shower and slid the door shut.

He would make this call short, he decided. He wanted to get into that shower before Toni got out. He'd been horny all through the *silat* class, and it hadn't gotten any better on the ride home.

'Alex? MI-5 says they are not having you surveilled. Is there something we ought to know?' She smiled.

He thought about it quickly. 'No, I think I'm just getting paranoid in my old age.'

'Hardly old,' she said.

'I'll see you tomorrow. Sorry to bother you at home.'

'Call any time. It's never a bother.' she leaned back, and the red silky shirt or gown or whatever gaped a little at her neck, showing the top of her cleavage.

He discommed, and as he did so, his male radar picked up a blip. Was that . . . interest? He'd only been with a few women. Since he'd gotten his divorce, Toni was the only woman he had been seriously interested in; he was out of practice, but it sure sounded as if Cooper didn't find him totally disgusting.

Interesting. Good for the old ego, to have a beautiful and bright woman possibly interested in him. Assuming he wasn't reading the signals wrong.

Not that it mattered. He had much better waiting for him here. He started for the shower, pulling his damp clothes off as he went.

'What did she say?' Toni called from the shower.

'She said it isn't her people,' he called back.

'Then we ought to find out who it is,' she said.

He pulled the shower door open and was rewarded with a blast of hot vapor that fogged the mirrors behind him. 'Tomorrow. Got room for me?'

She glanced down. 'If you stand in front. I don't want to get stabbed in the back.'

He grinned. 'Well, look at that. I wonder where that came from?'

'A present from Ms Cooper, perhaps?'

He frowned. 'What?'

'Well, you didn't have it before you got on the virgil, did you?'

Was she teasing him? She was smiling, but he wasn't sure.

While he considered that, the point became, well, *moot*.

Toni noticed. 'I was just *joking*, Alex.'

He was embarrassed. He grabbed the bar of soap and a wash cloth. 'Turn around,' he said. 'I'll wash your back.'

'Alex—'

'I'm really tired,' he said. 'It was a hard workout, I'm not used to it. I need to get some sleep.' It sounded lame and he knew she knew it. He rubbed the soap into the cloth, fast, worked up a thick lather. She turned around and he scrubbed at her back. Maybe a little harder than he should.

Something was going on between them, something he didn't understand. Whatever it was, he didn't like it. Not a damn bit.

Toni didn't pursue it, though, and he was glad. He didn't really want to get into a deep emotional discussion right now. He *was* physically wrung out.

He was tired, but, unlike Toni, who fell asleep a few minutes after their shower, Michaels sat reading for an hour. He finally got into bed, turned off the light, and tried to sleep. After lying there for almost another hour, he realized he wasn't drifting off to sleep any time soon. He was wound up, too tight to relax.

He got out of bed carefully, went into the bathroom, and slipped into jeans, a T-shirt, and running shoes. He dug his kick-taser out of his kit and checked the battery. The little wireless weapon used compressed gas as a propellant, was non-lethal, and fired a pair of charged darts that would knock a man on his butt if they hit him, even through clothes. The effective range was only a few meters, but that was where most gunfights were likely to happen. The old FBI shoot-out maxim concerning such encounters was, 'Three feet, three shots, three seconds.' If a guy was fifty meters away from you and pumping elbows and ass in the other direction, he wasn't real dangerous. The armorer at Net Force had told him that somebody had come up with an electromesh vest that would defeat a taser's charge, but a vest wasn't a full body suit – you could always shoot somebody in the leg or head. And it was a simple device. It had a laser sight on it. You put the tiny red dot on the target, allowed for a little spread of the needles in flight, and that's where the darts went when you pushed the button. If you weren't too far away. If your hand didn't shake too bad. He'd only had to fire the thing on the job once; it had worked well enough then.

He tucked the taser into his back pocket, put a windbreaker onto cover it, and quietly left the room.

Michaels left the hotel via a rear exit, circled around the block, and approached the front of the place from behind where the gray Toyota had been parked.

Where the guy in the Toyota was *still* parked, sitting behind the wheel. He had his window rolled down, and was smoking a cigar. He could smell it fifteen meters away.

The Commander of Net Force looped around the car as a bus passed, sending a blast of night air into the Toyota, backwashing the cigar smoke into the vehicle. The guy in the car ducked away from the bus's wake.

Michaels pulled his taser, scooted in from the driver's side – the right-hand side in this country – and put the taser on the windowsill as he squatted next to the car.

'Hi. Are we having fun yet?'

The guy, a thin and balding man of maybe thirty-five, nearly swallowed his cigar.

'Jesus Christ! Don't do that! You scared the piss out of me!'

American, no mistaking that accent. A westerner.

On the seat next to him was a small flatscreen computer, a digital camera, and a pair of binoculars. There was also a thermos, and a grease-soaked paper bag under a cardboard container with the remains of a fried fish and chips dinner. On the floor was a large-mouth jar, empty. In case nature called.

If there had been any doubt in Michaels' mind before, this put it to rest. Mr Cigar here was sitting surveillance.

'Okay, pal; so who are you and why are you following me?'

'What the hell are you talking about? I don't know you—'

'Look, we can do this easy or we can do it hard. You can tell me – or I can call my friends at British Intelligence and have you picked up as a spy, stuck in a cell so deep it'll take a month for the foggy sunshine to filter down to it.'

'Hey, I'm an American citizen, I got rights—'

'This is England, friend. They don't play by the same rules. Your choice.'

Cigar considered it for a few seconds. He'd been burned, and he wasn't going to talk his way out of it. He shrugged. 'I'm a private investigator from Boise.'

Michaels blinked. A private detective?

'Who hired you?'

'I know who you are. I know you can give me a world of crap. You can stick me in a dungeon if you want, but I can't tell you who hired me. Word gets around, I'm outta business. But you're a bright guy, figure it out.'

Boise. Oh, shit—

Megan. But – why?

Michaels tucked the taser away. He stood. 'Might as well go home. If I see you again I *will* have the local law take you away.'

There was a long moment, then Cigar started his car. Michaels watched him drive away.

He pulled his virgil. It was the middle of the night here, they were what – seven? eight hours ahead of Idaho on the clock?

Never mind what time it was there. Too bad if he

caught her at work. He tapped the memory button, clicked on Megan's number.

'Hello, Alex,' she said. Cool. Her voice was a warehouse full of ice in the winter at the North Pole. In the shade. 'Hold on a second, let me get where we can talk.'

She came back on in a moment, and she lit her cam. She was dressed for work, her hair up. She looked good, as always.

'Megan. How is Susie?'

'She is fine. You called me at work to ask that?'

'No. I just had a few words with your balding cigar-smoking private eye,' he said, his voice barely controlled. 'Why are you having me followed?'

'Self-defense,' she said.

'What the hell are you talking about?'

'After you beat Byron senseless at Christmas, you *threatened* me, remember?' The ice in her voice melted. Now she sounded like a volcano rumbling, about ready to let go. 'You told me that if he spent a night under my roof – *my* roof, Alex, not yours and mine – that you would have me declared an unfit mother!'

'I never said that. I never said you were an unfit mother—'

'Like hell you didn't! You said you would throw Byron up in my slutty face and go for full custody. Well, mister, two can play that game. Byron will be spending the night tonight, just like he did last night, and the night before, and just like he will be spending it tomorrow! And as many goddamned nights as I want him to be here! And you know what? He will be screwing my brains out, too!'

Just as she had always been able to do, she pushed his hot button. He lost control, snapped back at her almost reflexively. 'That won't take much, screwing your brains out. By the time he gets his zipper down it'll be done.'

She laughed, knowing she had made him lose his temper. When she spoke again, it was back to the ice queen: 'Funny. But laugh at this, funny man – I know all about *your* sleeping arrangements. About sweet-little-butter-wouldn't-melt-in-her-mouth Toni Fiorella. At least Byron is my age, not a child. Let's see how the court views you bonking an employee!'

Oh, *shit*!

'At least I'm not doing it in front of Susie,' he said. Not much of a response.

'So what you're saying is, it's okay to sneak around like a preacher with a whore, but it's not okay for an engaged couple about to be married to do it? I doubt the judge here in Boise will be much impressed with that argument. You were always good at twisting the story to fit your definition of righteous, weren't you?'

He should apologize, he knew. Pour a tanker full of oil on the troubled waters, calm her down. Tell her he'd lost his temper when he'd punched out her new boyfriend – who had grabbed him, don't forget – and said things he didn't really mean. The problem was, he *had* meant them. Still did, though this certainly put another face on the problem. She was right. A judge wasn't going to take Susie away from Megan unless he could show she was a bad mother, and the truth was, she was a great mother. He'd thought so when they were together, and he thought so now. And he didn't want to lose his daughter. If he was limited to visiting Susie once or twice a year on holidays, their relationship was doomed. She'd grow up thinking of Byron as her father. He'd be the one who'd take her to school and to the mall and he'd be the one helping her with homework and doing the things Michaels should have been doing.

He should apologize, try to get this resolved. But he waited too long.

'Goodbye, Alex. You can call Susie, I don't want her to think I'm shutting you out of her life, but you and I don't have anything else to say to each other. Give my regards to your teenaged girlfriend.'

She broke the connection.

Michaels blinked. He was in the middle of the sidewalk on a street in downtown London in the middle of the night, feeling as if he had just been slammed in the groin by a linebacker's knee. His ex-wife knew about his affair with Toni – who was a dozen years younger than he was, but hardly a teenager! – and he was going to have to hear that in court if he contested the custody hearing for his daughter. He and Toni were both adults, but he was her boss. That wouldn't look good. The FBI frowned on such relationships, and since he didn't have any history with the new Director, she wouldn't be ready to put her ass on the line to save his if this all blew up in his face.

He was, not to put too fine a point on it, fucked.

18

Thursday
Walworth, London, England

Peel's first real assignment from his new boss was a field operation – right up his alley. Much better than sitting in a drafty old shed of a church watching stats stream by on a computer's holoproj. Of course, almost anything would be better than that.

It seemed that a certain scientist, formerly one of Bascomb-Coombs' university teachers and now retired to a private consulting position, was poking around in computer territory best left alone. Old BC was about to unleash some new electro-devilry on the world and he didn't want his former professor to tread on him while he was about it. And while he didn't want to seriously injure his old mentor he did want him out of the way for a day or three. Could Peel manage that?

'Level Two,' Peel said to the three men in the car. 'Are we clear on that?'

The trio in the back – Peel sat in the driver's seat of the big right-hand-drive Chevrolet four-door – nodded. 'Yes, sir,' they said in unison. They were the youngest of his men, Lewis, Huard, and Doolittle, dressed now as lowlife rowdies, in Doc Martin steel-toed boots, baggy denim pants, and black shirts cut to reveal fake tattoos on their arms and chests. The outfits came complete with false nose-rings, earrings, and tight skinhead wigs that easily covered their military-short haircuts.

Here was a picture: A trio of thumpy boys, out for a lark, trouble on the prowl. It was exactly the right image, one that authorities would not look at twice without accepting. Coppers were good about that. You gave them an obvious picture, they didn't scurry around looking for hidden meaning in the brush strokes and hues, they nearly always went for the overall model.

Level Two. The code was one he'd learned from a commando in South Africa during a training seminar there some years ago. For direct physical violence not involving guns or knives, there were five operational levels:

Level One was the mildest, consisting mainly of threats or shoves, intimidation, without physical injury to the subject.

Level Two was mild to moderate damage, bruises, perhaps a broken bone or two, equivalent to a good bar-fight thrashing. A few stitches in the local doctor's surgery, some pain pills, and a day or two to rest up at home, and you'd be right as rain.

Level Three was damaging enough to require a stay in hospital; you'd be weeks or months recovering. A serious encounter.

Level Four meant you would carry reminders of the attack with you for the rest of your life: you'd be crippled with a torn-out knee or ankle, or perhaps crushed hands; you might lose your hearing or an eye, or be otherwise maimed. Recovery would be slow and painful – and you'd never be as complete as you had been before.

Level Five was terminal. A subject was to be made to suffer much pain, to know what he had done, and to have time enough to regret having done it before passing away.

The South Africans would deny having such codes, of course. They hadn't been used officially since *apartheid* days, but used they still were. Many military and intelligence services around the world had similar operational modes still in place, officially or not. One simply did not talk about such things where unfriendly ears might lurk. Peel recalled an Israeli official some years back, blabbing on in public about their official policy on torture. How it was, under some extreme circumstances, justified. Oh, but the Jews had been lambasted for *that* when it had hit the media. Of *course* they used torture when they needed it. Some raghead ready to join Allah in Paradise plants a bomb and they catch him before it goes off? Only a fool would sit and politely inquire about it: Excuse me Abdul, old boy, would you mind awfully telling us where the bomb is so we might disarm it? Some more tea?

Whatever else you had to say about the Jews, they were survivors. If you kicked dirt on their shoes, they would drop a mountain on you in return. Such things didn't bother fanatics ready to die at the drop of a Koran, but more reasonable governments kept that in mind before sending sorties against Israel. Getting hit back thrice as hard as you hit somebody was still a deterrent in some quarters. And the Jews never let it pass, never. You spat on them and sooner or later – likely sooner – you'd have a fire hose blasting you in the face.

If you wanted your country to survive its enemies you did what you had to do. No one needed to run to *CNN* and talk about having to shove a few needles under a terrorist's fingernails to save decent men and women from being killed, now did they? It was all part of the game. You got caught, you suffered the consequences. Unfortunately, that was how Peel had been forced to resign, being . . . overzealous with Irish terrorists – which, as far as he was concerned, was redundant. Whatever peace decrees were signed, the bloody Irish were never going to settle down and be civil. But some of them had died under his interrogations, word had gotten back to the rear echelons, and that was that.

Ah, well. Water under the bridge. That was when he had been a major in good standing, serving King and country. Now, he catered to another master, one who understood the reality of things, and he was already rich as a result. Not a bad trade, all in all.

The target emerged from the pub in a cloud of alcohol-fueled noise and good cheer. BC wanted him bent but not broken, just enough to put him out of active service for a few days, after which it wouldn't matter. It ought not to be too difficult to manage one old college professor.

'Here we go, boys. Move sharp, and be careful.'

The target, a rotund man of sixty in a twenty-year-old tweed suit and matching Irish rain hat, sported a mostly white beard and carried a furled umbrella.

'Right, Major,' Lewis said, grinning. He was the leader of the attack team. 'Here's a fierce old beaky. We'll keep our heads in.'

Huard and Doolittle laughed. They exited the car.

The plan was for them to amble toward the professor and, once close enough, jump him. A few good thumps and they'd be away, taking his wallet. The police would see it as no more than another sad example of youth gone bad, and tell the professor he was lucky to get off as easy as he did. They'd look for the trio of skinheads, but since those three wouldn't exist in an hour, their disguises burned and gone, it would be a fruitless search. A pickup vehicle waited around the corner for Peel's men, a stolen lorry with the license plates switched with those of a van parked at a nearby cinema. A simple operation, and untraceable.

The major cranked the Dodge Ram's engine to depart, which he intended to do as soon as he was sure the assault was proceeding as planned.

The three skinhead slackabouts, laughing and talking too loud, moved to intersect the professor's path. Lewis held an unlit cigarette, and he was first to reach the target. He waved the cigarette and said something to the older man. Too far away for Peel to hear, but he knew the gist. *Allo, Gramps, gottuh match, have ye*?

Huard and Doolittle drifted out to the sides, to encircle the old man.

Peel put the car in gear to drive off. It was going by the numbers, one, two, three—

Then, of a moment, the operation leaped past three to seventeen: The professor lunged like bloody Zorro, jabbed at Lewis with the tip of the umbrella, and caught him a hard stab in the solar plexus. The team leader lost his cigarette prop and his wind as he backed off and clutched at his belly. The professor twisted to his left, swung the umbrella like an axe, and whacked Huard across the face. The shock and surprise drove him backward, too.

'Help!' the white-bearded old boy yelled in a voice to wake the dead. 'Assassins! Help!'

Doolittle lunged and bounced a fist off the old man's shoulder, and the old fellow spun and slashed at him with the umbrella, missing only because the fake skinhead leaped back like he was Nijinsky doing steps from bloody Swan Lake.

'Help! Help, I say!'

Several men rushed out of the pub and saw the goings-on.

Wonderful. Bloody wonderful!

Lewis recovered, stepped in, dodged another rapier-like thrust from the umbrella, and managed to land a solid punch to the old man's nose. The professor stumbled and sat down hard on the sidewalk, but did not release his hold on his weapon. He swung at Doolittle's legs, caught a shin with a *whack*! Peel heard thirty meters away, and flailed his weapon back and forth, missing only because Doolittle did another quick little nancy-boy ballet step to get out of the way.

What a bloody cock up—!

The party was over. The three troops took to their heels as the growing mob from the pub rushed them. The boys were young and fit, didn't smoke, contrary to the fag prop, and should be able to outrun a bunch of middle-aged men who'd had a pint or two. If they couldn't they deserved what they got. Idiots.

Peel pulled away from the curb, made a turn, and glanced at the professor. He did not intend to relate exactly how the attack had gone, nor how it had slipped downhill. The old man probably had a broken nose, that should be enough – though it was likely he was less damaged than the three who had set upon him.

Peel watched in his rearview mirror as the first of the pub-goers reached the professor and helped him to his feet.

Hello all. Meet my friend, Corporal Disaster.

Hell's bells! He'd warned the lads to take care, but they were young and too full of themselves to even consider than one old man was a threat of any kind. Didn't expect they'd be up against John bloody Steed and his Samurai umbrella, now had they?

Well. They'd know better next time. Embarrassing and painful lessons were the kind that etched themselves into one's memory.

Christ.

Friday, August 8th
Somewhere in the British Raj – India

Jay Gridley stood there, machete in one hand, his revolver in the other. He hadn't even moved yet, and already he was dripping with sweat. The jungle lay in front of him, leaves and vines woven into a thick wall of tangles, too verdant, and altogether too alive. His heart pounded, and he was breathing hard. It took everything he had just to hold the jungle image, and even so, it wavered at the edges, threatening to collapse at any second.

It wasn't just the problem with concentration. Yeah, Saji's exercises had helped, the breath and meditation and all. And his grandfather had been a Buddhist, and he knew a bunch of them, so it wasn't that weird. The big thing was—

Jay was afraid. No, not just afraid, he was *terrified*. This was the jungle where the tiger had been, where it had leaped from cover and clawed him, ripped at his brain so he couldn't think. Maybe killing his ability to walk the web forever, and, if so, killing him, too.

He didn't have to be here. Nobody was making him go back into the jungle. But if he couldn't play computers he might as well be dead.

He took another breath. The little handgun wouldn't even slow the tiger down, he knew, but he couldn't work the machete and hold the big double rifle ready. If it came at him again he would get hurt again, maybe worse than before.

He could get help. Saji was willing to come with him. He wouldn't carry a gun, because he wouldn't shoot even a VR creature, but he could offer moral support. And there were other ops, some in Net Force, some not, who could link with Jay and share the scenario, some of whom would cheerfully tow a howitzer and who'd blast anything that moved. But that wasn't the way. Jay couldn't spend the rest of his life asking for help. If he couldn't walk in the valley of the shadow alone, he couldn't do his job, and if he couldn't do the thing he loved most in the world, what was the point?

He took yet another breath and let it out slowly. He was going in. If it got him, then it got him, but he was going to go down swinging the big knife and pulling the Webley's trigger if he went, and to hell with it.

He raised the machete. The VR wall of vegetation rippled and wavered. The image started to fade. Crap!

He came back into himself in front of his home work station, soaked with sour-smelling sweat, heart still thumping madly.

He'd been ready. He had. He was willing to do it.

Just not ready and willing enough to hold the scenario.

He blew out a sigh. Okay. He'd go back, try it again.

In a little while. When he'd had a chance to get his breath back, to rest a little. Really, he would go back. Really.

19

Saturday, April 9th
London, England

Mikhayl Ruzhyó, now looking like just another tourist, walked toward the Imperial War Museum. The building, with its centered dome and pillared front, could almost have been an Italian church – had not the approach been guarded by a pair of 15-inch guns, taken, according to the sign nearby, from HMS *Resolution* and HMS *Ramillies*.

Churches may have been violent places through the centuries but Ruzhyó had never heard of one protected by naval guns outside the front entrance.

To one side of the walkway, a tall concrete slab stood, a section of the Berlin Wall taken from near the Brandenburg Gate. He had been a teenager in 1989, when they had started taking the wall down, and the significance of it had been lost on him. What an American president had once called 'the evil empire' had been much closer to home. He had known very little about the world outside his homeland in those days. He had learned too much about the world since.

The piece of the Berlin Wall had been painted to look like a giant, cartoonish face, done in blues and blacks, with its mouth stretched wide open. Against a dark red background in the mouth were the words 'Change Your Life.'

Easy for you to say.

Ruzhyó had been to London several times, usually on his way elsewhere, once on assignment to erase a wayward colleague, and he had seen a few of the tourist sights: Buckingham Palace, the Wellington Monument, Abbey Road. He and Anna had almost come to England on a holiday once, before she got sick, but something or the other had prevented it. Since Anna had died, he hadn't been much of a tourist. Anna would not have enjoyed this place but these days, war museums were more to his tastes.

Inside, the main gallery was full of old tanks and artillery pieces; various airplanes hung from the ceiling. He strolled past a Mark V tank, a 9.2-inch howitzer, a Jeep. Gray-greens were the dominant colors.

The most impressive display was of a giant V2 rocket, the side cut away to show the engine – such that it was. The missile was huge, painted dark green. It looked to him like a cartoon rocket ship, a pointed cigar with fins on the tail.

Ruzhyó stared at the V2. How frightening it must have been to civilians to see this monster dropping from the skies during the Blitz. According to the placard more than 6500 of the V2s and smaller V1s fell on London and the Southeast in hard and explosive storms, killing a total of 8,938 people.

How, he wondered, how they been able to come up with the exact number killed? 8,938?

If the Germans had been able to manage a decent guidance system for these beasts, they would have killed a lot more. But while they had been fearsome devices, shooting them off had been rather like launching pop-bottle rockets. That they were able to hit London at all had been due more to luck than skill. Many, if not most, of the V1s and V2s had fallen harmlessly into the sea or in the countryside. And in a war, nine thousand civilians mean little in the overall casualty count. A few drops in an ocean of blood.

What men did best was kill other men. Especially when given leave to do so in battle.

Ruzhyó strolled past a searchlight, another item painted a flaky military-green; he looked at a shellacked and unpainted wooden fishing boat used during the evacuation at Dunkirk; he examined Monty's tank, in which he'd ridden during the North Africa campaign against Rommel, when Montgomery was still a lowly general and not yet the famous Field Marshal.

The monuments of killing.

There were also side rooms with cryptography equipment the museum-goers could play with, and on the lower ground floor, a World War One experience, designed to look like the trenches. This floor also had a Blitz display, and a Second World War area, as well as a more modern conflict display: Korea, the Cold War, Vietnam, the Falklands, Bosnia, the Middle East. Ruzhyó quickly passed through the more contemporary presentations; they held little interest for him. He knew about those kinds of wars. Chetsnya and the invading Russians lived in his memory as real as if it had taken place yesterday, and not almost twenty years past.

Even though it had been a sea of mud then, it was a much cleaner business in the trenches in France in 1915 than it was when Ruzhyó had been *Spetsnaz*. Cleaner in the sense that you knew who your enemies where, you knew where they were, and you had things laid out for you in black and white. Attack here, shoot there, live or die along the way. There was little skulking about and shooting people while they sat at a desk or lay in bed with a wife or mistress. Those had been his stock in trade. He knew about that kind of war.

It wasn't particularly satisfying, these monuments to war, but it seemed appropriate. He would book his flight out and leave, today, if possible. Perhaps by way of Spain, using another identity. Madrid would be warm by now, and the smells of Spain were more pleasing than those of England.

Saturday
Quantico, Virginia

John Howard knew he should have been at home, visiting with his wife and son, but he couldn't relax enough. He'd just sit there simmering and his family would feel it, which wouldn't be pleasant for anybody. Might as well be at work, though there didn't seem to be much he could do here, either.

He thought about Ruzhyó, wondered about him. How could the man be such a cold-blooded killer? He had started out a soldier, and killing sometimes went with the territory, but somewhere along the way somebody had recruited him for wet work. He had stopped being a soldier and become an assassin, a thing of the dark. Howard could understand that an adrenaline rush could pump you up for sneaking around in the back alleys two steps ahead of somebody chasing you, but the stone-hearted murders? That was different—

'Wool-gathering, John?'

Howard smiled at Fernandez. 'Just thinking about our quarry.'

'Wishing you knew where to find him?'

'That, too. But more wondering how he can do what does.' He explained, expecting Julio to agree with him.

To his surprise his friend shook his head. 'Not a lot of difference, way I see it.'

'Shooting men in the back of the head? You don't see the difference?'

'Would they be any deader if he had shot them in the front of the head?'

'Come again?'

'Those two we lost were soldiers, on guard duty. The risk goes with the job. If they'd been paying attention they'd probably still be alive – or at least they'd have gotten to shoot back. But when you get right down to it, how is it different, really? Somebody shoots you for evil and might, or they shoot you for goodness and right, you're still cold either way. Their reasons won't matter to you, will they? Dead is dead.'

Howard stared at Fernandez as if the sergeant had just turned into a big caterpillar puffing on a hookah: Whoo are youu?

Fernandez caught the look and grinned. 'You don't like spies and assassins but they're as much a part of an army now as they ever were. You want to go into battle with the advantages on your side, or at least not against you. So you send a spy into the enemy camp to find out where they plan to march. He's doing the same to you, so the side with the quicker, smarter spy gets a half-step on the other side. That game is as old as war, isn't it?'

'Spies aren't the same as assassins,' Howard pointed out.

'Yeah, that's true. But let me ask you a hypothetical question, Colonel. Suppose you could go back in time to Germany in the late thirties—'

'—and assassinate Hitler?' Howard finished. He had heard this one before.

'Yeah. Would you?'

'In a heartbeat. He was a monster. It would save millions of innocent lives.'

'You'd still be an assassin, then, right?'

'Yes, but in this case, the ends would justify the means. Sometimes it does, Julio. I'd take the moral heat.'

'No question, I'd pop him, too. But how do we know *what* our quarry's ends were? Why he got into what he's into? And think about what you might have done in his place, out there in the desert. We went to collect him, and if he had come out shooting, we'd have clotheslined him, right? Deleted him cold?'

'Yes.'

'So, tactically, he was surrounded, outnumbered, and outgunned. The way we saw it, he either gave up or died.'

'We saw it that way. We were wrong.'

'Yes, sir. He beat us, straight up, and he did it with the tools he had. I wouldn't have been able to do it. You wouldn't have, either, would you?'

'No.'

'You'd have gone down shooting.'

'Probably.'

'Me, too. And we'd be dead. Ruzhyó isn't. And he's on the loose.'

'You *admire* this guy?'

'Man beats me at my game, oh, yeah. I'm pretty good at what I do, so are you. This guy, he's a formidable enemy, and when push comes to shove, those are the ones we want to face off with, aren't they? You remember the shoot-out in Grozny?'

Howard nodded. He remembered.

'Those revolutionaries we took down weren't in our league. They never had a chance once we decided to scoop 'em up. Screwed, blued, and tattooed. You voiced your disappointment on the flight home. How . . . easy it was.'

'I remember.'

'This ice man we're after, he's not easy. He's in our league – hell, maybe he's better than we are. Catching him will mean something, won't it?'

'Damn straight.'

'It's not a war, John, but it's not a walk in the park. You're pissed off because the guy whipped us, not because he shoots people. The samurai killed a lot more people than the ninja ever did. It's not about body counts. It's about winning.'

Howard couldn't stop a small grin. 'When did you get to be such a . . . Taoist philosopher, Julio?'

'I'm about to be a married man with a child. It makes a man think.'

'Well, go home and take care of your bride-to-be, you aren't doing any good here.'

The warning chime on Howard's computer peeped. A flagged subject.

'Go ahead, computer,' Howard said.

'Subject A-1 located,' the computer said.

Howard reached for the computer. Damn! They had him!

Well, if they could get there fast enough. Wherever 'there' was.

20

Saturday
Old Kent Road, London, England

Peel stood watching Bascomb-Coombs, once again not having a clue what the man was doing. But BC liked an audience, so Peel allowed his running commentary.

'Here we go. We insert the passwords we have rascalled from the gatekeepers, thus . . . and we are in. A straight shot to the inner doors, which we also open with no effort at all . . .'

He tapped at the keyboard, his fingers dancing like little elves. He hummed to himself, and laughed softly.

'Poor sods. They've rebuilt their walls and made them twice as thick and high as they were but it doesn't matter, you see. There still must be the pass-through, and no matter how straight the gates, if you have the keys, you are unstoppable! Voila!'

He turned from the computer screen, awash with complex lines and clots of numbers and letters that Peel did not comprehend. 'How is your desire for power, Terrance?'

'Excuse me?'

Bascomb-Coombs pointed at the keyboard. 'Come over here and press this key, and for a few milliseconds you'll be the most powerful man in the world. You will have more of an effect on more people's lives than anyone else on the planet.'

Peel stared at the man but didn't move.

'Ah, you hesitate. You must know the dictum, "With great power comes great responsibility"?'

'Churchill?'

The scientist smiled. 'Spider-Man, actually. Sure you don't want to do the deed?'

Peel shook his head.

'Well. Onward and upward then.' He tapped the key once, smartly. 'That ought to give the rabble something to think about.'

'Commander Michaels?'

Michaels looked up from his desk. He didn't recognize the man standing there; he was just another of the young, clean-cut types running around the place, dressed in a suit and tie. Could have been an FBI agent, save that his clothes were tailored better. 'Yes?'

'DG Hamilton wanted me to deliver this to you, sir.' He handed a silvery disk about the size of a quarter to Michaels. 'If you'll thumbprint here, sir?' He held a print reader out. Michaels pressed his right thumb against a small gray panel on the device. The messenger looked at the readout and was apparently satisfied with the print match. 'Thank you, sir.'

Michaels looked at the tiny computer disk. If you were worried about your computer system being burgled and you didn't trust your electronic protection, there were ways to placate your fears. The easiest method was to disengage your computer from all contact with other machines and strip out all communications right down to the hardwiring. If it was unplugged and not firewired or optically-linked to any other computer in a network, local or external, you were safe.

Nobody could sneak in your house if you didn't have any doors or windows.

Of course, you couldn't get out, either, and that was a problem.

So if you isolated yourself, you accepted input only via secure and scanned disks. And if you needed to reach out to another computer, you sent them a hand-carried disk. It was slow, it was cumbersome, but it was safe.

Michaels stuck the disk into his reader and had his viral software crunch it. Even though it was supposed to be secure, you still checked – always.

The software – the best antiviral-antivermal-Betty Crocker program MI-6 had – dutifully reported that the coin-sized disk was clean, no sign of viruses, worms, or unwanted pastries.

Michaels ran the disk. Things were looking up on a few fronts. The airline reservation and flight-control computers were, by and large, back up and running smoothly. That was the good news.

The bad news was they hadn't been able to backwalk the hack that had caused the problem in the first place. It just . . . stopped past a series of firewalls and foolpits.

'Good afternoon, Alex.'

He glanced up at Angela. She was in a green T-shirt, faded and kind-of-tight jeans, and tennis shoes. His surprise at her outfit must have showed. She smiled and said, 'Casual Saturday.'

'Ah.'

'Anything new?'

'Afraid not. I was just going over the disk your boss sent over. The airlines are back online.'

She strolled in his direction, leaned in to look over his shoulder.

He felt her right breast brush against his back.

Apparently Casual Saturday meant no bra, too.

Damn.

She quickly leaned back. 'Well, that's good news, at least.'

The young man who had delivered the disk came into the room, not exactly running, but close to it. 'Commander, DG Hamilton would like to have a word. You, as well, Cooper.'

'Trouble?'

'I couldn't say, sir.'

Trouble.

Saturday
The Yews, Sussex, England

Lord Goswell sat in his study, sipping a gin and tonic, looking through the French doors. Seemed as if it might rain again. Maybe it would come down hard enough to drown the bloody rabbits; certainly his shooting hadn't been much good there. Perhaps he needed to have his eyes done sooner rather than later.

He heard one of the maids chattering madly at somebody in the hall. He smiled as he sipped his drink. He pulled his pocket watch out and looked at it.

'What is the problem, Applewhite?'

The butler came into the room, looking apologetic. 'Sorry about the disturbance, milord. The maid and Cook were distraught.'

'Whatever for?'

'It seems the telly has gone down. And the telephones are also on the blink.'

'Really?'

'Yes, milord. Can't even pick up most of the radio channels on the battery unit or in the automobiles.'

'Well, that would be distressing then, wouldn't it? Think it's the Russians dropping bombs?'

'I hardly think so, milord.'

'Well, I'm sure His Majesty's government will see to whatever the problem is soonest.'

'Yes, milord.'

Applewhite went back to calm the maid and Cook, and Goswell rattled his ice cubes around in his drink. Had to hand it to that scientist fellow, he was dashedly good at the computer business. Not only the airlines had been knocked down again, but worldwide communications had been whacked solidly, most of the satellites taken offline. And the telly and radio signals that depended on the network of satellites had been disrupted, along with telephonic operations. Quite a stroke. And, of course, operations in the U.K. would come back much sooner than the rest of the world, if Bascomb-Coombs' calculations were correct – and so far, they always had been. A brilliant fellow, he was.

A pity he would have to die. Good help was so hard to find.

21

Saturday
In the air over the Virginia Coast

Net Force's military arm had cranked up one of the old overhauled and refitted 747s for the hop to England, and John Howard sat in the thing wishing it was an SST. The sooner they got to the U.K. the better. Of course, he might as well wish for a time-travel machine so he could have gotten there yesterday. Government agencies went on diets and binges as often as attendees at a fat farm, and Congress had been in moderate belt-tightening mode when Net Force had been funded. It could have been worse, though. They might have come up with some old DC-3 prop jobs the DEA had confiscated from drug runners instead.

He wanted to get his hands on Ruzhyó right now, and though that was impossible at least he was on the way. He'd have to work the logistics with the Brits when they got there but they had an arrangement with His Majesty's government, and having Alex Michaels already in England wouldn't hurt. Howard couldn't imagine the British would give them any flack about collecting a former *Spetsnaz* killer. Of course, they didn't have the death penalty over there, and if they went through formal extradition that could be a problem. A lot of countries had gotten on their high horses about that, refusing to turn escaped scum over to the U.S. unless they agreed not to fry the bastards.

Well. It wasn't going to come to that. There wouldn't be any paperwork filed on the killer through His Majesty's legal system. If he didn't come back with them to face American justice, then it would certainly be because he was beyond any earthly justice.

You didn't kill Net Force people and get away with it. Not on Howard's watch.

He was dressed for travel and not the field, but he had his smaller gear pack on the empty seat next to him, and now he pawed through it. He tended to recheck his gear frequently when he went on a mission, even though not much was likely to have happened to it since he'd checked it five minutes earlier. It was a nervous habit, and he'd realized a long time ago he was going to do it, so he didn't worry about it any longer. Better safe than sorry.

He looked around and saw that Julio was all the way back toward the tail, heading for an empty washroom. Good. It wouldn't do for Julio to see what he'd done to his good-luck talisman, not yet anyway.

He removed the charm from the pack and looked at it. 'Talisman' was a funny way of thinking about a handgun. But this was an ancient Smith & Wesson .357 model 66 stainless-steel revolver, unlike the polymer H&K tacticals the rest of his unit had been issued. For years he had carried the piece as it had come stock from the box – well, except for a little action smoothing by the armorer and a set of hand-filing after-market grips. A six-shot wheelgun, plain iron sights, no bells and whistles. He was comfortable with it, it had been on his hip every time he had gone into a firefight, and like the old Thompson subgun he had inherited, there was a kind of energy wrapped around it. He wasn't particularly superstitious, didn't avoid black cats or worry about ladders or mirrors, but he did believe the Smith had some magic about it. Part of that was that the Smith was a trusted, dependable design, functional, nothing complex that might go wrong. Not that he was a technophobe or some kind of Luddite, but Howard had always liked the simple-is-better philosophy when it came to hardware.

The RA and Navy SpecForce elites, the Rangers, the SEALs, the green hats, had all kinds of new computer-augmented personal weaponry. Things like carbines with TV cams on them you could stick around a corner and shoot without being seen; pieces with built-in trackers, lasers, grenade launchers, the whole package, expensive as hell, and he could have put in for them, but Howard's Strike Teams carried plain-Jane – if top of the line – 9 mm subguns. They went *bang*! when you pulled the trigger, you could get the ammo anywhere in the world, it being the most common military handgun round; he figured it was the *operator's* job to make sure the bullet was on target. Sure, they had the modified SIPEsuit armor, and it had plenty of tactical computer stuff built in, LOSIR coms and headset graphics and GPS and all, but if those failed, you could at least still shoot your weapon manually. The principle of KISS for the lethal hardware had always appealed, and he'd never been shy about letting people know he favored it.

So when he looked at his trusty six-gun with the Tasco Optima 2000 dot scope mounted where the notch-and-post sights used to be, it felt, well, a little weird. And after all the years of shaking his head and calling the polymer sidearms 'Tupperware guns,' his new acquisition might be thought by those who knew him to have shaded right on into the hypocritical.

It wasn't all *that* complex, the scope. What you had was a tiny, clear plastic window mounted an inch and a half or so in front of a tiny red diode that projected a red dot onto the window. Unless the safety cap was over it, the sight was always on, and the battery was good for a lot of use. The way you turned the thing off was, you put the cap on it, and the tiny computer in the scope put it to sleep. How it worked in practice was also simple: You popped the cover off, held the gun up, both eyes open, and the little red dot floated in the air in front of you, just over the piece. Wherever you put the dot – once you had it zeroed – that was where the bullet went, assuming you didn't jerk too much when you dropped the hammer. No parallax. And unlike a laser, there was no beam or glowing dot for an enemy to see and target; the dot wasn't visible from the muzzle side, and if it had been it was only a 7 minute-of-angle pinhead.

The unit weighed about as much as a round of starfish ammo, didn't add much bulk, and was a lot easier to line up than standard iron sights. It was almost indestructible, too, according to the reports. While Howard didn't need glasses to read his newspaper yet, the front sight on his short-barreled pistol had seemed a little fuzzy the last few months. When the rangemaster showed him this little toy on one of the range pistols, he'd tried it, just for the hell of it.

And had shot fifteen percent better straight off.

For a man to improve his combat efficiency with a handgun by fifteen percent just like that was not something to dismiss lightly. After a couple more magazines, that efficiency went up a couple more points still.

At first he'd tried to ignore it. But on subsequent visits to the range he'd used the thing again. The armorer told him he could pull the back sight, grind the front post off and bead-blast the Smith, mount the electronic replacement, and get it done in a few days. Hell, he'd said, begging the Colonel's pardon, but at real close range you were gonna point-shoot that antique and not use the sights anyhow, and outside six or eight yards, the red dot would make the Colonel a better shooter. What was the problem?

Howard hadn't said, but mostly the problem would be the taste of crow.

Julio would never let him live it down.

It had taken a month or so but once he started down that road, it had been impossible to go back; there was no arguing with the numbers. Same gun, same ammo, and he was more accurate and faster with the dot scope. So it was a done deal and he'd had this technological marvel mounted on top of a weapon whose basic form went all the way back to Samuel Colt's first designs, in what – the 1830's? Even the double-action revolver wasn't a new invention, used on Robert Adams' self-cockers only sixteen or eighteen years after Sam Colt's early revolvers. The scope and the Smith thus made for an interesting marriage; seventeenth-century technology meets that of the twenty-first.

This was the May-December marriage Howard didn't want his sergeant to notice; not just yet. Maybe by the time he did, things would be so heated up it wouldn't require an explanation . . .

He looked up and saw Julio coming back from the can. He shoved the revolver back into his bag. At the same time one of the flight crew, the navigator, approached from the other direction. 'Colonel?'

He looked at the navigator. 'Yes?'

'We, uh, have a problem, sir.'

Saturday
Johannesburg, South Africa

The new light-rail shuttle train, carrying six hundred and seventy-four passengers from Pretoria to Johannesburg, blew through the scheduled stop at Tembisa Station at almost a hundred and forty kilometers per hour. The engineer threw the manual override, took control from the computer, applied the brakes, and the train began slowing. It would have been all right—

—except for the second passenger train stalled just south of Tembisa.

The shuttle was still doing more than ninety when it plowed into the back of the halted train that was supposed to be ten minutes ahead and moving at speed.

Both trains buckled and more than two-thirds of each left the tracks, accordioned like toys jammed together by a spoiled child.

Half the people in the rear car of the stopped train were killed instantly. Others were thrown from the smashed car to their deaths. A few were electrocuted by downed power lines.

The engineer of the moving train stayed at his

post and died there, along with scores of panicked passengers just behind him. His last words, as recorded by the black box, were, 'Oh, shit—!'

A fire, started by sparks from the impact or maybe electricity, set the interior of one of the stopped train's cars aflame. Smoke boiled forth and laid a black cloud over the scene.

Estimates of the dead were ballpark but the number was more than two hundred. More would doubtless die on the way to area hospitals, or later from injuries.

Nobody even worried about the third shuttle following ten minutes later. They should have. The engineer on this train frowned as he realized that his communications gear was out and that his vehicle was going too fast as it approached the station.

By the time he wrested control away from the computer it was too late.

His last words would never be known, as the impact was sufficiently violent to destroy this train's black box, leaving only a burned-out husk.

Saturday
Kona, Hawaii

The beacon switched off just as the L10-11C3 wide-body jumbo jet from Japan came in for a landing at

Kona during a tropical shower. The pilot apparently overreacted as the plane yawed, and JAL Heavy dropped hard enough to collapse the rear landing gear on the port side. The big craft slewed starboard, spun, and slid sideways across the runway, square into a Hawaiian Air MD-80 waiting to taxi for takeoff for the short hop to Maui. The smaller bird spewed flaming jet fuel, ignited, and the resulting fireball set the larger craft on fire. There was a terrific explosion. Tourists waiting inside the airport were killed as shattered aluminum sleeted like shrapnel through the open-walled designed terminal, cutting down everything in its path.

Pieces of the jumbo jet and human body parts rained down as far as half a mile away.

Four hundred and eighty died in the crash, fourteen were killed outright in the terminal or on the aprons, and fifty-six more were seriously injured.

Saturday
Perth, Australia

Despite heroic measures, eighteen polio patients breathing on respirators in the Dundee Memorial Hospital died when the backup generators failed after a power outage blacked out the city. The problem was worse because it was so dark in the building away from the battery-powered lighting that nobody could find some of the dead until almost an hour later.

Saturday
MI-6 – London

'Oh, Lord,' Alex Michaels said. 'He's killing people.'

The video of the South African train accident came from a security cam at Tembisa Station. The plane crash was recorded by a tourist waiting for a passenger on the JAL jet. The Australian deaths were vox-only, no video.

Just as well, Michaels thought. The idea of watching a score of people die trying to breathe might have been more than he could stand. At least the train and jet crashes had been quick for those who perished.

'Yes,' Cooper said. 'He's bollixed dozens of major systems. I don't see how it is possible.'

Neither did Michaels, but like the apocryphal ostrich with his head in the sand, not seeing it didn't make it go away. Communications, transportation, even traffic signals were screwed up. Who was this guy? How could he do such things all over the world at the same time?

They were in the office that MI-6 had provided; the building around them hummed with frantic energy that matched their own. He looked at Toni. 'We need to talk to our people at home.'

'Unless you have a fast carrier pigeon, good luck,' Toni said. 'The landlines that work via the Atlantic cable are jammed, and anything going up to satcoms is scrambled worse than Humpty Dumpty.'

'I can't believe it. He's managed to shut down virtually everything tied into a major computer net. The power is beyond anything we've ever seen,' Cooper said.

That was for damn sure. Worse, why was the hacker doing it? What did he stand to gain? Was he a terrorist? Michaels knew he needed to do something. But what could you do when the tools you normally used were all broken?

Better come up with some new ones, Alex, or this guy is going to bring the whole planet to a screeching halt. Maybe he's already done so. You can't get good intel, so how would you know?

'We got these vids and reports on our shielded and hardened lines,' Cooper said. 'We'll get as much input via them as possible. I'll go and see if we can obtain time on one to contact your agency in the States.'

She left, and Michaels stared at the desk. 'We've got to do something,' he said.

'I know.'

But what?

22

Saturday
London, England

Ruzhyó stood in front of the post office across from Westminster Cathedral. He was aware of the frantic scurrying around him. There had been a major power failure, it seemed. He had been buying stamps when the machine had gone blank and eaten his coins. As he left the building he'd noticed the traffic signals were out; there was kind of puzzled worry in the air. Policemen arrived and began directing traffic at the intersection. He listened to snatches of conversations from passersby and got the buzz of what they knew and didn't, and he wondered about it. But that did not distract him so much that he missed the man angling in toward him from the left, dodging traffic as he hurried across Victoria Street.

That the man was coming toward him – for him – was certain. The man was young, fit, smiling, but that meant nothing; Ruzhyó had smiled at some of the people he had deleted. It was disarming, a big smile, it allayed suspicion. How dangerous was a man grinning at you?

Such a man could be deadly, Ruzhyó knew. But was this one?

Dressed like a layabout in a leather jacket and jeans, the young man moved like a soldier, Ruzhyó thought. He had a definite military bearing to his step. This one had spent time in uniform, no question. Either that, or he was wearing a back brace.

Ruzhyó considered his options.

What should he do? Run? Stand his ground?

He looked around. No others were focused on him; at least none that he could see. If it was just the one, what did that mean? The smiling man showed no hardware, and though he certainly could have a pistol hidden under his motorcycle jacket, his hands were swinging loosely, making no move to draw a gun.

Ruzhyó was unarmed save for a small pocket knife, not a particularly formidable weapon. True, he could kill with the knife at grappling range, if need be, but if it came to that, the situation would be bad.

If he was bracketed by a collection or deletion team, one good enough that he could spot only the one who was making no effort to hide, then he was already caught or dead. They would be keyed on the smiling man who was almost all the way across the street now, and a gesture from the smiling man would end the game.

Ruzhyó put his own hand into his right trouser pocket and found the small knife. It had a three-inch blade he could flick open with his thumb as fast as a spring-loaded switchblade. But even so, if he was targeted, and if he took his hand out of his pocket with a weapon, he'd probably be dead before he could get the knife cleared. If he had been a designated shooter on a delete team, he would be aiming at the head, a central nervous system hit being the only way to be sure of an instant stop. A rifle bullet through the brain generally brought things to an end.

Were there crosshairs laid upon his brow? A jittery laser spot dancing on the back of his head?

He looked around again, but could not spot the shooter. Nor did he see anyone else on the street paying him undue attention. Were they there? Had he gotten so old he had lost his ability to spot death watching him? Or was the leather-jacketed man alone?

While he was ready to go if beaten by players better than himself, Ruzhyó found this scenario bothersome. He hadn't thought it would be this easy for them. He had expected to give a better account of himself in the final moves. Perhaps he was too far gone, too burned out, and perhaps this was his final play.

The smiling man reached the kerb and stopped three meters away, well outside the range of a quick lunge with a short knife.

'Mr Ruzhyó,' the man said. It was not a question. His right hand had drifted down to the hem of his jacket by his hip. There was a weapon there, a knife or a gun.

'Yes.' No point in denying it. This man wouldn't be taken in by a protestation of mistaken identity. If he'd had the knife out and opened, it would be no contest. Ruzhyó could move five or six meters and stab a man clawing for a pistol nestled in a concealed holster before the man could draw his weapon. This was not an especially challenging feat – any good knife fighter could do it; it was a simple matter of speed and reaction time. But with the knife in his pocket . . . Maybe he could get there first, maybe not. Probably he could take his killer with him, at the very least. But if there was a shooter in a car, or hiding in a building, already lined up? Well, in that case, any sudden move would end with Ruzhyó face down on the concrete, probably dead before he got there. It would be a clean, quick end. It was tempting to see.

'Hello, sir. I'm Corporal Huard. Major Terrance Peel sends his regards and wonders if you might be free for dinner this evening?'

Peel? How did he know Ruzhyó was in London? And what did he want?

The young soldier offered Ruzhyó a card. It had an address on it.

'About seven o'clock all right?' Huard said.

Ruzhyó nodded.

'Will you be needing directions or a ride?'

'No.'

'Right, then. See you later.'

Huard smiled, turned, and marched off. Ruzhyó watched him until the man was out of sight. Nobody else joined him. It made him feel a little better that Huard seemed to have been alone. But even so, he should have spotted him sooner.

He looked at the card. Peel. How interesting. It had been nearly two years since he had met the man. The major had trained one of the paramilitary units for Plekhanov, having been thrown out of the British Army for . . . what had it been? Torturing an IRA prisoner to death? What was he doing now? And how *had* he known Ruzhyó was here? On this corner, at this time? He must have had his men following him. Why?

And why hadn't he noticed a tail sooner?

He put the card into his pocket, the address already committed to memory. He would go and find out.

Saturday
Somewhere in the British Raj – India

Jay wasn't alone this time. He had brought a native guide to stand watch. Well, it was actually a 'motion detector' program, one that would squeal if anybody

– or any *thing* – entered his scenario uninvited, and warn him in time to get his gun ready. At least he *hoped* it would warn him in time.

Having the program look like a turbaned native guide was as good as anything. He had altered the scenario a little more, though – he was no longer carrying the old double-barreled elephant rifle lovingly handcrafted by a Victorian English gunsmith. Now the weapon he had on a strap digging into his shoulder and leveled, ready at his hip, was a shotgun. And not just an ordinary shotgun, but a South African Streetsweeper, a short-barreled, semi-automatic, drum-fed 12-gauge, with twelve rounds of 00-buckshot alternating with twelve sabot slugs in the magazine – and one more in the chamber. If something moved in front of him, all Jay had to do was point the gun and start pulling the trigger, and he could put up a screaming maw of deadly metal teeth that would chew up anything in their path. Nothing alive could eat that much lead and keep coming. The gun was heavy, but it was a comforting weight on the strap digging into his shoulder.

'Keep a sharp eye out,' Jay said.

'Yes, Sahib.'

Jay bent to look at the ground, using the new skills he had learned from Saji in the New Mexico desert and mountain scenario. Cutting sign, and looking as much for what wasn't there as much as what was. He knew that the tiger must have gone this way because, in the perverse logic of computer

VR, it couldn't have gone this way. And since he knew that, he should be able to track it. You couldn't move through this kind of brush without leaving a sign.

The smelly jungle heat washed over him like a dead man's final breath, cloying and nauseating, but he ignored it. He could have made a more pleasant scenario, a nice ski lodge in the Alps, or a sunny ocean beach at Malibu, with wheeling seagulls and bikini-ed starlets bouncing past, but this was the place where the tiger had jumped him, and this was the place he had to get back on the figurative horse. If he didn't, he knew he would always be afraid. And you couldn't webwalk if you were afraid; there were too many set-piece scenarios you had to live in, too many jungles out there to avoid them all.

The fear tasted like warm zinc in his mouth. He sweated, he trembled, he felt his wind nearly catch in a sob every other breath. Once upon a time he had been Super Jay, faster than a speeding bullet and more powerful than a locomotive, able to laugh at any and all dangers in any dark corner of the net. But not anymore. The tiger's massive claw had wiped that invulnerability away. It had shown Jay the darkness at the end of the road. The darkness where everybody had to go eventually, which though he had known intellectually, had not in his heart of hearts believed.

He believed it now.

He hated the tiger for that. For making

him afraid. For forcing him to acknowledge what everybody knew but nobody really talked about. Jay didn't believe in a benevolent god waiting to greet him at the pearly gates to some mythical heaven, no more than he believed in a malevolent ruler of some neverending hell. His faith had been in himself, in his own abilities; the tiger had taken that from him. Saji's talk of Buddhism had helped, drawn him to that religion because it was so pragmatic and based in earthly reality, but it hadn't erased the fear.

He saw a mark in the jungle floor, a slight depression on a patch of old leaves and twigs long-since rotted to damp humus. He glanced up at the guide, who stood scanning the jungle, then back at the mark. Not very deep for such a huge tiger, but it was part of a track, he was sure of it. It had gone this way.

Which meant that Jay was going to have to go this way, too.

He rose from his crouch. 'Come on, Mowgli. Through here.'

'Yes, Sahib.'

So far the scenario was holding steady; that was something.

He wondered how long he could maintain the surrounding imagery if he saw the tiger? Not very long, he figured.

Jay took a deep breath, adjusted the shotgun's strap, and started forward.

* * *

Peel smiled at Huard. Inside his office, the former church, the younger man looked somehow out of place. Probably hadn't been in a church since he was a lad – not that Peel could claim too many such visits himself. Outside of attending regimental weddings and funerals and this place, religion hadn't been his cup of tea.

'And your impression of the fellow?'

'Well, sir, he didn't seem all that swift. I mean, he didn't see me until I stepped in front of him, almost on his toes, and he just stood there with his hand in his pocket like he was playing with himself. I'd say he's lost most of his moves since he was with the Russians. If he ever had any moves. Sir.'

Peel nodded. 'You have the recording?'

'Right here.'

Huard tendered an infoball the size of a marble.

Peel slotted the infoball into the computer's reader and clicked it on. The holographic projection appeared at one-sixth scale over Peel's desk. The image of Ruzhyó from the minicam in Huard's belt buckle was remarkably sharp and stable. Ought to be, for what they'd paid for the bloody camera. The former *Spetsnaz* agent was across the street, his image blocked by passing vehicles as Huard started toward him.

'Computer, magnification, times two.'

The holoproj blinked and doubled in size. Ruzhyó stood on the street corner, staring into space. Yes, well, he did look distracted – hello?

'Computer, stop play. Rewind fifty frames, replay, magnification times three.'

Huard, still at a modified parade rest, frowned. 'Sir?'

'Watch, Huard. And learn.'

The image blinked and began again, larger, a closer view of Ruzhyó. There. Just as the image waggled a little – that would be Huard stepping from the kerb – Ruzhyó's eyes shifted.

Peel grinned. 'There's where he spotted you, Corporal.'

'Sir?'

'He's just seen you across the street. And without moving his head too much, he's checking out his surroundings. Looking for other players.'

Huard shook his head. 'I don't see it, sir.'

'No, of course not. Computer, normal-size image.'

The view shifted, just as Ruzhyó put his hand into his pocket.

Peel said, 'He's got a weapon in his pocket. Knife, or maybe one of the small South American keychain pistols.'

'How can you tell that? Sir.'

'Because that's what I'd have done if I saw you coming toward me across the street. If you had made any sudden moves once you got there, he would have cut your throat or put a couple of small-caliber bullets into you.'

'I was armed, sir.'

'Huard, this man was killing people when you were still in short pants. That you were unaware of him seeing you and preparing for your arrival is hardly unexpected. Had you reached for your pistol, I expect *we* wouldn't be having this conversation.'

Huard didn't believe him, but he said, 'If you say so, sir.'

Peel grinned. Youth was so wasted on the young. They thought they were going to live forever; it was amazing that as many of them lived as long as they did. If Huard survived, some day he might understand.

'That's all, then. Carry on.'

'Sir.' Huard came to attention, did an about-face, and left the building.

'Computer, replay sequence.'

The machine obeyed. Peel watched. He did enjoy watching a real professional at work. He was looking forward to seeing Ruzhyó again. Good men were hard to find.

23

Sunday, April 10th
London, England

Toni didn't have any spare time, not with the crisis as dramatic as it was, but she'd realized long ago that if she didn't exercise, she wouldn't be much good in the middle of a high-stress environment. She had to have a valve to bleed off the pressure, and if she went a day or two without doing *silat*, or at least some serious stretching, she got cranky and stupid. So when her days got really busy, when things started going to hell in a handbasket and there simply wasn't time to workout, she stole the minutes from elsewhere. Sometimes it was a skipped lunch, sometimes dinner. Sometimes, it was sleep. She could miss a meal or an hour of shut-eye and still function, but without exercise she was surly and out of sorts. She also made dumb mistakes, growled at people, couldn't focus or get herself centered.

So, this morning, the workout was going to have to come off the top. Not yet five a.m. and she was up, washing her face, the bathroom door closed so as not to wake Alex, dressing in sweats for a trip to the hotel's gym. True, it wouldn't be the best workout this early, but anything was better than nothing. It wasn't as if she *wanted* to be up before dawn and breaking a sweat, it was a *need*. An addiction, maybe, but it was putting money in the bank: today's deposit might not be as big as she'd like, but at least there would be something to draw on later if she needed it. And given how things were going, she would need it. So much for their vacation.

But in truth, she was a little excited: Carl Stewart was going to meet her in the hotel's gym. When she'd gone by his school and explained to him that her job was going to keep her from his class in the evenings, he'd offered to meet her for private sessions, and it turned out he was an early riser.

She'd laughed at that. 'Ah. One of those people who runs around throwing open windows, breathing deep the air and smiling at the sunrise?'

'God, no,' he'd said. 'Just a slave to my internal clock. I'm a wren, been that way all my life. Up at four, to bed by nine or ten, no help for it. I have learned to make the best of it. I usually get my workout done in the morning, though. Not a lot else one can do when most of the rest of the world is still beddy-bye.'

'Well, in that case, I'd love to train with you.'

'There's a decent gym in your hotel,' he'd said. 'Save you a taxi ride to the school.'

'And cost you one,' she'd said.

'Not really. I have a car. And it's not all that far from where I live. I have a flat in Knightsbridge.'

'Knightsbridge? That's a pretty nice area, isn't it? We drove through there. By Hyde Park?'

He looked embarrassed. 'Yes, well, my parents got a bit of an inheritance from my grandfather on my mother's side, and they have a small family business that does all right.'

As she headed for the hotel's gym through the quiet and empty hall, Toni grinned to herself. Before the computers had gone south she'd checked out the real estate in the area called Knightsbridge. Flats went for the equivalent of half a million U.S. dollars. Houses started around three million and went up. There was a four-bedroom semi-detached house – what they called a double condo in the States – for seven million. And offers had been made on most of the listings already.

Apparently the Stewart family business was doing all right indeed.

Carl was waiting in the gym, which was in itself interesting, since you supposedly needed an electronic keycard to be admitted. Toni inserted her own card into the lock and went through the heavy glass doors. They were the only two people there.

'Good morning,' he said. He seemed too awake and cheerful for this hour.

'Morning.'

He was warming up and stretching, and she

joined him. The gym had several weight-stack machines, a stair-stepper, an elliptical walker, and a treadmill, all of which were equipped with the latest VR interfaces. There was an aerobics area in front of a mirrored wall opposite, a twelve by twelve-foot square. No mats, but the carpet was padded enough, and there was more than enough room for two people to practice *silat*.

Ten minutes later they were ready to begin. 'Shall we do *djurus* for a few minutes?' he asked.

She nodded. That was how she always began her practice. The short dances were the basis for everything else. All of the combat moves could be found in the *djurus*, if you knew how to look.

For a long time, Toni had practiced the *Bukti* dances, the eight basic and slimmed down *djurus*, before she began the *Serak* moves; lately, however, she had been skipping straight ahead to the parent art. *Bukti Negara* was still used in a lot of places as a kind of test, to see if a student was serious about training. If, after a couple of years practicing the simpler stuff, a student was still hanging around, then she could be introduced to the more complex and demanding forms. *Serak*, so the story went, had been invented by a man of the same name in Indonesia. Serak, or Sera, also known as Ba Pak – 'the Wise' – was Javanese, and had been a formidable fighter – despite having only one arm and a club-foot. That the man could function at all was noteworthy; that he had developed a martial art that made him equal or better as a fighter against other trained men who had all their limbs was truly amazing.

After ten minutes of *djurus*, Carl stopped. 'Want to work some combinations?'

'Sure.'

Once again Toni thrilled to the knowledge that Carl was a superior player. None of her attacks and counter attacks got through. He blocked them effortlessly, it seemed to her, always keeping the centerline. She had to work hard to keep his second and third series of counter punches and kicks from landing – especially the sneaky rising punch, a strike that wanted to come under a high-line defense, but over the low-line block. She managed to stop him from connecting solidly with her, but he brushed her chest once, and another time tapped her on the chin. Not hard enough to hurt, but enough for her to realize he would have tagged her if he'd wanted.

This was great. Just what she needed.

He was showing her a take-down he liked, they were pressed together, her groin against his thigh, his right hand on her butt, levering for a hip sweep when she caught a glimpse of somebody watching them from the hall. She didn't have time to look as Carl completed the throw, taking out her leg and dropping her to the carpet, following up with a kick and punch.

When she got to her feet, the watcher in the hall

was gone. Probably a bellboy delivering somebody's breakfast.

'Again?' Carl asked.

'Yes.' She grinned. This was really great.

She stepped in with a punch.

Alex felt a sour pain in his belly, a churning, twisted feeling. He had felt it before and he knew it for what it was: jealousy. He had watched them together in the workout room, Toni and the English *silat* instructor, seen them glued together, the man's hand on her ass. Yeah, sure, it was part of the deal, he knew enough of the art to know that, but still it bothered him as he hurried down the hall toward their room. She hadn't seen him, and he didn't want her to know he'd been there. Normally he'd have been asleep at this hour, but he'd woken up as she shut the door on her way out and couldn't drift back off. So he'd gotten up, thrown on some clothes, and gone to watch them workout. Maybe he could learn something, he'd figured.

Yeah, right. He'd learned how to feel up somebody's butt.

He knew he was being unreasonable. It wasn't the man's hands on Toni that bothered him as much as how much she was obviously enjoying herself. Probably it was just the *silat*, being able to workout with a guy as good as Stewart was. Probably. But he couldn't get rid of a nagging worry: What if it was more? He and Toni hadn't been getting along that well in the last couple of weeks, that business about not sending her on assignment and all. Maybe she was interested in the big Englishman in some way other than as a sparring partner?

Yeah, okay, she said she loved him. But Michaels' ex-wife had said that, too. Her reasons for the divorce had to do with his career, with him being gone all the time, not being there for her or their daughter, but she had once loved him and now she didn't. Maybe she even hated him, after he punched out her new boyfriend.

He reached his room, carded the lock, stepped inside.

He didn't need this, no way, no how, not given the other crap falling from the sky right now. Why couldn't life be simple? Why was it that every time things seemed to be rolling along smoothly, something always popped up in the road ahead, puncturing tires, sending his happy trip skidding and slewing off the pavement?

And why did it always have to be so damned *emotional?*

The way he'd been raised, a man didn't walk around with his heart on his sleeve, whining and blubbering about his problems. His father had been career Army, and Michaels had never once seen the old man cry, not even when his dog had been run over. The old man hadn't had a lot of deep conversations with his son, but one of the deepest had been about what men did and did not do: You took a hit, you sucked it up and you kept going. You never let anybody know they'd gotten to you. If it's killing you, you smile. That keeps your enemy off-balance.

As an educated man raised in a society where emotions other than laughter or anger were now okay for men, Michaels knew he didn't need to hold himself so tight, that it was no sin to *feel* things, but those old rules from his childhood were hard to get past. Knowing it was okay to let go, intellectually, was not the same as being able to actually *do* it.

It wasn't just his career that had killed his marriage. That don't-show-emotions lesson had been part of the problem with his ex-wife, he knew. And now it seemed to be part of the problem with Toni.

What to do about it?

He shook his head. he couldn't deal with this now. He had a job, a nut with some magical computer gear killing people, bringing the world more grief. He had to deal with his problems the way the samurai warrior Musashi had spoken of it: When faced with ten thousand, you fight them one at a time – the most dangerous ones first.

Of course you need to be pretty damned quick to beat ten thousand, so best he get back to it right now. His emotional life would just have to wait.

He left a note for Toni, then called for a cab to take him to MI-6.

24

Sunday
Washington, D.C.

It was a beautiful sunny morning, no wind, a perfect day to throw. Tyrone glanced at his watch. Ten a.m. Where was Nadine? She was supposed to meet him at the soccer field at – wait, there she was, coming around the gym, a backpack slung over one shoulder. She saw him, grinned, and waved.

'Hey, Tyrone!'

He waved back.

There were a couple of guys practicing at the goal on the south end of the field so they headed for the north goal, then unpacked their gear. Tyrone had brought four of his favorite 'rangs, along with pixie dust and his timer; Nadine had three 'rangs, some fingerdip wind-check, and a stopwatch.

The watch was odd-looking. It was an analog, round, big, silvery.

'Wow, where'd you get that?'

'My dad bought it on a trip to Russia,' she said. 'You hit this button to start it, same button to stop, the big sweep hand gives you seconds, the little inner dial gives you minutes. Doesn't use batteries.'

She handed it to him and he looked at it.

'Solar-powered?' He didn't see a cell.

'No, an internal wind-up spring. Good for, like, hours, then you wind it again.'

'Exemplary. I got a radio like that, you crank it, it plays for an hour, never needs to be charged.'

'My dad says we could save a lot of dump space for batteries if we used more springs and gravity-powered devices,' she said.

'Yeah. It's the next surge.'

They warmed up, rolled their shoulders and waved their arms back and forth, shook out their hands, something Tyrone had learned from watching the older throwers. There were special stretching exercises, too, to keep the muscles of the shoulders and back limber. He'd seen articles on the net about serious boomerangers who had torn ligaments and stuff by throwing too hard without warming up first, and he didn't want to put himself out of commission that way. Of course, most of the guys who hurt themselves were old – in their twenties and thirties.

Nadine went to take a few practice throws, and he watched her carefully. She was in good shape – you could see that vein in her upper arm – and she had excellent form when she threw. She used her whole body and not just her arm, what you were supposed to do. You could learn a lot watching somebody good work.

They'd been throwing for about half an hour,

getting to the point where they could do some serious MTA stuff, when Tyrone saw three or four people watching them from across the field, standing in the shade of a sycamore tree by the fence. That happened a lot when he was throwing and usually he didn't pay much attention, since if you took your gaze off your 'rang for a second, it might disappear. He knew too many guys who had lost a bright orange boomerang on a newly trimmed field, poof, just vanished. Sometimes they angled in and somehow managed to bury themselves in the grass just enough so you couldn't see them; sometimes they just . . . vanished. He had lost a red quad-blade once on a golf course where the grass was like half a centimeter high, no way, but there it was.

It took only one quick look to see that one of the watchers was Belladonna Wright.

He jerked his gaze back to his 'rang, found it floating toward him about thirty meters out, and stayed with it until it came close enough to catch. He managed to trap the 'rang without dropping it, but he was rattled.

Though he was trying hard not to look at Bella, Nadine picked up on it.

'Well, well. Looks like that old fire might not be out after all, hey, Ty?'

'What?'

'You and sweetiepie over there under the tree. You kinda acted like you didn't know her real well, but from what I hear, you and she spent some quality time together.'

'So what if we did?'

'Nothing, nothing, not my business. I just hate to see you get cooked, is all.'

'What do you mean?'

'Come on, Tyrone, gimme a bye here. Pretties like that go through guys like toilet paper. Use 'em, flush 'em, there's plenty more where the last one came from. She's got a string of guys waiting to run around behind her and kiss the ground she walks on, just to enjoy the view from there.'

'Yeah? How would you know that?'

Nadine stared at the ground. 'You hear stuff.'

'Anything else you hear?'

'I'm not trying to start a fight.'

'Could have fooled me.'

She looked up, hefted her MTA. 'I came to practice. You interested in that? Or you want to wait for Miss America to crook her finger so you can go running?'

'I don't go running. For your information, it was *my* idea to break up with Bella.' Well, that wasn't strictly true, but he had opened the conversation that led to it. And when given the choice of being one of her string, he had told her he wasn't interested. Sort of.

'Good for you. You gonna throw?'

Tyrone glanced at Bella, then back at Nadine. 'Yeah, I'm gonna throw. Get ready to start your watch, I'm gonna hang you out to dry.'

'In your dreams.'

She flashed him a small grin, and he returned it, but even as he did, he wondered about what she had said. What if Bella crooked her finger? If she waved him over, told him she wanted him to drop by and sit on her couch and kiss him like she had kissed him before. Would he go running?

No way. No. Fucking. Way.

Easy enough to say that when he was pretty sure it wasn't gonna happen. But if it actually did, would he drop everything and trot over?

That was a hard one. He didn't want to think too much about that one.

He gathered himself for the throw. Three steps, one, two, three—!

The boomerång soared high into the air, an artificial bird climbing for the sun. And it was gonna be a long hang time, too. He could tell. That ought to shut Nadine up about whether he'd come to throw.

Sunday
Somewhere over the Atlantic Ocean

Flying the big jet wasn't a problem for the Net Force pilot, and landing it manually wasn't either, assuming the weather in England wasn't so foul they needed a ground beacon to locate the airport. The 747's self-contained instruments weren't affected by the international snafu that had ensnarled the major computer systems. But trying to land in heavy traffic at Heathrow or Gatwick without some help from the ATCs on the ground was not at the top of any pilot's list.

'No way in hell, sir,' the pilot had put it to Howard.

Fortunately, there were military bases that were self-contained in the U.K., at least insofar as flight operations went, and they could put the big bird down at one of these, even though the wait would be fairly long. Most of the still-operational bases had been hauling in civilian planes affected by the snafu, or allowing takeoffs and landings by those non-military aircraft that simply had to fly – hospital planes, those moving organs for transplants, or assorted heads of state. They might be stacked up a while waiting to land.

Fine, he had been stacked up before.

Fortunately, most military organizations were, by their nature, paranoid, and few of them put all their eggs in one basket. That half the planet's computer systems had been screwed up was bad, but not so bad that it totally paralyzed the world's armies and navies. Good soldiers always worried about such things, and good soldiers could usually convince the bad ones to have some kind of backup plan. Looked as if that chore might get easier after this, too.

They could have turned the 747 back and landed in the States, but Howard wasn't interested in letting his quarry get away again, not if they could help it. The good thing was, if they were having problems travelling, so would Ruzhyó. And he didn't think the assassin would get far on foot. Although tracking him without computers might be something of a problem itself, it would be easier if he sat still for a while.

Julio drifted down the aisle and stopped next to his seat.

'Colonel.'

'Sergeant.'

'You still think we can collect this boy?'

'Oh, we'll get him.' Howard mentioned his reasoning.

Fernandez laughed. 'Begging the Colonel's pardon, but bullshit. If the guy's IQ didn't drop by fifty points when he landed, he's plenty smart enough to figure out how to rent a car or boat or even a plane from somebody and get out of England. He waves a handful of that funny Euro money at some college kid or poor fisherman or broke pilot with an ultralight, and he's got wheels or floats or wings. I'd guess the frogs or the Spanish or anybody else across a body of water from Jolly Olde are gonna be busy trying to stop opportunistic crooks trying to smuggle trains or steamships past 'em while the computers are whacked out. His chances of getting nailed in all the hubbub are probably so close to zero as to practically *be* zero.'

'You're assuming he wants to leave England that bad,' Howard said. 'Why should he? He doesn't know we're on his tail. He probably thinks he's gotten away clean.'

'Would you assume that, were you in his shoes?'

Howard grinned. 'Hell, no.'

'Me, neither.'

'Maybe he won't want to risk it,' Howard said.

'I don't think this guy worries an awful lot about risk, given what we've seen out of him so far, John.'

Howard nodded. That was true enough. And there was nothing to be done about it.

Julio said, 'But, shoot, we could get lucky. He might step off a kerb and get hit by a double-decker bus or something. Be waiting for us in a hospital somewhere, nothing but a tongue depressor to fight us with when we show up. "Course, with our luck so far, he'd kill a couple of us with it, and wouldn't that look good on the obituary page? "Assassin Kills Net Force Personnel! It was depressing, Sergeant Julio Fernandez said." '

'I can always count on you to cheer me up, Sergeant.'

'I do what I can, sir.'

Sunday
London, MI-6

Michaels sat hunched over a stack of hardcopy, reading that instead of using the computer. It was slow going. Toni had arrived, but left again to collect some material from a satellite recon site that still had a viable uplink. They didn't want to risk sending the stuff from there to here, even with protected landlines. It was more reliable for somebody to collect it physically.

His neck and upper back were stiff and sore. Part of that was probably from being stuck in a chair reading for hours; part of it was tension from all the other crap going on in his head. Megan and the private eye, Toni, the whole ugly situation with this mad man screwing with the world.

'Knock, knock?'

Angela Cooper came in, tapping at the doorframe as she did so. She wore a dark blue blazer and a matching short skirt, with a paler blue blouse. She closed the door behind her. 'How goes the war, Alex?'

'Our side is still losing.'

'We've gotten a bunch of systems back online,' she said. 'We're recovering. So far, no permanent damage to sensitive material.'

'That's something.'

She moved to stand behind him and looked over his shoulder.

'Statistical analysis of transcontinental telephonic transmissions? My! This must be fascinating reading.'

'Oh, yeah, right up there with freshman philosophy papers on German existentialists written in Chinese by Bantu Bushmen.'

She laid on hand on his shoulder. 'Oh, dear. You're like a rock.'

'I've been more relaxed,' he admitted.

'You should let me work on you.' She put her other hand on his other shoulder and started to knead the muscles. He had a moment of alarm. He should not allow this. But mmm, it felt good. Her hands were much stronger than he would have thought.

'You don't have to do that.' Weak. Not the same as telling her to quit.

'I don't mind. It's one of my few talents. My mother was a therapist for a time. She knew some of the more esoteric elements of massage-reiki, shiatsu, Aston-Patterning. I picked up some of it along the way.'

God, but that felt good. He could feel the knots in his traps. It also felt as if his head might just nod forward and fall off his neck if she kept this up. It was not sexual, but it was certainly sensual.

'You really ought to lie down to get the full benefit,' she said. She continued to work her fingers into his neck and upper back, digging in with her thumbs, working in elliptical spirals.

'However, the couch is too soft, the desk too short. But the carpet is clean. Lie on the floor, on your stomach, next to the desk there.'

Like a man in a trance, Michaels obeyed. He hadn't realized just how tight he was. She was finding spots in his muscles so hard they felt like ball bearings.

Face down, he felt her straddle him, and he

opened his eyes enough to see her short skirt riding up as her knees pressed into his sides. Her butt was only lightly touching his; she wasn't putting very much weight onto him.

Oh, yes . . .

'It would be better with your shirt off, but perhaps we ought to wait on a more private setting for that. Wouldn't want tongues to wag.'

The way Michaels felt with her working on his back, he didn't care if all the tongues in MI-6 wagged like a pack of starving dogs being offered liver treats. An involuntary moan escaped, pressed out of him when she dug the heel of one spiraling hand into the flesh over his right scapula.

It hurt, but it was a good hurt; he could feel himself loosening under the hard pressure.

She slid backward, hovered over his hamstrings, and leaned onto her hands against the small of his back. She pressed her thumbs into his buttocks, slid her fingers over his hips, circled to his back again.

Oh, man. He could get used to this.

Used to it? It could become an addiction.

It occurred to him after ten minutes or so that this would be the worst time in the world for Toni to come back. This would be difficult to explain. He should make her stop. Now.

But he didn't.

And Toni didn't come back, and after twenty minutes, Angela slid backup his body, did some stuff to his scalp, then climbed off him and stood.

He could barely move but somehow he managed to get to his feet.

She was flushed, had worked up a sweat, was glowing.

'Thank you. You just saved my life.'

'It wasn't much, really. To do it right takes an hour, an hour and a half, and you have to work both sides, back and front. I have a massage table at home. Maybe you can drop by and let me give you the full treatment sometime.'

A warning flash strobed his brain: *Danger! Bad idea!*

Then he thought about Toni and her *silat* workout. Stewart had put his hands all over Toni, hadn't he, so what was the difference? It wasn't sex, it was harmless. It was . . . therapeutic.

'Yeah, maybe we could do that,' he heard himself say.

She smiled at him and he smiled back.

'I must look awful, like an old sweaty cow,' she said. 'I must go and repair myself. See you later.'

After she had gone, he found that a small bit of tension quickly returned, despite the skilled rubdown he had just gotten. It had nothing to do with work.

What, he wondered, are you getting yourself into here, Alex?

25

Sunday
The Yews, Sussex, England

Goswell sat in his study, in the good leather chair, and sipped at his iced gin. He sighed, and looked at the photographs for perhaps the tenth time. In this age of computer miracles, it was certainly possible to fake such things, he knew. An expert could easily put one man's face on another's body, could erase or add elements that never existed. He recalled seeing a movie once of Sir Winston Churchill – a damned fine PM according to his father – seated next to the American President Abraham Lincoln, chatting away, when, in truth, the latter had been assassinated eight or ten years before Churchill had been born.

He shuffled the pictures. Yes, certainly it could be done, but in this case he was just as certain that it had not been done. These were genuine enough, for the man who had taken them had not had a reason to fake them. There sat Peel, talking to Bascomb-Coombs, right there in a public eatery. Of course, Goswell thought, Peel was his security chief and Bascomb-Coombs one of his employees, and a valuable one, as well, so one could easily argue that such a meeting was well within the normal scope of Peel's duties. It was his job, after all, to keep tabs on such people, and talking to them directly was not out of the question.

Goswell took another swallow of his drink, and looked at the grandfather clock. Nearly seven, supper would be ready soon.

No, Peel could certainly justify speaking with Bascomb-Coombs easily enough. The damning thing was, he had not *done* so. Nowhere in his reports was there any mention of such a meeting. Nor of the subsequent meetings. While not all such instances had been edited from the tally of his observations and actions, some of them certainly had been. There were other photographs.

Goswell shook his head. Damned bad show, this. Was he to believe that Peel's formerly faultless memory had begun to malfunction? And only in instances concerning Bascomb-Coombs? What a terrible world it had become when one had to have a trusted watcher himself being watched.

The question was, of course, what were these two about? That they were in league together certainly meant something.

Well. He had not gotten to be a general of industry without learning how to figure such things out.

He rattled the cubes in his nearly empty glass rather loudly.

'Milord? Another drink?'

'Yes, please. Oh, and Applewhite? See if you can find Major Peel, would you, and have him drop round after dinner?'

'Certainly, milord.'

Goswell stared into the depths of the melting ice in his glass as Applewhite went to fetch more gin. He would take the quisling Peel's measure, one way or another. A damned shame, really. Good thing the boy's father was gone. It would break his heart to know his son had betrayed a trust.

Sunday
London, England

A light rain had begun falling, and Ruzhyó figured this would be a perfect excuse.

It was Sunday, and in some cities that meant much of the commerce would be shut down, but not here in London. He caught a cab near the British Museum and gave the driver the address he wanted. It was not far from a shop on a side street close to Regent's Park, a tiny slot of a store-front, long and narrow, that specialized in hand-crafted umbrellas and canes. You could easily drop a couple of hundred in such a place on a handmade walking stick or bumbershoot, considerably more if you so wished. They were big on such things here, the accoutrements of a gentleman, and likely the shop could make ends meet just with such sales alone; however, there were other items to be had by a knowledgeable buyer.

The cab arrived a block from the destination. Ruzhyó paid the fare, reflexively gave enough of a tip so the hack wouldn't remember him as being either cheap or extravagant, and alighted from the taxi. The rain was coming down a little harder, and Ruzhyó made certain he didn't appear to notice the man following him as he walked. Not that his shadow was totally inept, but it would take somebody far better to tail him unnoticed once he was looking for such a thing.

When he arrived at the shop he wanted, he made a show of looking irritated at the weather, shook the water from his windbreaker, and offered what he hoped would seem a spur-of-the-moment decision to duck into the place.

It would all be for nothing if Peel knew what the shop's merchandise included, but unless things had changed recently, the Brits did not have a clue about the umbrella store.

The meeting with Peel had been interesting. His claim that he had spotted Ruzhyó by having every passport picture of every foreigner entering the country compared to a list of known agents seemed far-fetched, but Peel *had* managed to spot him somehow. And he had managed to put a watcher on him. Perhaps it was just luck. Or perhaps Peel's claim was true. Either way, the offer of employment had been forthcoming. Ruzhyó hadn't been all that interested in work, but then again, it wasn't as if he was in a hurry, and Peel could make it easier for him to travel, especially given all the computer problems of late. A short stopover might be to his benefit. The assignment, to stand by for a possible elimination of an English Lord who just happened to be Peel's employer was intriguing – although Ruzhyó doubted he would actually attempt the deletion.

Peel's flimsy explanation as to why he couldn't do the job himself, or have one of his men do it, wasn't fooling anybody. It was obvious that he needed a scapegoat, a foreign agent who could be blamed for the assassination, and who better than a sneaky CIS former *Spetsnaz* killer? One who might well be shot full of holes himself in the aftermath of the killing while trying to escape, thus tying up all loose ends?

Ruzhyó allowed himself a small smile as the umbrella shop clerk took notice of him and nodded. Were he Peel, that's how he might set it up. Hire an expendable shooter, then delete him once the job was done, all very neat, if not terribly smart. Sooner or later, somebody would get around to asking why a man on the run from US authorities would bother to stop off for a bit of murder in the UK, motive being a necessary part of such a thing. And even the plodding British authorities would turn over every rock in sight investigating the murder of such a highly regarded man. They were still very class-conscious here. But the Brits were short-sighted about some things, always had been. Had they been paying attention they'd probably still rule most of the world. Hubris did awful things to an empire. Likely it was that Peel had a touch of that himself.

'May I help you, sir?'

'I need a special umbrella. One with more . . . heft than the ordinary.'

The clerk's smile never wavered. 'Ah, yes. I'll have the manager, Mr O'Donnell, right out.'

The clerk disappeared into a door behind the counter. Ruzhyó pretended to browse. There were fantastic handles on some of the canes and umbrellas, made of ivory or exotic woods, carved in fanciful shapes. Here was a tiger, there a snake, over here a nude woman arched backward in a graceful half-circle.

'Good afternoon, sir. I'm Mr O'Donnell. I understand you need a special umbrella?'

Ruzhyó nodded at the tall, sandy-haired man in the dark suit. 'Yes.'

'Might I ask who recommended our shop to you?'

'That would be Colonel Webley-Scott.'

'Ah, I see. And how is the Colonel these days?'

The identity code was the same. Ruzhyó said, 'Still dead, last I heard.'

The manager smiled and nodded. 'If you will step this way, sir?'

'I have a tail. No connection to you.'

'Not to worry. He won't see through the window unless he has x-ray vision. Is he likely to come in?'

'I doubt that he is that stupid.'

'Well, if he does, he'll see you come out of the door to the WC.'

Ruzhyó followed O'Donnell through the water closet and through a hidden door to a small private room. There was a tall, green, antique safe on claw feet in one corner. As the manager opened the safe, he said, 'Would you be wanting something edged or projectile, sir?'

'Do you have a multiple projectile model?'

'We have. A five-shooter. Small caliber, I'm afraid, only .22.'

'That will do.'

'Here we are, then.'

He offered what appeared to be a standard umbrella to Ruzhyó, with the J-shaped wooden handle perhaps a hair thicker and heavier than normal.

'Handle unscrews here . . . inside, you'll notice the back of the cylinder. It's a revolver, you see.'

Ruzhyó looked at the five small holes in the tiny cylinder inside the umbrella shaft. The firing pin and rest of the action was in the removed J-section. Ingenious.

'One puts the shells in like so, threads the handle back on until it locks, thus. Trigger unfolds from the handle, thus, use this little notch, much like a penknife blade . . .'

He used his thumbnail to bring the flush-mounted lever out.

'It is double-action only, of course, and there aren't any sights, but a man proficient with firearms can point-shoot it rather well. Barrel is rifled steel, as good as most commercial long arms. The end cap is a soft rubbery material, no impediment to the bullet if you don't have time to remove it, and actually offers a bit of sound-damping, though it must be replaced after several shots. The weapon comes with spare end caps, of course.'

Ruzhyó took the disguised carbine, hefted it. Normally he did not like to go about armed if he did not specifically need a weapon. This was not a normal time.

'You have fired it?'

'I have.'

'And is there a place where I can test it?'

O'Donnell nodded, approving. 'That box over there – it's full of baffles and has a steel backstop.' He wasn't offended. Only a fool would trust his life to a weapon he had not personally tested to see if it would work.

'Ammunition?'

'I have some Stingers, solids and hollow-points.'

'Excellent,' he said. 'How much?'

'Two thousand.'

'Done.'

O'Donnell smiled.

The tail was across the street in a sandwich shop, watching through the somewhat foggy window. A young man, hair cut short, who from his general look could have been Huard's brother. The rain was still coming down, so Ruzhyó held his newly acquired and fully loaded short carbine up and utilized the secondary function. The black silk canopy expanded crisply on its titanium struts and locked into place. The thing had fired five rounds without any problem. It worked fine as an umbrella, too. A wonderful and deadly toy. Most people did not realize that an ultra-high velocity .22 solid bullet fired from a long barrel would punch right through standard police-issue class-II Kevlar body armor. Police agencies understandably did not like to talk about such things.

Ruzhyó smiled to himself as he walked away from the shop.

Peel would get him weapons, of course, but it was much better to have a hidden trump, just in case.

Better to have it and not need it than to need it and not have it.

26

Sunday
Somewhere in the British Raj – India

The heat and dampness were oppressive and the sour odor of the tiger's spoor permeated the leaden air. He was close, the tiger, and the scent of his scat was mixed in with the stink of Jay's own fear.

Jay and his native guide followed the footprints across an open stretch of ground, easily seen now in the soft dirt. No doubt of it, no way to mistake the trail. It led across the open stretch into a dense patch of brush; fat-boled trees, short, thick bushes, a bordering stand of big bamboo.

Jay shifted his sweaty grip on the Streetsweeper, took a long and ragged deep breath, and exhaled slowly. The tiger had gone into that thicket, and if Jay wanted it, he was going to have to go in after it. The prospect filled him with a dread as cold as a bucket of liquid nitrogen, a fright bordering on the edge of stark, gibbering terror.

Jay stopped walking. What he wanted to do was bail from this scenario, pull off his gear, and shut down his computer. He wanted to find a South Sea island somewhere in Real Time, to go there and lie in the sunshine on an empty beach for a month, to do nothing but bake and drink something cold with rum and coconut in it. The last thing on Earth he wanted to do was traipse into that fecund wall of jungle ahead, stalking the thing that had crashed his wetware and put the fear of death into his mind. And if he did it, it might well *be* the last thing he ever did.

So he had to go. If he didn't, he might as well hang it up as a player; if he didn't find and destroy this beast, he was as good as brain-dead.

He took another deep breath and let it out. 'Let's go,' he said.

They were almost to the wood when his native guide said, 'Sahib! Behind us!'

Jay spun and saw the tiger charging them, impossibly fast.

He had maybe half a second, and he knew it wouldn't be enough. 'Bail!' he screamed.

Washington, D.C.

Jay fell out of VR in his apartment, heart pounding, the panic filling him. The tiger! The tiger! He couldn't even breathe.

At his core, he knew he had to go back. Before it got away. He had to go back. He wanted to scream,

to cry, to run, anything but what he had to do.
Instead, he said, 'Resume!'

Somewhere in the British Raj – India

Jay arrived in time to see the huge tiger sinking its terrible fangs into his detection program – the native guide – mangling it into a bloody ruin.

Poor Mowgli.

Jay snapped the shotgun up as the tiger realized he had returned. The great beast coughed, roared, and spun to face him. No hesitation, it charged—

—Jay stood his ground, aimed—

—fifty feet away, forty feet, thirty—

—he squeezed the trigger. The shotgun bucked against his shoulder, lifted from the recoil. He fired again, too fast, too high—

—but the first blast hit the charging monster. It screamed in surprise and pain, sheared off, and ran for the forest. Jay saw blood on one of the tiger's shoulders as it wheeled around and ran.

He had hit it! It was fleeing! It wasn't invincible!

A surge of triumph washed his fear away. Jay had faced it down, shot it, driven it off!

The victory was shortlived, though.

Now what he had was a wounded man-eater hiding in the bush. That wasn't going to make things any easier.

But it didn't matter. He had to go after it, and he didn't have time to call up another warning program, he had to go *now*!

Jay ran for the jungle.

The Yews, Sussex, England

Peel stood by the greenhouse, wishing he had a cigarette. He had quit smoking years ago, a matter of discipline more than anything, a test of his will. Everybody knew it was bad for you, but as a soldier, he had always expected he would die in the field somewhere; he didn't expect to live long enough for the fags to get him. Besides, his grandfather on his mother's side had smoked two packs a day for almost seventy years, and had died at ninety-four from injuries sustained in a fall, so he figured a lot of it was genetics. Drank whiskey every day right until the end, too. No, Peel had stopped because he wanted to prove to himself that he could. What was the old joke? Quitting smoking is easy, hell, I've done it a dozen times.

The rain had stopped, there was a patch of clear sky directly overhead, and the gathering darkness sported a few stars. It was quiet, calm, with no signs of any problems from his troops around the estate. Goswell had called him in for a visit, they'd had a pleasant drink. There was all that money sitting in a bank. Bascomb-Coombs was about his business, and if it went as well as it had gone thus far, Peel would be rich and powerful beyond belief in the not-too-distant future. Especially since, once the scientist's plans came to fruition, Peel planned to take him out and take over himself.

On the face of it, Peel didn't see how things could be much better. However . . .

Something was wrong.

There was nothing to point a finger at, no focus for his unease, but on some instinctual level he felt it. There was danger lurking here somewhere. Perhaps a cigarette wouldn't help him figure out what it was, but smoking had always settled his thoughts, had given him time to ponder problems. Like Sherlock Holmes with his pipe, perhaps.

Well. He wasn't about to light up again because of some vague disquiet. A walk around the grounds might serve as well, and he was trying that, but so far nothing concrete had loomed. It would present itself, if indeed it existed, in due time. It always did. The only question about that was, would he figure it out in time to marshal his defenses against it?

Whatever it was.

There was the question.

Monday, April 11th
Washington D.C.

Tyrone walked down the hall toward his first class, threading his way through the other students, each hurrying toward his or her own rendezvous with education.

'Hey, Ty.'

He stopped and turned, recognizing the voice from those two words.

Belladonna Wright.

'Hey, Bella.'

She wore a tight-wrap blue dress that fit like spray paint and stopped a foot above her knees, matching thick-sole sandals that added four inches to her height, and she had her long hair up in some kind of curly do that made her look taller still. Two steps and he could touch her.

'How you doin'?'

He shrugged. 'Okay. How about you?'

'Okay. I saw you out with your boomerang the other day.'

'Yeah.' Why was she talking to him? After he had seen her kissing that slackbrain at the mall and called her on it, she had dumped him flatter than two-dee. They hadn't spoken since. And here she was, passing the time of day like nothing had happened.

'Haven't seen you at the mall lately,' she said. She smiled.

'Haven't been there much.'

'You should check out the new food court. It's terrif–aboo.'

'Yeah, maybe I will.'

She flashed another of her perfect smiles at him. Took a breath deep enough to push her chest out a little. A wonderful, beautiful, fabulous chest. He swallowed dryly.

'Well. See you around,' she said.

'Yeah,' was all he could manage.

She walked off, queen of all she passed. From the back, she was just as gorgeous.

Tyrone's brain hurt. What was that all about? She smiled at him, practically *invited* him to the mall, acted like she was glad to see him! Last time they had talked, months ago, she had verbally kicked him in the nuts when he'd called her on having other boyfriends, told him to lose her number! What the hell was going on?

The bell went off, and Tyrone jerked himself out of his trance and hustled his butt to his class. He wished his dad was in town. Maybe he would know what this meant.

Monday
MI-6, London, England

Michaels suddenly realized how quiet things had gotten at the office, and he looked at the computer's clock. Lord, it was almost midnight.

He was bushed. Hunched over the computer all day had knotted him up again; his mind was foggy. Most of the British computer systems had come back online, but other European nations were still having big problems. Toni had taken the Chunnel to Paris, to coordinate infoflow with the French authorities. She wouldn't be back until Tuesday evening.

He had been making stupid mistakes for the last hour, words on the holoproj running together and not making sense. Time to shut it down and get back to his hotel.

He slipped his windbreaker on – what was it somebody had called it here, a windcheater? – and left the office. Probably wouldn't be a lot of taxis standing out front. He pulled his virgil to call for one as he headed for the building's exit.

'You work late hours,' Angela said from behind him.

Michaels turned. 'Yeah, well, you're still here, aren't you?'

'Just leaving. You need a ride?'

'I was just calling a cab.' He waved the virgil. 'I wouldn't want to put you out.'

'No trouble, really,' she said. 'It's practically on the way to my flat.'

'In that case, okay, sure.'

London was a big city, it never shut down, and even at midnight the streets were still clogged with traffic. There were twelve? fifteen million people here? Too many in too small a space.

'Making much progress?' she asked as they wound their way past a pub that spilled laughing patrons onto the sidewalk.

'Not much.'

'Us, neither,' she said. 'Much of the British grid seems to be back up, but the rest of the world is still putting pieces back together.' She waved at the happy-looking people coming out of the pub. 'Fancy a pint and some late supper?'

As she asked, Michaels realized that he was hungry; he'd had a sandwich at his desk at noon, nothing since. 'I could eat.'

'There's a nice quiet place not far from my flat. They serve decent fish and chips.'

Again the little danger signal cheeped in his mind but he was tired and hungry and he didn't feel like bothering with it. What harm could there be in a beer and a little fried food?

'Sure, why not?'

The pub was moderately full but, as she'd said, fairly quiet. They ordered fish and French fries – chips – and took pint glasses of beer to their table to wait for the food.

He took a couple of swallows of his beer, dark brew called Terminator Stout. She nodded at his glass. 'Came from America originally, that,' she said.

He looked at the beer. 'Really?'

'Indeed. Some microbrewery on the west coast. Chap from London passing through tasted it, liked it, started importing it. Only taken a couple hundred years for you Americans to produce decent beer. Another hundred years or so, you might make a decent roadster.'

'I beg your pardon,' he said. 'Chevrolet did that with the Corvette in the 1950s.'

'Know about cars, do you?'

'A little.'

'Well, it didn't take them long to muck it up, the Corvette, did it? It might have started out okay, but after a few years, it ballooned into a monster, didn't it? Bigger body, bigger engine, electronic this and that, until it was as huge as a town car – and cost more than a Cadillac sedan.'

He grinned. 'Well, yes, that's true.'

'Now, you take a classic 50s or 70s MG . . .' she began.

He snorted, cutting her off. 'Please. Take it to the dump. They should have offered the thing with a mechanic as standard equipment. Your average vintage MG spent more time in the shop being tuned than it ever did on the road.'

'Well, all right, some of them were a bit finicky,

but that's a small price to pay for the driving experience.'

'Ha! You mean the towing experience. You tell the Automobile Club you own an MG, they won't even take your phone calls.'

She smiled at him.

The food arrived, and the smell of the batter-fried halibut and potatoes enveloped them in a wonderful aroma. He wasn't just hungry, he was starving!

After ten minutes of chowing down and a second round of beers, Michaels felt much better. This was nice, having a late dinner and enjoying a conversation not connected to work. They talked about Japanese and Korean roadsters, the new South African Trekker, and he told her about the Prowler and Miata he had restored.

Next thing he knew, it was two a.m.

'We probably should get going,' he said. 'Work and all.'

'How is the muscle tension?' she asked.

'Not as bad as it was.'

She put her hand on his neck, slid it lightly down to his shoulder. 'You're still tight as a violin string.' She paused. Said, softly, 'My flat is just up the road and around the corner. Would you like me to give you a massage?'

Maybe it was because he was so tired. Or maybe it was the two pints of beer and the good food. Or maybe it was because she was really a handsome and intelligent woman who obviously enjoyed his company.

Whatever the reason, Michaels nodded at her. 'Yes. I'd like that.'

27

Tuesday, April 12th
Somewhere in the British Raj – India

Jay moved with all the stealth he could manage. Which wasn't very much, considering how rattled he was and the terrain through which he moved. Tracking the beast was not a problem: the brush was trampled and smeared with blood, and the trail led in a straight line, a sign of animal panic. The tiger ran, making no attempt at stealth.

Or so it seemed. It had sneaked up behind him once before, and Jay wasn't going to get caught unawares again. He kept a constant watch, head swivelling as if he were watching a tennis match in the round.

At the base of what looked to be a huge boab-like tree, the blood trail disappeared.

Jay looked up.

Thirty feet above the ground, the tiger coughed and charged down the tree trunk, *ran* against gravity as if he was on level terrain!

Jay didn't think. He whipped the shotgun up, spot-welded his cheek to the weapon, and fired. He recovered from the recoil using his whole body and fired again—

The tiger fell off the tree. Jay dodged to his right, swung the gun around at waist level, and pulled the trigger as the thing hit the ground hard five feet away, hard enough to shake Jay where he crouched, gun blasting.

He lost count of how many times he shot, it seemed like one continuous roar – *boomboom-boomboomboom*! The coppery smell of tiger's blood rose and joined the stink of burned gunpowder, and when he stopped shooting, the ground was littered with green and red plastic shotgun shells, at least a dozen of them, maybe more.

Now, the tiger wasn't even twitching.

Now, Jay drew a shuddery, deep breath, his first in a while.

The animal that had clawed his brain apart was dead. He had killed it.

Even as he bent to examine it, though, he knew it wasn't the thing he sought. Oh yeah, it had attacked and damaged him, but now that he had killed it, he knew this was but a security program, not the creature that had ripped open the unbreakable cages of the world's most advanced computer systems with impossible strength. It was the most dangerous thing Jay had ever faced in VR, but this was just a watchbeast, put in the jungle to take care of snoopers, nowhere near the power of what had casually left it behind.

The real monster was still out there. And Jay knew this shotgun wouldn't slow it down if it spotted him.

Jesus.

Tuesday
Paris, France

It was three a.m. and Toni couldn't sleep. The big bed in the French hotel was comfortable enough, the room insulated and high enough above the city streets so the traffic noise was but a quiet drone. She'd had a fairly quiet day, gotten a lot of material collected and assembled, and had a delicious, fattening supper. She'd even gotten a workout in the hotel's gym, and spent half an hour in the spa, letting the roiling hot water bubble and relax her. She should be conked out like a baby.

Her mind was buzzing, and the sense of disquiet she felt might be due to the work, but it wasn't that. No, it was Alex. Something was wrong between them, and she didn't know what it was. He was upset with her, she could feel it, even though he denied it, and she didn't know what to do about it.

Oh, she had tried to find out: *Alex? Is everything okay?*

Yep, everything is fine.

You sure? Have I said or done anything to upset you?

No, Toni, everything is okay. I'm just tired, is all.

Then he'd flashed her a tight smile that looked sincere but was hollow.

How could you get past that? How many times could you ask without being a nag? Once you'd asked and been answered, how much could you harp on it? Wasn't it his responsibility? If he said everything was all right, didn't she have to accept that?

Well, with men, no. Not in her experience. They weren't wired the same way as women. They'd say one thing and mean something else entirely.

Who could she talk to about this? She had girlfriends who would listen and offer advice, back in the States. Or maybe she could call her mother. What was the time difference between Paris and the Bronx? Six hours? It would be nine o'clock in the evening there, Mama would probably be dozing out in front of the flatscreen TV by now. Besides, this wasn't really the kind of thing you talked about with Mama. She'd been dealing with Papa for so long there was only one way to do such things in her mind, and besides that, Toni doubted if Papa had ever voiced a complex emotional thought to anybody in his whole life: *Whaddya, some kinda* sissy *goes around whining about your* feelings? *Geddoutta here.*

No, she'd just have to deal with this on her own, somehow. When she got back to London, she'd find some time – would *make* some time – sit down with Alex, and get him to open up. They'd get it worked out. She loved him, he loved her, how hard could it be as long as they had that?

Tuesday
London, England

Angela's flat was one of a row front on Denbigh Street. It was a small place, but very neat and clean, with a sitting room, kitchen, bedroom and bathroom. And she did have a massage table set up in the small sitting room. Michaels remarked on that: Did she do so much massage that she left the table out all the time?

No, she'd said. She'd gotten it out and put it up just today.

A small alarm went off in his head. *Uh oh.*

She handed him a bed sheet. 'Take off your clothes and lie face down,' she said. 'Cover up with this. I'll get out of my work clothes and put on something less constricting.'

She moved off into the bedroom, and Michaels found himself standing in the apartment of an attractive woman he barely knew, holding a folded sheet, contemplating the removal of his clothes.

This was a bad idea.

Then again, she did have a real massage table,

and she did seem to know a lot about body work.

He blew out a deep breath. What the hell.

He stripped to his underwear – a pair of black silk bikini briefs Toni had bought for him – stretched out on the table face down, and pulled the sheet over himself.

When Angela came back into the room, he saw she wore a pair of gray sweatpants and a tank top. Sweatpants. Sweatpants were good.

'Ready?'

'Sure.'

She started by digging her elbow into his upper back, and after a couple of minutes, he relaxed into it. Some tiny part of him was maybe a little bit disappointed – it *was* going to be a massage – but the larger part of him felt relief. She was bright and beautiful but his life was already complicated enough. A back rub wasn't something he had to lose any sleep over.

She spent about thirty minutes working on his back. She moved to his legs, and he felt himself tense a little, but Angela was matter-of-fact about it, pummeling his hamstrings hard enough to be slightly painful, uncovering one leg at a time and folding the sheet so that the rest of him was under the thin cloth.

She worked on his feet and calves then moved to his butt, hands under the sheet. 'This won't do,' she said, and she peeled his briefs off, slid them quickly over his legs and his feet.

'Uh . . . Angela . . . ?'

'Relax, Alex. I can't work the muscle properly if it's covered up.'

He tried to do as she suggested, but with her fingers stroking his ass that was hard. And, unfortunately, that soon wasn't the only thing hard about him. At least he was face down, so that wasn't too embarrassing – just a little uncomfortable.

After five minutes of kneading his buttocks he was beginning to relax again when she said, 'Okay, turn over.'

'Excuse me?'

'The back is only half of you. I need to work the front.'

Crap. How could he say this? How to handle his, ah, current *condition?* 'Uh, well, I, uh, well, turning over might be kind of, that is—'

'Got a bit excited? Don't worry about that, Alex. I've done this before. It happens all the time.'

She lifted up the sheet. 'Turn, I'll hold this.'

He wasn't thrilled with the idea of rolling onto his back and showing her where his mind had gone – when she let go of the sheet, it was going to look like a tent – out all right, fine. He kept his eyes closed and rolled over.

'My. How lovely,' she said.

He opened his eyes as Angela dropped the sheet to the floor and climbed onto the table to straddle him.

Her sweatpants were gone – how had she done

that? – and she wasn't wearing anything under them. In another second later, he was going to be wearing *her*, and he knew if that happened, his mind would shut down completely. He would be lost.

'Hey, Angela?'

'Mmm?'

'Look, I really can't do this.'

'You obviously can. And certainly you want to. I can tell.' She pointed at him.

'Yes. But the thing is, I *can't*. I'm involved.'

'She'll never find out from me. Nobody will ever know.'

He shook his head. 'I'll know.'

She leaned back, looked down at him. 'You sure about this?'

He sighed. 'Yeah.'

Michaels came out of a troubled doze back in his room with the sound of his virgil playing 'Bad to the Bone.' Man, was *that* ever true.

Toni!

Oh, man!

He was in deep shit now.

The virgil kept telling him it was b-b-b-bad, and he got up and went to find it. Yeah, okay, he hadn't actually *done* anything but he should never have gone to Angela's flat; he knew at the time it was wrong, and he had done it anyway. And if they could hang you for thinking, he'd be swinging by now. The last thing he wanted to do now was talk to anybody, and he especially did not want to talk to Toni.

He left the visual off. 'Hello?'

'Hey, boss.'

Jay Gridley. Thank God. 'Jay. How are you?'

'Doing a lot better. I tracked down the security program that thumped my head and wrecked it.'

'Congratulations.'

'This is the easy part, boss. I still have to find the guy who created it. But it ought to be easier with that out of the way.'

'Good.'

'Uh, is, uh, Toni around?'

Michaels felt a cold hand squeeze his guts. 'Ah, no. She's in Paris. Be back this afternoon.'

'I'll give her a call, there's some stuff in her files here I need to access.'

'Fine.'

'How's London? You having a good time?'

Was he having a good time? Well, no, not exactly. He was busy becoming the biggest unfaithful, lying turd in all the world. All right, technically he might not have been unfaithful, but it sure felt as if he had been. He'd been inches away from it.

'Yeah,' he said. 'I'm having a great time. Talk to you later, Jay. Keep me advised.'

He shut off his virgil. Jesus Christ. How could he have been so fucking stupid? A few drinks, some good food, and a massage didn't sound so awful. His neck had been sore, right? Taking off your clothes in front of a doctor or a massage therapist, there wasn't any harm in that. But the thought that it might continue into something had rattled around in his head, he had to admit it. It was only by the slimmest margin that he could claim any kind of victory, and it felt more like a loss.

He was going to have to tell Toni about it, of course.

The question was: *How* was he going to tell Toni? Oh, by the way, while you were in Paris, I dropped round Angela's place, took off my clothes and let her rub my back, and almost let her rub my front?

When was *that* going to come up in conversation?

Man.

28

Tuesday
London, England

Goswell glanced over the top of his *Times* at Sir Harold Bellworth, who sat brooding; his cigar had gone out from lack of attention. The old boy called for Paddington to fetch him another match, and Goswell figured this was a good time to broach the subject he had in mind.

'I say, Harry?'

Bellworth looked up from his dead cigar. 'What? Eh?'

'You recall that business you had with that . . . Armenian fellow a few months ago?'

Bellworth snorted. 'I could hardly forget that! Blasted rogue, the man was, mucking about in my business!'

'I heard he met with an . . . unfortunate accident, the Armenian.'

'I should say he did. Fell off of a platform in the tube station and was squashed by a train. Served him right, and no loss to the world at all, bloody foreigner!'

Goswell waited as Paddington returned. Paddington struck a match against the box, let it flare, then bent and held it so Bellworth could rekindle his Cuban torpedo. A cloud of fragrant smoke billowed as the old boy puffed the cigar back to life.

'Decent of you, Paddington,' Bellworth said.

Paddington moved the ashtray a hair closer – Bellworth was notorious for flicking the cigar residue onto the rug – 'Not at all, sir. Will there be anything else?'

'No, no, this will do it.'

'Very good, sir.' Paddington ghosted away.

Bellworth looked back to Goswell. 'Why on earth are you bringing up such a distasteful subject, Gossie?'

'Well, I'm embarrassed to admit it, but I have a somewhat similar problem myself. I do believe I need someone . . . discreet.'

Bellworth took another puff, held the cigar away and peered at the lit end, nodded through the gray cloud. 'You have your own people to attend to such things, surely?'

'I'm afraid one of my own people *is* the problem. Having one of his underlings take care of him wouldn't do at all, would it?'

'Heavens, no, bad for morale and all that, I understand completely. Well, then, shall I put in a call to my fellow, have him ring you up?'

'If it wouldn't be too much trouble, Harry.'

'Not at all, not at all, consider it done. Now, what do you make of Lord Cleese's proposal about bringing back the poorhouses? I thought it was rather a clever idea myself . . .'

Goswell smiled. Here was a subject on which they could certainly agree. Putting the poor to work instead of carrying them on the dole. Bloody socialists would be the death of the country if somebody didn't stop them, and such suggestions were, for Goswell's money, right on the mark. It would never happen, of course, but it would shake people if Parliament actually considered such a thing. Indeed it would.

It would seem he was going to have to take direct control of his own personal war on the world's foolishness, given as how his primary tools had somehow gotten bent. He sighed. One should expect such things in this day and age, but they still came as rather a surprise. You simply could not get dependable help these days, not of the caliber that once was. Such a pity.

London, England

Toni didn't expect to see Alex waiting for her when she got through the throng at the Chunnel train station, but there he was. She was tired after the ride from Paris, and the air the English Channel had seemed particularly stuffy, though that was probably just psychological. All that unseen water weighed heavily upon you. Good thing she wasn't claustrophobic. She was beat but her spirits lifted immediately when she saw him.

'Alex! What are you doing here?'

They hugged, he took her bag and said, 'I missed you. Welcome back, sweetie. How'd it go?'

'Okay. They really are well-mannered, most of the French. It's only the few who give them such a bad reputation. Well, okay, more than a few, but it wasn't so bad. As long as you don't pretend to understand the language and try to speak it, even the waiters aren't too nasty.'

'You always liked anybody who liked Jerry Lewis,' he said.

'He was a comic genius. Good slapstick isn't easy, you know.'

He laughed. It was an old joke between them. But Jerry Lewis *was* funny, he had created that monkey character, built from it, and some of his later dramatic roles were as good as any actor working. He was underrated.

'Anything happening here?'

'No . . . not really. Well, except that I got a call from John Howard. He's landed at an Air Force base north of here.'

'The Colonel? Why?'

'Plekhanov's hired gun, Ruzhyó. They traced him to England.'

'Great. One more brick on the load.'

He didn't say anything to that.

'You look tired,' she said.

'I didn't sleep well.'

'I bet I can help you fall asleep tonight.'

'I bet so.'

She squeezed his arm. He smiled at her. They'd been passing each other in the dark lately; it was time to get back on the same track. She said, 'You talked to Jay? He called me. He's doing better.'

'Yeah. I'm glad to hear that.'

'And he says he is making progress toward finding our hacker.'

'About time we had some good news on that front.'

He seemed a little bit stiff, but just look at him, he was obviously tired. A nice hot shower and crawling under the covers together would do wonders for both of them. She had missed lovemaking with him. And, truth be known, she was getting horny from all the working out with Carl. Best drain that tension and be done with it.

Cambridge, England

Howard sat in the back seat of the Ford behind Julio and the driver loaned to them by the RAF. They were on the M11 heading south toward London. He passed signs for Bishop's Stortford and Sawbridgeworth, and except for the colors and shapes of the signs, it could have been an American freeway in the countryside of New York or northern California. The greenery was similar, the look of civilization not all that different.

Well, except for being on the wrong side of the road.

Julio sat where an American would be at the steering wheel back home, and he seemed a bit more relaxed on the motorway than he had been on the surface streets. Leaving the base, every time they'd rounded a corner and seen cars coming from the opposite direction Howard had seen Julio tense, his foot going for an imaginary brake. He understood the feeling; he had put his own braking foot against the back of the seat a few times.

Why on Earth had the British chosen to drive on the wrong side of the road?

It may be a little easier because the driver's controls were on the right but it would take some getting used to before Howard wanted to do his own driving here.

They were still thirty miles from downtown London, the driver told them, but they were also zipping along at about seventy-five, and Howard knew that was miles per hour and not kilometers. They were going to MI-6 to meet Commander Michaels and fill him in on the hunt for the Rifle, the meaning of Ruzyhò in Russian. The guy had a warped sense of humor to go along with everything else.

'You doing okay up there, Sergeant?'

'Just fine, sir. Enjoying the lovely countryside.'

The driver, a British airman, grinned. 'I went to visit my uncle in New York City once,' he said. 'I thought I'd go mad first time I got out on the road in his car. Why'd you Yanks decide to drive on the wrong side of the road that way?'

'You are in error, limey,' Fernandez said. 'What's the brandname on this beast? F-O-R-D, isn't it? We invented cars, so we got to pick which side of the road first.'

'Begging your pardon, Sergeant, but where did you get *that* notion? Henry Ford was a Johnny-come-lately, now wasn't he? Making a lot of them is not the same as making them *first*, is it?'

'You're not gonna sit there and try to tell me with a straight face that the *English* invented the automobile, are you?'

'It's the King's Truth, Sergeant.'

'Bullshit it is.'

The driver grinned wider. 'Well, everybody knows it was the frogs what made the first *steam* carts, Nicolas-Joseph Cugnot, with his tricycle-steamer in 1769. By the 1830s everybody and the King's nephew had steamers up and running, in England as well as half of Europe. Even had those in the States by the end of your Civil War. But we're not talking about scaled-down steam trains that ran on dirt roads now, are we? We're talking about *automobiles*.

'The first *real* car, what with an internal combustion engine? Well, that was built and driven up Shooter's Hill in London by Sam Brown in 1823–1826 if you believe old Sam himself, who was admittedly a bit hazy on dates. Ran on carbureted hydrogen, it did. I make that a bit sooner than John Lambert, who put the first one together in the U.S. in 1891. He beat the Duryea brothers by almost two years, though they usually get credit for the first 'un, but that's only a drop in the bucket compared to *sixty* years, innit?'

'Great,' Fernandez said. 'Just my luck to sit next to the fucking Royal Historian slumming as an Airman driver.'

The driver laughed. 'Man ought to know his tools, right? I drive 'em, I might as well learn a little something about 'em, eh?'

Fernandez laughed. 'Score one for the home team. Which side of the road do they drive on in France?'

'Who cares?' the Airman said. 'They're the bloody *French*, aren't they?'

Even Howard laughed at that one.

London, England

Ruzhyó met Peel at a corner in front of a giant Coke sign that flashed thousands of lights overhead. They were to discuss his assignment, but when he asked about it, Peel shook his head. 'Let's leave off on that for a moment,' he said. 'I've got something else I need you to do.'

Ruzhyó raised one eyebrow. 'Yes?'

Tourists bustled along the sidewalks. A group of school children in uniforms, holding hands in pairs, snaked past like a blue and white caterpillar.

Peel looked nervous. He checked his surroundings constantly, if unobtrusively, as if he was being watched. 'I need somebody to cover my back,' Peel said. 'I think maybe I stepped on somebody's toes.'

Ruzhyó nodded. 'All right. Do we know whose?'

'Not for certain. I have an idea, but I'll have to check further.'

'Why me?'

What he was really asking was more involved than that: *Why trust* me? *We don't know each other that well. Surely you have your own men?*

Peel answered the unasked part of the question: 'Because you don't have any reason to want me dead.'

Ruzhyó kept his face deadpan. 'Not that you know of.'

Peel smiled, short and tight. 'Have you obtained a gun?'

'Not yet,' he lied. He kept his voice bland.

Peel produced a small, zippered, dark blue nylon pouch from his inside jacket pocket and handed it over. 'Beretta, model 21A, .22 caliber, Italian, but this model was American-made. Six in the magazine, one in the chamber, double-action first round if you wish, tip-up barrel.'

'I am familiar with the weapon.'

Peel nodded. 'There are two extra magazines, already loaded as well. CCI Minimags, solids. I could have gotten you a bigger gun, but I understand that *Spetsnaz* ops have a fondness for the smaller calibers.'

'It will do. And it shoots how?'

Peel nodded, as if he expected the question, but nonetheless pleased to hear it. 'I didn't have time to have the armorer smooth it out, so the double-action pull is a bit stiff, probably twelve or fourteen pounds. Single-action is fairly tight, five pounds or so, but with a little creep. Shoots dead on at seven yards, two inches high and slightly right at twenty-five yards.'

'I understand.'

'I would appreciate it if you would keep it handy. And if you should happen to see somebody sneak up behind me with intent, shoot them for me, would you?'

Ruzhyó gave him a choppy, military nod, slipped

the pouch into his pocket, and unzipped it. He removed the pistol, and thumbed the safety off. Given the stubby barrel, the Beretta would not be as accurate as the umbrella gun, but it was added firepower. And the little weapon would also be the Devil that Peel knew about.

The Russian faded into the background, just another foreign tourist with an umbrella, to keep potential trouble off of Peel's arse. Peel felt a little better, a little safer. Maybe it was all in his mind, a figment of his imagination, being stalked, but he hadn't kept body and soul together by ignoring his inner alarms. Now and again he was wrong and nothing amiss ever turned up, but why take the chance?

Once, he had been on a bivouac with a drop squad doing training in the middle of some woods in NSW, Australia. They had backpacked in more than fifteen miles off the beaten track, into the foothills. They were only a couple thousand feet up, in a dry area where the dust was red and thick on everything, raising in clouds every time they took a step outside the tents. They were camped in a small clearing amidst trees and scrub so thick it was like there were solid walls all around them.

Just before dark, as the men were settling down to cook the evening meal, Peel got spooked. A sudden, overwhelming fear rose in him, so fast and powerful that he wanted to run, to get away from the area as fast as he could move.

It was totally irrational. There was nothing threatening around, no other people for miles – as far as they knew. He tried to reason with himself. God, he was a trained officer, a battle-tested lieutenant, young, brave, armed to the teeth, with six veteran men who could chew nails and pee needles, likewise armed, and there wasn't anything in the bloody woods that could seriously bother them. But that didn't matter. His sense of imminent doom was undeniable. Without explaining, and making it seem as if it was some part of their training, he ordered his men to pack up and be ready to move out in five minutes. It took them almost seven, but as soon as they were ready, they force-marched six miles before Peel's sense of danger faded. They reestablished camp, posted a guard, and turned in.

Early in the morning hours before dawn, the sentry woke Peel and pointed out the orange glow in the sky. A forest fire.

Later, when he checked, Peel found that the fire had begun just below their original campsite. It had swept up the hills so fast that fleeing deer had been caught in the deadly flames; had he and his men stayed above where the fire raged, none of them would have survived.

His men had been impressed.

How had he known? Some faint hint of smoke in the air nobody had caught? Some frightened animals in the woods whose fear had been powerful enough so that he could somehow sense it? He had pondered it, but never came up with an answer that satisfied him. More important than 'how' was that he had done it. Some sense had told him death was near, and he had had enough sense to go with it.

Similar things had happened in various firefights and patrols since, though nothing quite as dramatic as the Australian event, and when he had felt the cold touch of it on his shoulder, he had harkened to it. More times than not, such actions had saved his life.

There was no enemy in sight here but he felt the fear. The only cause he could figure was the scientist. Nobody else knew what he was doing, and the man certainly had something to hide. It didn't make sense, not with Bascomb-Coombs giving him a bloody million and making him a kind of partner in the scheme, but who else could it be? And in truth, he hadn't *seen* the money stacked up neatly on a table somewhere, had he? It was all electronically vouched for by the Indonesian bank, and normally that would have been enough, but Bascomb-Coombs was owner and operator of the world's nastiest computer, wasn't he? Surely he could fool somebody not computer-savvy enough to know the difference, if that was his wish.

Why would he wish to do that?

Peel did not have a clue, but something was lurking out there and he did not plan to become its victim. Best he take steps to find out, and best to be quick about it, too. And if it was Bascomb-Coombs, well, all his genius wouldn't stand up to a knife between the ribs or a bullet to the back of the skull. When push came to shove, the sword was a much better weapon than the pen, no question.

Peel walked toward the train station, feeling a bit better now that he was taking action.

29

Tuesday
Washington, D.C.

Sojan Rinpoche was coming to see Jay. He was coming here, to his apartment, in the flesh, and Jay was more than a little nervous.

The advantage of VR was that you could craft your image into anything you wanted. True, Jay tended to look like himself in a lot of scenarios, because it was more trouble than it was worth to create a persona to impress somebody. Okay, so he touched himself up at the edges; maybe he looked a little taller, more muscular, had lines that were a teeny bit sharper. But not so much you couldn't recognize him in RW if you met him. After you had been a player for years, you more or less disregarded what you saw when it came to other players in VR anyhow. You'd meet them offline in some RW conference or whatever and you couldn't quite reconcile the real person with the net persona. A lot of times, they would build an image that looked totally different yet not bother to change their voice, and hearing them speak from a completely unrecognizable body was weird sometimes. Or they'd change the voice but not the face, and that was strange, too.

Truth was a very subjective thing in virtual reality. The term itself was almost an oxymoron . . .

Saji had told Jay on the net that he was going to be in D.C. for a couple of weeks, and asked Jay if he wanted to meet in Real Time. Jay had agreed, though he had a few reservations. Saji had saved his butt, no doubt about that, and he owed him BTDS – big-time-damn-sure – but there was that little gnawing worry that the real Saji might not jibe with the virtual version. Buddhists had dealt with illusion a long time before computers had been invented, and maybe he'd look like Saji and maybe he wouldn't. Sometimes you hated to meet somebody for whom you had great respect, for fear the reality wouldn't live up to your imagination. Once, when he'd been a kid, Jay had happened across the host of a television show he'd loved. On the air, the guy had been smiling, avuncular, the kind of man kids wanted for a father. He'd been Jay's hero. The show host had spotted Jay, and the first words from his sweet lips had been, 'Jesus, who let that little dickhead in here?'

So much for childhood heroes.

Jay had killed the tiger, but compared to what he had left to do, that was the easy part. Now he was hunting tyrannosaur, he was stalking a dragon, and he was gonna need a bigger gun. And more nerve.

Saji was going to make him spill his guts about it, about how he felt, and that wasn't gonna be fun, either. In some ways that was scarier than the thunder lizard. Who was it said the unexamined life wasn't worth living? Plato? Aristotle? Yeah, maybe so, but if you spent too much time digging into your own psyche, it got spooky. Maybe the overexamined life wasn't worth living, either.

In Betty Bacall's throaty, sexy tone, the house computer said, 'Jay, you have a visitor.'

Saji was here.

He was ready for anything. Jay took a deep breath and went to the door. Opened it.

A petite, short-haired brunette woman in blue jeans, a black T-shirt, and cowboy boots stood there. She looked to be about twenty-five, maybe five feet tall even in the boots, and had big dimples around a beautiful smile. She could have been Tibetan, he supposed, but there didn't seem to be any Oriental cast to her features.

'Hello, Jay,' she said.

Well . . . *shit*. He realized he wasn't ready for *anything* after all.

'Saji,' he said. It was not a question. Son-of-a-bitch. Not only was Saji a *woman*, she was young and beautiful. This was not *fair*!

Son-of-a-bitch.

Tuesday
The Yews, Sussex, England

'Telephone call for you, sir,' Applewhite said. He came into the room carrying the instrument. 'A gentleman by the name of . . . Pound-Sand, milord. He says you were expecting his call.'

Goswell paused and looked through the tubes of the shotgun he had been cleaning. Pound-Sand? He didn't know anybody named that, did he? Did anyone? Someone was pulling Applewhite's leg, surely? He blew hard through one of the barrels, causing a hollow, hooting sound; lint from the cotton cleaning patch floated out into the room, drifting downward in the rays of the afternoon sun.

'He says he was told to call by an old gentleman fond of Cuban cigars.'

Ah. *That's* who it was. He reached for the phone and waved Applewhite out.

'Hello?'

'Lord Goswell?'

'Yes, it is I.'

'A moment, please, sir.' The voice seemed cultured enough, some education and decent background in it. There came an electronic tone from the other end of the connection. 'Excuse the delay,' the man said. 'One cannot be too careful, can one?'

'You just did a voice analysis?'

'Yes, my lord. And the line is secure, our

conversation is quite scrambled. I trust no one is listening in on an extension on your end?'

Goswell nodded to himself. Good show. He said, 'No, we're alone, Mr – ah, Pound-Sand.'

The man chuckled. 'I hope you'll forgive me the little joke, my lord, Sir Harold has indicated that you have something of a delicate problem . . . ?'

'I'm afraid so, yes.'

'Would you like this problem resolved temporarily or permanently?'

'Permanently, I'm unhappy to say.'

'I shall attend to it immediately.'

'You'll need particulars.'

'Just the name will be sufficient, my lord. I can determine the rest.'

Goswell grinned. Capital!

He gave the killer Peel's name.

'Thank you, my lord, I'll take care of it. Goodbye, then.'

Goswell hung up the phone. No discussion of money or tawdry details. How wonderful. He felt better. At least there were still a few good men out there.

London, England

Alex Michaels walked along the bank of the Thames near the Jubilee Gardens, watching tourist boats cruise by and wishing he could turn back time. His life had become a fucking soap opera. His investigation was stalled. His ex-wife wanted sole custody of their daughter. He was having a relationship with his second-in-command. Worse, he had damned near slept with someone *else*, which would have been only the third woman he had been with in a dozen years. How could he tell Toni that? What could he say? Oh, yes, while you were out of town I came that close to rolling around and breaking furniture all night with the gorgeous British secret agent Angela Cooper. Sorry about that.

Yeah. Now, he had a monkey riding his back, clawed fingers dug into his neck and shoulders, legs wrapped around his torso like a vise, and it was so heavy he could barely stand. He had never felt so guilty in his life. He had never done anything like this before, ever. How could he have been so stupid? How the hell was he going to make this right?

Was it even possible to make it right?

He couldn't stand the idea that he might lose Toni. But if he told her – no, *when* he told her – that could happen. She could slap his face and stalk out. She could also break his bones and stalk out, though that didn't scare him as much as the hurt he'd see in her face.

What the hell had he been thinking about?

Sure, he could try to blame it all on Angela. She had worked pretty hard to get him to her place, had set it up with the massage and all, but he wasn't fooling himself with that rationalization. She hadn't held a gun to his head. It took two to tango. He could have politely declined the offer and gone home.

You can't spike paper without a paper spike.

Okay, fine, so you didn't actually *spike* anything, but, like horse shoes and hand grenades, close counts here. Ah, Jesus.

Some Japanese tourists on a barge-like boat with a bright colored canopy over it smiled and waved at him. Probably thought he was a local; not much difference between an Englishman and an American to look at, was there?

The tourists didn't have a clue that the idea of throwing himself into the Thames and diving to the bottom and staying there held a certain morbid appeal just at the moment.

He waved back. 'Eat shit and die,' he said, smiling falsely.

How could men do such things, cheat on their wives or significant others as he had done? Almost done. Once, he'd had drinks with a lawyer he'd met on the job, a tall, handsome, rich guy who was married to a beautiful woman. They had three children, a great home in Virginia, money, dogs, cats, every measure of happiness imaginable. They started talking. After a couple of drinks the lawyer confided in Michaels. Once, not long ago, he said, he'd been to a fundraising breakfast in D.C. Aside from his wife, there were four very attractive women at the table, some married, some not, ranging in age from twenty-two to forty. He had, the lawyer said, slept with all of them during the past year, and looked forward to doing it again with each of them. None of them knew about the others. It was a peak moment for him, he'd boasted.

Michaels had nearly choked on his drink. The man must be mad. The idea of sitting at table with five women, all of whom he had been to bed with, filled him with terror. In such a situation, he would have dropped dead from fright, no doubt about it. The tension would have been unbearable. He could see his head just . . . exploding, like a cherry bomb on New Year's Eve.

His experience was small, but he believed that women could tell these things somehow. A wrong look or word from Angela, and Toni would *know*. That was the last thing he wanted to happen, that she find out from somebody other than him.

The second-to-last thing he wanted to happen was that she find out from him.

Oh, man! What was he going to do now? No matter how he looked at it, this was a no-win situation.

Should have thought about that when you shucked your clothes and rolled over on that massage table, pal. Should have put your brain in gear before you put your hydraulics in motion . . .

Ruzhyó followed Peel, keeping his rented car one or

two vehicles back in the traffic. He did not consider himself an expert in surveillance – he had known men who could follow a damned soul through Hell's Main Gate without the Devil knowing it – but it was much easier when the subject knew you were tailing him and *wanted* you to be there. It was true he had shadowed people before, usually just before he killed them. And it was true he knew the basics of moving surveillance, how to use cover, how to blend into the background, when to back off and let somebody go to keep from burning them. Such skills were part of his trade, and he was adept, if not a master.

Ruzhyó glanced at a street sign as they drove past. Old Kent Road. And there off to one side was something called the South East Gas Works. He made a mental note of these.

One of the tricks that beginning operatives learning how to tail somebody often missed was to pay attention to where you were. There was a tendency to concentrate on your subject to the exclusion of all else. You might not see his friend, laying and watching for just such as you. Or you could stay with a subject through various twists and turns, sometimes even when he got cute and tried to see if he was being followed, but if you were not paying proper attention when the subject stopped, you looked up and did not have any idea as to where you were. In a familiar city this was not a problem, but in a strange town, it could cause difficulty. If you did not have a good local map or a GPS, finding your way back to your base might be a chore.

And there were worse things. There were areas in every city where you simply could not park for several hours and wait for a subject to return to his vehicle and depart. A residential street in a well-to-do neighborhood was a bad place to stay. Rich people had things they wanted protected, and they also felt that the law and its officers should offer them priority. It might be a public street and you might have the right to park there legally, but if the local captain of industry glanced out his mansion window and saw you sitting in your automobile in front of his property, he *would* call the police and they would come and check you out. *If* the private security patrol didn't get to you first.

Parking and sitting for long periods in front of a bank were also unwise actions.

If you drove into a strange area and found yourself near a primary school, close enough to view the children playing, you could safely bet everything you owned against a plugged ruble that police would be arriving shortly to see if you were some kind of molester waiting for a chance to expose yourself – or do worse – to the children. If you did not have an excellent reason for being there – and no reasons *were* excellent enough to convince the police that a man should be perched and watching children, except possibly that you were one of them laying in wait for someone like they thought *you* were – you would be directed to move along.

In such a situation, it would be to your advantage to have some knowledge of where else you might go to watch for your man leaving.

Peel turned into a parking lot in front of a small gray two-story building.

Ruzhyó drove past the lot and spotted a parking place on the street only a few meters ahead, under the overhang of a smallish oak-like tree. He grinned. The first rule of automobile surveillance, as taught to him by Serge, the old Russian *Spetsnaz* operative who had trained him in the basics, was: Always park in the shade. The warmer the day, the more important this becomes.

Ruzhyó pulled the car into the slot, killed the engine, and looked to make certain nobody followed Peel into the parking lot. Nobody did.

Peel alighted from his car and headed for the building, giving no sign he saw Ruzhyó. Peel had already told him the building to which he was going was secure; there was no need to follow him inside.

Ruzhyó shifted in the seat, and looked for signs of anybody who might either be there already or arriving to position himself so as to watch Peel's departure. If he saw anything he considered threatening, he would call Peel using his mobile, and they would decide how to proceed from there.

Seated in the car with nothing to do but watch, Ruzhyó thought again about going home. The travel problems had mostly resolved, and he could easily figure out a way onto the European mainland. There had been another case in the newspaper just yesterday of some fool who had managed to bypass the fences and security camera and guards to get into the Chunnel on foot. It had taken him all day to walk from England to France, and it was a wonder the slipstream of the trains, barreling along at a hundred and sixty kilometers per hour, hadn't sucked him off the narrow ledge to his death. Several others had died thus in the last few years.

Such a thing just proved that if a man wanted to get somewhere bad enough, he could find a way.

He owed no allegiance to Peel, and the money he was being paid meant nothing. He had plenty of money. But he would give this a few more days. It was mildly interesting, and Peel *had* managed to spot and surprise him. That meant something in his business. A few more days wouldn't hurt.

30

Tuesday
Washington, D.C.

Tyrone stood more or less hidden inside the sporting goods store, looking out at the food court. He'd cut classes to come to the mall. Bella was there, seated at a table in front of the Tor-tee-ah Mah-ree-aa, surrounded by half a dozen girlfriends and a couple of boys. The guys weren't anybody Tyrone recognized as belonging to Bella, just some small moons orbiting her bright star. Bella laughed and they all laughed. When she talked, they listened. She was something.

He had mixed feelings about her though. On the one hand he hated her guts for how she had dropped him. No warning, blam! Right between the eyes, and hasta la vista, Ty-rone! She wasn't used to having guys tell her they didn't like how she was behaving, and he had sure done that. And then just like that, it was end game, and don't bother to put another coin in, because you don't get a replay.

On the other hand, just look at her . . . She was so beautiful, the center of every room she entered, guys would line up just to kiss the ground she walked on. And, once upon a time, she had bestowed her favors on *him*. Kissed him, touched him, let him touch her, and the thought of being able to do that again, to walk around knowing he had her attention, well, that was something magic, no question, no Q. He'd once had his hand on that perfect breast, tangled tongues inside that perfect mouth. It was so exciting to think about it it was lucky he was between two racks of ski clothes so nobody could see just *how* exciting it was.

She had practically invited him to the mall. He could walk out of this store, kinda amble over to where she sat, and see what was what. Would she smile and welcome him into the fold, have him sit next to her? Because, in the end, she respected him for telling her how it was? Or was it some kind of sicko-sticko where she'd dry-ice him in front of her friends, embarrass the hell out of him, make him look like a total fool? He didn't think she'd do that – she could have done it a lot of times before now and why wait so long? – but he wasn't sure.

Once upon a time not too long ago, he'd have run as fast as he could move and never worried about it for a nanosec. He had *loved* her. He thought she loved him, too. But that was then. Life changes a lot in a few months, no feek.

When he thought about Bella Tyrone felt like he was a washcloth, twisted, wrung out, tossed onto the edge of the tub still in a knot without even being hung out to dry. This could be the time to find out where he stood, to know for sure.

Thing was, did he really want to know? Being dumped once was awful. Being humiliated in public on top of that would be zero cubed. He could hear Jimmy-Joe and the rest of the geek patrol now: 'Whoa, slip, I hear you got driced by The Belladonna (donna-donna-donna-wah-wah-wah-whaah) right in the middle of the mall! Count Zero, cold cut, got your card *maxed*. How you feel about *that*?'

Tyrone shook his head. He didn't want to play that scenario in RW *or* VR, thank you very fucking much.

Nothing ventured, nothing gained. But nothing *lost*, either, right?

But if it got Bella back, got you to her house on the couch, got you another chance at putting your hands on that perfect body, those lips against yours, wouldn't that be worth the risk?

Oh, yeah.

He took a deep breath, let it out slowly. Took another. Worse-case scenario, he'd look like a big fool. Best case?

He had an imaginary flash of Bella, naked, hair spread out on a pillow. It was vivid enough that he forgot to breathe. He was fourteen, and that was an image to die for – never mind that it was also to go to jail for, even if she was older than he was. Bella. Naked . . .

Jesus Christ!

When he remembered how to breathe again, Tyrone headed for the door. Do or die, slip. Do or die.

Tuesday
London, England

John Howard stood outside the MI-6 building, watching his boss walk across the street and head toward him. He waved and saw Michaels see him and wave back.

'Colonel. How are you?'

'Pretty good, sir. All things considered.'

'Anything new on the search for the assassin?'

'Yes and no,' Howard said. 'We know he was on a flight out of Seattle on Wednesday. We know he came here. We have confirmation via a scan of passengers going through customs. Fiorella pulled up arrivals from the U.S. early Thursday morning. We got a photographic match.'

He tendered a hardcopy color print of a man strolling through the airport. A grid of fine lines had been superimposed over the photograph.

'You sure this is him?'

'It looks like him. Right place, right time. Computer says the ears and hands match our reference, so unless he has a twin brother, it's him all right.'

Michaels nodded at the building. 'Shall we go inside?'

As they passed the guards and headed along the hallway, Michaels said, 'It's been almost a week, he could be anywhere by now.'

'Yes, sir, that's true. He could have moved on before the travel computer systems all went south. We've got mainframe time on Baby Huey, and with British cooperation, Lieutenant Winthrop is back home using it to crunch flight and train and auto rental information, even boat rentals from London to anywhere else. Even a fake passport picture will have to look something like him.'

'He could get one with a phony beard and a wig,' Michaels said.

'We're redballing any male traveling alone who is anywhere close to the right height, weight, and age.'

'He could hire an escort and travel with her.'

'Yes, sir, and he might find a witch doctor who could turn him into a gorilla, too, sir, but we've got to start somewhere.'

Michaels smiled at that.

They arrived at the office where Howard had left Toni Fiorella.

Inside, Fiorella and a tall, striking, short-haired blonde stood and looked at an enlarged holoproj image of dozens of faces lined up in rows.

'Got the first run of photos from Jo Winthrop, Colonel,' Toni said. 'All with either ears that match our size specs, or are covered by hair so we can't see them clearly. Hi, Alex. Have a good walk?'

'Yeah, thanks,' Michaels said. He looked uncomfortable. Pale.

'Oh, excuse my manners,' Toni said. 'Colonel John Howard? This is Angela Cooper. She is our liaison to MI-6. Colonel Howard is the head of the Net Force Strike Teams.'

The blonde extended her hand and smiled at Howard. 'How do you do, Colonel. Pleased to meet you.'

He shook her hand, returning the smile. He caught a glimpse of Michaels peripherally. The man had a sickly grin pasted in place but he looked to Howard as if he was about to throw up.

Cooper released Howard's hand, and he caught her flick a quick gaze at Michaels. He followed it, and saw Michaels glance away, refusing to meet her look. It was nothing, no more than half a second's worth of what might be his imagination. But—

Oh, my.

Howard usually went to church on Sundays with his wife and son but he didn't consider himself any kind of prophet, able to see more than everybody else could see. Then again, he'd been around the block a time or two, and he liked to think he was not too bad at reading people.

Something was there. Something in the glance that the good-looking dishwater-blonde had thrown at Michaels, the way he had refused to engage her.

Howard, like most men away from home a lot, had been tempted by the possibility of extramarital liaisons from time to time. There had been more than a few women interested in getting to know him horizontally, and a couple of them had been attractive enough so the thought had crossed his mind. Who would know? Who would be hurt by it? How did the old song go? If you couldn't be with the one you loved, couldn't you love the one you were with?

No harm, no foul, right?

Fortunately, in all the years he'd been married, all such thoughts had died before they had gotten more than a few steps from wonder toward action. He didn't think of himself as particularly righteous – he'd sowed a fair number of wild oats as a young soldier before he got married – but he'd put all that aside when he'd said 'I do.' Maybe he was luckier than most; he hadn't slipped since. But he had known a lot of men who had chosen to go and sin some more. He'd seen plenty of these men standing next to women they pretended not to know as well as they did know them.

He couldn't have sworn to it on a Bible in a court of law, but that little exchange between Michaels and Cooper told Howard something he'd just as soon not know, too: These two had *something* going on together. And more than that, from how she acted, Toni Fiorella *didn't* know it.

Oh, boy. All of a sudden, Howard was very glad he was not Alex Michaels. Very glad.

London, England

Ruzhyó saw the shooter the second he opened his car door.

It was good luck, really; he'd just happened to be right next to the car and looking that way as he walked along twelve or thirteen meters behind Peel. If he hadn't looked at just that instant it might have been too late, but he had seen the glint of sunlight on stainless steel as the man pulled his jacket shut to hide the handgun tucked into his waistband on his right side. Half a second later, he'd have missed that, and not known for sure the shooter was anything other than just another pedestrian hurrying to a late appointment, or to pick up something before the shops closed.

The shooter came out only a meter or so behind Ruzhyó, who just kept walking, drifting to his right slightly, as if window-shopping at a hat store. The shooter, a tallish man with thinning, sandy hair, dressed in a windbreaker over a tan polo shirt, khaki slacks and running shoes, walked past, intent on his target.

Ruzhyó glanced around. He didn't see a backup man. He moved away from the window and onto the shooter's tail, hurrying his pace. He reached down to where his mobile phone was clipped to his belt and tapped the 'send' button.

The number was preprogrammed, one of two Peel

had given him, and the mobile on Peel's belt would now be vibrating with the call. Nobody else had the number, Peel had told him, and if it vibrated, that meant Ruzhyó had spotted a deadly threat too close to use the other number to call and talk about it.

Peel made an immediate right turn and into the door of the closest shop. A bookstore.

The shooter angled that way to follow.

Ruzhyó speeded up so that he reached the bookstore's door half a meter behind his quarry. It would be easy enough to blast the shooter, put him down and out, but they wanted to keep him alive long enough to find out who had sent him. That might be a little trickier on the street, but inside a shop, with fewer witnesses, it should be easier.

Peel knew what was needed, and he quickly led his would-be assassin down an empty aisle bounded by tall shelves of musty books. Before the shooter could get to his weapon, Ruzhyó got to him. He shoved the little Beretta into the other man's spine and said, 'Move and you die.'

The shooter was a pro. He froze.

'Clear,' Ruzhyó said.

Peel turned around, his hand under his sport coat at the right hip. He smiled. 'Henry? I thought you retired?'

The sandy-haired man said, 'I should have, so it seems.'

'Bit late now,' Peel said. 'Let's go somewhere and have a little chat, shall we?'

'That won't do, Terry, you know that.'

'You can't win, Henry. My man there is ex-*Spetsnaz*. He can make you a paraplegic and we still get to have our talk. Why don't we keep it civilized? We might even be able to work something out so that nobody has to feed the worms.'

'Really, Terry, I hoped you'd think better of me than that—'

With that Henry leaped to the side, a move unexpected enough so that Ruzhyó shot missed his spine and punched a small hole over the man's left kidney. The blast was loud, channeled by the books and shelves so that it lapped back over the three men. They had a few seconds left to finish this at most.

'Alive!' Peel shouted, pulling his own gun.

Ruzhyó tracked Henry's right hand, knowing that was the one closest to his hidden pistol. He would shoot for the hand, and if he missed, an abdominal shot with a .22 wouldn't be immediately fatal—

Maybe Henry realized he couldn't get his own pistol out fast enough to outshoot them. He didn't even try. Instead, he shoved his left wrist to his mouth and bit down on his watch band. Ruzhyó knew what the move meant, and apparently, so did Peel, who said, 'Bugger!'

Ruzhyó put his pistol back into his pocket, turned, and headed for the exit at a fast walk. Peel was right behind him. People, even bookworms, would come to see what the noise was about.

Whatever poison pill Henry had just bitten into was undoubtedly fast-acting, and there was no way to torture information from a man who would rather kill himself than reveal it. A pro, all right. Henry would probably be dead before any medical help could reach him. Ruzhyó respected a man who died well. If you knew your time was up, it was better go out the way you elected to leave. You lost the war, but if you could cheat your enemy of anything at that point, you could carry some small satisfaction with you to your grave.

Outside on the sidewalk again and moving moderately fast but not running, Peel gained past Ruzhyó and headed for his car. He said, 'I rather liked old Henry. A shame.'

As he followed him, Ruzhyó considered how he was going to rid himself of the Beretta. He would have to lose it somewhere as soon as possible. A man was dead in a bookstore, and it would be poison that caused his demise, but even a hollowpoint sometimes retained enough of itself to be matched ballistically to the gun that had fired it. And a gun that could be connected to a dead man was a bad talisman to have around.

31

Tuesday
Washington, D.C.

Jay brought Saji a glass of water, shook his head, and said, 'You're really enjoying this, aren't you?'

Seated in the overstuffed chair, she smiled. 'More than I should, yes.'

He went to sit on the beat-up gray leather couch he'd bought at a garage sale. There was a faint smell of patchouli in the air. Her perfume? Residue from incense clinging to her hair? God, she was gorgeous. 'I should know better after all my years on the net, but I didn't expect this.'

'Does it bother you that much?'

He thought about it for a second. 'No. Not really. It's the mind that matters, not the body.'

'That's to your credit, Jay. You really believe it. If I had known that when we met I wouldn't have bothered with the disguise.'

'So satisfy my curiosity, why did you?'

She swirled the ice cubes in her glass. 'You want the quick answer or the lecture?'

'Oh, go for the lecture. Condensed books are usually boring.'

She smiled. 'All right. Buddhism is like a lot of traditional religions, in that for a long time virtually all of the ranking practitioners were men. Oh, there have always been nuns and women laity who walked the path as well as any man, but for a lot of folks even now there is a gender bias. And in most traditional holy books – the Bible, the Koran, the Upanishads, and most Buddhist literature – when women are referred to at all, it is with a paternalistic and condescending tone, even while supposedly singing their praises: Women are the keepers of life, the bearers of children, the weaker, needs-to-be-protected-from-the-harsh-world sex. Blah, blah, blah. Most old-style religions see women more as property than as people. A man has a farm, goats, cattle, and a wife. Women have had the vote in this country for less than a hundred years. You still with me?'

'Flow on, I'm here.'

'Okay. So, the philosophies want to keep the girls barefoot and pregnant, tending the home fires while serious business is conducted by the boys. With few exceptions – various kinds of Goddess worship and Wicca and the like – until very recently, women were not really considered major players when it came to doctrine or practice, even in the more 'neutral' religions. There still aren't any Catholic priests who are women. In some of the Moslem countries, women still can't show their faces in public. It isn't as bad in Buddhism as some of the others, and great strides have been made in the last hundred years, but there is still a kind of unspoken belief among serious students that women aren't quite as good at it as men. Physicality discounted, women don't think the same way as men. Female chess players at the highest levels don't beat the male champions. Most men are better in spatial tests, in pure left-brain thinking than women. Men – and some women – see this as reason that they should be in charge. Equality has been a long time coming, and in most places it still does not truly exist.'

Jay nodded. He knew this. And he could see where it was going, but he said, 'Still here.'

'In a lot of circles, if they think you're an old man, you get a lot more respect than if they think you're a young woman. Truth is truth, but a lot of people look to see who delivers it before they accept it. You know the old Hollywood joke about the producer and the writer? The writer sends in a script to the producer who is in a hurry for it. Weeks pass, the producer doesn't call back. Finally the writer calls him. Says, "Well, did you read the script?" "Yeah, I read it." "So, what did you think?" The producer says, "I dunno what I think – nobody else has read it yet." '

She shook her head. 'That's how it works in religion sometimes. If you have a choice between a seventy-year-old man and a twenty-something girl offering nuggets of wisdom, when push comes to shove, you pick the old guy. Old and wise are better than young and stupid.'

'That's dumb,' Jay said. 'If you can walk the walk as good as an old guy, it shouldn't matter. It's *what* you say, not *who* says it that counts.'

She rewarded him with a big smile. 'I love you. Marry me,' she said.

He blinked. 'Huh?'

She laughed, a deep and melodious sound. 'We'll get back to that part of the Dharma later. How goes the monster hunt?'

He sighed. 'About to get really scary.'

'That's why I'm here. I think I should go with you.'

Wednesday, April 13th
London, England

Stephens drove the Bentley along at a proper pace toward the computerworks. Goswell reclined in back, the scent of fresh mink oil hand-rubbed into the leather a familiar and pleasing smell. Traffic was, as usual, awful, but Stephens was quite capable of dealing with anything London could throw at him. Goswell leaned back and enjoyed the ride.

A short while later, Stephens said, 'Milord. There

is a telephone call for you. Sir Harold.'

'Yes, I'll take it.'

Stephens passed over a mobile phone. 'Hallo, Harry.'

'Hallo, Gossie. Out and about, are we?'

'In the car, yes. Off for a bit of an inspection tour of one of the facilities. Can't let the help get too complacent, can we?'

'Certainly not. Er . . . I say, Gossie . . . that is, hmm.'

'Something bothering you, Harry?'

'Well, yes. You had a conversation with a man by the name of, er . . . Pound-Sand recently? Regarding a matter of some delicacy of which we spoke at the club?'

'I do recall that, yes.'

'Er, well, it seems that Mr Pound-Sand has . . . passed away.'

'Oh, dear.'

'Yes. Quite unexpectedly.'

'A sudden illness?'

'Very sudden, I'm afraid. I am given to understand that it happened even as he was attending to that very matter of delicacy. That, er, it was a more or less direct result of that very thing.'

'How unfortunate.'

'Isn't it.'

'Well, these things happen.'

'Yes. Would you like for me to give Mr Pound-Sand's associates a jingle? See if one of them might be interested in continuing the matter?'

Goswell thought about it for a second. 'That's decent of you, Harry, but perhaps we should wait a bit on that.'

'As you feel best, Gossie. I'm awfully sorry about this.'

'Tut, not your fault at all, Harry. It's obvious I underestimated the problem myself. Think no more about it.'

As Goswell handed the mobile back to Stephens, however, he thought about it. So Mr Pound-Sand was now Mr Pushing-up-the-Daisies. Which meant that Peel was either lucky or good, or perhaps both. On the one hand that gave Goswell a certain feeling of pride, that his man was adept enough to thwart an assassination by another professional. On the other hand, that also meant Peel would now be on his guard more than ever, and if he had been difficult to remove before, he would be doubly so now.

Hmm. That was certainly food for thought, wasn't it?

'We're very nearly there, milord.'

'What? Oh, yes. Quite.'

Well. One thing at a time. First he would be certain that Bascomb-Coombs was out of the loop. Then he would figure out a way to deal with the turncoat Peel.

Wednesday
London, England

'We got a break, Colonel,' Fernandez said.

Howard looked up from the stack of reports he was reading. They were in Michaels' temporary office, and the Commander and his second were down the hall talking to one of the MI-6 higher ups.

'How so?'

'Miz Cooper just came up with this.' He passed a hardcopy wax-laser drum photograph over.

Howard looked at the wazer image. 'Ruzhyó!'

'Yes, sir.' There was a long pause.

'All right, Sergeant, get off the dime. Where and when?'

'Sir.' He grinned. 'Yesterday the London police were called to an incident at a small bookstore near Piccadilly Circus. They found a body on the floor, shot. The dead man is one Henry Wyndham, a former MI-5 agent who ran a 'security service.' Cooper says that the local authorities suspect Wyndham was a high-priced and very discrete ice man for rich clients, but nobody has ever been able to pin him down. Turns out the bullet didn't kill him – he apparently croaked from a fast-acting poison. This picture was from the store's occult door cam, one of two men who left about the time patrons heard the shot. Here's the other man.'

Fernandez offered another picture.

'Anybody we know?'

'Not us. Cooper is working on an ID.'

Howard nodded. 'So, he's still in London. And he just killed somebody. I wonder why.'

'Why he's here? Or why he killed somebody?'

'Both.'

'Well, it could be a coincidence, he just happened to be browsing for a nice Agatha Christie novel to while away the hours when somebody got capped the next aisle over.'

'Right. Can we backtrack the dead man?'

'Cooper is working on that, too, sir.'

Howard nodded again. 'Good. Would it do us any good to go and talk to the bookstore employees?'

'Cooper is sending over the police reports, says we can access 'em on the computer in a couple of minutes. But she says nobody saw the two men come in or leave.'

'I bet the late Mr Wyndham saw them come in.'

'But not leave. The cops haven't seen anything like this before. The dead guy was armed. The guess is, somebody shoved a gun into his back, he tried to get out of the way. He took a small caliber round at contact range, probably a .22. It wouldn't have killed him, the examiner says, but he must have figured he was gonna lose, so he erased himself. The poison was one of the new explosive-pellet neurotoxins. Guy had ninety seconds once he bit the capsule and it spewed.'

'Interesting.'

'Yeah, ain't it?'

'Well, don't just stand there, go see if Ms Cooper can find some use for you. He's close, Julio. We're going to get him. I can feel it.'

'Yeah.'

Wednesday
Washington, D.C.

It was sunny, no wind, a perfect day for working the 'rangs, and Tyrone headed for the soccer field, full of himself. Bella had given her smile back to him, she wanted him around, wanted to see him, had invited him to her *house* this very evening! Life was better than good, life was great.

When he arrived at the field there, Tyrone saw Nadine. Dee-eff-eff!

But when he got to where Nadine was, she was already packing up.

'Hey, Nadine.'

'Hey, Tyrone.'

'Where you going?'

'My arm's a little sore. I don't want to overtrain.'

'I've got some Ibuprofen gel.'

'That's okay. I got some at home. See you.'

Something was wrong, he could feel it, but he couldn't see what it was. 'You okay?'

She looked him straight in the eyes. 'I told you

my arm was sore, you forget to turn on your implant?' There was a definite hard edge in her voice.

'Whoa, dial it down, I wasn't calling you a preva, I was just asking, that's all.'

She went back to loading her backpack. 'Why do you care? You don't need to be skulking with people like me. You got Belladonna.'

'What's that got to do with anything?'

She crowed the pack shut, lifted it, swung it over her shoulder. 'C'mon, Tyrone, you know what it means. You sweat with the jocks, you don't hunch chair with the gamers. You breakfast with the dressers, you don't eat lunch at the scuzz table.'

'What are you *talking* about?'

'You gonna make me say it, aren't you? You skulk beautiful, you don't skulk ugly.'

'Who is ugly?'

She gave him a sad smile, a little one. 'You telling me I'm in Bella's league, Ty? You'd rather be seen with me than with her?'

He was stunned, he couldn't get his mind online. Why was Nadine babbling on about this? Of course Bella was prettier. She was prettier than everybody in the school! What was the point?

He was trying to figure out what Nadine meant, and what he should say, when she shook her head. 'Yeah, I hear the dial tone. Copy you later, Ty.'

She slipped her other arm into the backpack and walked out.

Tyrone watched her go, and while he hadn't done anything wrong he could think of, he felt guilty. Somehow he had just failed some kind of test – and he didn't even know what it was.

Damn. He wished his father was home. Dad knew about stuff like this. He needed to talk to him.

32

Wednesday
London, England

Something was wrong, Toni knew. The small cracks in Alex's facade had been plugged up, spackled over, leaving a solid wall in front of his emotions. It wasn't so much what he said or did, but an unseen though somehow detectable shift in his posture. From her years of martial arts training, she had a tendency to view things in terms of physical engagements. What it felt like was, all of a sudden, Alex stood in a defensive stance. When they'd met, his guard had been up, but he had relaxed it when they'd gotten together, allowed her to get closer. Now, he was hunched over, face covered, backing away.

Sitting in a strange office halfway around the world from her roots, Toni worried about it. What had happened? Sure, he had a lot on his mind, the looming custody battle, the mad hacker and their relationship had a few bumps in the road but none of that seemed to be enough to account for this sudden distance between them.

'Ms Fiorella?'

She looked up. Cooper. 'Yes?'

'Your Colonel Howard has some information on his assassin. He'd like your opinion on it. He's in the small conference room.'

'Okay. Be right there.'

Cooper left, and Toni shook the worry about Alex. She did have a job to do, and while Alex certainly was a complicating factor in it, she couldn't sit here worry-warting about her love life all day. She picked up her flatscreen and headed for the conference room and John Howard.

Howard glanced away from the holoproj as Toni Fiorella entered the room. Julio was there, but Angela Cooper and Alex Michaels were meeting with one of the MI-6 higher-ups and would be a few minutes.

'John. What's up?'

'Toni. The Commander will be along in a little while, Ms Cooper went to collect him, but I wanted to bring you up to speed on the Ruzhyó matter.'

'Sure, fire away.'

He laid it out for her, using the holoproj images to punctuate the briefing. He did a fast sitrep through the stuff she already knew then got to the new information.

The holoproj image shifted to the occult cam view from the bookstore. 'This man left the store after the incident, at almost the same time as Ruzhyó. According to what Ms Cooper and her people have found, this is Terrance Arthur Peel, a retired British Army major. Julio, would you lay out the rest?'

'Sir. Ma'am. Peel had a fairly decent career until he was posted to Ireland a couple years back as part of the standing British force at one of the permanent treaty bases. The peace there is fairly fragile, oddball groups still agitating, and from what we're able to gather, Peel was responsible for an incident that might have threatened it. Caught some of the locals doing things they shouldn't have, and beat confessions out of them. Apparently he and his people were . . . over-zealous. There were some serious injuries, even deaths, as a result.'

Toni nodded. 'Uh huh.'

Fernandez continued: 'The British Army is relatively tight-lipped about all this, but Peel was apparently given the choice of falling on his own sword or being drummed out, so he retired, and the incident was swept under the rug. Next time he surfaced, he was providing security for a local bigwig, Lord Geoffrey Goswell. Peel's new boss is not only a nobleman, he is also richer than Midas, a crusty old billionaire who owns half a dozen companies producing everything from computers to catsup.'

Toni considered the information for a moment. She had an idea where this was going, but she wanted to hear Howard's take on it. She looked from Fernandez to the colonel. 'I see. And this leads you to believe . . . ?'

Howard shrugged. 'We really don't have enough information to make a conclusion yet. But it seems awfully coincidental that a former intelligence operative gets shot and poisoned in a bookstore, and a few seconds later a known killer *and* a disgraced army major busted for killing prisoners both saunter out the door. If I was a gambling man, I'd be willing to bet these two had something to do with the death. And with each other.'

'You think Ruzhyó is working for Peel? Hired to catch or kill the guy in the bookstore?'

'Like I said, it's too soon to make that stretch for sure, but it certainly seems as if we ought to have a chat with this guy Peel. Even if he is totally innocent, at the very least he was there when the trouble went down, and he had to have seen Ruzhyó when he left. If Ruzhyó had been a second slower leaving, Peel would have stepped on his heels.'

Toni nodded again. 'All right. How do we go about it?'

'Cooper will set it up. We can go along as observers. No guns needed. Apparently Lord Whatshisname is quite well connected and beyond reproach.'

Fernandez said, 'Right. We knock on the door, have a spot of tea, then politely ask the major, 'I say, old bean, did you shoot somebody in a bookstore recently?' and he says, "Happens I did, old boy. Is there a problem?" They are all very civilized here, pip, pip, eh, what?'

Toni laughed.

From the sound of her laugh, Howard figured she still hadn't gotten around to discussing Angela Cooper with the Commander. Well. It sure as hell wasn't his business, and he wasn't going to—

His virgil peeped, the tone indicating it was a personal call. He frowned. He wasn't really in the field, so he hadn't shut off everything but tactical reach yet; still, it was unusual for his wife to call. 'Excuse me a moment,' he said. He walked away from the table and pulled the virgil from his belt. Mindful of where he was, he kept his visual transmission off.

'Hello?'

'Hey, Dad.'

'Tyrone. Everything okay? Your mother—?'

'Mom's fine, we're three by three and go ahead here, Dad.'

Howard relaxed. Nobody had gotten into a car accident or anything. 'What's sailing, son?'

'I don't want to bother you if you're busy.'

'I'm not that busy. Shoot.'

There was a pause. It stretched.

'We are talking transcontinental rates here, Tyrone.'

'Sorry. Well, there's this girl at school . . .'

Howard listened to his son pour out his problem, and felt himself grinning. Whenever anybody asked him if he'd like to go back and live his life over, he'd always told them no, not a chance. He hadn't made so many mistakes that he would go through puberty again to make up for them. No, sir.

Fiorella and Fernandez ignored him, looking at the computer visuals, and after a little while Cooper and Michaels arrived.

Finally, his son ran down. 'So, whaddya you think, Pop?'

'Well, I could be wrong, but I think your boomerang girl likes you. And she's maybe a little jealous of Bella.'

'Oh, yeah?'

'Yeah. And she might have a point, too. Why do you like hanging around with Nadine?'

'She can *throw*, Dad. She's smart, she's funny, and she's got an arm to sell your comic collection for.'

'But she's not much of a looker?'

'Not really.'

'And Bella?'

'Jeez, Dad; she's gorgeous!'

'And if my memory serves, she's also got a mean streak. You remember talking to me about her when she cut you loose before?'

'Yeah.'

'She thumped you pretty good once before. You got any reason to believe she won't do it again, if it suits her?'

'Uh . . . no. But maybe she realized she made a mistake.'

'And maybe you're more desirable because somebody else wants you.'

'Nadine? No offense, but I can't see that Bella

would be the least bit worried about Nadine, Dad. She's fun and all, but she's not somebody you'd cross the street to get a better look at.'

'If Nadine is athletic, smart, and funny, some people might find that intimidating, especially if they aren't.'

'You mean *Bella* is *jealous* of *Nadine*?'

Howard chuckled. Tyrone spoke in the same tone of voice he might use if he'd just heard his father say he was going to fly home by jumping into the air and flapping his arms real fast.

'What else changed, son, since she dropped you?'

'Nothing.' Another silence. Then, 'Man.'

'It's nice to be wanted,' Howard said. 'But you have to ask yourself who wants you, and why. You can't blame anybody for the face and form God gives them, but they can't take any credit for those looks either. Unless maybe they've paid for a lot of expensive plastic surgery.'

'What are you saying here, Dad?'

'If Bella wasn't beautiful, if she was plain, or even ugly, would you want to spend time with her? Has she got something going for her other than what she looks like? Would you cross the street to talk to her, if you couldn't look at her when you did it?'

This dead air was getting real expensive.

'Uh . . .'

'Think about it. Let it perk for a while and see what comes out.'

'Oh, man. I guess I better go. Uh, thanks, Dad.'

'Say hello to Mom for me.'

'I will. Discom.'

'Bye, son.'

Howard hooked the virgil back to his belt. He was a soldier, and he was going to be gone a lot, that was the nature of soldiering, but he worried about not being there for his son. A man had to do his job, but a man also had responsibilities to his family. Whatever else was going on, he had a son who needed a father's help. There were values that needed to be passed on, lessons to be taught. He had to remember that. It was important.

33

Wednesday
Upper Cretaceous
What will be Western Europe

Ferns as tall as pine trees loomed in the sweltering heat, and dragonflies the size of hawks flitted among the lush greenery, hunting mosquitoes that could pass for skinny sparrows. This was primeval, primordial, hot, wet, and dank in ways far beyond a tropical rainforest.

The wide-base Humvee hit a dip and a mound of humus that might grow up to be part of an oil field in twenty or thirty million years. The front wheel on the passenger side bounced into the air and clawed at nothing, but the other three studded tires had enough traction to clear the decaying lump before dropping the vehicle back on all fours.

Jay's teeth clacked together, hard.

Belted into the passenger seat, Saji said, 'Damn, Jay! You want me to drive?'

Jay gunned the powerful engine. The Humvee lurched forward. 'Like you could do any better.'

'I don't see how I could do any worse. Unless maybe I drove off a cliff.'

The damp ground leveled out a little and the tire studs dug in and pushed the wide-track along a little faster. 'It's not as easy as it looks.'

'Well, the way you do it, easy isn't the word that leaps to mind.'

He was trying to come up with a killer comeback when he spotted the smashed ferns. He slowed, crept a few feet closer to the downed plants, then pulled the UV over and put it into neutral. He glanced at Saji. 'You can stay here while I go look. Stand by the gun, if you want.'

There was a .50 caliber water-cooled belt-fed Browning machinegun mounted on the uncovered rear deck of the Humvee. Clipped to the deck was also a shoulder-operated, laser-guided anti-tank rocket launcher and half a dozen rockets. Jay had considered bringing rifles and shotguns but decided not to bother. Anything smaller wouldn't do the job. He would have preferred a tank and spent-uranium armor piercing rounds to shoot from it, but, relatively speaking, the rocket launcher was the biggest thing he could carry in this scenario. Anything more powerful simply wouldn't work.

Unfortunately.

'I'd rather not,' Saji said. She wore a set of bush khaki shorts and shirt, with Nike waffle-stompers and knee socks rolled down. She was gorgeous in the tropical clothing. He wondered what she looked like without any clothes.

'All right. Slide over and take the wheel, then. Leave the engine running. We might need to takeoff in a hurry.'

He alighted and walked toward the smashed fern boles over fairly springy ground covered with what looked like green moss.

He could hardly have missed the footprint. Three toes and a pad, no heel. A little water had seeped into the bottom of the print, which was big enough so that if you completely filled it you could sit down and take a bath.

Jay swallowed dryly. Jesus, look at that thing. He followed the direction of the toes. Twenty-five feet ahead was another footprint, and there was a definite path through the brush ahead of that, as if somebody had driven a big diesel tractor-trailer through the forest, knocking down anything that got in its way.

Jay stared at the trail of destruction. It wasn't a truck. Nope. It was Rex Regum, the king of kings, Carnosaur Supreme, the ultimate predator. Made your average Tyrannosaur look like somebody's pet iguana. The thing could run from one end of a football field to the other in a dozen steps. Probably was fifty feet tall, not even counting the tail.

Following its trail wasn't gonna be a problem. But like a dog chasing a car, the question was, what would he do if he caught it? That machinegun might not be enough to accomplish the job, and if he got close enough to use the rocket launcher and he missed, he wasn't gonna get a second shot. He turned and headed back to the car. 'Move over,' he told Saji.

'Doesn't look as if cutting sign is going to be a problem,' she said.

'No, I don't think so.' He put the car in gear and started following the monster's trail.

Since his brain had more or less stared working again, albeit somewhat slowly, Jay had turned the problem over and over, trying to come up with an explanation – any explanation – as to how such a brute could exist. What could have created it? And with technology as he knew it there simply wasn't an answer. But as they drove down the VR path looking for the beast, he thought again about the old Sherlock Holmes dictum about eliminating the impossible and dealing with the unlikely remainder. Nothing he knew about had this kind of power, and he knew a lot about computers. But, given that the thing existed, what could be responsible? What would it take? There weren't too many possibilities, but only one made any sense and that was theoretical – the hardware didn't exist to make it work.

But what if, by some miracle, it *did* exist?

'Better go left here,' Saji said.

'Really? I thought I'd just drive into that big tree instead.'

'Just trying to be helpful.'

He shook his head. 'Sorry. I'm distracted.'

'Something on your mind?'

'A theory.'

'Want to bounce it off me?'

Jay looked at the swatch of destruction that ran through the VR jungle. He had to catch up with Godzilla's nasty brother, but the more he knew about him, the better. Anything to clarify his thoughts was good. 'Sure,' he said.

Wednesday
The Yews, Sussex, England

His Lordship had gone off to his club, escorts fore and aft, and Peel was in the little church on the telephone, currently on hold. Outside, along with Peel's regular crew, the man from Chetsnya waited in a rental car, watching for potential enemies. He should be safe here, Peel figured, but he couldn't bet his life on that. What was he going to do about the bloody scientist? Should he kill him now?

Naturally, the first thing Peel had tried to do when he started worrying that maybe Bascomb-Coombs wasn't on the level with him, was to withdraw the million from the Indonesian bank. Had he been able to transfer the money into England, he would have felt a lot better, and that would also have gone a long way toward assuaging his fears.

Unfortunately, all kinds of electronic transactions had been disrupted, courtesy of Bascomb-Coombs' infernal computer. All Peel had been able to get from his computer login was a 'transfer pending' notation, awaiting some final clearance that never happened.

Given the computer problems worldwide, this could have been a legitimate response. It was possible.

But it was also possible that this might be a clever ruse by Bascomb-Coombs, one easily hidden by the chaos he had himself caused. By the time things cleared up, Peel might be dead.

'This is Vice-President Imandihardjo,' came a man's voice. 'How may I help you?'

Peel turned his attention back to the phone. At last, the bloody Indonesian banker. 'Right. My name is Peel. I need to check the status of my account.'

He could almost hear the man frown. Check an account? For this you needed a vice-president? 'Your name and password, please?'

Peel gave it to him.

There was a long pause. 'Ah, Mr Bellsong, yes, I see it.'

Peel shook his head. Bellsong. The song of a bell, and thus Bascomb-Coombs' little joke: 'Peal.' Same sound, different spelling.

'You have my account information?'

'Yes, sir, I certainly do.' The VP's voice shifted; it now had that obsequious tone that big chunks of money sometimes brought from those who weren't rich. This was good.

'I should like to transfer part of the account into another bank.'

'Certainly, certainly. If you will give me the particulars?'

Peel rattled off his English account number and password. He would move it, and once he was sure it had cleared he would breathe a lot easier.

A moment later, the banker said, 'Ah, Mr Bellsong, there appears to be a problem with our system.'

'Really?'

'Yes, sir, I'm sure it's nothing major, but I'm afraid I can't access anything but the balance. The computer won't let me make a transfer.'

Peel nodded to himself. Well, well.

'Hmm. It seems that there are several dozen accounts affected. I'm sure it's only a temporary aberration.'

'You mean I can't get my money out until it's fixed?'

'Ah, well, I'm afraid so, yes.'

'I see.' That was all Peel needed to hear. His bowels clenched and went cold. He had a sudden, deep suspicion that what the Indonesian bank would find on closer examination would be electron money-demon dollars that glittered brightly if you looked at them peripherally, but that would turn to smoke and vanish if you tried to lay your hands on them. Bascomb-Coombs was having him on.

'I'm sure this will be cleared up very soon. If you will give me a number where I can reach you, I shall call as soon as we've resolved the problem.'

Right.

Peel gave his number but he wasn't going to hold his breath. He'd been skewered, and he knew who was holding the shaft, too. Time to go and have a chat with Mr Bascomb-Coombs. Yes, indeed.

Almost as he thought this, his phone buzzed. The private line.

'Yes?'

'Hello, Terrance.' Well, well. Speak of the Devil.

'Hello.'

'I'm afraid we have something of problem. It seems His Lordship has given orders cutting my access to my ah toy. He has shut down all the apparent external lines and posted a guard to keep me from physically entering the building.'

'Really? Why is that?'

'I suspect the old boy doesn't trust me.'

Good bloody reason for that, Peel thought. Then another thought popped up. ' "Apparent external lines," you said?'

Bascomb-Coombs had his visual mode off, but Peel could almost see him smile. 'Very good, Terrance. Naturally, I have a few digital and microwave transceiver links carefully hidden around the hardware. Even a landline wired into the power supply, if anybody thinks to use jammers. They'd have to take it down to the floorboards to cut off my connection, and since they don't know it's there, they won't. If they shut it off, they know they might not ever be able to get it up and running again.'

'I see. And what does this mean?'

'I believe we shall have to deal with the old boy. Using *your* area of expertise.'

'You think so?'

'I'm afraid I do. I must ring off now but I'll call you back shortly. Give it some thought, would you?'

The scientist broke the connection. Peel stared at the wall of his office. God, the man had brass balls. Here he was trying to have Peel himself iced, and pretending as if nothing had happened as he ordered him to kill their mutual employer. Bloody nerve, all right.

He would, Peel realized, be better off with both of them gone. Bascomb-Coombs had to depart this mortal coil, of course; a man who tried to have you assassinated could hardly be allowed to live. And Goswell might be in his dotage, but he wasn't completely senile. Sooner or later, he might tumble to the fact that his security chief had sold him out to the mad scientist, and that would be extremely bad. He doubted the old man would reach for his blackpowder shotgun to blast him, but certainly he would be able to see to it that Peel never worked in the U.K. again. With a million in the bank, such a thing hadn't worried him, but if the money was no more than a ruse by Bascomb-Coombs, then Peel would be, in a word, screwed.

If Bascomb-Coombs went missing, and His Lordship fell over with a stroke or heart attack, then Peel would be in the clear, nobody to tell tales. He might not be rich, but he would still be marketable. With a spotless record under His Lordship, some other rich fool would find him worthy.

Victory was better than defeat, but there were times when you had to cut your losses and retreat, to survive long enough to try another tack. He had pulled in Ruzhyó because he needed a goat for taking out the old man, but now, given the change of situation, it was better that Goswell die of natural causes, so his security chief wouldn't look bad.

Bascomb-Coombs would simply disappear in such a way that nobody would ever find him.

Peel smiled. Yes. This was all unfortunate, but not beyond repair. Time to fix things and get on with it. Kill them all – God will know his own. One of the early Popes had said that, hadn't he? *Better them than me.*

34

Wednesday
London, England

During a lull in the increasingly frantic activity at MI-6, Toni got on the com to call Carl Stewart.

'Hello?'

'Carl?'

'Ah, Toni. How are you?'

'Fine. Look, I'm up to my eyebrows in work and I can't see any way to get out of it for class tonight. Sorry.'

'Not a problem. We'll miss you, but I understand.'

'Thanks.'

After a short pause, he said, 'Well, you do have to eat, though, don't you? Perhaps we can have lunch or dinner later this week?'

Toni's stomach did a small lurch. It wasn't the words but the tone of them that raised the alarm. Was he asking her out on a date? That would have been her most direct question but Toni wasn't quite ready to ask it. Should she follow that up? Or brush it off? It was moot if she said she was too busy. But no. She had been doing more waffling lately than she liked. It was time to start facing these things head-on.

'Are we talking about two *silat* students getting together for a bite, Carl? Or are we talking about something else?'

'Well. I was thinking along the lines of two people who found each other's company interesting and who had a deep interest – *pentjak silat* – in common.'

A date.

Toni's kneejerk response was to tell him she was involved with somebody and decline politely. The window for her comment opened . . . and stayed open. He was a vital man, attractive, and he had a skill she much admired. If she and Stewart went to the *gelanggang* – the fighting floor – for a serious match, he would win, she did not doubt it. She couldn't say that about many people she knew. She was sure that even her own guru, now in her eighties, was no longer up to her level, and she was pretty confident she could keep up with most martial artists, men or women, when it came to one-on-one, however egotistical that might be. But she knew she couldn't defeat Carl. And that was, in its way, a large part of the attraction. She had a momentary vision of what it might be like to lie naked on a bed with this powerful and skilled man, and it was not an unattractive daydream. Not at all unattractive. In fact . . .

She felt a shard of guilt stab her. 'I'm pretty much

involved with Alex, Carl, and I appreciate it, but I think maybe we ought to keep things strictly professional.'

'Ah, too bad. But certainly I understand. I appreciate your candor. Let me know when you can come back to class.'

'I will. Thanks.'

After she hung up, Toni had a sick feeling, a cold stirring in her gut. It had, for a moment, been tempting. More so than she wanted to admit. She could have gone down that path, and it bothered her that she had even considered it. She admired Carl, maybe even had a bit of lust for him, but she *loved* Alex, and there was a world of difference between those two things. For just a moment there, however, she had wondered, had felt indecision, had *considered* it.

'Can't hang you for thinking' was an old saying that was true because nobody could know what was in your mind, but you couldn't fool yourself for very long. How could it have even crossed her mind? This was bad. Bad.

Wednesday
The Yews, Sussex, England

Ruzhyó adjusted the 9mm Firestar pistol in the clip-on holster on his hip under his windbreaker, canting the butt forward slightly to make it more comfortable. The previous handgun Peel had furnished him, the American-made Italian .22, was at the bottom of the Thames, wiped clean and broken into pieces, the frame and the barrel of which were separated by more than two miles. If anybody happened to dredge the parts up before they rusted out, assembled them, and ran ballistic tests and determined that the bullet in the dead man in the bookstore had come from the pistol, it wouldn't matter; there was nothing to connect Ruzhyó to it. But if you left nothing to chance, then chance would not be so likely to sneak up behind you and fasten its teeth in your back.

He did not much care for the new weapon, but he could use it. It was solid, well made, a single-action chrome-plated steel semi-automatic that operated much like the old Colt .45 military models, a reliable, small, if somewhat heavy, piece. The gun carried seven jacketed hollowpoints in the magazine and one more in the chamber with special, scored noses that would expand in a human, causing much damage. The thing had not been designed to punch paper at a range, or to plink old cans in the woods, but to shoot soft targets and seriously damage or kill them.

Ruzhyó smiled. For the last several years, especially in the US, gun makers had been under legal attacks by anti-gun forces. The more recent tactic had been to sue the manufacturers for not providing adequate safety devices or warnings of danger. He could not believe how foolish this was. Carried to its extreme, there would be similar warnings necessary for automobiles, knives, even matches: Caution! You might be killed if you collide with a big truck while driving this small car! Warning! This knife has a sharp edge – do not press it against your throat! Danger! Matches can create fire that can burn you!

This gun labeling scheme seemed to him monumentally stupid to anyone with half a working brain. It was one thing to require a lock that children could not easily open, another thing to stamp on the barrel of a gun: Caution! Do not point at someone and pull the trigger! Anybody who did not understand what a gun was and what it did would not be able to read such a warning anyhow. It reminded him of the old advertisement that used to be on the electric buses in Chetsnya when he'd been young: 'Are you illiterate? If so, please contact . . .'

The 9mm would do the job for Ruzhyó, and there was the umbrella to back it up. In addition, he had bought a Benchmade tactical folder, a knife that could be flicked open with a thumb, to lock its four-inch *tanto*-point blade rigidly into place. Given the local laws, with two guns and a knife, he was probably armed better than almost anybody walking around in this country, including most police officers. As he had in the Nevada desert,

Ruzhyó felt the need to have the weapons. Things were about to go bad here, he could feel it.

He considered leaving. Simply catching a boat or train or plane for a short hop out of the country, then heading home, staying on the round to avoid directional tracking. He could do it, and Peel wouldn't miss him in time to stop him, even if he wanted to.

Ruzhyó, however, was tired. And looking over his shoulder made him more tired. He had the Americans back there somewhere, and eventually they might figure out how to track him. He did not need another enemy dogging his trail. No, he would finish this business with Peel first, and when he left, it would be on his own terms. One way or another, he would resolve things. Once he was home, then what came, came, and he would deal with it.

Peel came out of the converted church and nodded in his direction before setting off for his own car. Ruzhyó nodded in return and started his car's engine. They were going back to see the computer scientist where Ruzhyó had spotted the surveillance that had ended with a dead man in a bookstore. Apparently Major Peel had plans for the man in that building that Mr Bascomb-Coombs would not in the least enjoy.

Ruzhyó didn't care about the scientist. He would stay with Peel until the right opportunity came up, and then he would take his leave. And it would be soon, he reflected as they pulled out of the estate. Soon.

Wednesday
Washington, D.C.

There had been an all-hours assembly at school, and when it was done Tyrone drifted down the hall, waving at Jimmy-Joe in passing. The hall-monster Essay had indeed been expelled, for at least two weeks, and while there were other denizens to be avoided in the corridors, they weren't in the big idiot's league.

As he headed for the bus queue he saw Bella, book reader in hand, walking and laughing with three girlfriends. She spotted him and smiled. 'Ty, hey, over here.'

He felt that rush of belly-clenching cold energy that radiated excitement all the way to his groin. He started toward her, holding his steps slow so as not to seem in a hurry. He tried to look sparse, matter-of-fact, and AF – almost frozen – he was so cool. Bella wanted to see him? That was DFF and all, but no huge kluge, hey? Amble. That was the look he wanted. But he moved maybe a little too fast to pull it off. Kind of a twelve-frames-per-second amble that would look a lot better at twenty-four.

'Hey, Bella.'

'We're going to the mall. You want to come along?'

He smiled. And at that second, just when he was about to deliver a liquid-oxy AF 'Sure, why not?' he glanced past Bella and saw Nadine walking down the hall.

Nadine saw him, then looked away.

Bella caught his look and flicked her own gaze in that direction. It was quick, her peek, and she pretended not to notice, but Tyrone got it. Nadine had been inspected, stamped 'failed,' and dismissed, all in a half-second glance, thank you very much.

And all of a sudden, Tyrone Howard, pushing fourteen, found himself at the crossroads of the rest of his life. Looming here were two paths at right angles from each other, and not likely he would be able to switch from one to the other once he made his choice.

You got the com in your hand, Tyrone. Who are you gonna call?

Maybe he could still do both. He said, 'Why don't I meet you at the bus? I got something I have to take care of first.'

Bella might not be the brightest diode on the board but she wasn't so dim she couldn't see immediately what he was doing. She let him know she knew, too: 'We're going to the mall *now*, Ty.' What was left unsaid, was *Now or never, Tyrone. Your call.*

Well . . . shit. It would be great to be able to have his cake and eat it too, but that wasn't gonna happen, no way, no how, DSS-data scrambled stupid.

The moment stretched for a couple million years. He felt like he was going to explode. Damn, damn, damn! You could skulk one or you could skulk the other, but you didn't get both. Hell with it. He made his decision. 'Nadine! Hey, Nadine! Hold up a second!'

Nadine turned, surprised, he could see. He didn't dare look back at Bella, though he wanted to see her face. He'd been given a second chance to get into paradise, and he'd just put it in the trash and emptied that sucker. He wanted to run and hide.

Nadine smiled, and her face didn't seem so plain. When he got there, she said, 'Your girlfriend just left without you. Didn't look real happy, either.'

He shrugged. 'So what?' He felt bad, but he also felt good at the same time. 'How's the arm? You want to go throw some?'

'You sure about this?'

'I'm sure.'

The smile got bigger. 'My arm is a lot better now. Yeah. Let's go throw.'

As he walked along next to her Tyrone felt his own smile begin. Something his dad had told him. When you do the right thing, it almost always feels better than when you don't.

Score another one for the old man.

35

Thursday, April 14th
Upper Cretaceous
What will be Western France

'Looks as if it can swim,' Saji said.

Jay pulled the Humvee to a halt and shut the engine off. The monster's tracks led to the edge of a sea, disappearing into the water. Small, silky waves with pristine whitecaps rolled machine-like tubes onto the shore. 'Looks like,' he said.

'What now?'

'We change vehicles. Boat or helicopter. I'm favoring the copter.'

'I can understand that. Better to be a few hundred feet above it than sailing along and having it come up under us like Moby Dick.'

Jay nodded. 'The disadvantage is that we can arm the boat better than we can the helicopter. We're limited to weapons we can physically carry, so if we see it from the air, one of us has to lean out and shoot at it. You don't want a rocket launcher going off inside a copter. The exhaust gases would cook us as dead as if we got hit by the rocket itself.'

'There's a pleasant image. Why the limits on weaponry?'

'Well. Even in sim, you have to think about what the real situation is like. This thing is bigger and stronger and faster than we are, and we can't just lob a nuke at it, 'cause we don't *have* one vis-à-vis the hardware and software we are up against.' He stepped out of the car and looked at the shore. He pulled a GPS handheld from his jacket and consulted it. 'This is a cheat in this scenario,' he said. 'I should be looking at a paper map, since there are no global positioning satellites in this time. But we can get away with this. Not with a Seawolf-class sub, though. Too bad. And I'm not really sure this body of water would be here, either. My knowledge of geological history is not that great.'

Saji climbed out of the car, stretched, and said, 'Where is "here?" '

'Coast of France. What will be Great Britain is over the horizon that away.'

'So in RW, that's where the trail leads?'

'That's what it looks like, yeah.'

'Is that any help to your theory?'

Jay nodded. 'Yeah. Maybe.'

'Are we going after it?'

'Oh, yeah. I want to drop out of VR for a while to check some stuff and give the boss a call first. I think it would be a good idea to run my theory past him. Just in case.'

Thursday
London, England

In the MI-6 conference room, Michaels sat waiting for Jay's visual to appear on the call-waiting holoproj that floated bluely over the table. With him were Toni, Howard, Fernandez, and Angela Cooper.

Michaels said, 'I wanted you all to hear this, so I had them route Jay's com in here. We'll get to him in a minute. Any other business in the meanwhile?'

Howard said, 'We've got an appointment to see the retired major out at his employer's estate in –' he looked down at his flatscreen – 'in Sussex this afternoon.'

'A lovely drive,' Angela said. 'Beautiful country, if somewhat narrow roads.'

'No more attacks on major webs or military systems to note,' Toni said. 'Looks as if our hacker has backed off, at least for the time being.'

'I'll take any good news I can get,' Michaels said. 'Let's get Jay off hold.'

The holoproj flickered, and Jay Gridley's face appeared in the air. 'Hey, boss.' His voice sounded almost normal, just a trace of a slur. He was recovering fast.

'Jay. This is Angela Cooper, of MI-6. You know everybody else.'

Jay murmured greetings.

'Okay, tell us what you've got.'

Jay sighed. 'Well, it's not much. We – I have been on the program's track and it looks as if it's leading in your direction. Could be passing through, could be it lives there, I dunno. I'll get back after it as soon as we discom.

'I've been thinking about the problem. No working computers we know about could brute-force prime-number encoding the way this thing has, even working in multiple-series-parallel, so it's got to be something else. The first thing that comes to mind when you ask yourself what kind of computer *could* do it is, of course, a QC – a quantum computer. We talked about that before. The thing is, none of those are past the small experimental stages, so none of them would have the power needed to pull off what has happened.'

'I'm dense,' Fernandez said. 'What is a quantum computer?'

Jay gave them a short lecture, explaining about Qubits and multiple quantum states. Michaels was familiar with the concept, but as Jay had pointed out, nobody had come up with a full-size working QC, so it wasn't something they had seriously considered.

'But what if somebody had one?' Jay continued. 'A fully operational model? Something with a hundred or two hundred Qubits? It would blow through prime-number encryptions like a tornado through a straw house.'

'Big *if*,' Toni said.

'Yeah, but I've done a little poking around. None

of the various militaries and corps who have gone to the new AMPD standard – that's abstract-multidimensional-point-distance encryption – were bothered by these attacks. Could be coincidence, but a QC wouldn't be able to crack those. It wouldn't matter how fast it could crunch numbers, AMPD standard would be immune. Of course, only a handful of people have shifted to the new method.'

'All right,' Michaels said. 'But if somebody had created such a thing, wouldn't we know about it?'

'Eventually. You couldn't keep it hidden forever, but maybe you could for a while. The technology and gear necessary wouldn't be something you could cook up in a high-school computer lab or in the corner of your Uncle Albert's electronics hobby shop. We're talking a multimillion-dollar operation, custom-made hardware, lots of bells and whistles, a support staff, programmers, all like that. Sooner or later somebody will stumble into this from outside; it's just not something you can hide with a piece of camo net. But even if you knew where it was, as long as it was the only one out there, it'd sure be a big damned wolf among the sheep.'

'A QC seems kind of slim,' Toni said. 'Any corroborative information?'

'Nothing I can lay on a table and prove,' Jay said. 'Then again, if such a thing existed, it would perfectly fit the parameters.'

'And in your expert opinion, this is what you think it is?' That from Howard.

'Yes, sir. Nothing else comes close. I've searched the web and found everybody serious who's ever published anything in the field. On the list are a couple of guys in the U.K. One of whom – a man named Peter Bascomb-Coombs – did some flat-out brilliant theoretical work a couple of years back. He's head and shoulders above most, and I can't begin to stay with him. I don't even *know* anybody who can stay with him. He used to be in London, but he's dropped out of sight.'

Howard said, 'Are we looking at him as somebody to help us out? Or as a suspect?'

'Either way, I'd talk to him if I was there. I can't find a public e-address for him. It seems odd a guy that sharp would just disappear. He was too young to retire, and if he'd croaked there would have been something about it in the news.'

'Give us what you have on him and we'll check it out locally,' Michaels said.

'Already uploaded,' Jay said. There was a short pause, then he said, 'I've got to get back to the hunt. I think I'm gonna be able to run this beast down, I'm close.'

'Be careful, Jay,' Toni said. There was no need to remind him why. If anybody knew, he did.

'Yeah. Thanks. I'll keep you posted.'

Angela had been tapping commands into her flatscreen, and she looked up as Jay discommed. 'Got the information about Mr Bascomb-Coombs. I'm running a search . . . hello?'

'What?' Michaels said.

'Here's our man,' she said. 'Employed by ComCo U.K. They are a privately held computer company that produces, among other things, high-end work station motherboards.'

'He's a computer geek working for a computer company,' Fernandez said. 'Is this a big surprise?'

'Not in itself, no,' she said. 'But ComCo U.K. is owned by Lord Geoffrey Goswell.'

Where had he heard that name before? Michaels wondered. Then he remembered.

Howard beat him to saying it. 'Is that the same guy whose security chief is the one in the store with our assassin and the dead guy?'

'Yes,' Angela said.

'Well, well,' Howard said. 'Small world.'

'Probably doesn't mean anything,' Angela continued. 'Goswell owns several companies, and has thousands of employees scattered all over the country. Anywhere you go in England, Scotland, Wales, or Ireland, you are apt to run into somebody who works for him, or who knows somebody who works for him.'

Michaels shook his head. He didn't like coincidences. Stranger things had surely happened, but this had a fishy smell all of a sudden. 'Tell you what, put off that interview with Peel for now. Pretend it was nothing, tell him you've gotten things resolved, you'll call him back later if you need to see him. I think we need to know a little more about his boss before we go blundering into his den.'

Howard nodded, as did Fernandez and Toni. Angela gave him a small smile, and he felt his heart stumble and bang into the wall of his chest. He did not look at Toni. He couldn't take the risk.

London, England

As he drove away along Old Kent Road, passing the gasworks, Peel was royally pissed. Bascomb-Coombs had taken the day off yesterday, and when he'd gone to find the man, he'd missed him. According to his operatives, Bascomb-Coombs was not in evidence at his flat, nor did he have his automobile, which was parked at his garage where it had been all day. He was not answering his phone either.

Another pass by the office suite was also a waste of time.

Where the Devil was he?

It was his own fault, Peel knew. He had pulled his men off because he wanted to deal with Bascomb-Coombs himself. He did not want them around when he did it, and so when the bastard went missing he had no one to blame save himself. Where had the bugger gone? And why?

His phone chimed at him.

'Hello, Peel here.'

'Major Peel? Angela Cooper here.'

The woman from Intelligence. Another brick on his already overloaded lorry. They called him from time to time about all that Irish business. Whenever some flaming shanty potato-eater blew something up, they always called, as if Peel were somehow responsible for those lunatics. 'Ms Cooper. I haven't forgotten our appointment this afternoon.'

'As it happens, sir, we won't be needing to speak to you after all. The, ah, matter at hand has resolved itself. Sorry to have bothered you.'

Thank God for tiny favors. At least he wouldn't have to deal with these bloody idiots again. 'Quite all right.'

'I'll ring off now. Thank you for your cooperation.'

After the disconnect, Peel looked in his rearview mirror to make certain he had not lost Ruzhyó. He had not.

Well, where to now, Peel, old man? Our rogue scientist seems to have flown the coop, he's not at his digs or usual haunts, and surely that only confirms it. He's lied to you, tried to have you offed, and cheated you out of a million EUs as well. Best you find him and take care of the problem before it gets worse.

Easier said, however, than done.

It was a warm and sunny day, and Howard, in civilian clothes, strolled along the sidewalks a few blocks from MI-6's HQ, enjoying the weather and city. London was quite a cosmopolitan place. People walked past in strange outfits, speaking foreign languages, looking very much at home in the English city.

Next to him, also dressed in civvies, Julio smiled at a pair of teenaged girls wearing microskirts and platform shoes with soles as thick as a Washington D.C. phonebook. The girls smiled back at Julio, and gave Howard a long and appraising look. Christ, both men were old enough to be their fathers. And if they fell off those monster shoes, they'd surely break an ankle, or worse. Howard raised an eyebrow at his sergeant.

'Hey, you know what they say, a thing of beauty is a joy forever.'

'And jailbait is jailbait no matter where you go. Aren't you getting a son and a wife soon?'

'You need to loosen up, John. Looking isn't the same as doing.'

'You've been a bachelor for a long time, Julio. You sure you are going to be able to make the transition?'

'To be absolutely honest, I don't know. I think so. I'm gonna give it my best shot. But you know as well as I do that no battle plan survives first contact with the enemy.'

'You looking at marriage like a war, Sergeant?'

'Not exactly a war, but certainly unfamiliar territory. I mean, I love Jo, I want to wake up to her every morning, and she's gonna be the mother of my child, but I'm not some eighteen-year-old recruit fresh off the farm and never been to town.'

'That's for sure.' He let that sit for a while, then said, 'So what do you think about this business?'

He shrugged. 'This Goswell guy being part of the old-boy network and above reproach and all that doesn't sound all that different from home. Maybe he doesn't have anything to do with anything. But every rich and famous businessman or politician I ever heard of who got a bright light shined into his closet showed some skeletons hanging in the back. And it seems real odd to me that our ice man Ruzhyó is hooked up with this major who works for Mr High and Mighty.'

'That's how I see it, too.'

A gorgeous, cafe-au-lait woman in a black and red silk dress strode along the sidewalk toward them. With the heels she was wearing, she was a couple of inches over six feet, easy. A model, maybe. She went past them in a subtle cloud of expensive perfume. Julio turned to watch her and Howard glanced over his shoulder, trying to be unobtrusive about it.

'Looks good from the back,' Julio said. 'Wouldn't you say, Colonel?'

He'd noticed Howard's quick glance.

He smiled, caught. 'I have to admit she does.'

'Married as you are and all?'

Howard just grinned.

'So what now, John?'

'We let British Intelligence gather everything

they think we ought to know and then we see what's what. Then we take care of it and go home. All these women make me miss my wife.'

Fernandez laughed. 'I hear that.'

36

Thursday, April 14th
London, England

When Toni came back from the loo into the conference room, Alex and Cooper stood at the end of the conference table, talking. They almost literally had their heads together, close enough to be breathing each other's air.

Toni felt a pang of jealousy. They looked up, saw her, but didn't move. That was good. If they had jumped apart when they saw her, that would have been something to worry about. Still, she didn't have any reason to be uneasy. She knew Alex.

'Anything new?' she asked.

'We've got the intel on Goswell and Peel,' Alex said. 'And some interesting developments. Colonel Howard and Sergeant Fernandez are on their way here.'

Even as he said it, the two men arrived.

'Angela, if you would?'

Cooper stood as the others took their seats. She touched her flatscreen and a projection lit over the conference table.

'Lord Geoffrey Goswell's estate in Sussex,' she began. 'It's called The Yews. He spends most of his time there. The place sits on several hundred acres that include the main house, smaller cottages and various outbuildings.'

More images flashed into view.

'Except for staff, His Lordship – he's a widower – lives there alone. He has places in London, Brighton, Manchester, a villa in the South of France, and various houses or condominiums in Wales, Scotland, Ireland, Spain, Portugal, India, and the United States. Here is a list of the companies he owns all or part of. His personal fortune is estimated at just under two billion.'

'Must be hard,' Fernandez allowed.

Cooper continued: 'Peel, whom we've discussed at some length before, heads Goswell's personal security. He's got anywhere from half a dozen to ten men, all ex-military, all heavily armed, patrolling the estate at any given time.'

'I thought guns were more or less illegal here,' Howard said.

Cooper said, 'For ordinary citizens, yes. No handguns, and all rifles and shotguns must be locked up except when actually in use for target shooting or hunting. No military-style assault weapons allowed in any case.'

Fernandez said, 'Let me guess: When you have a couple billion in the old piggy bank, the rules are different, right?'

Cooper gave him a tight smile. 'Just so.'

'Please continue,' Alex said. 'Let's keep the editorial comments down, shall we?'

'We've put a couple of teams on the roads leading to the estate, and less than an hour ago a rental car arrived there. A check of the car agency records indicate it was rented yesterday in Southampton by Peter Bascomb-Coombs. Our operatives managed to get a blurry picture of the driver and it appears to be the computer scientist.'

That got a nice reaction.

'Major Peel, also under surveillance, is currently en route to Sussex on his way from London. It will take him another hour or so to get there.'

'No sign of Ruzhyó?' Howard asked.

'No.'

'Could he be at the estate?'

'It is possible,' Cooper allowed. 'We won't have any spysats in position to footprint the area for another ninety minutes. Even so, and even if he is strolling on the grounds, we would be hard-pressed to identify him from that alone. We have, under the aegis of National Security, tapped the landlines into the estate, as well as having scanners recording wireless activity.'

'Must be nice to be able to get a wiretap that easy,' Alex said.

'It was not exactly easy,' Cooper said. 'But so far nothing of importance has been forthcoming. And essentially, that is the situation as we now know it.'

'Sounds like most of the eggs are in the basket to me. We need to take a little run out there and have a chat with some folks,' Fernandez said.

Cooper stared at the holoproj image, then down at the table. She looked uncomfortable, a thing that didn't bother Toni much. Cooper said, 'Well, yes, that would be the logical next step.'

'But . . . ?' Howard said.

'This is a bit awkward,' she said. 'We can't just pop out and do that.'

'Why not?' Toni asked. 'We have a suspect in the computer crime that has rattled half the planet and we know where he is. I can't believe you don't want to have a few words with him. And with the guy who he works for, too.'

Toni saw Julio and John Howard nod in agreement, and Alex also looked ready to hear her answer.

Cooper said, 'This is true. However, things aren't done that way here. What if you were in the States and you suddenly had to question a billionaire who was also a powerful political figure? A senator or even the President? You couldn't just knock on his door and demand to come in, could you?'

'No,' Alex said. 'But if we had enough reason to suspect he was involved in a major crime, in which hundreds of people were killed as a result of something he did or had done, we could get a judge to issue a search or an arrest warrant. We've had our President testify when he didn't want to. Even impeached.'

'After weeks of consultation with his lawyers,' Cooper said. 'And the impeachment was a wristslap – he wasn't tried and found guilty, was he?'

'The effort was made,' Alex said. 'No man is above the law.'

'Men are not above the law here, either, Alex, but this is a small country, and despite our attempts to bring it into the twenty-first century, still very caste-conscious. Lord Goswell is at the acme of power here. He went to school with the senior members of the House of Lords. He knows the blue-blood wealthy, he knows the most powerful barristers and solicitors, and he knows the judges, the high police officials. Every couple of weeks he has tea with the head of the Conservative government. He can get more done with a wave of his hand than Parliament can do in a week. He plays bridge with the King. Getting the wire- and wavetaps were small miracles, and managed only because Goswell didn't know about them. This is not a man upon whose door you knock and demand anything. If you want to go and beard this lion in his den, you need to enter into negotiations with a delicate touch, your hat in hand. It's one thing to call up and tell his head of security you are going to drop round for a chat; it's quite another to demand the same of one of the richest and most powerful men in the country.'

Nobody had anything to say about that for a moment.

'Bullshit,' Julio said.

Toni suppressed her smile. She had to agree with that one.

'That may be, Sergeant, but I am here to say that His Majesty's government will not be approaching Lord Goswell, save through his attorneys, and cautiously at that.'

'Even if we suspect he's involved in the computer assaults?' Toni said.

Cooper turned to face Toni. 'Even if we knew for sure he was responsible and could *prove* it, Ms Fiorella. Which we do not. We have no real evidence other than some very thin circumstantial material – Bascomb-Coombs, who might or might not be involved himself – works for Lord Goswell and is there visiting him. That doesn't prove much of anything, now does it?'

Toni knew that Cooper was right. But she also knew in her gut that Bascomb-Coombs was tied into this, and Peel and Ruzhyó were somehow connected to it. But what could they do if the local authorities wouldn't let them even *talk* to the parties?

Alex said, 'We can't barge into His Lordship's house without an engraved invitation. All right. Can we shortstop Peel?'

'I beg your pardon?'

'Can you have your field ops pull Peel over and keep him from getting back to the safety of Goswell's estate?'

Cooper stared at him. 'Why would we want to do that?'

Alex said, 'Okay, follow my logic here. Let's suppose that Bascomb-Coombs is responsible for the computer disruptions.'

'All right, for the moment let's assume that.'

'If he is, he has to be doing it with help. According to Jay Gridley, this isn't something you can do cheaply, so somebody substantial has to be backing him.'

'Yes. So?'

'Occam's razor. He's working for Goswell. He's at Goswell's house. How many people can fund a multimillion-dollar project and keep it secret? Wouldn't that have to be somebody with a lot of clout? Like somebody who owns lock, stock, and barrel a high-end computer company? That gives us Goswell. And wouldn't Goswell's chief of personal security have to have some idea who Bascomb-Coombs was? Any op worth his paycheck would surely run background checks on people who cozied up to his boss. If it was me watching over a rich man's health, I'd want to know everything about everybody who walked in the door. I'd make it my business to know what visitors had for breakfast, where they ate it, and how big a tip they left.'

'You're saying that Bascomb-Coombs is the mad hacker, that Goswell knows about it, and that Peel also knows. Your logical chain is weak, even assuming the first link in it is as solid as steel.'

'Stands to reason if they are all sitting around having tea together, doesn't it?'

Cooper gave him a small smile. 'Come now, Alex, people who have tea together don't share all their secrets, do they?'

Alex flushed. John Howard turned and suddenly found a fascinating spot on the empty wall to stare at. Cooper's smile grew bigger and warmer. These actions didn't prove anything, but taken together, on a sudden, deeply intuitional level, an icicle of solid nitrogen formed and stabbed Toni in the heart:

My God. Had Alex slept *with this bitch*?

How? When?

God in heaven – *why*?

Alex cleared his throat and said, 'Look, we know Peel is connected to Ruzhyó and the death of a suspected ice man.'

'The fellow in the bookstore was, according to the coroner, a suicide.'

'After Ruzhyó or Peel shot him! Peel knows something about all this. You know I'm right. Pull him in and let's sweat him before more people die and millions of lives are disrupted.'

There was a long pause. Toni stared at Cooper with the new suspicion still piercing her to her soul. All of the rest of this was nothing. It didn't matter about Peel or Goswell or Ruzhyó. None of that was important.

Had Alex betrayed her? Surely not. He couldn't have. Could he?

She felt sick.

Cooper said, ‘All right. I’ll have to get DG Hamilton to sign off on it, but I suspect we can do that much in the interests of National Security.’

37

Thursday
M23 – South of Gatwick

Ruzhyó took a couple of deep breaths and blew them out, trying to relax. He had been growing more tight as he drove, gripping the wheel harder, hunching forward, and it wouldn't do to be tense when he needed to be loose. A tight man could not move properly. Even knowing that, it always happened. You had to work to overcome it, despite all the years and bodies.

Ahead of him and one lane over, the gray Neon with the two men in it who had been following Peel since London cruised fifty meters behind the major's car, using traffic as cover. They'd been so intent on tailing Peel they had not noticed Ruzhyó.

As soon as he had spotted them, Ruzhyó had made the call and had spoken but one word: 'Company.' That had been enough to alert Peel.

He'd replied. 'Got it. I'll call back later.'

They had passed Gatwick Airport a few miles back, still heading south on the big motorway as if going to the Sussex estate. The mobile phone on the car seat next to him rang. Ruzhyó picked it up. 'Go ahead.'

'Have they made you?'

'No.'

'Good. We're getting off at the next exit, about two miles ahead, heading east. Down that road three miles, there is a large oak tree, at an intersection with a narrow road to the right. Two miles down *that* road, on the left is a big sheering barn. We'll have a chat with our company there. Why don't you go on ahead and get set up?'

'Yes.' Ruzhyó thumbed the connection off. He accelerated and pulled smoothly ahead of the surveillance car, passed Peel, and was half a mile ahead of them when he turned off the highway at the next exit. The shadowers paid him no attention.

The oak tree was where it was supposed to be – Ruzhyó measured the distance with his odometer – and the barn, in front of a field of grazing sheep, sat alone and quiet in the middle of a long stretch of nowhere. A perfect place.

Ruzhyó pulled his car into the barn and shut the door behind it. The place was dusty and smelled of dry hay, wool, and something like hot candlewax. Farm smells, bringing with them quick lances of memory from his days with Anna. He checked out the exits. There were two more at ground level besides the one he'd pulled the car into, and two openings on the upper level, with hoists and ropes and pulleys dangling from them. Peel was a professional; he would pull his car in and get out in such a way as to allow somebody hiding in the barn a clear shot at his followers when they left their car. Probably in front of the smaller door on the building's south east side, he figured.

Ruzhyó checked the magazine in the Firestar, making certain that a round was chambered. He cocked the hammer and put the safety back on. There might not be any shooting at all; if it became necessary, he had eight shots, and seven more rounds in a second magazine; should he have to reload. No semi-auto was jam-proof, but he had adjusted the magazines and polished the feed ramp, and the bullet ogive was clean and rounded enough so there shouldn't be a problem. After firing a few rounds when he'd gotten the piece, he had hand-cycled a hundred cartridges through the action without a misfeed. At this range, if he had to shoot he'd only need a few to work, and the first one was already there.

He heard the sound of an approaching engine, easily discernible in the quiet pastures. He took another deep breath and let it out, stretched his neck, and rolled his shoulders. He was ready. He would follow Peel's lead.

Peel pulled his car onto the hard-packed dirt next to the barn, and circled to his left to force the following car to pull in between him and the building. He stopped, loosened his pistol in its holster, and alighted from his car. He kept the door open and stood partially covered by it. He didn't see Ruzhyó, but he had noticed the fresh tire prints leading to the barn, so he knew the man was in there. If it was him, Peel would set up behind that door right across from his car, and he bet that the ex-*Spetsnaz* shooter was already there. He felt a lot better having an old pro watching his arse.

The Neon pulled off the road and right into perfect position. The car stopped in a light cloud of dust, and as the reddish-gray powder settled two men got out. They wore windbreakers, and they had the moves of men carrying firearms hidden under their jackets. But they didn't look like coppers, at least not civilian ones. One was a medium-tall brunette, the other a shorter, stockier man with mouse-brown hair cropped short. Were they Military? Or Intelligence? What the bloody hell?

'Good afternoon, gentlemen. May I help you with something?'

Mouse-brown said, 'Major Peel. We wonder if you would come along with us, sir.' Not a question.

'If you'll explain who you are and what you want, maybe we can keep this civilized.'

'We didn't come to answer questions. We'll send somebody for your car. You'll be riding with us.'

'I shouldn't think I'd want to do that,' he said.

'Then we must insist,' Medium-tall said. 'Please step over here, sir. And keep your hands in plain sight.'

'Insist all you want. I'm minding my own business, and I don't believe it is any of yours.'

The two exchanged glances, and without speaking, split up and drifted away from each other. This was standard procedure if you were facing a man you considered armed and dangerous. Even if he was very fast on the draw, he would have to swing his weapon from one to another with two opponents, and the farther apart they were, the harder that would be, especially if both opponents were prepared to shoot back. They still had not pulled their own weapons; that was to his advantage.

'Let's not make this difficult, Major,' Mouse-brown said.

'Gentlemen, I advise you to stand still and keep your hands away from your weapons.'

Medium-tall grinned and said, 'Begging your pardon, Major, but either one of us is ten years younger and ten years faster than you. You don't really think you're good enough to take us both?'

'Maybe. Maybe not. It would be more risky if I were alone.'

Mouse-brown said, 'There's no one else in your car, Peel. How stupid do you think we are?'

'Fairly stupid, I should say. Why do you think I stopped here, sonny? At this particular quiet spot in the country?'

Mouse-brown paused in his sideways drift and shot his partner a quick glance.

'He's having us on,' Medium-tall said. 'A bluff.'

'You think so?' Peel said. He smiled. 'You've been behind me since we left London. You think I didn't know that? I've had plenty of time to have a colleague arrive here. You seem like decent lads. Tell me who sent you and what you know and perhaps you get to walk out of this. Otherwise . . .' He gave them a broad, theatrical shrug.

'Forget it,' Medium-tall said. 'We weren't born bloody yesterday!'

Peel raised his voice. 'Mr Ruzhyó! Are you there?'

The barn door swung up with a creak of rusted hinges and Ruzhyó appeared in the doorway, though he did not step out from his cover. 'I am here,' he said. He held the silvery pistol in both hands, pointed at Medium-tall.

The two men started, surprised.

Men who had been under the gun, under fire, would have known they didn't have a chance. You could be faster than Billy the Bloody Kid from the holster but that wouldn't be nearly quick enough to outdraw a gun already aimed at you.

The two panicked and went for their guns.

Ruzhyó had Medium-tall, so Mouse-brown was Peel's. But before he could clear his weapon, Ruzhyó fired-*pow! pow! pow!* the tiniest hesitation, then *pow! pow! pow!* again. Six rounds at maybe five meters, and it was so quick it sounded like two bursts of fully automatic submachinegun. Damn, he was fast!

Medium-tall and Mouse-brown went down like sickled wheat.

'Shit!' Peel yelled. He finished his draw and hurried toward the downed men. Both were wearing body armor under their jackets, he could see that as he got close. The vests had stopped two rounds each, just as they were supposed to. But the armor had not stopped the rest of Ruzhyó's Mozambique Drill: Two to the chest and one to the head. Both men had been shot between the eyes, and they were effectively dead before they hit the ground. Peel had never seen the drill performed better, not even in practice, much less in a hot scenario. Ruzhyó was a master shooter.

'Damn, how am I supposed to find out anything if you don't leave one alive to question?'

Ruzhyó gave him a Slavic shrug. He popped the magazine from the pistol, let it fall to the ground, reloaded the handgun with a second magazine from his pocket then bent to pick up the fallen magazine. When he straightened, he reached up with one hand and pried a silicone earplug from one ear, then the other, and dropped those into his pocket along with the nearly empty magazine.

Good God. Ruzhyó was so cool as to think about bloody *ear* protection before he had calmly blasted two armed men as neat and quick as you could possibly please. The man must have ice water in his veins.

Well, there was not any help for it now. Best find

out who these two were, if he could. Peel fished in Medium-tall's pocket until he found a wallet. He opened it, then stared at the ID card behind the clear plastic window. 'Oh, Lord! These blokes are MI-6! We've just killed two of His Majesty's SIS agents!'

Ruzhyó shrugged again, scanning the countryside for witnesses.

Aside from the sheep, who seemed unaffected by the gunshots, there weren't any prying eyes.

Peel shook his head. 'Come on, help me move the bodies,' Peel said. 'We've only got a few minutes before they are missed.'

They were in the crapper now, weren't they?

London – MI-6

'We have a problem,' Cooper told Michaels. 'We've lost contact with the team following Peel.'

Howard, Fernandez, and Toni had gone to the cafeteria to grab a quick bite, and Michaels was once again alone with Cooper in the conference room. 'Lost contact with them?'

'More than half an hour ago. Their last report was that they had pulled off the M23 near Balcombe and were about to detain Peel. We've been unsuccessful in our attempts to reach them since.'

'Do you have a way to find them?'

'Not exactly. The location transponder in their car stopped sending its signal a few minutes after their last transmission. We know where they were. We've sent a military strike team via helicopter to check it out.'

'They're either taken or dead,' he said flatly.

'We don't know that.'

'You wouldn't have scrambled an air strike team if you didn't think it was likely.'

She sighed. Put one hand on his forearm. Her touch was warm. 'We do fear something has gone awry.'

He stared at her hand. After a beat, she broke the contact. 'No chance for us, is there?'

'I – it wouldn't be a good idea. I'm sorry.'

'But you did enjoy yourself? As far as it went?'

'Ah . . . yes. I did.'

She smiled, but it was hollow. 'The good ones always get away . . . A pity. Your Ms Fiorella is lucky, you know.'

'I think I'm the lucky one.'

She stepped back, out of his space, and glanced at her watch. 'Should be hearing from the strike team shortly.'

'Can we still stop Peel? If he is on his way to Goswell's estate?'

'Given the current situation, I doubt that DG Hamilton would want to risk another team. It would be safer to bottle him up at The Yews, if that's where he's going, and deal with him later.

* * *

In the MI-6 cafeteria, Fernandez swallowed a bite of what looked like Salisbury steak and mashed potatoes drenched by a half gallon of brown gravy and said, 'What's with the Sub-Commander?'

Fiorella had come to the cafeteria with Howard and Fernandez but had quickly excused herself and left, looking pale.

Howard glanced down at his Thai chicken salad. He wasn't a gossip, but he had known Julio all of his adult life; the two of them didn't have many secrets from each other. And from Toni's face, the nickel had dropped. She had figured out about Michaels' extracurricular activities. Howard didn't need to get that specific, though, so he said, 'I think she and the Commander might be having some personal problems.'

Julio washed another bite down with a glass of water and nodded. 'Cooper,' he said. 'Boss got Biblical with her?'

Howard raised an eyebrow.

'She's gorgeous, smart, and she's been giving him looks,' Julio went on. 'And the boss stares at his shoes every time Cooper gets too close. She looks possessive and he looks guilty. And that looks like a done deal to me. Not that I'm telling you anything you don't already know. You picked it up.'

Howard nodded. 'Yes.'

Julio took another mouthful of the brown and steaming goop. 'I don't understand what all the fuss about how bad British cooking is about. Nothing wrong with it far as I can tell,' he said.

'Spoken like a true meat and potatoes man.'

'Yeah, well, Br'er Rabbit, why don't you have some more of that grass and twigs you got.'

A young man approached the table. 'Colonel Howard? Commander Michaels would like to see you, sir, as soon as possible.'

Julio shoveled another mouthful in, hurrying, as Howard nodded once and got to his feet. Now what?

38

Thursday
Near Balcombe, England

MI-6 had sprung for a second 'copter, and it landed with Alex, Howard, Fernandez, Cooper, and Toni. The strike force 'copter was still on the ground, and a dozen soldiers in Brit camo and berets, weapons at the ready, moved around the big old barn as the Net Force team piled out of the second bird into the dusty prop wash.

Toni had tucked her personal pain away into the box of professionalism and locked it tight. Even so, she hadn't been able to look directly at Alex during the short flight.

A British captain approached and spoke with Cooper. Toni walked around, bent to examine the ground in a couple of spots, then drifted toward the barn. There was a new car parked inside and it hadn't been there long enough to get dusty. The floor was earth, under a light layer of dry hay. She walked back out and circled the area again. The ground was soft and chalky enough in places to take footprints, but the military force had obliterated a lot of them, their combat boots leaving a distinctive tread. She thought about what might have happened here, given what she knew and what she had seen.

Alex said, 'Toni?' He stood next to Cooper and the British captain.

She could do this. She could keep her feelings at bay and do her job.

'This is Captain Ward,' Alex said.

Cooper said, 'Why don't you bring Sub-Commander Fiorella up to speed on what you think might have happened here, Captain?'

A flash of anger enveloped Toni. Bring her up to fucking *speed*? Yeah, right. She wanted to smash Cooper's smug face. Instead, she tamped it down and said, 'It's pretty obvious, isn't it?'

Cooper blinked. Did she hear the challenge in Toni's voice? 'Oh, really? Why don't you tell us, then?' Yeah, she heard it.

'Sure. Peel had a backup man, that's his car in the barn. It will be a rental, and won't have a backtrail, probably some dummy corporation post-office box and phony ID used to get it.

'Your agents must have missed the backup. Odds are it was Mikhayl Ruzhyó, who must have some kind of link to Peel. Maybe they were old college buddies, or they met in some police action in Africa or SA somewhere. They have history. Otherwise, it's too coincidental.

'Peel led your men here, right into a trap. Ruzhyó

sneaked up on them – no, strike that. You couldn't really sneak up on this barn from the road in a car and it's too far from anywhere to walk, so probably he was already hiding when Peel arrived. How am I doing so far?' She looked at Alex and his face was frozen into a half-grin. He felt her anger, she knew. She nodded at him. *I know, you bastard. And now you know I know.*

Cooper didn't speak, nor did Alex or the captain, so Toni continued: 'There are two small spots of blood on the ground, still visible, though somebody kicked dirt over them, there and over there—' She pointed. 'Were your men armed? And wearing body armor?'

Cooper just glared at her, and it was the captain who said, 'They carried sidearms, and as for the vests, yes, they should have worn them. It's standard for this kind of operation.'

'Right. So Peel or Ruzhyó shot them, most likely in the heads. That's where they fell. Then they shoved the bodies into their own car, and left here driving that and Peel's. I imagine if your troops haven't stomped all over them, you'll find his tire tracks and those of your men's car leaving. By now, I'd guess they've driven the car with the bodies in it somewhere it won't be found for a while. Two missing agents are a concern, but not as high profile as two dead ones. If I were in charge, I'd have the local constables drag any big ponds or lakes within a few miles of here. Deep water is a good place to hide a car.'

The captain shook his head. 'Overall, it's a bit of a stretch, isn't it? Aside from the blood, we found no other evidence. There weren't any shell casings.'

'Ruzhyó would have picked his up, and I'm assuming Peel is smart enough to have done the same. By the time we catch up to them, the guns used will be long gone anyway. I don't know much about your Major Peel, but Ruzhyó is very much a professional. He doesn't leave you much to work with.'

Ward nodded, as if confirming that he wasn't as concerned with her explanation as he wanted to hear her reasoning for it. 'The scenario you postulate is not impossible. As soon as he figured out with whom he was dealing, Peel would have known about the transponder in their car and disabled it. We've set up roadblocks, but we may be behind the curve here.'

We're behind the curve, all right. Toni gathered herself and gave Cooper the sweetest smile she could form. 'Anything else you need to know, Ms Cooper?'

'Not at the moment, Ms Fiorella.' Cooper gave Alex a quick look, and in it Toni saw a measure of what she thought might be concern. Pity, even.

So, Cooper had figured out that Toni knew, too. And the British tart was feeling sympathy for Alex because of it. Great. Now we're all just one big, unhappy fucking family.

* * *

Michaels pulled his virgil and put in a priority call to Jay Gridley.

'Yeah, boss, what's up?'

'If I gave you an address, a physical address for where this QC hardware might be, would that help your search?'

'Couldn't hurt. Might be able to spot a trail if I'm close enough to it, though there's no guarantee.'

'Stand by, I'm uploading it now. We found Bascomb-Coombs and where he works. We can't lay our hands on him just at the moment, but maybe you can figure out something from your end.'

'Thanks, boss.'

'Be careful, Jay.'

'I copy that, decibel and crystal. Discom.'

Michaels walked to where Cooper stood. 'Does this change things? Can we go to Goswell's and grab Peel?'

'I can check with the DG, but I'm afraid it won't matter. We have missing agents, but not much to tie them to His Lordship or even Peel. For all we know, Peel drove off before they could speak to him and our men were coincidentally attacked by sheep rustlers.'

'Yeah, right.'

'Sorry, Alex, but that's how it is. Our hands are tied.'

On their way back to the helicopter, Michaels lagged behind. 'Hold up a second, Colonel.'

Howard slowed.

'Cooper says MI-6's hands are tied. They can't go traipsing into Lord Goswell's estate without an engraved invitation.'

'Wonderful,' Howard said. His voice dripped sarcasm.

'Colonel, I don't know how good your grapevine is, but I've put you up for a promotion.'

Howard hesitated a second, then said, 'I had heard the rumor, Commander. Thank you, I appreciate it.'

'I mention this only because an international diplomatic incident might squash your chances. Probably would.'

Howard grinned. 'If that would let me catch Ruzhyó and this mad hacker, I could live with it.'

Michaels smiled back at him. 'Somehow I knew you'd feel that way. When we get back to MI-6, I think our crew needs to take a break. Go for a ride in the country or something.'

'Yes, sir.'

Michaels looked at the 'copter, squinting against the dust blown up by the prop wash. Most of the time he colored between the lines. Now and then, he had to go outside the boundaries. There was a difference between justice and the law, and sometimes the end did justify the means. Generally in his line of work if you took a risk out in territory where your ass was bare and you pulled it off, you could rationalize it afterward. If you failed, you got skewered. They were hunting terrorists, killers both by remote means and with their own hands. The worst that could happen to Michaels if he screwed this up was that they'd fire him in disgrace and put him in jail for twenty or thirty years.

As he watched Toni climb into the helicopter, pointedly not looking at him, he knew there were heavier prices to pay for screwing up – or in this case, almost screwing some*body*.

Maybe, if he was lucky, he'd get killed in this clandestine operation . . .

Upper Cretaceous
What will be London

On foot, the rocket launcher slung over his shoulder, Jay sniffed the air. The usual jungle odors were there, plus another smell that washed over the others, insistent in its demand to be noticed. Impossible to ignore, actually.

Next to him, Saji wrinkled her nose and said, 'Lord, what is that stench?'

'Not to put too fine a point on it, it's monster shit.' He pointed.

Ahead of them was another thicket of prehistoric jungle, representing reams of coded packets, an electronic locus, a nexus that, in RW, corresponded to a computer company in London. Upon the path that led to that jungle, forming a rough triangle with two huge footprints, was a mound of scat, a pile of reeking excrement, brown, the size of a dumpster, and beset by a flock of busy flies.

Off to the sides of the path were a dozen or so other mounds, dried and hardened into the beginnings of giant coprolites. Welcome to Feek City.

The two of them circled around the fresh deposit. This close, they could see undigested bits of bone stuck in the pile, could feel the heat coming off it. The stink was so thick you could almost lean against it.

Jay said, 'Not to pretend I'm any better at cutting sign or anything, but I'm pretty sure it went this way. And I'd bet it came out here to do its business because it lives in there.'

Saji stared at the mound. She shook her head. 'I don't much like the idea of going in there after it,' she said.

Jay unshipped the rocket launcher. 'Me neither. Stand to the side there,' he said. He shouldered the weapon, aimed it at the jungle, and squeezed the trigger. The rocket *whooshed*! away on a flaming tail, arced into the woods, and blew apart in a fiery *kaboom!* that spewed leaves and other bits of trees all which way.

'Couple more of those ought to get its attention,' Jay said.

The Yews, Sussex, England

Peel alighted from his car and slammed the door shut a bit harder than necessary. He got a grip on his irritation, nodded at Huard, who was standing watch at the rear of the main house, then turned to watch as Ruzhyó got out of the passenger side. The car with the two dead agents in it, along with the gun that killed them, was at the bottom of a thirty-foot-deep sinkhole in a stock pond on one of His Lordship's farms in East Sussex, not far from where they'd shot the pair. Well, where Ruzhyó had shot them. The SIS or local police would likely get around to finding the car and its cargo eventually, but probably not immediately. He should have plenty of time to clean up the loose ends and get the hell out of the country. A pity, that, but it was going to be too hot to stay, that was for certain. And while he wouldn't be getting that phantom fortune from the Indonesian bank, Goswell had a safe in his house that would surely yield running-away money. His plan was to ice Goswell, that bastard Bascomb-Coombs, and Ruzhyó – this last with great care, from behind when he wasn't expecting it. Some artful arranging of the bodies so that it would seem as if the ex-*Spetsnaz* agent had killed the other two, then been shot by one of his men – Huard, say, who'd have to be iced as well – and Peel would be off. His situation was bad, but not fatal, and while he would have preferred things to have turned out differently, he could survive it. He was a trained soldier, an officer with command experience in the field, there was always a market for his services somewhere in the third world. He could train an army in one of the CIS countries, or command a battalion in central Africa, or work security for an Arab prince. War dogs were never completely out of fashion, no matter how peaceful things might be. You never knew but that your neighbor was eyeing your territory, and you had to be prepared to protect it regardless of how wide his smile was or how open his hand seemed.

Not his first choice, but better than the options.

'Stay here and keep your eyes open,' Peel told Ruzhyó.

Ruzhyó saluted with his rolled-up umbrella. He'd likely need that soon: The sky threatened rain, dark clouds rolling in from the North Atlantic in a cool front. Perfect, a storm to make things even gloomier.

Peel walked over to Huard. 'Tell the boys to move out to the perimeter,' he said. 'We might have company. You watch the back door.'

'Yes, sir.'

Peel headed into the house. He would get it all done. And he'd wait until well after dark, so that he could take off on foot across the fields, just in case anybody was watching the estate. He had to figure that if they knew who he was, at least enough to have an SIS team on him, they knew who he worked for. They wouldn't storm the bloody gates at The

Yews, oh no, but they might be waiting for him to leave. If he hiked out on foot far enough, he could boost a car from one of the neighbors, drive to the south coast, and take one of Goswell's boats across the channel. There was no shame in retreating from a superior force. You could always regroup and come back later. A lost battle was not necessarily a lost war.

Goswell was having a drink in the sitting room. 'Hello, Major.'

'Your Lordship. Where is Mr Bascomb-Coombs?'

'Down the hall, in the study, I believe. Playing with his portable computer. I had his access shut off to the special unit, but he has his way around that, I am sure. His portable computer peeped at him, he got quite agitated, and excused himself to go deal with whatever it was. A drink?'

'Splendid idea,' he said. Applewhite materialized – too bad he would have to die as well, he liked old Applewhite – and Peel held up two fingers, to indicate the depth of his scotch. Oh, what the hell – he added a third finger. He had to last until dark, didn't he? And it had been a long and trying day. Nobody could blame him for needing a stiff drink.

A sudden breeze rattled the window casement, and the first drops of rain spattered on the glass. Well, it was going to be a stormy evening, to be sure, in more ways than one.

39

Thursday
London, England

The Net Force team rode in what Howard called his Mobile On Scene Command Center – essentially a large RV he had hurriedly rented – with Julio Fernandez driving, and cursing as he did so.

'Why don't you stupid bastards drive on the right side of the road!' he muttered angrily.

The rest of the Strike Team had already piled into cars and trucks at the military base and were on their way to the meeting place – in this case, a fire station in Sussex.

Howard had a computer set up on a small table, and Michaels and Toni sat next to it, watching. Howard brought up an image, an augmented aerial view of a big house and some smaller structures. 'This is Goswell's place,' he said.

'You get this from MI-6?' Michaels asked.

'No, sir. I had Big Squint – USAT – footprint it this morning.'

'Before we knew we were going to do this?' Toni asked.

'Yes, ma'am. Never hurts to keep the 6P principle in mind.'

Michaels nodded to himself. Everybody here knew what that meant: Proper planning prevents piss-poor performance. Howard was just doing his job.

Howard continued: 'We'd be a lot better off if we had a couple of days to study things, to run tactical scenarios, and play with alternative plans, but since we don't, we KISS it and hope for the best.'

Another acronym: Keep it simple, stupid.

'Here's how I see it,' Howard said. 'We wait until after dark before we hit the place. My men do the tango with the estate's guards while Sergeant Fernandez and I and a couple of others hop the fence and head for the house. We set off some flash-bangs and some puke lights and take out any guards there, go in and round up everybody, haul the ones we want out, and hightail it for the border. Ruzhyó, Peel, and Bascomb-Coombs will do, and we can feed any incriminating information about Goswell back to our hosts later and let them deal with him if he's involved. With any luck, by the time the locals figure it out, we're on our plane and halfway across the ocean.'

'One small addition,' Michaels said. 'I'll be going in with you. And yes, I know, it isn't the wisest course of action, but we've had this discussion before and since I get the heat, I get to make that choice.' He glanced at Toni, about to say that she'd be staying at the command center.

The look in Toni's eyes was reptilian. She knew what he was going to say. And he suddenly knew if he said it, whatever chance he might have of patching things up between them was going to die right here and now. So instead he said, 'And Toni will be going in, too.'

She gave him a short nod. 'Thank you.' Her words were cool and crisp, you could use them to frost beer steins, but at least she was still talking to him. Better than nothing.

When they got to the fire station, near a little town called Cuckfield, the Net Force Strike Team was already there. But when Toni stepped out into the rainy evening, there was a surprise waiting under the overhang of a carport next to the main building:

Angela Cooper was there, too. She wore combat camo, pants, shirt, and boots.

'Oh, shit,' Fernandez said quietly. 'Looks like the game is about to be cancelled.'

They moved to the carport, out of the weather. Alex stepped forward, but before he could speak, Cooper raised one hand to his objections. 'If I wanted to stop you, Alex, I wouldn't be here alone.'

'What *do* you want?' he asked.

'Officially, His Majesty's government cannot condone any action against Lord Goswell without much more evidence than we currently have. However, the DG and our MP know what we've found out and, unofficially, they believe what we all do – that Bascomb-Coombs is very likely responsible for the computer terrorism, and that Major Peel and Goswell are privy and part of it as well.'

'So you've decided to look the other way?' Alex said.

'Yes. Provided we have an unofficial observer to make certain our unofficial position is kept, well, unofficial.'

Toni said, 'So we get to do the dirty work, take care of your problem, and if it all blows up in our faces, you get to keep your hands clean.'

'Can't put anything past you, can we, Ms Fiorella? Well, that's probably not strictly true, is it, Alex?'

Years of martial arts practice gave you a certain amount of physical self-control. If you knew you could seriously injure or kill somebody with your hands, elbows, knees, or feet, it tended to make you think before you made any sudden moves. You had to be able to move almost reflexively fast once the action started, but you also had to know when it was appropriate. Once, in college, a dorm-mate had sneaked up behind Toni and grabbed her in the hallway, intending to tickle her. His practical joke had cost him a visit to the campus clinic and a concussion. It had taken her a few more years to get past the reactive stage, so she could usually assess the situation before decking somebody who didn't really mean her any harm.

That hard-won self-control was all that kept Toni from stepping forward and destroying Angela Cooper. She really wanted to do it, bad. Instead she managed a smile. She said, 'Oh, I'm a bit slow sometimes but I eventually catch on.'

'All right,' Alex said. 'Colonel Howard will run it down again. We've got a couple of hours until we go.' He looked at Toni, shook his head a little, then gave her an open-handed 'Sorry' shrug. He looked pale, almost gray, and she hoped he felt bad. He should.

Ruzhyó leaned against the stone wall of the big house under the substantial roof overhang. The wind had died pretty much as the rain began, and the gutters piped the water away to drain chains at the house's corners, so he was dry enough even in the damp evening. And he had his umbrella, of course, and a feeling he would be needing its hidden functions before the night was over. Intelligence services of every country he knew of took a dim view of anybody who killed any of their operatives. It was bad for business. *Spetsnaz* had always been notorious for its vengeance. Once, in one of the ever-troubled mid-eastern countries, one of their ops had been caught by a group of zealots and slain. A week later sixteen of those zealots were found lined up neatly in a ditch, their severed penises stuffed into their dead mouths, their eyes plucked out.

Kill one of ours and we destroy a village of yours.

It made even zealots think.

The British were more polite and less savage but they would assume by now their men were dead, and they would know who was responsible. At least they would know of Peel, and if they knew enough to find and follow him, they doubtless knew for whom he worked and where his employer lived. Peel would realize this, and he would have a plan in place by now, a way to escape being captured.

Huard, dressed in rain gear, walked a circuit around the back of the house, looking at Ruzhyó but not speaking as he moved from sight. Huard didn't like him, but Huard was a child.

So, in Peel's shoes, what would he do? Flight was the only real option; even Goswell could not protect him if he stayed here. And timing was critical. Peel would have to disappear before things grew too warm. Were he Peel, he would already be gone. Certainly before morning light offered his pursuers too much help in spotting him. And he would wish to depart without any telltales left behind. Peel had sent his men to the property's borders, leaving only Huard and Ruzhyó here. They, along with everybody inside the house, were expendable. That's how Ruzhyó would see it in Peel's place.

So. Sometime during the night, Peel would call him inside. Or perhaps use the com to tell Huard to do it, to kill him? No. He wouldn't trust Huard. And if the boy failed, his master would know that Ruzhyó would have to come for him.

Ruzhyó could simply disappear into the rainy darkness in a few more minutes. None of Peel's men would find him, or stop him if they did find him. He could trek away, catch a ride, steal a car, and be in France tomorrow. This game was nearly over, and what was the point in waiting around for the expected end?

He mentally shrugged. No point at all, actually. And perhaps that was the reason. There was nowhere he had to be. One place was as good as another. Did it matter where the sands of one's hourglass ran out? In the end, did anything matter at all?

Next to the parked lorry, Howard slipped his helmet on, and checked the LOSIR com. 'Perimeter team, sound off, by the numbers.'

The Strike Team obediently replied. All ahead functions there.

'Entry team, sound off.'

'This is E1, Cooper.'

'E2, Michaels.

'E3, Fiorella.'

'E4, Fernandez.'

And he was E5. Five of them should be enough, if everybody did what they were supposed to do. He and Fernandez would work the heavy shots, and while Michaels and Fiorella weren't trained assault troopers, he'd seen them in action enough to know they had balls. The only unknown was Cooper, and if she was a field agent for MI-6, she ought to have at least some basic moves. It was hurried, it was slapdash, it was hung together with string and bubble gum, but it was what he had to work with, and it was about to be a go. They all wore the light SIPEsuit configuration, mostly just armor, coms, and the tactical comp to run the helmet. They all carried the simple but reliable H&K 9mm subguns and tactical pistols, save for Howard and his .357 revolver. And as soon as he'd brought that out, Julio had howled.

'Why, Katie Mae, I must be going blind,' he'd said, 'my tired old eyes completely shot. What is that ugly lump on top of the Colonel's antique good-luck charm? Is that a dot scope? It can't be!'

'Julio . . .'

'No, I must be on drugs, or maybe just out of my mind. The Colonel John Howard I know would never in a million years upgrade to hardware just because it was state-of-the-art and *useful!*' He started looking up at the rainy sky.

'What are you looking for, Sergeant?'

'I dunno, sir. Some sign or portent. A big meteor about to fall on us, a gathering of angels, a rain of fire, something to let us know the end is near.'

'Never let it be said that your commander is a total Luddite,' Howard said. He smiled.

Now, they were on their way. They'd split into two groups a couple of miles from here; the perimeter team would hit the gate, and they'd go over the fence. Howard took a deep breath and let it out slowly.

'All aboard,' he said.

Peel glanced at his watch. Almost nine. Still raining, but not as hard as it had been, judging from the sound on the slate tile roof. Bascomb-Coombs hadn't come out of the study. He was hunched over his computer, wearing a headset and finger bands, deep in some VR scenario. Well, fine. He could die never knowing what had hit him for all Peel cared, and good riddance.

Goswell had tottered off into the dining room for a late supper, and Peel had the sitting room to himself, working on his third scotch, a small one this time. He didn't want to drink too much. There was Ruzhyó to consider.

He'd have to get started soon, but he was stalling. Had to be done, of course, but there was a certain reluctance to get to it. Another page turning in the book of his life, and a big one. Ah, well. That's how it went. Win some, lose some, but the important thing was to live to fight another day.

He took another sip of his scotch.

The monster, which looked like a cross between Godzilla and a giant Spielbergian raptor, stomped out into the clearing that served as his toilet and let loose a bellow that shook fronds off the ferns. It was still pretty far away, a couple of hundred meters.

Probably could cover that in maybe four or five seconds once he got moving. One shot, maybe two.

'There he is,' Jay said redundantly.

Saji looked up. 'No shit.'

Jay swallowed dryly, put the laser sight crosshair onto the monster's chest. The cross bounced around a little, but finally the holographic image blinked red, indicating that he had a lock. He jerked the trigger – and had a moment of panic as he feared he'd pulled it too hard.

The rocket streaked away. Smacked into the monster's chest and exploded.

When the fire and smoke cleared, the monster was knocked down.

'All right, Jay!' Saji yelled.

The triumph was shortlived. As they watched, the monster rolled, used its tail as a prop, and got back to its feet. It looked around for the source of the attack.

Ohhhh, *shit*!

Saji was already shoving another rocket into the bazooka-style launcher before Jay could speak. She slapped him on the shoulder. 'Loaded!'

The rocket lanced into the beast again. Boom! Again, it knocked the thing asprawl. Then it climbed back to its feet again, and roared loud enough to wake everything that had died since the beginning of time. It leaned forward, stuck its big tail straight out behind it, and spotted Jay and Saji. It looked like a giant hunting dog on point at a covey of quail.

Man! At least it was having an effect. Thing was, they had one more rocket and then the party was over. They could bail from VR if it got too close, but they'd sure as hell have to do that. Given what the little tiger had done to his brain Jay had a feeling that if this beastie got its claws on them, VR image or not, they would be in real physical jeopardy. If they had to bail, the thing would win, and Jay did not want to let it do that. More than anything he had ever wanted in his life, he wanted to beat this thing. Not just beat it, but to kick its ass seven ways from Sunday, to stomp the crap out of it big-time.

But it didn't look good for the home team, no sir.

'Reloaded!'

Jay took a deep breath and readied his last shot.

Sure enough, Bascomb-Coombs was still there in the study, waving his hands around, wiggling his fingers, and directing some unseen computer wizardry. Peel glanced up and down the hall. No one around. He slipped into the room. He pulled the small Cold Steel Culloden boot knife from the sheath on his belt. The knife was short, pointed like a stiletto, with a hard, rubbery handle that gripped well. He stepped up behind the computer scientist, reached out and caught his forehead with his left hand, then drove the knife into the base of his skull with his right. Bascomb-Coombs stiffened—

The monster opened its toothy mouth, flashed fangs

the length of a man's forearm, and screamed that terrible scream again. Then it froze in that position, jaws agape.

'What is it doing?'

Jay shook his head. 'Hell if I know. But there's my target.' He lined the crosshairs up on the thing's open gullet. Held his breath and pulled the trigger—

Bascomb-Coombs jittered a few times, then collapsed, his suddenly-dead weight more than Peel could hold up. He bent and pulled the knife out of the man's hindbrain, wiped it on the dead man's shirt, and put the blade back into the sheath.

'Sorry, old man, but you mess with the bull and sometimes you get the horn.'

The knife was the way to go, all right. He didn't want to attract any attention. Once he was done in here, he would use his gun to do Ruzhyó. He didn't want to get too close to that one.

Now let's see. There was Goswell, the maid, the cook, and old Applewhite left inside, then Ruzhyó. Huard he could save until last, the boy would never have a clue. Then pop the safe – whose combination he'd had for months – take whatever cash and baubles were there, and a lively stroll through the rainy fields and away. A long and hard day and it wasn't over yet, but there it was, you did what you had to do, and God save the King.

He went down the hall toward the dining room to have a word with His Lordship.

* * *

This time when the rocket exploded, so did the monster's head. Ersatz brain and bone and blood sleeted in all directions, some of it hitting Jay and Saji, but neither of them cared.

'You got it! You got it!'

'You seem awfully joyful for a Buddhist, under the circumstances.'

Saji hugged him. 'What, for shutting down a computer program? That's all you really did, isn't it?'

'*All* I did? Hey, this was no ordinary computer program, woman!' But he hugged her back. He had done it. He had redeemed himself. And it felt better than pretty damned good, it felt absolutely great.

Jay Gridley was *back*!

40

Thursday
The Yews, Sussex, England

The entry team made it to within a few hundred meters of the house without any trouble. Michaels had expected to hear shooting from the perimeter team when it got to the gate but either they were too far away or things had gone better there than expected.

In the headset, Howard said, 'See anything, E4?'

Fernandez was on point. 'Negative, I – wait. There's one just passed under the light by the back door. Looks as if he is walking patrol.'

'Copy. Let's move in.'

Michaels waited until Howard passed him before he got up from the wet ground where he'd been prone and started moving in a low crouch. *Stay low, move slow*, that's what Howard had emphasized.

Toni and Cooper followed him, and the tight feeling in his bowels was not altogether from his worry about being shot.

Ruzhyó caught the movement in the field during a

lull in the rain. It wasn't much, just a dark shape outlined against the distant outdoor light from a neighboring farm, but it was enough to gain his attention.

A few seconds later, he caught another glimpse of something. Could be a lost sheep, maybe. A calf that had wandered away from its mother. But he didn't believe that. Dark shapes coming across the field in the rain? British assault team was more likely. And sooner than he – and Peel – had expected. Since he hadn't heard any gunfire, Ruzhyó had to assume they had gotten past the guards. Not a real surprise. Peel's men were good soldiers, but the estate was too big for them to cover properly.

Ruzhyó moved deeper into the overhang's shadows, circled away from the house, and headed toward the building that Peel used for an office. He could use that for cover until he saw how many of them had come. Then, if he was lucky, he could still slip away. There could be a dozen or a hundred of them, and without knowing where the gaps were, it would be risky to try and run.

Goswell wiped his lips as Peel came into the room, wearing a rather smug smile. Ah, well. Here we go.

He had sent Applewhite upstairs with the maid and cook, and told them to lock themselves in the upstairs office and stay there until he personally told them to come out. The office door was steel, with a stout lock and a policeman's bar behind it, installed as part of a security room under Peel's aegis. Rather ironic, that.

Now he could finish this unpleasant business. He put his napkin back into his lap and left his hands there with it.

'Do have a seat, Major.'

'I think I'd rather stand, if it's all the same to you, Geoffrey.'

Geoffrey? Good God, Peel has gone round the bend. Somewhat flustered at the overly familiar tone, Goswell sought to collect himself. 'Did you see Bascomb-Coombs, then?'

'Ah, yes, that I did. I just left him in the study. Quite dead.'

'Dead, you say?'

'Yes. A sudden attack of brain fever. Brought on by this.' Peel pulled a wicked-looking little dagger from under his jacket and held it up. The bright steel glittered under the lamps of the electric chandelier.

Goswell considered that. 'Killed him, did you?'

'I'm afraid so.'

'A pity. He was quite brilliant.'

'And he was also a psychotic willing to do your bidding and who also tried to have me killed.' Peel turned the knife this way and that, looking at the steel almost as if hypnotized.

'Did he? Well, apparently his assassins fared no better than mine, then.'

Peel frowned. 'Yours?'

'Yes, of course. I'm afraid perhaps you've made a mistake and poor Bascomb-Coombs has been made to suffer for it. It was I who had people trying to kill you, sir.'

'But – why?' He seemed genuinely perplexed.

'Really, Peel. For conspiring with that very same Bascomb-Coombs you have slain in my study. Did you think me such a fool that I wouldn't remember that someone must watch the watchers?'

'Ah, so it was *you* having me followed. And that fellow in the bookstore.'

'I am sad that it was necessary. Your father would be most unhappy with you. I thought you were made of better stuff, Major.'

Peel laughed. 'Well, I've got to hand it to you, your Lordship, I never tumbled to it being your doing. I stand corrected. And it's not as if Bascomb-Coombs was some innocent who didn't deserve his fate. Though I must say, you are awfully calm for man who is about to have his throat cut. A gentleman to the end, eh?'

'I should hope so. Although I confess that I don't expect that end to occur this evening.'

With that, Goswell brought his Rigby double up from his lap and pointed it right at Peel's heart.

The old man was slow and half-blind, and there was a moment there if Peel had moved quickly that he could have gotten around the point-blank line of sight and stabbed Goswell. But such was his shock at seeing the gun come up, so unexpected was it, that he froze. By the time he recovered, Goswell had him covered. He might not be able to hit a rabbit hopping about in his garden fifty feet away, but at ten feet he'd play hell missing a man-sized target. And a load of even birdshot would be fatal in the right spot.

'Are you going to shoot me?'

'I'd rather not get blood all over the dining room, but if you bat an eyelash crooked, certainly I will. Applewhite would hate the cleaning, but he is very discrete.'

'What, then?'

'I was rather hoping we could step outside, you could have a final cigar and a brandy or whatnot, and we'd . . . part company there.'

He was serious. Goswell was going kill him. After cigars and brandy.

Not while he had a knife in one hand and a pistol inches from the other hand, the old fool wasn't. He would distract him and bet on his younger reflexes. It was the only way.

'Well, all right. If that's how it is to be. I think I'd like one of the Cubans and maybe a snifter of the Napoleon—'

With that, Peel lunged—

'All I see is the one,' Fernandez said. 'You want me to put a couple of rounds in him, pick a spot and say when.'

Howard considered his options. The guard had a submachine gun slung and ready, and he might cut loose if he heard a twig snap. Subgun pistol ammo wouldn't pierce their SIPEsuit armor, but it would surely make enough noise to warn people in the house they had company. So would a flash-bang or puke lights. Howard had been expecting a firefight, and in that case you did what you had to do to control the situation, but so far, with no shooting, it seemed possible they could pull this off without anybody getting blasted. He'd rather do it that way, considering how delicate the politics were. Michaels had gone out on a limb a few times for Howard, the least he could do was return the favor.

'I'm moving up,' Howard said. 'I'll get his attention. While he's focused on me, you take him out. Non-lethally, if possible.'

'Copy non-lethal, E5.'

Howard crawled to within twenty yards of the house, then fifteen. The guard was turning and heading in his direction, and he had to attract and keep his attention long enough for Julio to get to him and choke him out.

He needed a noise that would make the guard curious but not afraid. A cat's meow might do it. He did a pretty good imitation of a kitten looking for its mama. Even if the guard was some kind of pervert who liked stomping kittens, he'd have to see it before he did that. Should be enough time for Julio.

'Meow. Mew. Mew. Mew!'

Sure enough the guard started heading his way.

'Mew! Mew!'

The man grinned. 'Kitty! Here, kitty, kitty. Aw, you lost in the rain? C'mere, I'll dry you off.'

Good, he was a cat-lover.

It was going to work. And it might have – if somebody hadn't fired a shotgun inside the house just then.

The guard spun toward the door, saw Julio coming at him at a dead run, and whipped his gun up.

Well, shit, Howard thought. Then he opened up with his own subgun, a triplet into the guard's back. The guard wasn't wearing armor. He went down.

'Go!' Howard yelled into his comset. 'Back to Plan Able!'

Peel looked at the bloody hole in his belly, felt the burn of the lead, and knew he was not going to recover from this gut-shot. Thick smoke clouded the lights, the burned powder smell was awful, and from the floor, he wanted only one thing: to take fucking Goswell with him. He grabbed at his pistol, pulled it free—

Goswell stepped closer and aimed the shotgun at Peel's face.

'Sorry,' Goswell said.

The next explosion blew out Peel's lights forever.

Howard rolled through the door and into the

kitchen. He came up ready but, save for Julio, already on guard, they were alone. He pointed down the hall, and Julio nodded.

They cleared rooms. When they got to the study, there was a body on the floor next to a portable computer. The dead man wore portable VR gear. They rolled him over and saw his face.

'Bascomb-Coombs,' Julio said. 'Deader than last week's liberty.'

'Yes.'

Over the headset, Howard heard somebody outside suck in a harsh breath.

When they got to the dining room, they found the second corpse, a messy one with half its face blasted away, and an old man sitting at the dining-room table with an open double-barreled shotgun in front of him. White smoke hung like dense fog in the room.

'You shooting black powder in that thing?' Julio asked.

The old man was Lord Goswell. Howard recognized him from his pictures.

'You don't look like any of the security boys I know. Americans, are you?'

'Yeah, we're new,' Julio said. 'What happened here?'

'Major Peel went mad, I think. He killed Bascomb-Coombs and came for me. I had to shoot him, I'm afraid. A terrible business.'

Peel and Bascomb-Coombs, both dead. Howard shook his head. 'Jesus.'

Over his com, he heard Cooper echo that word. Or maybe it was Fiorella.

Julio said, 'Where is Ruzhyó?'

The old man frowned. 'Who? Oh, you mean the new Russian fellow Peel hired? I expect he's around somewhere. He was here earlier.'

'Stay here,' Howard said. 'We'll be back. Heads up out there, people, Ruzhyó is still loose.'

They headed out. Michaels, Fiorella, and Cooper were covering the back, and Julio said into his com, 'E4 and E5 are coming out the back door, nobody shoot us.'

As they stepped out into the yard, the rain stopped. The heads up in Howard's helmet lit with a flash on channel tac-2. He toggled the second com unit on.

'E5, this is P1. We have secured the perimeter.'

'Copy, P1. Keep half your unit there and send a squad our way. We have one unfriendly loose and running around, armed and the worst of the bunch. Stay awake.'

'Copy awake, E5.'

Howard said, 'Split up. Commander, you are with me. Cooper and Fiorella, you are with Fernandez. Do what he says. Let's go find him.'

From where he stood, hidden by the outbuilding's corner, maybe five meters away, Ruzhyó could hear the American's voice, though he could not quite make out the words. Five of them, and more out in the fields and doubtlessly on the way. They were wearing body armor impervious to his weapon, and it was unlikely they would flip up their visors or remove their helmets, knowing what had happened to their men who did that the last time they had tried to take him. He was outnumbered, outgunned, and outflanked. Once upon a time, he would have considered those things a personal challenge. Not tonight.

He might bank a shot under a visor with jacketed bullets, but the .22s were soft lead and wouldn't bounce well, though they would spatter if they hit a hard surface. Possibly he could blind one, but that wouldn't do him much good.

The only other weak points were the gloves, which were of thin Kevlar so they could have relatively unimpeded use of their hands. But a broken bone in the hands would hardly be fatal.

No, if he wanted to live, best he take his chances in the fields. Run, and with luck get past the line and away.

He sighed. He could have run a long time ago. He could be back in Chetsnya by now. But that wasn't really home without Anna. Wherever she had been had been his home. With her death, he had been cut loose, adrift, a sere leaf blown by the winds of fate.

He sighed again. Enough of this.

He unfolded the trigger from the umbrella's handle and stepped out from behind the cover of the building and into a cone of light. The five were only a few meters away, backs to him.

'Save yourselves the trouble,' he said.

They turned almost as one, all of their guns leveled at him.

'Drop it!' one of them yelled. 'Drop the – the umbrella?'

He saw them relax slightly. He had given up. They had him.

He snapped the umbrella up and started point shooting.

Howard felt the impact of the bullet on his weapon, and when he tried to return fire, the subgun fired one round, which was way low, then jammed. He let it go and snatched at his revolver.

He heard the others yelling, though he couldn't separate the voices in the LOSIR from each other or the people standing close to him.

'Shit—!'

'Fuck—'

The S&W came out of his holster, the cover to the sight popped off, tethered to the holster as it was. He jerked the revolver up, too high, found the glowing red dot and brought it back down—

—why the hell wasn't anybody else shooting at him?

—brought the dot down, centered it on the man's chest, and cooked off two rounds – *boom! boom!* – and watched him fall, crumpling in slomo—

—and the son-of-a-bitch was *smiling* as he fell!

Howard ran to the fallen man, stood over him. Both .357 rounds had hit him square in the middle of the chest, heart shots, both, he was out of it, and even if the medics were here, they couldn't fix that.

The dying man looked up at Howard. 'Anna,' he said. That was all.

It was just about wrapped up. Fernandez came over, carrying the umbrella Ruzhyó had used. He held it so Michaels could see the gun mechanism inside. 'Five-shot revolver, see? Ingenious little thing.'

Michaels nodded. He also saw the bandage on Fernandez's right hand where the small caliber bullet had hit it. It hadn't penetrated the glove, but it had smashed against it hard enough to keep him from shooting. Michael's own weapon had been disabled by a bullet that hit the magazine. Toni had a small wound on her right hand like Fernandez's, and Angela's glove had failed to stop the bullet and had broken her thumb. Howard's subgun had taken a round against the bolt.

The man called Ruzhyó had hit all five of them hard enough to keep them from shooting back, and it was only Howard's handgun that had finally put an end to it. It was amazing. Nobody here had ever seen anybody shoot so well. If he had had an armor-piercing weapon, he could have killed them all.

'Too bad he wasn't on our side,' Fernandez said. 'He'd have made a helluva small-arms instructor.'

'You sorry he's dead?'

'No. And, well, yeah. Kinda.'

Michaels understood that.

'All right. Let's get out of here,' Howard said. 'The party is over.'

EPILOGUE

Friday, April 15th
London, England

Toni had taken another room, without discussing the situation with Michaels. As he headed to the lobby of the hotel to meet her, he wondered what she was going to say. They were supposed to go home today. The flight was booked. It would be a long trip if she didn't want to talk to him.

He took the stairs, wanting to be alone.

The case was over. The Brits had cleaned up the mess at Goswell's. There was nothing to tie the old man directly to anything. The witnesses who could have implicated him were all dead.

Bascomb-Coombs' miracle computer was also dead. Some kind of timed destruct code that didn't get turned off when he wasn't there to disarm it. The Brits had the machine, but they didn't know what it was they had. Maybe someday they could puzzle it out.

So, no international incident. Bad guys mostly dead. It could have been worse.

But there was Toni, standing near the big potted

plant in the lobby. She hadn't talked to him about Cooper, had refused to listen to him say anything about it.

She looked at him, and her face was so sad he thought she might cry. So sad it wanted to make him cry. He had to fix this somehow.

'Toni, I'm sorry, I—'

'No,' she said, cutting him off. 'Not today. Your flight leaves in a couple of hours.'

'*My* flight?'

'Yes. I'm staying here for a while.'

'But—'

'No. I have a lot to think about, Alex, and so do you.' She looked at him, and he saw the tears forming, starting to spill.

'Toni, you don't understand—'

'No. Not now. Don't say another word about it.'

Tears streamed freely down her face now.

She didn't know he hadn't actually slept with Cooper. She must believe that he had. And when it got right down to it, did it really make that much difference? He had wanted Cooper. He had damned near had her. Lying naked on a table with a woman who was naked, did it really matter that they hadn't consummated things? He had to tell her, but the look she gave him froze the words in this throat. Would it make things better? Or worse?

Would she even believe him?

'Okay, sure, take some time, whatever you need.

We can . . . deal with this when you get back to work.'

'No, we can't. I'm not coming back to work. It's too much for us to have professional and private lives mixed together. I quit, Alex. As of today, right now, this minute, I'm no longer working for Net Force.'

'What? You can't!'

'You aren't going to tell me I can't do anything right now, maybe not ever. Goodbye, Alex. I – I'll miss you.'

With that, she walked away.

Michaels watched her leave, unable to speak, to move, even to breathe.

Oh, God, Toni! What had he done?

He stood that way for a long time, as if in a trance, and when he came out of it, she was gone.

Gone.